Tim Gautreaux

Born and raised in Louisiana, Tim Gautreaux lives there still with his wife and is writer in residence at Southeastern Louisiana University. His work has appeared in *Harper's*, the *Atlantic Monthly*, *GQ*, *Zoetrope*, *Prize Stories: The O. Henry Awards*, and *Best American Short Stories*, and he has published two collections of short fiction. *The Next Step in the Dance*, his first novel, won the 1999 SEBA Book Award and his second, *The Clearing*, was published in the US and UK in 2003 to wide acclaim.

Also by Tim Gautreaux

The Next Step in the Dance

TIM GAUTREAUX

SCEPTRE

First published in 1998 by Picador USA
First published in Great Britain in 2004 by Hodder and Stoughton
A division of Hodder Headline

A Sceptre Paperback

1 3 5 7 9 10 8 6 4 2

All characters in this publication are fictitious
and any resemblance to real persons, living or dead,
is purely coincidental

A CIP catalogue record for this title is available from the British Library

ISBN 0 340 83454 4

Typeset by Hewer Text Ltd, Edinburgh
Printed and bound by Clays Ltd, St Ives plc

Hodder Headline's policy is to use papers that are natural, renewable
and recyclable products and made from wood grown in sustainable
forests. The logging and manufacturing processes are expected to
conform to the environmental regulations of the country of origin.

Hodder and Stoughton
A division of Hodder Headline
338 Euston Road
London NW1 3BH

For Florence and Minos

Acknowledgements

I would like to thank John and Renee Grisham, whose support of the Southern Writer in Residence program at the University of Mississippi enabled me to revise this novel. My wife, Winborne, and my children, Robert and Tom, deserve credit for their patience and support. For advice on the manuscript, I owe a debt to both Reagan Arthur and Peter Matson. I would also like to thank the National Endowment for the Arts and Southeastern Louisiana University for their support.

One

The electric sign on the roof of Tiger Island Bank showed a temperature of eighty-eight degrees at 9:00 P.M. When Colette got out of the tellers' meeting, she glanced up at it and frowned. She drove the few blocks to her rent house and parked in the front yard, which smelled of the tall, bitter weeds that made her nose itch. It was the last Wednesday of the month, the night she had to stay late for the bald man from Baton Rouge to come and explain computers to the girls who worked behind the worn marble counters of the old bank. The bald man was tall, with a long neck like a marsh hen, and the only thing she remembered about his talk was his Adam's apple going up and down like a bony elevator for words. She went into the small wooden house and sat on the sofa, brushing grass seed off her dark panty hose. Her husband had promised a week ago that he would cut the lawn. The phone rang, and it was Aunt Nellie Arnaud calling from her car phone.

"Colette?"

"Yes." She pictured Aunt Nellie cruising through town in her old white Lincoln, an explosion of bleached hair brushing the roof.

"Paul's not there, is he?"

She sighed. "Now what?"

"Well, I don't want to spread gossip."

Colette straightened her narrow back. "What?"

"I just passed the Silver Bayou Drive-In and saw him and a young woman turning there."

She made a face, remembering that her aunt did not trust men in general. "You sure?"

"A fact is a fact."

"It wasn't his sister, Nan?"

Her aunt laughed long and loud. She had buried three husbands. "Colette," she keened. "Colette."

Colette could imagine her aunt accelerating toward Beewick, shaking her head. She yelled into the phone. "He's done a lot of things, but not that." Her aunt was gone in a stuttering crackle of static, and Colette looked around at the paneling and the dusty venetian blinds. She'd been married a year and a half and had hoped to do better than this by now. Paul, her husband, worked like a mule, but he also thought like a mule and pulled his plow in a straight line. He was a machinist and wanted to be a machinist. Ambition was not his long suit. His picture grinned from the top of the television, a big face, not bad-looking, the best fish in the pond, people said. But Colette read *Cosmopolitan* and *Woman's World* and had begun to think that Tiger Island was a small, muddy pond. She put her shoes back on and got into her little brown Toyota to buzz down River Street to where it became a thin strand of blacktop plunging through a sugarcane field. Two miles southeast of town, she saw the broad clamshell entrance of the Silver Bayou Drive-In, the back of the screen an expanse of corrugated tin disappearing into the misty night sky. Russell LaBat handed her a ticket with a bony, pale hand and gave her a long look.

"Russell, is Paul inside?"

"Paul who?"

She arched an eyebrow. "Pope John Paul."

"Ask me no secrets, I'll tell you no lies." He put her three dollars into a cigar box and went back to reading a copy of *News on Wheels*.

She cruised the dim shell lanes in front of the viewing humps, her parking lights glowering, and in their jaundiced beams she saw people she knew, cousins even. Working the grassy lot from back to front, she finally spotted her husband's ten-year-old pickup in the front row, where the grass hadn't been cut in weeks and *jonc cupon* and thistle sprang hood-high. The movie was a colorful rectangle rising out of a grassy plain. She backed onto an earthen ramp behind him. Her husband was turned toward a woman she did not recognize, and before she could stop herself, she sprang out into the grass. Her high heels buckled under her as she crossed the shell lane and jerked open the truck's door, banging it into the metal pole that held the speaker.

"What the hell are you doing with her?"

Her husband seemed drowsy and only mildly surprised. He opened his mouth but managed only a sleepy smile. His hand went up as if to support something he would say, but he said nothing. The young woman with him put an elbow on her armrest and lowered her forehead into a palm. Finally, Paul Thibodeaux said, "This is Lanelle. She said she couldn't find anyone to come watch this movie with her."

Colette squinted at the screen. "This is *The Train*. It's about a million years old, you fool." She thrust a vicious chin at Lanelle. "She can rent it for a dollar if that's what she's so hot to see."

A middle-aged man with Elvis sideburns leaned out of the car next to them and called, "Colette, baby, I can't hear the movie."

She turned like a released spring. "My husband is out with another woman and you want me to talk like I'm in church?" She gestured to the weedy lot stippled with dew-covered cars. "Does this look like a church, Mr. Larousse? What is it, the First Church of Messing Around?" The man rolled up his window as a car on the next row flashed its lights and a voice from the dark piped, "Give it a rest."

Her husband put his big machinist's hands palm-up in his lap. "Hey, c'mon. We wasn't gonna do nothing but watch a movie."

"Yeah. Right now. What about later?" She was winding up, her voice sailing. The locals liked to look at Colette because she was slim and fair-skinned, with dark hair, a straight nose, and eyes like little rain-soaked pecans, but her voice when she was angry was a diamond on glass. "What about now?" she yelled. "I'm sitting at home picking cockleburs off my panty hose because you won't cut the damned lawn, and you're kicked back in the drive-in watching Nazi movies with another woman."

A voice came from two rows back: "Colette, shut your trap, baby." Her head snapped around, but the speaker did not show himself.

Paul leaned out to her. "You better not raise too much racket. This place is full of bad asses from Tonga Bend."

"Since when am I scared of levee rats?"

Even the blond woman looked at her. "You want to land us all in the hospital, keep talking like that."

Colette put her face into the truck. "Why are you with my husband?"

"I wanted to see this old movie and nobody would bring me."

"It's a damned depressing movie. Who would want to watch this crap?"

"Colette." He put a hand on her arm. "I promise I'll cut the grass tomorrow."

The blonde leaned over. "Bring me back to the lounge, will you, baby?"

Colette brushed off his hand as she would a spider. "So you picked her up in a bar? You brought her here where half the town could see what you were doing while I was at work?"

On the other side of the pickup, a cowboy stood up in his convertible. "Y'all hush up, now."

"Go back to Texas if you don't like my voice," Colette told him.

"I paid three dollars to get in this movie. You gonna give me my money back?" His huge white hat was blocking a little patch of screen, and the car behind him flashed its headlights, so the cowboy sat down.

"I'm just watching a movie with a friend," Paul said.

Colette stared at the woman's big hair, her bulging silk blouse, and wondered how many times he had been out with other women while she was wrapping pennies at the bank after hours. Her heels sank into the dirt of the Silver Bayou Drive-In as she gathered a lungful of air. "That does it. I'm throwing your lying ass out. The next time I see you, it'll be in divorce court."

Paul slid partway out of the truck. "We're not doing anything, you hear? It's you who's got your head in a toilet."

A woman two cars down yelled, "Flush it." Russell LaBat began struggling through the high grass, carrying a flashlight. The PA from the storm-wasted snack shack and projection room came alive in a deep vacuum-tube thunder. "Will the group by dat Ford pickup please refrain from makin' any more noises." Two cars flashed their lights and four began honking.

Colette started to cry. "You bastard. If you come home tonight, I'll shoot you in the foot." He began to step all the way out of his truck, but she slammed the door and jammed his leg, ducking away as he cried out at the pain. In a second she was in her Toyota, spinning out of the clamshell lot, peppering the parked cars with little sun-bleached shells and raising an obscuring cloud before the patched screen, drawing yells, horn blasts, flashes, and curses from the dark ridges of automobiles fanning out toward Zeneau's swamp.

Colette drove back to the rent house and fixed a cup of tea, which she drank smoking-hot, straight down. When she finished, she looked at the empty cup and wondered where the tea had gone. She scoured the dishes in a cloud of steam, as though punishing them for their sins, and then looked around for something else to do. In the bedroom, she began sorting the pile of laundry on the mattress. She pulled out Paul's machine-shop coveralls and threw them against the wall. She folded her panties and brassieres as if they were presents and placed them in her underwear drawer. While she was folding her husband's briefs, she began thinking about the last time they'd made love; she stared at the bed, slowly folding six pairs of drawers and six T-shirts, tucking the smooth cotton under an elbow. She fished out his socks, which were all white and exactly the same, except for a dark pair he'd worn to go dancing with her Saturday night and to Mass on Sunday morning. These last, she snatched in a strangling hand before putting his things away. One thing he could do well was dance twelve different variations of the jitterbug. In fact, Colette thought he danced too well, and too long, as if dancing were a drug and he could never get enough. He moved in such a way that other people watched him, and that was all right; she could even match him for a couple of hours. Then she would get tired of all the motion and sweat. Sometimes she would drive home and leave him at the Big Bayou Club or at the Cypress Dance Hall, and he would come in at 2:00 A.M., smelling like an ashtray.

The last thing she picked up in the bedroom was a pair of Thom McAn loafers, which showed her their heels from under the dust ruffle of the bed. Lifting the shoes, she remembered the first time they had danced together, when they were fifteen, in the high-school gym. The sophomores had hired a ragtag band out of New Orleans that played mostly disco, now and then throwing in a country tune or an oldie so the chaperones could pretend to dance. Paul had hung back against a cinder-block wall, eyeing suspiciously all the no-touch wiggling, shoulder shaking, and hand clapping. Since first grade, he'd been in the corner of Colette's eye, but she'd had no reason to exchange more than two sentences with him. She'd seen him dance before, though. He was from a blue-collar family, and he'd told her once that he'd learned to dance from his younger uncles when the family would go out to the Big Gator on Saturday afternoons to eat boiled crabs, drink beer, and twirl to a jukebox loaded down with Van Broussard, Tommy McLain, Rod Bernard, and the Boogie Kings, a type of Cajun rhythm and blues fit only for medium-paced jitterbug or a stutter-stepped belly rub.

Before long, the band broke out with "Hello, Josephine" and she walked over and asked him to teach her the bob step. He'd given her a slow smile, as though she'd asked for a secret drink of whiskey. "You want to learn some real dancing, huh?" And as though he'd been waiting fifteen years for her to ask him for a lesson, he took just the fingertips of her right hand and showed her the pattern of the dance. She watched his glossy shoes as he taught her to count steps in her head. He told her how to hold her arm stiff when she rocked back on her heel before a spin, and then they practiced turning her right, then left, then a double turn, and finally a behind-the-back pass. She asked the band to play another one with the same beat, and the two of them actually danced this time among their shoulder-jerking friends and two jitterbugging chaperones trying to stay away from each other's feet. Colette found it easy to move with him. When she turned and looked down, their steps matched; when she put out her hand, it went right into his on the downbeat. They didn't talk that night, but they did dance.

It was two months before they were out on the floor again, at the Big Gator with his aunts and uncles, where he twisted his Neolite-soled loafers in the cornstarch and fed off the good moves she learned from him. He began hanging around her house, fixing things for her father. Colette admired a boy who could make broken things work again. She wondered what it would be like never to be defeated by the mystical world of machinery: dead hair dryers, buzzing light fixtures, snickering automobiles. He even repaired her music box, realigning a button-sized gear and oiling a hairspring with the tip of a toothpick. She liked his sense of humor, though she seldom laughed because of it. She valued it mostly because it meant he was smart. Smart people eventually went places, her mother told her, and Colette wanted to go places.

She threw the polished loafers into the closet and slammed the door on them, wondering where he was, what he had on his feet. It had to be his work boots. This somehow comforted her. At least he hadn't been dancing with that person she'd found him with. She grabbed a silky rope of her long black hair. She looked at it and narrowed her eyes, thinking of the blond woman. "She can wash his greasy clothes," she said aloud, putting a hand over her eyes.

Two

Sometimes Paul Thibodeaux's judgment was faulty, but he had enough understanding of Colette to make him sleep at his *grand-père's* old house on River Street. He told himself before he dozed off in the iron bed in the front room that Colette would cool down, and he could go by the house and smooth things over before she left for work. He was used to her anger, had learned already to endure it, knew that sometimes he deserved the sting of her voice. His wife wanted a better rent house with a paved driveway, not a mud hole dotted with a few clamshells. He would get around to looking in a couple of months, when they'd saved enough.

Before dawn he began hearing things. He was the kind of man who could wake up in the morning without opening his eyes, letting a new day come to him through sound instead of light. This morning he listened to shrimp boats and tugs, long-winded with their whistles, complaining in the fog. A trawler blared out for the railroad bridge, and a big upriver push boat squalled a crossing signal with its long-bell air trumpets. He heard, too, the sawmill whistle spilling its hoarse note onto the town, griping about sunrise.

He opened his eyes, feeling the idea of Colette flow through him like blood tingling in a waking leg. His bruised leg. Getting up in the dark bedroom, he searched above his head for the pull cord to the light. He felt the tingle on his wrist and closed his fingers on it. In a minute his *grand-père* appeared in the open door in a starched khaki shirt, scratching an elbow. He hadn't put his teeth in yet.

"Hey, boy. *Comment ça va?*"

"*Ça va.* Why don't you rewire this place and get some regular light switches?" He pulled his jeans on and buckled his belt.

The old man sniffed. "Hah. My 'lectricity ain't ashame of the wire it's in. Why should I be ashame of that, me?"

"You gonna burn this place down."

"Some people ought to worry about they own house." He looked down the hall toward the kitchen. "What's wrong with yours that you got to sleep here with me in my little place?" He pointed a thick finger at the linoleum.

"Nothing."

"Hah. Colette, she threw your ass in the street. Something's wrong in that house."

"Damn. Who'd you talk to?"

"Little Russell's daddy. He gets up early, so I called him and he told me that." He back-stepped into the hall, and the kitchen light gave life to his iron-gray hair, which was oiled back out of his way. "You know, I was married sixty-one years, and your *grand-mère* never had to lock me out the house."

Paul bent to comb his hair in the foxed mirror above the mahogany dresser. "You coulda talked all day and not said that."

"Maybe you need to hear it, you." The old man toddled closer and Paul could smell the Old Spice and coffee. "You married to the prettiest girl in six parishes and all you do is read books on machines, drink beer, and play the accordion."

Paul brushed by and slid into the hall. "Hey, that puts me right up there with Charles Manson, don't it?"

"Who?" The bushy eyebrows went up like wreaths of stickers.

"Never mind. You got some breakfast?"

"*Pain perdu.* You scared Colette won't fix you none?" His *grand-père* waddled after him.

He gained the kitchen and looked at the two places set on the porcelain table. It seemed he was already out of his house, misplaced. He brushed back his dark hair and sat down, staring long at the chipped plate.

The sun was coming out of a brake of second-growth cypress behind his rent house at the edge of town when Paul turned his pickup into the shell driveway. Colette's car was gone. On the front porch was everything he owned, his coveralls, his boom box and shoe box full of tapes, his suitcases, shotgun, La-Z-Boy recliner, everything stacked in a neat pyramid with his Acadian ten-button accordion at the peak. He stepped up on the little porch and walked slowly around the pile, going in to use the phone. He found her at her mother's.

"Colette, I'm sorry."

"Me, too. I'm sorry it took me over a year to see I was wasting my time with you." She didn't sound angry, and that scared him. She sounded like her eyes had been opened to fact. He trembled at the tone of her voice.

"Me and the lady wasn't gonna do anything. You got to believe that. And I know I shouldn't'ta done it."

Her voice snapped like a cap gun. "I want you out of the house. I'm tired of you sitting around not shaving and talking to old winos for hours about machinery and going out and drinking beer and putting two hours a day into that windstorm of an accordion."

"Baby," he started.

"I'm not your baby. Every woman I meet tells me she's seen you dancing with this one or that one. They're your babies. Not me."

He looked down at his work shoes. "Is this about money again?"

"No. Maybe. What are you gonna be in ten years?"

"A better machinist."

"A wife doesn't want to hear that, Paul." He heard an unexpected sigh on the other end of the line. "Don't you have any dreams?"

He thought about this a minute. "To be the best machinist in the world?"

It went this way for a quarter hour, and when they finished, he went out onto the porch, grabbed a box of underwear, and walked toward his truck.

Holding the box, he leaned his back against the hood and looked at the peeling green house, at the vine of poison oak rooting up the porch's corner post, at the brown lizards sunning on the screens. Already it seemed a place out of his past, and he wondered how things had begun to fall apart for them. He knew that Colette had been unhappy for months, and he suspected it had to do with her tiny salary. Every two weeks, she'd open her pay envelope and bite her lip at the deductions. Sometimes she gave him a little speech about the lard-ass men in the bank who earned twice as much while getting half as much work done as the women. She'd also said that it made her feel bad when he danced with other girls, but he didn't understand this. For him, dancing wasn't a hustle; it was a hobby.

He stared down at the weeds, trying to remember the last time she'd laughed out loud. And she *could* laugh. At their wedding reception down at the Lion's Club hall, there had been a lounge band, three skiffs up on sawhorses loaded with ice and bottled beer, and two hundred people, but the only thing he remembered plainly was the white arch of Colette's teeth as she threw her head back and laughed with him. They drank Schlitz and champagne mixed, threw cake at the ugly children from Grand Crapaud, and when it was time for the first dance, they did a barefoot jitterbug so dazzling to the cousins and aunts that they had to put on their shoes and spend the rest of the afternoon dancing with relatives. For a honeymoon, they went to New Orleans and ate for three days in expensive restaurants. In Brennan's and Gautreau's, Paul told her how much better she could cook than the city chefs. And this, for the most part, was true. The first meal she made in their rent house was a dark crawfish stew garnished with shallots and translucent slices of hard-boiled egg that he gladly would have driven a hundred miles to buy. Whenever he'd tasted her food, he'd known that she loved him.

The telephone started ringing in the rent house's living room, and he looked up at the rattling noise. In there on the couch, the second month of their marriage, he had been sick as death with the flu. Colette had tended him better than a hospital nurse, had put a cool white hand on his head and pulled the fever out of him. He remembered that she sat in a chair and watched him that few days, amazed that he could get sick.

She began to look at him a great deal. When he spent a thousand dollars on his little accordion, she stared at his eyes, at his fingers testing the buttons, and she asked him to practice with the squalling thing outside on the porch. He had not thought much of it at the time, but now he remembered the way she started looking at him, as though he were a complicated automobile she had bought and didn't quite know how to handle. The first time he'd refused to come home early on a Saturday night, she'd given him an angry stare before leaving the dance hall. He tried to remember her dark ball-bearing eyes that night when he did finally come in, tipsy and with Georgette Ledet's perfume on his shirt. He'd only *danced* with her, he'd told Colette. "I know that," she'd said, crossing her arms against him. He'd felt then that they had begun speaking two different languages.

The telephone continued to ring, and the house key in his jeans seemed to heat up, but standing there with his drawers in his hands, he didn't feel it was his phone anymore, nor his house.

* * *

He took his belongings to his parents' old place down on River Street, and after three weeks, he was still there. His mother tolerated him as long as he kept his mouth shut about her trips to the Boggy Belle Indian Casino and her Wednesday-night bourrée games. She was a sharp-eyed woman of fifty-five who kept her graying hair permed up in a nest of iron curls. His father, an inventory clerk at an oil-field supply company, was glad to have him around to repair broken screen doors and the leaky, singing faucets, but Paul suspected that when all the ruined and worn-out things around the rambling cypress house were restored, even his father would begin to fret over his son's unaccountable presence.

His mother fixed his breakfast as usual, grits, boudin, and a cup of strong coffee, which stayed on the back of his tongue as he walked to LeBlanc's Machine Shop, taking the levee that snaked past the backyard and along the Chieftan River. He spent the morning patiently turning a long propeller shaft in a lathe, seeing his worried face in the tool-polished Monel. At noon, he used the gritty phone in the spare-parts room to call Colette at the bank. He shook the sweat and metal shavings from his arms, then dialed her number, buzzed her extension.

"Hello, Paul, what do you want?" she said as soon as she picked up the receiver.

He waited a beat. "How was your morning?"

"Come on. What do you want?"

"Today's what, Friday? The casino calls heating up?"

There was a disgusted snort on the line. "Half the morning I wasted on the phone with local housewives over at that Indian place. When somebody drains the checking account and maxes out the Visa playing the slots, they call to transfer funds from savings, and the switchboard gives them to me to deal with. I'm supposed to advise them to lay off, but they're like bugs drawn to colored lights. I was put on earth to deal with dumb asses."

He winced, but listened to more of her complaints, closing his eyes to store the ring of her voice in his memory for the empty days ahead. And it did ring. Even when she was scolding him, it held a fine, anvil-like music.

"Why are you calling?"

"Maybe we can talk over a nice lunch?"

"Where we gonna get a nice lunch in Tiger Island? At the Little Palace? The table by the men's room, so I can smell the toilet?"

"There you go again."

"Well, it's the truth. If I want a fancy meal, I have to fix it myself."

"You want me to drive to New Orleans for lunch?"

"You could move there. They pay good in New Orleans."

"I'd rather live in the piss trough at the Little Palace."

There was another snort on the line. "Suit yourself. Look, I got to go. A light's blinking on my phone. Some other intellectual giant is amazed that a slot machine hasn't made her rich."

"Wait." He choked on the word. "Why won't you take me back?"

The line was quiet for a moment. "Maybe I can't trust you to take care of me anymore."

The back of his neck became hot. "We got a good marriage. I take you dancing. We eat out. When we get some money put by, we'll get a house. Why do you hate me all of a sudden? I got the separation papers in the mail."

"I don't hate anybody. Hating is a waste of my time."

"Then let's talk."

"I don't think so." The line fell quiet again. "Not alone, anyway. It'd have to be in a public place."

"Colette, I'm your husband."

"With somebody else along for the ride."

He frowned. "You want me to bring my shop foreman?"

"Don't get nasty. I'll take Clarisse."

"Your cousin from the bank? The kind of soft one?"

"She joined an aerobics class. She's a nice person."

"Nice and big."

"Hey, you want to talk to me?"

The phone seemed to glow in his hands. "Okay, okay. Where can we meet?"

It was a while before she said anything. "Big Gator. Tonight. They'll have hot boiled crabs at seven." She hung up.

The Big Gator. He wondered if he could call back and try to change her mind. The Big Gator was mostly an old folks' dance hall, and between the noise from the Cajun band and the big bug zapper over the bar, it would be hard to carry on a conversation. He tried to think of a better place, maybe in the next town, but the whole region was much like Tiger Island, small villages spread out along the Chieftan River, peopled by Cajuns, Cajunized Germans, maudlin Italians, and a sprinkling of misplaced Bible Belt types, whom Paul's grandfather called *les cous rouges*. Tiger Island was the most knuckle-knocked of the river towns: The only theater was the Silver Bayou Drive-In; the largest building was a metal shed where oil-field equipment was sandblasted. The best restaurant was in the Big Gator, next to the dance floor, where Nelson Orville's band would sing French versions of old rock songs, accompanied by pawnshop guitars and a ten-button accordion. The favorite sport of the town's young men was still fistfighting, which broke out as indiscriminately as swamp gas on Friday nights. Six thousand people lived inside the city limits, patronizing twelve churches and eighteen bars. Paul never could put his finger on it, but something about Tiger Island was slightly out of balance, a little too littered, sun-tortured, and mildewed. Most of the houses were old. A band of big weatherboard family places spread along River Street, but away from the levee, the houses were small, on small lots, as if they had been steamed and shrunk by the welding-hot morning sun and the daily afternoon thunderstorm.

Out on the machine-shop floor again, he pictured his wife and then the restaurant full of hotbloods from Tonga Bend and Pierre Part. All afternoon, he bit his cheek as he straightened the glaring blades on a tugboat's bronze propeller.

After work he went to Bernstein's, the only men's store in town. In the old brick building on Dupuis Street, he bought an imitation designer shirt, violently striped. At his parents' house he steamed the machine oil out of his skin and slapped on handfuls of his father's spicy aftershave. Driving south on River Street, he came to the city limits, where the pavement dropped off with a bump into a wide shell road. He could see Colette from a great distance, waiting under the crimp-tin awning of the Big Gator, separate from and unlike everything around her. She wore a loose white blouse and tan slacks, her glossy dark hair waving down past the bone-white skin of her neck. Next to her was her cousin, Clarisse, slouching against the door frame like Marilyn Monroe. When he drove into the rutted parking lot, he saw a serpentine necklace lying against Colette's skin, a golden reminder that she was the only drop-dead beautiful woman in Tiger Island. At twenty-three, she still owned the pearly glow of a child's complexion, as though she had hardly changed from the girl he had first seen in kindergarten at St. Mary's School.

He parked at the edge of the shell lot, which was giving back the day's heat. "Hey, babe," he told his wife.

"Hello," she said, her eyes unreadable.

"Hey, T-Bub." Clarisse waved like a parade queen. "That's a nice shirt you got on."

"Ah. Clarisse." He touched her arm and a little smile formed on her lips.

They went inside a long box of a room, plank walls painted with gray deck enamel, a rain-splotched Celotex ceiling. A bar ran the length of the room, at the end of which were two swinging doors to a cavernous dance floor. Three oil-well cementers were at the bar, wearing hard hats and coveralls, arguing over who would buy the next round. One grabbed another's arm to make a point, and a puff of cement rose into the pearlized light of a beer sign. A horsefly hit the bug zapper over the bar, and the men looked up at the raspy crackle. From the dance floor came the snort of an accordion, the thump of a beer-soaked drumhead, the caroming thud of a bass guitar, the waspy drone of a fiddle, and finally the nasal falsetto of Nelson Orville singing "Bad, Bad Leroy Brown" in French.

Paul ordered a round of beer and was trying to tell Colette something when Clarisse stood up and pulled on his hand. "Come on and dance with me."

He looked at Colette, and she waved them off. They went through the double doors into the blue thunder of the over-populated dance floor. Bare hardwood tables stacked with beer bottles jammed the walls. Everyone, even the few teenage couples, were jitterbugging, so he dropped his left hand, stuck out his rear, and put his feet in the pattern: three steps left, three steps right, left foot rock back. He did a little push-off jig with her so they could talk. "How mad is Colette with me?" he yelled. He noticed that Clarisse had lost weight, but she was still a little slow in her turns.

"Oh, T-Bub, you don't want to know."

He turned her right, rotated under her upraised hand, and slid past her back like an oiled wheel. "Help me out."

Clarisse shook her head in time to the music and mouthed the words: "*Mauvais, mauvais Leroy Brown, le plus mauvais boog dans toute la ville, plus mauvais que vieux King Kong . . .*"

"I got to know where I stand."

She swung and gave him a smile. "I think you two are blowed up."

"Aw, come on."

"That's no lie. She's mad about a whole raft of things. She really don't like the fighting."

He turned her into his side, then threw her out into a double spin. "I haven't been in a little fight in months. It's just playing, anyway."

Clarisse rolled her eyes. "It gets in the newspaper," she yelled over the music.

The band ran out of steam and gave up. Paul and Clarisse walked back to their table, past a group of Tonga Bend men wearing tight dark T-shirts, young fishermen who could have been thirty or seventeen. It was hard to tell after a few years in the sun. "What can I do?" He put his hand in the small of her back.

"Promise her you'll stop fighting, at least."

Colette looked away as they sat next to her. She was frowning. "You two have a nice time?"

Paul put his elbows on the table and clasped his hands. "You ready to talk with me?"

Her eyes were dark and hard. "You think we need to talk." She shook her head once. "We've gone over this already."

"Come on. We're married. The priest married us." He put a hand palm-up on the table. "We didn't just jump over a broomstick. *Donne-moi une autre 'tite chance?*"

"You can't speak French worth a damn. You stole that line from an old song."

He watched her bite her cheek, trying, he thought, to avoid giving him a smile. "I promise I'll never get in a fistfight as long as I live."

She passed her eyes over him quickly, from side to side, pretending to look at something across the room. "I'm scared you'll bring home some disease from a whore you pick up at Scadlock's."

He leaned back in the wooden chair and looked toward the dance floor. "You won't believe this, but I never cheated on you."

She turned her head, giving him the white landscape of her face, moonlight on still sand. "You're out of control," she told him, but the electrical snap had gone from her voice. He decided then not to push things, hoping that the broken pieces of their marriage could be welded together. He knew that Colette wanted to leave Tiger Island to do what other people with good looks and brains would do—which is to say, examine at least one other place in the world. Tiger Island was dragging her down in its humid, sun-blistered way. She was a local girl to the bone, related to half the town, and it would be hard to leave the ceremonies of kinship, her food and dance and the cemetery where her people had been buried for two hundred years.

She leaned toward Clarisse, who was buffing her press-on nails. "I wish they'd hurry with the crabs."

"You hungry?" Paul asked his wife.

"I know I am," Clarisse said, uncrossing her legs and scooting closer to the table.

"The sooner we eat, the better," Colette said to the wall. "I want to get out of here before it gets too busy." She ignored two men walking past slowly, taking her in.

Paul knew she wanted to get out before the fighting started. Friday nights were when a few high-school dropouts from Pierre Part, or Partians, as they were called locally, would stroll in, looking for Tiger Island men to fight. Sometimes combatants would roll around in the parking lot, grunting and hugging to the shouts of the spectators, but once or twice a year a general punching match would break out among most all the men at the dance, and the Big Gator would take a pounding, a type of internal hurricane, leaving broken doors and overturned tables in its wake.

But the Big Gator was the least dangerous of a group of levee-road honky-tonks that included T-Man's, Black Alice's, Scadlock's Boiler Room, and, down the road in the white-trash section called Tonga Bend, the Machine Gun Inn. Like the rest, the Big Gator was built above the swamp on creosote-soaked stubs and made of scrap material—some weatherboard, some plywood, some tin, all painted the color of stolen paint, like Louisiana Department of Highways orange or Exxon blue. It catered to a mixed crowd of Cajun trappers and fishermen, outlander river men, and oil-field roughnecks, plus a few third-generation Tiger Island Protestants.

Every man in the restaurant section stole looks at Colette. Paul stared at the battered swinging doors that led into the dance hall, noticing that they had been once again screwed back on their hinges. Clarisse excused herself to speak with a friend at the bar.

"So, how's work?" Colette asked, folding her smooth, perfumed arms on the newspaper. "What wonderful piece of machinery did you bring back from the dead today?" Her eyes told him to ignore the sarcasm, but he knew there was substance to it.

"We pulled the heads off the old main compressor down at the ice plant. What can I say? I enjoyed it."

"I know. You don't have to tell me. You work on those machines like they were people. You shoulda been a doctor."

He made a face. "I'd have to get my hands dirty."

She looked down at his fingers, which were hard with muscle. "I see you're still keeping your hands clean. For a machinist."

"That's the way you told me to keep them."

She nearly smiled one of her narrow smiles, and the nearness of the motion made him straighten his back.

In a few minutes a fat waitress wearing a black rayon dress dumped a beer box of crabs on their table. Colette cracked open a claw with a knife handle while Paul tore at a big smoking body, pulling out the hot white meat. The air was overloaded with nose-tickling cayenne. Clarisse sat down and sneezed.

Paul leaned toward his wife. "Why you treating me like this?" As he spoke, he pulled a feeler off a crab and winced.

"It's something I have to do." She looked a passing gawker in the eye. "I might even move to New Orleans."

His mouth formed a straight, hard seam. "Sure."

She cracked open another claw. "Have you ever looked at this town? Really looked at it? You know, when you live in a place all your life, you can't really see it."

"I've looked."

"There's got to be a better place."

"A good place is wherever you are, if you've got the right attitude." He hoped she would believe it.

"You're smarter than that," she said, scowling, ripping a crab, her face disappearing in a burst of steam. "You've got to live someplace else. See what it's like. This town is a mud hole."

"Aw, look . . ."

"Remember that old drunk of a history teacher, what he told us in high school? Even the first explorers who came through went back to France and told their children that if they were real bad, someday they would be sent to Louisiana."

"Aw, those guys were just passing through," he said. "They weren't born here." He banged on a claw and drew the meat out of the red shell. "It's not as bad as——"

"Mud and snakes and piles of roadside garbage. Little burned-out fishermen and——"

"Now how the hell would you be eating these big crabs if it wasn't for them little burned-out fishermen, you tell me that."

She looked over to the bar for a moment. "I don't know."

"You want 'em to catch crabs wearing a tuxedo? Think the crabs would be impressed?" He could tell that she was trying not to laugh. "You've fished for crabs yourself, you and your brother. And shot coon, too."

"That was just on weekends in ninth grade."

He leaned back and looked at her eyes. "You know, babe, until just now, I never thought you might leave town. You hate me and the people around here that much?"

"I don't hate anybody. Not even you, I don't think. Except when you come home stinking of diesel oil and leave steel curls in the bathtub."

He looked down at his beer. "I won't fight anymore."

She seemed to consider this. Clarisse sneezed again.

"Damn this pepper."

He leaned over to her blond frizz and whispered that her nose was running.

"Oh." She fumbled for her purse with wet fingers and headed toward the bathroom.

Colette looked down at the heap of broken shells between them and shook her head. "If it weren't for the people here . . ." She picked up a barnacled crab and hefted it, weighing the problems of the parish. "Everybody aims so low. Most people are so rough."

He thought he might point out to her that she had tried to break his leg in a truck door in front of half the town. "Baby, this is oil country. Fish country. You don't wear a suit to those jobs and you don't listen to Beethoven in your truck."

She shook the crab in his face. "Damn it, I want to know people who sparkle."

He made a slight sideways movement with his head. "I've got to admit, that's a tall order for Tiger Island." He dismantled another crab, working out the sweet flesh with a thumbnail.

She looked at the door that led to the parking lot, and she frowned. "There's no glitter on these guys, that's for sure." As she said this, the Larousse twins, Vincent and Victor, walked through the door, looking around like overgrown schoolyard toughs. They wore shiny floral shirts unbuttoned halfway down their woolly chests, alligator belts with lacquered toothy heads for buckles, and tight dark slacks. Their faces were acne-scarred and their noses had been broken into steps. On their big forearms were identical tattoos, naked girls drawn with green ink, except for the nipples, which were red.

"Oh boy," Paul said.

Colette's cheeks flushed. "It's starting already. Don't you see—"

He waved a crab claw at her. "Eat. Maybe we can get through the meal."

"How can we get through life together if we can't get through a meal here?"

He tilted his head to the side. "I'll turn over a new leaf."

From the dance hall came the buzz of an accordion, and Nelson Orville's band cranked up a chanky-chank waltz. Several old barflies slid off their stools at the counter to claim a dance from any unattached woman.

"I wish I could believe it," she told him, watching three Partians slide into the restaurant and stand against a plywood wall. The largest one smiled, showing a rotten incisor.

"You can believe," he told her, raising his eyebrows. "I want you to stay with me so bad, I might even move out to Pervert City with you."

"New Orleans is not Pervert City."

"Whatever." He spat out a piece of shell.

"Paul, I . . ." Victor Larousse bumped her chair as he walked over to stand under the Pearl beer clock as Vincent sidled over to the dance floor entrance. Etienne the giant came in from the parking lot dressed in Halliburton coveralls. He walked to the counter and ordered a beer from the barmaid, who looked at him hard, her mouth drawn to a stitched hole as she handed him a Schlitz. Etienne was king of the Partians, famous up and down Highway 71 as the man who had won a fight by tearing a toilet out of the rest room and throwing it at three attackers, bowling them down like pins.

Colette looked at the men with contempt, but Paul was unable to feel one way or another about young men who mostly followed the old codes when they fought for sport. They used only their fists as weapons, not really hating their opponents. They were just bored and restless, healthy from hard work, needing something other than time to age them.

"I want to try to talk with you," she said between her teeth. "And I appreciate your offer. About not fighting, I mean. It's a start."

He looked into the dark wood of her eyes and said nothing, feeling her anger begin to turn from him. He didn't want to risk even one comment to spoil things. When he had eaten enough, he finished his third beer, got up, and pushed through to the dance floor to wash his hands in the hot, dim rest room, which smelled like an oven full of piss. Turning on the tap, he felt a puny rill of cistern water trickle over his fingers. Five men were lined up at a galvanized trough, relieving themselves. One of them cursed the man next to him and put his fist through the Sheetrock wall. Paul dried his hands on his jeans and wondered if he could get to the door while it was still on its hinges. He went out onto the dance floor, where Nelson Orville was singing *"Mon cœur fit mal . . ."* through his nose to thirty couples, mostly men in their fifties pushing their hard, gumbo-fed wives around the dance floor with a stiff, practiced grace, hands clasped and stuck in the air like pump handles. Outside the kitchen door, at the edge of the dance floor, a cook had set up a forty-gallon garbage can and was boiling crawfish over an old water-heater burner. The room was dark with blue light, and Paul could barely see across the wide floor. He heard cursing and beer bottles toppling over a chorus of women's whining. *"Mon cœur est tout cassé,"* Orville moaned, and an old gent threw out a leg in a wide waltz turn, giving the smoking garbage can a glancing blow. Paul saw it slowly cascade over, many gallons of foaming juice charging into the dark dance hall. He wanted to get through the swinging doors to Colette before the building came apart at its orange seams.

The peppery, boiling water roiled under a long table, burning the feet of a dredge-boat crew from Texas, and the staccato pop of their curses filled the dance hall. Two of them leapt over a table and grabbed the old dancer who had caused the flood, then sailed him through the air like a paper plane. Paul watched him land facedown in a forest of long-neck bottles. The cook cried out as two men in cowboy hats turned him upside down into the still-smoking can, and then the Tiger Island friends of the old dancer arrived, throwing punches. Etienne the giant pushed open the swinging doors to the dance hall and smiled at a little red-faced Texan pulling off his shoes and hobbling toward him.

"That a new step?" Etienne asked.

The Texan threw down a brogan. "Get the fuck out my way, nutria face."

Etienne knocked him over with a backhanded swat and stepped on his groin. *"Mange la merde et meurs, Texas."*

The band began to play a two-step. Paul remembered Colette and slid along the wall toward the swinging doors. One of the dredge-boat crew ran up to him and swung wildly over Paul's ducked head. Paul grabbed his shiny shirt and tore it open, pearl buttons spraying into the room. The man glanced down at his chest, and without looking up, he landed a punch in Paul's belly. In reflex, Paul hit back with an uppercut, splitting the man's lip. Two fighters fell against Paul, flinging him through the doors and onto the floor of the restaurant, where three Partians had shoved a Rockola jukebox at the Larousse twins, pinning them against the plywood wall.

"Paul," Victor pleaded. "Kick one of these guys in the nuts." But he got up and went for Colette instead, who was standing by the door, clutching her handbag, hiding behind Clarisse. He was about to touch her, feeling that if he could, her soft skin would work a charm and transport him out of the fire of the brawl, but as he reached out, a tall deckhand pulled him around by an arm and let him have a fist on the cheek, solid as a brickbat, and he went down hard on his back. He saw a dark pair of cowboy boots leap over him toward the thunder coming from the dance floor, and he lay flat, feeling the bones of his spine burn against the planks. He was smarting and angry. Picking up his head, he saw Colette holding open the front door, gesturing. A beer mug crashed next to his shoulder. Victor called out for his help. Ah, Colette, just a second, he thought.

He jumped up, saw the Larousses turning white behind the jukebox, four beefy men pushing on it like tugboats. The heavy electrical cord had been torn off in the fight, and he picked it up, looping it once around the neck of the biggest Partian, putting a knee in his back and reining him like a stubborn horse. He fell over backward and the Larousse boys wriggled free, the tattooed women on their forearms jiggling alive as they hammered at the other men. Etienne the giant blew through the swinging doors like a cannonball with four men on him, and Paul charged toward Colette, pulling her and Clarisse outside, where they bolted for his truck, jumping in and spinning out of the lot, spraying clamshells over a little man chasing them with an upraised fist. A mile down the levee road, they met three sheriff's cruisers lolling along through the dust, their flashers off, taking their time.

Three

He slowed the pickup, watching the lawmen fade into the white cloud. He realized that he was panting. "Aw, man. What a mess. Did you get to pay the tab?"

"Bring me home." She sounded hurt, and he froze for a moment. He pulled onto the white band of shoulder and put his arm around her. "Please take your arm off me." She grabbed his hand and moved it.

"What?" His arm hovered above her, as though she were a hot stove.

"You told me you weren't gonna fight. A minute later I look up, and there you are, rolling in cigarette butts with those dredge-boat worms." Her voice grew big and sharp. "I must have been stark raving nuts to think you could do one thing the way I wanted you to."

"Aw, come on. I'm sorry." He leaned toward her.

Clarisse's puffy face appeared next to Colette's, and he jumped. He'd forgotten she was in the cab. "Paul was just defending himself," she sang.

Colette flipped her glossy hair over her shoulders. She wiggled against the seat, willing to grow smaller, concentrating like an unstable element. "How can I trust you if you can't keep a promise for five minutes? You lied to me. Bring me home *now*."

He floored the accelerator, fishtailing shells up into the moonlight like spinning coins. "All right, that's where your ass is going." When the truck charged into the drive of the rent house, she hopped over Clarisse and was on the overgrown lawn before the truck stopped moving. His mouth hung open as he watched her narrow back flash through the front door.

Clarisse looked through the windshield at the porch light winking off. She gave her hair a toss. "Well, it's early yet. Before you drive me all the way past Tonga Bend to home, I could use a highball." Paul put an elbow on the window ledge and grabbed a fistful of his dark hair. He thought of his wife's face, as unblemished as the new milling machine he had uncrated that day down at the shop. That's what she was like, a machine that was trying to shape and mill and saw his raw, unfinished self into something different. It scared him to think this, but what scared him more was next to him now: Clarisse's cast-iron perfume, her pickup truck of a body with its smooth ride and deep upholstery, and all the open dance halls between where he was and where he ought to go.

Colette sat on the sofa and got up immediately because it smelled of her husband, not an unpleasant scent, just a mix of Old Spice and a molecule of thread-cutting oil that was his odor alone. Nothing interested her on television and she didn't feel like staring at the plain wooden doors with their dozen coats of paint, so she got into her little car and drove to her parents' house, a rambling two-story high up on piers, built before the levee systems kept out the wandering Chieftan. Her father, a retired principal of the little rough-and-tumble high school, was asleep in the glider when she walked up on the porch. Both her parents were old. She had been an afterthought even for them. Before she went into the long, wide hall, she touched her father's shoulder.

"Huh?" Mr. Jeansomme's spectacles were two halos reflecting the streetlight. "Who is it?"

"Colette. You fell asleep. You'd better get in out of this dampness."

"I guess so," he said. She knew he would be stiff, so she helped him up. "Did you have a good time at the Gator?"

She pushed the screen to the side with her foot. "No. The crabs were good, but a fight broke out."

"Ah, Lord. It's Friday, I guess. How did Paul do?" He ran a hand through his white mop and walked out of her arms and down the hall like a figure in a dream.

"He lost this time," she called after him as he started up the stairs. Her mother had gone to bed by this time, so there was no one to talk to. She went to the end of the hall and opened a door into a small room showing two walls of narrow windows. It was an old reading porch left over from a time before television. In it was a dark George Steck upright, a relic of her girlhood, when she took piano from the old maid next door, who taught her to play songs no one on earth had ever heard of, music of no style or school, with titles like "Long Fingers Walking Through the Cloud Banks" or "German Salamander Night Waltz." She sat down and began playing from a book left open on the music rack for over a year.

The first time she had really talked to Paul was when her father had hired him to cut the lawn. She had been practicing piano, hearing in the background the sputtering of their smoky lawn mower and then the cattle-munching sound of grass being pulled by hand along the piers of the house. She finished playing that day and walked to the window, where she looked down on the top of Paul's head. He was sitting with his jug of ice water between his legs, which were stretched out on the fresh grass clippings. She could tell he had been listening to the music rain down on him from her open window. That first day, when she had gone out to meet him and size him up, he had tried to explain why the lawn mower was burning oil. She pretended to listen, but, like every pretty girl of fifteen, she was interested only in the fact that Paul had muscles, thick dark hair, and wasn't half-bad-looking. He seemed nice, and clever, though even then there was a kind of denseness to him, a heavy earnestness she could see by watching his eyes. That first day he had explained how a lawn mower worked and she didn't hear a word. From that point, things had never changed.

She played another page of notes and thought about quitting the bank and moving to New Orleans, breaking loose from all those silver cords of relatives and friends, the gumbos of the aunts, the homemade sausage of the uncles. As long as she stayed in Tiger Island, she would be a little girl in their minds, and Paul would think of her as what? The good dancer? The prettiest girl in town? The hardest hitter when she was angry? She stopped playing and wondered what went on in his mind. What had he been thinking when he'd asked her to marry him?

She turned to another sheet of music and stared at the title: "Firefly Dancing with a Moonbeam." She pressed the soft pedal and began to play.

On the way to her apartment, Clarisse slid next to Paul and asked him to stop at the Church Key Lounge so she could buy herself a drink. He arched an eyebrow and looked at her. She was his wife's first cousin. It would be like drinking with his sister. What could it hurt? He wasn't sleepy, and the old, familiar, dangerous boredom had set in, so when they reached the dusty parking lot for the Church Key, he turned the wheel.

A five-piece band of middle-aged men called Boogielicious was thumping out some early sixties rock and roll for a few couples swinging in the black-light dark. Paul and Clarisse sat at the bar and drank two rounds. He scowled at the slicked-back musicians because he wanted to talk about what Colette had been telling Clarisse for the past week. Choosing not to scream out questions about his personal life, he sulked until the band took a break.

After a third drink Clarisse sank against the padded bar and smiled a slow and sticky smile. "Paul, you enjoy looking worried? Is it maybe a new sport?"

"Hey. This ain't New Year's Eve for me."

Clarisse scooted back on her padded stool. She was big, bottom and top, but with a small waist. "Aw, Colette might take you back. It's not like she's never been pissed off at you before."

He held up a finger at the bartender. "I don't know."

"Hey. Me, too."

He looked at her empty glass and blinked. "You used to drinking sloe gin? You don't maybe want to eat something to soak it up?"

Her head fell back limp. "Get me a couple pickled eggs and one of those weenies in vinegar." She giggled when she said the word *weenie*.

A few new couples came in, blue-jeaned welders and cementers with their frizzy, bleached wives, and the place began to warm and fill with smoke. The bass player for Boogielicious strapped a guitar against his gut, thumbed a note, and frowned at the drummer, who rapped out the starting licks of "Jailbird."

After the band had played two numbers and started on a third, slow piece, Clarisse slid off her stool, her dress bunched up and sticking to her behind. "Matilda, Matilda, I cried for you . . ." she sang. "Come on, T-Bub, let's dance."

He looked around for people who knew who he was, and saw, at least, no relatives. "Okay."

Clarisse was clammy, sticky to the touch, but she could follow his movements like a shadow. He tried to keep a little daylight between them, but she was acting as though she would fall asleep in his arms. Her perfume grew salty and thick as steam. As soon as the band stopped the slow number, they hopped on an old jitterbug tune. Clarisse stuck an arm straight up, bent her knees out, and began moving her feet like windshield wipers. Paul jerked her into a double spin and they were off into the song like pinwheels. Clarisse's dancing was fueled by sloe gin, her eyes half-closed in her round face, every part of her body powerful and unconsciously accurate in movement. Paul tested her with fast turns all through the song, and when the music stopped, they were panting like runners. After two more drinks, they were bopping again. He flung her out and she banged an old man off the dance floor. Paul felt the music flow into him like alcohol and Boogielicious got tight and hot like the room, the oily pompadours of the gray musicians lunging through the smoke. They danced one after another until Clarisse began to get out of control, straightening her arms too much, dropping a step, breathing with her mouth open. The band went on break, and she sidestepped to the bar, where she washed down another pickled sausage with a sloe gin fizz.

"Let's go outside and get some air," Paul told her at last, gathering in her damp waist and propelling her to the door. The smokeless atmosphere was a shock. Inside the lounge, everything was loud and spinning and they were part of the large organism of the dance. Outside, the air was like syrup, and Paul stood in the gravel under a yellow bug light, trying to think of something to say. He wagged his head as though trying to shake water from his hair. "Man, that was a workout."

Clarisse gave him one of her slow smiles. "You sted nuff," she told him.

"What?" He looked into her pale green eyes.

"Sif langs labial."

"Aw, Jeez, Clarisse. You ain't even here anymore." He grabbed her upper arm, scared that she would go down at any moment. Clarisse looked up at him with the most open, trusting, adventurous face he'd ever seen on a woman, her eyes filmed over with romance. "Hey," he told her. "Don't look at me like that. You having some kind of estrogen tornado inside or what?"

"Pal," she said, "lesko fride nadark."

"Whatever. Time to go home." He pushed her toward his truck, his own steps a little sideways and creaky, though he had drunk only beer. The truck pulsed and vibrated under a flickering mercury-vapor light. Clarisse grabbed three times for the door handle, and he had to boost her rear into the high seat. When he climbed into the driver's side, she put an arm beside him and once again turned a dreamy, eager face to his. "Straighten up, now," he said. Paul was ashamed that he enjoyed the heat of her, the kind of rounded-off, well-padded fun of her, and he quickly started the truck. But before he put it in gear, he turned for one last slow look at her face, which was still half-smiling and shiny with dance, a little cross-eyed from all the twisting steps, soft, and a bit too pale, maybe too shiny, her mouth open as if she was trying to figure out how a mouth worked. "Erik ohms," she said.

"Oh no," he yelled, his dizzy butt dancing on the suddenly electrified upholstery.

The next morning, he was taking his truck apart on his parents' front lawn, had the front bench seat out on the grass, and was working carefully with towels, a bucket of pine oil, and two cans of Lysol. There was a sour pond on his dashboard, little bits of vinegar sausage in his tape deck, an egg yolk–colored mist gumming up the little pill-shaped buttons of his radio. With screwdrivers and pliers, he removed his air-conditioning vents, which were awash with acid-fried bits of Slim Jim, milky pink sloe gin, and crab meat. On the complex dashboard, every control lever, fan switch, digital readout, and seam gave off a clabbered, alcoholic, sun-tortured vapor.

He had pulled out the carpet and was giving it a vigorous hosing when Father Clemmons, a middle-aged priest, stopped on the oak-shaded sidewalk and called to him. Paul had spotted him first but had pretended not to see him.

"Good morning," said the priest, a pale outlander from Indiana. "Are you having a little car trouble?"

Paul smiled in spite of a headache, hoping his eyes weren't bloodshot. "I guess you might say that." The priest had run the parish for twelve years but still seemed fresh from the wheat fields, unaffected by the south Louisiana ways of hard drinking, poverty, white heat, and green humidity, the general funk of the place. He was bald, optimistic, and tall, unlike everyone else in the parish.

The priest walked closer and took a winesap apple from his pocket. "How are you and Colette getting along?"

So he had heard already. "I guess we're hitting a few bumps in the road. We ought to be able to work it out."

The priest took a bite out of the apple, folded his arms. "What's her complaint, Paul?"

He twisted the nozzle and turned off the spray. "I don't know."

"She didn't tell you?"

"Yeah, something about staying out too late."

"Do you?"

"Hey, Father, I don't need much sleep. I can't sleep is more like it. Not until late." He soaked a hand towel in Lysol and leaned in to work under the windshield, realizing that he would have to remove the heater vents from under the dash.

"Most people watch television." The priest bit the apple as though he were trying to hurt it.

"I like to dance. Listen to live bands. You really think some late-night TV will make me a better person?"

"Would Colette like to go dancing with you?"

Paul threw the cloth into a bucket and grabbed a fresh one.

"About once a month, she'll come out on a weekend. But you got to understand that she runs out of gas about eleven o'clock. She's not a night person." He was not sure how much the priest knew. He looked up at him, his sweating bald head, his worried eyes. "You had a bad morning, Father?"

The priest swallowed hard. "I did two counseling sessions this morning. Couples heading into divorce. You know, this is a bad era, even for Catholics."

"Well." Paul picked up a long screwdriver and leaned in under the dash.

"Nobody wants to earn love," the priest said.

"Yeah?" Oh God, he thought.

Father Clemmons stepped closer and bobbed the apple core in the air before him. "People think love is something you decide, something you will. It isn't that at all." It showed in the priest's face that Paul was ignoring him, so he pursed his lips for a moment. "Paul, how long did it take you to learn to play that little Cajun accordion?"

"Aw, man, I wore the nickel plate off those buttons before I even learned to keep time. Sometimes I wanted to throw that thing down and kick it across the yard. But I know what you going to tell me. That marriage takes practice and you got to be patient and all that sermon stuff. That might work on paper, Father. But if you had to live with a woman that was like a bomb with a short fuse, the answer wouldn't be so clear." He pulled a segmented hose out from under the dash, dropping it on the lawn with two fingers.

"Okay," the priest said, holding up his free hand. "I'd better get going. If you and Colette need any advice, give me a call."

As the priest turned, Paul saw Colette's Toyota jounce into the driveway. "Don't go just yet."

Colette got out and walked up with her fists balled white, like a runner waiting for the gun. She looked at Father Clemmons and back at Paul. "You . . . snake," she said between clenched teeth. Paul imagined all the adjectives she was leaving out for the priest's benefit.

"Colette . . ."

"Don't Colette me," she said. And then her face knotted up like an angry child's. "My own first cousin." She glanced at the priest. "My own childhood playmate."

Paul stood up and wiped his hands. "What?"

"Someone told me."

"Told you what?"

She nearly gagged on the word. "Clarisse. You took advantage of her."

Paul glanced at the priest. "All we did was dance," he yelled.

"She was on you like flypaper, I heard."

The priest cleared his throat. "Well, I've got to be . . ."

Paul gave him a pleading look. "Don't go yet."

Colette put a fist to her mouth for a moment. "You were dating my first cousin. Clarisse and I made our first communion together."

"She was holding on to me, I wasn't holding on to her."

Colette gave him a killing look. "You got her drunk."

"Baby, since when can I keep Clarisse from drinking?"

"You came on to her, I heard it."

"Pardon me, Father, but that's bullshit." The priest waved his apple core, giving his blessing to the argument.

Paul pointed at the ground with a forefinger. "She asked me to buy her a few rounds and I thought she was sweating it off and soaking it up with all the bar stuff she was eating."

"She ate a pickled pig foot, I heard. Do you know how drunk Clarisse has to be to eat a pig foot? But no. You weren't worried about her. Just like you don't worry about me. Now everybody in town knows my husband is dating my first cousin. It feels like incest."

He threw up his hands. "I did not date Clarisse. *You* invited her along."

Colette opened her palms to the priest. "He puts a woman in a car—"

"I had to bring her home and—"

"He brings her to a dance hall. . . ."

"She bugged the hell out of me for a drink. . . ."

"He gets her drunk. . . ."

"She ordered, damn it. She ordered and she—"

"He dances with her like she's his wife. . . ."

"She's a decent dancer. . . ."

"Takes her out into the parking lot in the dark—"

"I was bringing her home. . . ."

Colette looked away from the priest into Paul's eyes, and he felt that something big was coming. "Then he feels her on the behind as she's getting in his truck. . . ."

"Feels her behind? What? She was so shit-faced she couldn't raise her legs to—"

"Then when he's in the truck, does he start it right away and drive her home? Nooooo." Colette wound up an arm like she was getting ready to throw a softball underhand. "He lets the poor woman slide next to him and he looks her in the eyes. . . ."

"Damn it, she was looking *me* in—"

Colette slowed down and made her voice deep. "And then, and then . . ."

"And then she blew up all over my truck."

"It was her defense mechanism," she shouted.

"Defense, hell, Colette. The woman was like a big balloon somebody pumped up with puke. I mean, she flew around."

"And when you saw you weren't gonna get any action, you finally drove her home. She had to beg you to stop and let her throw up some more."

"That's a lie. I stopped five times for her to open the door and lean out. I like to've ralphed myself, the truck was so full of her. I had whitecaps on the floorboards."

Colette turned to the priest again. "And you know what he told her the last time she made him stop?"

"Aw, Colette." Paul put up his hands. "It was a joke. You remember. An old joke from high school."

"You want to know what he told my sick first cousin?"

"Colette, she wanted me so bad she was cross-eyed. And I wasn't gonna do a thing."

"The last time she leaned out over the road, he said, 'Hey, if you throw up a little round thing, you need to save that,' and Clarisse asked, 'Why?' and he said, 'Because that'll be your ass-hole.'"

Father Clemmons began to back away. "That was not very compassionate," he said quickly, "and if you want to talk, I'll be in the rectory all afternoon." He began to cross the street.

"Father," Paul called after him. But the priest was already on the opposite sidewalk, waving backward over his shoulder.

Colette pointed a slender finger at him. "You can date all you want. Check your mailbox every day, because more separation papers are coming, T-Bub."

He walked toward her, but she backed away. "Come on, now."

She flipped her hair behind her shoulders and pointed a long fingernail at him like a weapon. "And you know what? I think I'll go on a date tonight."

He froze. "A date? Who would date you?"

"You bearing-head bastard. Bucky Tyler has been hitting on me at the bank."

Paul squinted. "Who the hell's that? That guy from Texas? The cowboy?"

"He's got money and style."

"He's a worm for Texaco. He screws old people out of their mineral rights. Come on, let's talk about this. You can be sweet."
He felt threatened, truly threatened, for the first time.

"Can't. I got to call for a date." She bobbed off to her little car like a schoolgirl and was gone in five seconds. Out in the river behind the house, the bridge tender blew a warning signal for a tugboat. Paul put his head into his truck cab and pulled it out again, turning for the hose. I have to get everything put back together, he thought.

Four

He didn't see his wife for several days. His parents demanded a raft of repairs and he puttered around oiling hinges, changing faceplates on outlets, replumbing the kitchen sink. The morning of the third day, he was tired of replacing the old thin-skinned brass pipes on every sink in the house, so he walked away down the levee to visit his *grand-père* Abadie, who was so old that nobody went to see him anymore. When he was in his late sixties, everyone in the family enjoyed checking on the dried-up fisherman to help him out. When he was in his seventies, the family members continued the tradition of visits and little gifts. But then *Grand-mère* died, the old man sailed into his eighties, and people didn't come around as much, as if to say, It looks like you'll be around forever, so why should we bother you? And why are you living so long? Paul found him in the kitchen of his unpainted wooden house, making morning coffee for the second time.

"Hey, *Grand-père*."

The old man turned from the stove and arched an eyebrow. "Ey, T-Bub." He shook his silver head. "Ey, T-Bub."

"What's wrong?" He sat down at a small table near the varnished window frame.

"Mrs. LeBlanc called me and told me Colette was out with another man at the Big Gator this weekend sometime. I think it was Saturday night. What the hell's wrong with you?"

"Me? She's the one stepping out."

His grand-père sat down across from him and narrowed his eyes. He hadn't combed his hair yet and looked like some wind-blown oysterman just landed from the Gulf. "You didn't talk to her? You didn't find the guy and whip his ass?"

Paul put his hands on the table and swung his head. "Aw, we having some problems. You know. And it's my ass-whipping tendencies that she's pissed off about."

"When you got problems, you solve 'em." The old man opened a hand toward the window. "I can't understand you children nowadays. You all like a bunch of marshmallows. They's nothing to you."

Paul closed one eye. What his grand-père told him hurt. "Aw."

"Aw," the grand-père mocked. "Prettiest girl in the parish and you just throwing her away like that."

"She wants me to change."

"Change! Hell, boy, you got to change your drawers in the town square if it means keeping your wife." He banged his coffee cup on the table in disgust.

"I'm not sure she's worth keeping. She cramps my style, you know?" He thought of her hair. He didn't believe what he'd just said.

"Your style?" He pronounced the word slowly, dragging out the s. "What kind of style you got? All you do is read machinery books and hang over the piss trough at the local dance hall."

"Hey, I came to visit. Let's talk about something else."

"Okay, new topic. Your wife, she's going to California on tomorrow night's train."

"What?" He was reaching for an ironware cup of coffee his grand-père was handing over, and he dropped it on the table with a bang. "Get me a rag. What?"

His grand-père mopped at the coffee, keeping it from streaming onto the floor. "You heard me. She told Melinda Ongeron in the bathroom at the Big Gator that she was tired of living in Tiger Island, yeah. She wanted to see another part of the world."

"California!"

"That's a long way off, T-Bub."

Paul raised a hand and let it fall. "California. Where is that?"

At eight-thirty he was hiding around the corner of the little yellow stucco railroad station, out of sight of Colette and her mother and father, who were standing at trackside talking and now and then glancing toward the east. He looked west, past Railroad Avenue's sleepy wooden houses, their tin roofs turned to pewter in the moonlight. He didn't want her to leave Tiger Island, but he didn't know how to ask her to stay. He thought and thought for words. When he saw the station agent come out with orders for the engineer tied to a stick, he knew he had to try something.

He walked up to them, and her parents gave him polite smiles.

"Well, look who's here," Mr. Jeansomme said.

"Paul." Mrs. Jeansomme patted his shoulder.

Colette looked at him as if he were a stray dog that had wandered up.

He took a deep breath. "I heard you were going and I came down to ask you to stay."

"For what, Paul?" She was so still, it was as though the voice came from somewhere else. She wore a beige blouse with a button-down collar, but the cloth seemed white against her dark hair. He realized that he was hungry for the sight of her, and he already wondered what the days ahead would be like.

"I want you to stay for us."

The railroad bridge whistled out four times and began to swing closed. "I don't think there is an *us* anymore," she said, looking west toward the bridge. The agent clicked on an electric hand lamp. He seemed worried.

◆

Paul kicked lightly at the roadbed. "I never thought I'd make you mad enough to leave town."

"Maybe I'm going *to* something, not away from you."

"Like you went to Bucky Tyler." He knew it was a mistake to say this as soon as he said it.

She looked him in the eye. "I just wanted to dance."

"I'm sorry," he said. He started to say something else but felt an arm on his shoulder. It was the agent, Mr. Lodrigue. "Am I glad to see you. You know what's coming? Right? That's why you're here?"

"What you talking about?"

"The steam locomotive. It's the seventy-fifth anniversary of this train and the railroad decided to pull tonight's run as far as Houston with a big steam locomotive." Mr. Lodrigue was a short man with rabbity teeth, and he couldn't talk to people without grabbing on to them.

"That's nice." He looked back to Colette, who was biting the inside of her cheek.

"Nice, hell. The crew radioed New Orleans saying they were having trouble in the cab and the superintendent called me to find a machinist who knew something about steam fittings. I told him, 'No way.' Then you walk up like the answer to a novena."

Paul shrugged off the agent's arm. "Hey, I'm here with these people, that's all."

Colette turned around at the sound of a distant whistle. "Go on, do what you're interested in."

"Colette." Her parents backed away, disentangling themselves. From two miles away, he could hear the five-chime whistle of the locomotive filling half the parish with its rising, angry note.

Colette turned west, looking past him. "When you first came into my house when we were children, you repaired my music box but hardly said a word to me."

"At least I fixed it," he said, looking east down the track to where the gold headlight swam above the illuminated rails. The whistle came, a big seventh chord searing the night air. The locomotive, a hissing thundercloud of iron and spinning brass, undulated past them and slowed, a jet of steam blasting out from under the cab as the coaches squealed and stopped.

He turned to her, put his hand on her arm, realizing that she had been watching him, not the train. "Colette . . ."

"I'm sorry, Paul," she said, stepping away. "Look, go dance with your machine." She turned to her parents and hugged them.

Mr. Lodrigue was pulling his arm. "Come on. They're waving at us from the engine." He towed Paul toward the head of the train, and after a minute he was standing with the engine crew, looking at a screaming pipe under the firebox of the locomotive.

The engineer, a smooth-faced blond man dressed in a new set of pinstriped overalls, yelled above the noise. "The agent says you can work on old stuff. Can you do anything with boiler injectors? We have to move out soon or they'll let a slow freight past us and we'll have to follow him to Texas."

"What's wrong with the injector on the fireman's side?" Paul looked at the glossy black paint, the gilt and lacquer in the cab.

"We're losing steam and water both through this one, and I don't think we can keep the boiler fed.

Paul pulled on the grab irons and climbed up into a vibrating forest of gauges and levers, forgetting everything but the locomotive, ignoring the crew behind him. He checked the water level in the boiler and tried to turn off the steam valve that fed the injector, but the stem screwed all the way down, and the leak roared on. The fireman clicked the overhead light, and Paul knew what the problem was as soon as he saw the maker's name and code cast into the side of the brass valve. He grabbed the engineer by an overalls strap and pulled him close so he would hear. "Whoever restored your engine put an eighty-year-old water valve in your injector line. Part of the valve disc's fallen off and blown through into the injector. Get me a thirty-six-inch pipe wrench. You've got quick-breaking unions on these pipes, so I can get you rolling in twenty minutes if the injector's not damaged."

The engineer looked at the arcs of hot pipe, the enameled valves. "It'll take hours to pull that assembly apart."

Paul looked at the men around him carefully, at their new overalls. "Get me a big wrench from your kit or call a diesel to pull your train."

The engineer looked at his watch. "We don't have twenty minutes. Can you make the repair while I operate the engine? You can invoice us for whatever you want."

Paul looked up at the brass face of the steam gauge. "We'll see. Fill the boiler full as you can with the fireman's injector, cut off the main appliance valve, and run slow. If I get the injector on this side fixed, I can jump at Patterson."

"I'll tell the agent to pick you up," the engineer said, twisting the knobs of a radio bolted to the roof of the cab. "I just hope you know what you're doing."

The big locomotive came alive, its exhausts rasping out as it left the station behind and made hollow thunder on the railroad bridge. Paul spun two unions loose, pulled down a hot section of two-inch pipe, reached into the injector with a pair of long-nosed pliers, and fished inside.

The engineer blew a crossing signal for Cotton Road and pulled the throttle wider. "Can you see what you're doing?" he yelled.

"Don't have to. This is a Hancock inspirator. I've got a book on it." Paul pulled out a broken valve seat with the pliers and put it into the engineer's glove. "Souvenir."

He reassembled the injector piping and climbed into a nest of hot steam lines on top of the boiler to turn on the main appliance valve. Steam pressure hammered the pipe, but there was no leak. He pulled back on a brass lever and the injector sucked up a charge of water from the tender and sent it whistling through to the boiler.

The engineer watched his water indicator inch up. He nodded

once. "Get ready to jump," he yelled. "I'm slowing for the first Patterson crossing." The locomotive rocked on the bad track coming out of Badeaux's swamp, and when the whistle sang out for the first road, Paul got down on the lowest cab step, feeling the train drag. He hopped to the asphalt road and ran a few steps, grabbing the pole of a crossing sign. The engine's exhausts cracked like gunshots, and the coaches lurched as they gathered speed.

He leaned on the pole, watching the bright windows float past. When the diner approached, he looked up at the broad light-filled windows, the silver menu holders, the shining bud vases. Only a few people sat on his side, a man in a brown suit, two old women, and then like an electric shock came the face of Colette, staring out into the dark, seeing nothing, certainly not him, her face more beautiful than he had ever seen it, full of energy and excitement. Before he could move, she sailed by and was gone. He caught a glimpse of dark hair flowing over her shoulders, and then nothing, a baggage car and an empty coach, the end of the train. He was left in a dark, windy guilt. He had fixed the giant machine that was taking her away, had forgotten that his love was on the train. He began to sense what he'd lost, and as the steam whistle fluted a huge warning a mile to the west, he tried to remember her face, her perfume. He cupped his hands over his nose, hoping for some trace of her there, but he smelled only the oily scent of machinery.

The next morning he lay in his bed, feeling like an old sack washed up on the riverbank. He kept his eyes closed, listening. In the kitchen his mother threw his lunch box on the table. A skillet banged on a stove burner; the coffeepot rang as she charged it with grounds. He opened his eyes and rolled out of bed, hoping that his mind would not come with him, that for one day at least, he could be just a body.

He found his mother scrambling a hill of eggs, the bottoms of her big arms swaying as she skimmed the spatula around the hot metal. He sat down and braced himself.

"Did you talk to Colette at that station?"

"Not much," he said patiently.

Her arms continued to tremble above the skillet. "What did she say?"

"She was leaving me. Going to California for a job. You probably know more than I do."

She gonged the spatula on the skillet. "I always did." Turning around, she touched his face and made him look at her. "You don't sound so sad, you. Don't you want her to come back?"

He shrugged. "She left me. She can do what she wants."

She shook her head and went back to the stove. "You know, you're spoiled. You and Colette both."

"Aw, yeah. We're millionaires."

"Don't get sassy with me, little boy. Just because you're twenty-four doesn't mean you can talk to me like that." She shook the hot spatula in his face. "When I got married, your father was making ninety cents an hour and we barely had electricity. Think of what you have that we didn't."

He looked through the screen door into the backyard, then beyond to the grassy rise of the levee three hundred feet away, all but obscured by the fog. Somewhere a boat hooted a deep signal, and he narrowed his eyes, deliberately not thinking of what his parents didn't have. "I hear the old *Gruenwald* up by Smoke Bend," he said.

His mother lifted out a load of egg. "You changed the subject."

"I'm listening to a boat signal."

"I'm glad I don't have ears like yours. I couldn't sleep any at night, hearing everything for five miles around the way you do."

After his meal he grabbed his lunch box, walked through the

backyard and up the levee, turning south at the top and walking toward LeBlanc's Machine Shop. His *grand-père*'s little tin-roofed shotgun house was between his parents' and his place of work, and the old man was standing in the fog, looking at the river through the willows. "Here's a early *ouisseau*," his *grand-père* said. "Is this a fog or what?" Paul squeezed the man's shoulder. "Early again," said his *grand-père*. "You must be bucking for a raise."

"I just wanted to get away from Mamma."

"Ah. She ask you about the station?" Paul looked downriver into the fog over the levee. He remembered that when Mr. Lodrigue, the station agent, got off work, he went to the Little Palace Bar, which his *grand-père* visited nearly every night to play cards in the back room. He and Colette were continually reinvented by the imagination of townspeople who knew more about their marriage than they did themselves.

"I don't have time to stop right now. You ought to get in out of this dampness."

"Baby, it's eighty degrees. I don't live in no air-conditioned house. Why you and your mamma think dampness is going to do something bad to me?"

"Got to go." When he was a quarter mile down the levee, he saw the old man still standing in the grass, hands in his pockets, looking after him.

As the church clock across the street rang seven, the high riverside door to LeBlanc's Machine Shop thundered open on its rusty rollers. Maurice LeBlanc walked the sliding door to the side and hit the handle on a switch box with his palm, the lights coming on, the rooftop fans humming alive and pulling in wisps of fog onto the concrete floor among the milling machines and lathes. Paul headed for his tool locker, anxious to get busy at once and stay busy.

* * *

Around nine o'clock he was milling a keyway in a shaft, his mind filled only with the work. Mr. LeBlanc walked up, shadowed by a hunched man wearing overalls. Nobody in Tiger Island wore overalls. They were farmer clothes. LeBlanc yelled over the noise. "Hey, Thibodeaux. Bring Gatlin down to the icehouse to take the heads off number-two compressor." Gatlin put a thumb under an overalls strap and frowned. The other men in the shop called him LeBlanc's redneck. He was too tall and ruddy. His hair was the yellow of scrambled eggs. Gatlin was from up north, around Caddo Parish.

"I can do it alone, if you want to save labor," Paul said.

"Nah. Work with this guy and teach him something." LeBlanc tilted his head and an oiled strand of iron-gray hair fell out over an ear. "You hear?"

"Yeah. We'll get it."

Gatlin, who was either forty-five or had drunk his way to thirty, turned up his lip in a smile of sorts but said nothing. The two men loaded into the shop's dusty truck and drove downriver a half mile to People's Ice Company, a worn-down brick building with thistle and pigweed growing along its roof line. Paul parked the Dodge next to the compressor room and dragged a toolbox off its bed.

The old two-cylinder vertical-piston machine had not been keeping up pressure on the ammonia line. Paul walked into the building and looked over to the tall twin blocks of the overbuilt compressor, eighty years old and made of porcelain-finished cast iron and lathe-polished brass to last forever. He climbed the five-foot flywheel and sat on its rim. The head of the compressor was eighteen inches in diameter, an inverted cast-iron bowl held down by eight one-inch-diameter bolts. He put a socket over a bolt head and connected a three-foot breaker handle. Jake Gatlin came up on the other side of the head, waving an air wrench. "I'm hooked into the plant's air," he said. "Why bust your ass with a breaker bar when you can use this?" He pulled the trigger twice and the silver wrench rasped two breathy *zips*.

Paul looked at him for a long time. He remembered the lanky Gatlin drunk and fighting with two local boys who got him down on the dance floor at Scadlock's and beat him like a drum. "I've seen you at the Big Gator," Paul said.

Gatlin's face brightened. "Yep. I seen you there, too, in the restaurant part. You was with a nice-looking woman, if I remember right."

"Yes." He pulled a slow strain on the breaker bar.

"Real pretty. What's her name?"

"Colette."

"Local gal, huh? I'm not one for dark hair, but she's the smoothest-looking bitch I've seen in this town." He put a socket on the air wrench and proceeded to place it on a head bolt.

"Great gal," Paul said. He wondered if he should let Gatlin snap a head bolt in two pieces and get himself fired. As he drew back on the breaker bar, he looked Gatlin in the eye and saw what a rawboned redneck he was, and he also thought of what a burden it was to be that way. Gatlin had been beaten up by the Larousse twins, the best fighters in Tiger Island. Anyone in his right mind should have known better than to tangle with a set of muscular twins. He recalled a girl he had seen Gatlin with that night, a beanpole blonde who worked at the truck stop over in Beewick.

"This engine was made before your grandpa was born, Gatlin. The bolts might be crystallized or froze up in the block, and you'll break them with that air wrench. They need to be backed off careful, by hand. Watch."

He put both hands on the end of the bar and leaned away slowly, pulling with his waist and shoulders at first, then drawing back his arms as though rowing in slow motion, willing all the strength in him to flow into the bolt. He could feel the bolt shaft twisting, the threads not moving, so he held his pull on the bar steady, waiting for the threads to follow the power. And it happened. Slowly as a minute hand at first, the bolt relented, and his arms turned to rock as he drew harder, bringing it around a quarter turn.

"Damn," Gatlin whispered. "I never seen nobody have sex with a engine before."

When the lunch whistle from the Louisiana Sawmill Company moaned out, Paul was back at the shop. He sat with his *grand-père* Abadie on a church pew under a live oak in the shop yard. From a thermos in his lunch box, he poured nose-snapping coffee into a plastic cup for the old man, who told him *merci* and wiped his eyes and took a sip. Paul stared at a cloud shaped like a locomotive and wondered what sights Colette had seen through the train's windows, what she was thinking at that moment.

"You know," his *grand-père* began, pausing to chew a section of sandwich Paul was sharing with him. He was a simple old Frenchman who said only what he meant, and Paul could tell what he was going to say seconds before he could get out the words. "Sometime a man can make a mistake and not know he did that."

"Is that right?" Paul nodded politely, wondering whether anyone in town was talking of anything else. He studied the ground where the shadows of millions of leaves leapt and ran. A gust of wind rolled over the levee, and the two men faced west, letting the breeze leech the heat from their moist shirts. The old man finished eating and struggled up the levee, and Paul walked into the equipment room, a jumbled storage area containing thousands of pieces of machinery and a greasy oak desk where a black rotary phone rested in a nest of invoices. He often sat in there on his lunch hour among the cables and gears, reading old machinery manuals, learning about steamboat engines and windmills. Placing his hand on the phone, he imagined it ringing and heard Colette's voice singing in from the West Coast like a silver arrow.

Paul had never been more than two hundred miles from home. He had attended a local college for a year and had done well, despite the jammed and windowless classrooms. He'd soon realized that if he ever graduated from the dinky school, he would wind up holding an indoors job, unable to spit on the ground, forever looking for a window, forever sitting at a desk, filling out paperwork and swallowing snot.

Colette had made straight *A*'s in her two-year associate program, getting on at the bank and leaving everyone there in awe of her brains and looks. Paul was sure the tellers were talking about her at this moment, for they went to lunch in a gaggle at twelve-thirty.

At four o'clock everyone in LeBlanc's Machine Shop began replacing tools and turning off grinders and drill presses. Paul picked up his airy lunch box and mounted the weed-ridden levee, listening to the exhaust fans wind down and the riverside door grind closed as LeBlanc grunted against it. On his left was the wide Chieftan River, and floating near the edge was his *grandpère*'s gray cypress skiff tied to a willow.

Paul's father was in a plastic chair on the screen porch, reading the New Orleans paper. He was a small, dark man who never said much but who found pleasure in listening to others. "Hey, T-Bub," he said, lowering one corner of his paper.

"Hey," Paul said, putting down his lunch box and settling into a rush-bottom rocker. "Has the mail come?"

"I don't think Colette would write this soon." He drew his face close to an article about Norway.

"Well, did you check?"

"Nobody writes to me." His father wet a finger and turned a page.

Paul walked out to the front porch and thrust his hand down into the tin pocket of the mailbox, feeling only dead leaves.

Colette had been gone six weeks. It was now the end of August and the weather turned vicious, hot and steamy as an overworked engine. The machinists at LeBlanc's labored wet as retrievers at their lathes and band saws. In the afternoons, he would sit on the front porch, red-faced and dehydrated. He saw no reason to keep renting a house, and his parents got used to having him around again like an extra piece of furniture. After supper he would go out and play cards with the old men at the Little Palace or meet a friend at a local lounge. He would dance only with the date of another man, avoiding single women as though they were made of hot iron. Once, he went into the Big Gator, saw Clarisse waltzing with a pipe fitter from Pierre Part, and left before the bartender returned with his beer.

That same night he went home and tried to watch television, but a thunderstorm rolled up from the Gulf and knocked the power out. In the dark he thought of something Colette had said, that Louisiana was a land of limited ambition. He suddenly wondered if he would ever own LeBlanc's Machine Shop. Was that ambition, to want to own a machine shop? Two machine shops? A chain of machine shops strung out along the Chieftan River like franchise hamburger stands? Colette would like that. MacLeBlanc's, over one billion crankshafts repaired.

In the afternoons he would check for a letter that never came. When he called her parents, they would tell him they had received only one letter, one brief call. She was working in a bank. No, she had not told them to tell him anything.

One night he dreamed his left arm had been cut off by the shop's band saw. He woke lying on his side, his arm drained and asleep, and he leapt out of bed to turn on the light. He stood there panting and wet, his whole body feeling like a sleeve with no flesh in it.

The next day he woke with the idea that he had ruined his marriage. By noon he was sitting on the pew in the yard of the machine shop, thinking that it was Colette who had done the damage. Later, on the front porch of his parents' house, his hand in the empty mailbox, he decided he would try to go out to the clubs in town, get a buzz on and dance. He needed to cheer up, burn some gas.

He began with a Dixie beer at a sedate paneled lounge in town called the Moonbeam, but he quickly tired of the flat black walls and of being ignored by the lesbian bartender. He stopped by René's for a beer and then worked his way out to the levee road south of town. The more he drank, the more he craved to be in a place befitting his sinking self. He drove to the trash-lumber Big Gator, watched them rebuild the swinging doors to the dance floor, and then he drifted down the road to a lounge built like an apple crate, called Black Alice's, a moldy place cooled by a giant homemade box fan that roared near the entrance and occasionally sucked in a drunken patron. Five minutes after he sat at the bar, the fan's blades ripped a woman's skirt off, and the men at the tables pointed and yelled, turning over one another's drinks. The woman was dark-haired and slim. She cursed the men, pulled off her shoes one at a time, and threw them into the bar. He watched the ghostlike blur of her slip drifting across the dim parking lot.

Eventually Paul's self-esteem tumbled enough for him to drive his truck slowly down to Scadlock's Boiler Room, a one-time equipment shed near Tonga Bend, open twenty-four hours a day, windows cut into its sides with a chain saw and covered with nailed-up screens. The bar was hot and bug-infested in the summer, and drafty as a prairie in the winter. Zumo Scadlock had bought the building from a bankrupt shipyard and moved it to the edge of Bayou LaFont, propping it up on cypress stumps. The bar's rear hung over the bayou. Inside, the walls were made of smoke-stained one-by-six lumber—wooden tables to the left, a dimly-lit bar to the right, two narrow rest-room doors at the end of the leaning bar, and one innocent-looking unpainted hollow-core door in the rear wall at the end of a short hall. Behind the bar was an entrance to a kitchen, where Zumo boiled crabs and crawfish. Paul went in and sat at the bar next to Zumo's cousin Ray-Ray, who had just been paroled from Angola. He looked the cousin in the face for a long moment.

"Ray-Ray," he yelled.

"T-Bub. What's happenin', man?" He grinned, showing five upper teeth, widely spaced. Paul ordered a round of drinks as though Ray-Ray were a long-lost friend, though he could remember speaking to him only two or three times in grammar school.

"You, uh, just got out?" Paul asked.

Ray-Ray swung his beer bottle in a wide, slow arc. "Yeah, man. I wore out three hoes in them soybean field with my black brothers." He took a long draw off his bottle.

"Were you glad to get back to Tiger Island?"

Ray-Ray looked at the girl on the Schlitz clock and stroked his narrow, furry face. "Yeah, man. I was in that place for almos' three years, and I didn't know nobody when I got there, and I didn't know nobody when I left." He took another long swig. "My people's here."

Paul wondered what Colette would think of skinny, sunburned Ray-Ray, whose cotton shirt was burned through in several places by cigarettes, whose polka-dotted welder's cap was turned backward, its crown rising like the tip of a pistol bullet. What would she think of the fact that her husband was drinking with the wiry, mustachioed parolee in Scadlock's, buzzy drunk and unhappy that he was now considering his birthplace the way an outsider might. He drew deep on his long-neck and banged it down on the bar, hard. No one looked up.

After an hour, a new face appeared through the cigarette smoke, a man wearing a cowboy hat and a denim vest unbuttoned over a hairy chest. Paul took one look at the man's pointed boots and thought of the West, where Colette's train had gone.

"Uh-oh," Ray-Ray said under his breath. "East Texas white trash." He turned his cap around and stared with one eye into his beer bottle.

"I've seen him in town before. Who is that?" Paul squinted toward the door.

"Name's Tyler, I think."

Paul's mouth fell open slightly. "Bucky Tyler."

"That's it, man."

"He dated my wife."

Ray-Ray ducked his head. "Whoa."

The cowboy sat on the next stool and ordered a Pearl. He turned to Paul and smiled like a movie star. "Hey, coon-ass, where can a man get laid around here?"

Paul glanced at him as though he were a piece of machinery that needed to be taken apart quickly. He didn't look for fistfights, but at the moment he felt a high-pitched keening in his head and a stiff but airy tension in his neck and shoulders, as though he needed a bit of sporting exercise to adjust his mood. He focused on the cowboy hat, a cheap white straw thing bought in a feed store.

"Me, I don't speak English so good, monsieur," Paul began. "But if you want a good *morceau de chou*—how you say, piece of ass—then pass through that back door to Madame LaFont's." He directed Bucky Tyler's attention to the unpainted door. "You got to walk through quick now, so the bouncer, he can't stop you."

The cowboy looked at the door and then at Ray-Ray as though for confirmation.

"*Mais oui,*" Ray-Ray volunteered. "On the nother side that door, they got some *jeune filles* for forty dollars what look like them Dallas Cowgirl. But you got to be fast to get past the old man at the door who ask too many damn question."

The cowboy motioned to Zumo, who came up and killed a roach on the bar with an empty bottle. "Is there a whorehouse through there or what?"

Zumo stared at him just one second before answering. "Shit yeah, man. We got a whole Comrade Hilton back there." The bartender walked away to check a cooler and Bucky Tyler slid off his padded stool.

Ray-Ray leaned close to Paul's ear. "Hey, man, if he walks out that door, it'll be like walking outside a spaceship, only worse, you know, when you think about the drop-off and that pile of garbage."

Paul remembered that Scadlock threw his crab shells, fish guts, and tons of bottles and cans right out the back door into the bayou. There was a healthy five-foot drop to the swamp pit of glass, tin, and rot.

Bucky pulled his hat down over his eyes and sucked in his little paunch. Ray-Ray and Paul kept an eye on his back as he walked to the door, opened it with a flourish, and stepped out into the blackness, disappearing instantly. They heard the rattle of cans and the tinkle of bottle glass. One or two bar patrons turned to look through the open door as a gaggle of moths trembled into the light. Paul and Ray-Ray drew on their beer bottles and watched the front door. After a full five minutes, the cowboy appeared, his hat gone, his arms scratched up, a red gash over his nose.

"Hello, baby," Ray-Ray said. "You get you a quickie?"

Paul began taking off his shirt. "People from Texas never could stay in the saddle long."

Bucky Tyler walked up to the bar and kicked Ray-Ray off his stool with a pointed boot, and Paul grabbed his leg, spilling him like a wheelbarrow. When he got up, Paul hit him square in the face, but the cowboy took it and returned two more, putting the machinist on the floor. The punches were like gunshots coming out of a foggy night, and Paul became angry with himself that he was too drunk to put up his best fight against the man who had dated his wife. Before he could get to his feet, Tyler turned and shoved Ray-Ray against a table. Paul grabbed his shoulder and the cowboy turned for him. They traded punches and slipped to the floor, wrestling in spilled beer and cigarette ashes. Paul got in three hard uppercuts, and the cowboy began to holler that he had had enough.

"Hol' up, now. You gonna kill me."

Paul stood and staggered back against the bar, his body struggling with beer and the electric excitement of the fight. A flash at the cowboy's hip told him to jump and a skinning knife arced past his stomach. Paul gave Ray-Ray a flicker of a look and they ran, putting a heavy plank table between them and the cowboy, picking it up and sailing it off in his direction. Bucky Tylor dropped his knife to fend off the flying furniture, which ironed him out against the floor. Paul and Ray-Ray each grabbed a boot and dragged him into the men's room, a foul and slimy place with no urinal, just two boards ripped out of the floor next to the rear wall, Bayou LaFont gleaming darkly below. "Listen up, son of a bitch," Paul told him. "This is what Cajuns do to shitheads who pull knives." Ray-Ray put his foot on the man's stomach and Paul towed him next to the wall and twisted him through the hole. There was a watery splat, followed by a little twangy moan.

A big hard hat swayed into the tiny box of a rest room, nodded to Paul, and began to urinate into the darkness below, trying to hit a moth that flew up from outside. From under the building came a roar of cursing, and Ray-Ray punched Paul lightly in the ribs. "Hey, T-Bub, I'm gonna get myself down the road in case John Wayne call the cops when he crawl out the shit pit." Together they went into the parking lot, an oyster shell—covered, spinning moonscape.

"Ray-Ray," Paul cried, "don't go off. I got a truck here some-place." He pulled his shirt on inside out. "You got to drive me."

"Okay, man, but I ain't had no license in two years, ten months." He got under the steering wheel and gunned the engine. Not a mile from Scadlock's, Paul began to dream with his eyes open and woke up when his head hit the dash. He figured he had to talk to keep from passing out.

"Ray-Ray neg, did you ever get married?"

"Man, what you mean?" Ray-Ray shook his head slowly. "That's why I wound up in the pen. My old lady run off to Houma with a punk-rock motorcycle freak. I caught up with them and whipped his ass so bad, he couldn't wipe hisself for a month." A wheel dropped off into a muddy rut and they were quiet until the truck was going straight again. "But what they really got me for was cutting his ten-t'ousand-dollar motorcycle up with a blowtorch. Good thing they got to me before I shoved them pieces up his butt. Yeah, man, the women around here, they something else. All they want is your paycheck, and then it's off to Wal-Mart to live high on the hog buying ceramic pussy cats and imitation-velvet shower curtains and shit like that." The truck rolled over the center line a moment. Ray-Ray was apologetic. "I haven't drove no car with power steering in a long time." He ducked his head and looked ahead toward town. "You ever got married?"

"Yep, still am, until the divorce gets finalized."

"Yeah, you used to go out with that white-skinned girl. What's her name? Claudette? Her old man threw me out of high school."

"Colette," Paul said, rubbing his eyes with the heels of his hands.

"Yeah, man. She was drop-dead good-looking." Ray-Ray looked over to the passenger side. "She married you? Man, I thought she'd a been married to a movie star by now, with her looks."

Paul wondered if there was one person in the entire town who didn't know who Colette was. "She wants to move away from here. She thinks the people around here are, uh . . ." He opened his hands, looking for a word. "Rough." It wasn't the right one, but it would have to do.

Ray-Ray laughed. "It don't take no Elbert Einstein to see that."

"Would you ever consider moving away?"

He shook his head and pushed back his cap. "I got my family to live off of here. You know, it's like the little girl in the movie about the wizid says, 'They ain't no place like home.' Stay in you own backyard, know what I mean?"

They were riding under live oaks. Paul squinted at the silvery Spanish moss hanging ahead. Colette looked nothing like Judy Garland.

Five

The next morning he felt a raspy hand on his foot, rocking it back and forth. Paul did not open his eyes. "Hello, Daddy."

"You got a headache, I bet."

"Who told you?" He opened one eye and focused on his father's khaki shirt.

"Never mind. Just be glad that poor fellow they fished out the toilet ain't hurt bad."

He sat up and blinked, working his tongue through the cloudy mass in his mouth. His father, round-shouldered and tawny, watched him. Through the window, the backyard shone bright with midday sun. "My God, what did I do? I remember some kind of fight at Black Alice's. Did I get sucked into the fan?"

"Scadlock's," his father corrected. "T-Bub, ain't you getting kinda old for that stuff?"

"Awwwww." He rubbed his head with both hands.

"Here," his father said, holding out a parched palm. In it were three headache tablets.

"How's the Texas dude?"

"He's all right. They used a gallon of peroxide on him at the clinic and turned him loose. He's not no common white trash, you know. He's a lease buyer. You lucky he didn't press charges."

"He just didn't want it to get out what I did to him."

"How you feeling?"

He felt his left cheek. "Sore inside and out."

His father looked down at his bulky work shoes. "You ever hear from Colette?"

"No." Paul put his head down in his hands.

His father handed him a glass of tap water. "Why not?"

He drank and looked out of his window. "Daddy, I think I might never see her again. It's like she's on the moon."

"Just be thankful she can't see you right now. Clean up and come out on the porch and let's us talk."

In a half hour he went out into the sun, pale and trembly, trying not to spill an ironware mug of dark-roast coffee. Across the grass of the backyard, the silver whorls in the lumber of the gray cypress shed leapt at him and he stepped back. Slowly, he lowered himself into the green rush rocker. "Daddy, you think this is an ugly town?"

The old man rocked and scratched an arm. "Hell, I don't know. When a man lives somewhere all his life, he don't know if that place is ugly or not. I guess it was better when I was a kid, before the oil people came and set up all these tin buildings and yards full of junk."

Paul took a long sip of coffee and felt it burn all the way down. "Did you ever spend time anywhere else?"

"Before you was born, Uncle Medric passed away up where he had moved to in north Alabama. I had to go up, up, way up the country. He lived alone, and nobody else where he lived would do it, and I had to sell off everything he owned. Took me a month to clear things up. He had a house and two barns plumb full of stuff."

"Was living there different from here?"

"Well, they had mountains. You could see stuff far off, not like down here, where everything's flat as a lawyer's ass. You'd get up in the morning and the grass would be dry. Even on a hot day, the walls wouldn't sweat, and hot was about eighty. The streets in that town went up and down like a washboard and on the sides of the mountains you could see real rock, not just sand and mud like here. The only rock we got in town's that gravel on the railroad track."

Paul closed his eyes, trying to picture what a real mountain looked like. "Could you have lived there?"

His father touched his chin. "I don't know, T-Bub. Maybe if I had some family around. Family was more important them days than it is now. But the damn food couldn't be eat, and everybody talked that twangy twang, so you couldn't understand half what they said."

Paul looked out to the wine-colored rust on the shed roof. "I wonder if I could live somewhere else, like Colette's doing."

His father crossed his legs and took a deep breath. "Some people are like birds and can live wherever they light." He put his head back and closed his eyes. "Some people."

Colette's parents were waiting for him after Sunday Mass. They seemed to have gotten grayer since he had seen them at the train station two months before. Mrs. Jeansomme was fifty-eight, her husband nine years past that, and this cloudy morning they seemed like old birds on a wire waiting out a drizzle. Mr. Jeansomme was just beginning to be senile, he'd heard, now and then putting on his wristwatch upside down, getting lost coming back from Communion.

"Paul," Mrs. Jeansomme began, "have you heard from Colette?"

He shook his head. "I don't guess she feels like writing to me yet. And you?"

She glanced at her husband. "Not much. She's got to be busy." She grabbed Paul's arm and gave it a squeeze, then herded her husband toward the street. Their son, Mark, came up and slapped Paul on the back.

"Paul."

"Big M. How you doing?"

"Okay. You heard from the ice woman?" Mark was a tall, friendly man with the olive skin of a heavy smoker.

"Not a snowflake."

"Well, I can see that, considering who she's not writing to. But what's sad is she's not calling home. Momma doesn't deserve that." He banged Paul on the shoulder with a fist and walked backward toward the street. "Later. I got to drive them home so Daddy won't roll into a ditch."

"Wait." Paul raised his hand the way someone might flag a taxi. Mark stopped and squinted at him. "Did you ever figure why she left town?"

"She doesn't like the looks of the place anymore, T-Bub. It's the town as much as it's you, you dancin' fool." He waved and got into his father's faded Chrysler.

Later Paul sat on the squeaky bed in his room, looking out the window. Next door old lady Fontenot hacked at her garden, mixing in a wheelbarrow of manure with the dark soil. He could not see her face, but he knew it was a nest of wrinkles, her eyes two sharp dots at the end of the tunnel of her sunbonnet. She was singing something in French, the notes jerky with the work of her hoe. He had never paid much attention to her, but Colette said it was stupid for a ninety-year-old woman to kill herself in a garden for vegetables she could walk to the store and buy. He stared at old lady Fontenot, trying to figure if she was one of the ugly reasons Colette had left.

The next afternoon after work, he got into his truck and rode around Tiger Island looking for ugliness, hanging a sour face out the window. He saw the strip of plywood bars on Water Street, the Blowout, the Dropped Anchor, and, in the woods where the road gave out, the No-Name Inn, a flat-black box of a building without windows or a sign of any sort. At night the building disappeared, making it hard for the police to find when they received a complaint. Battered iron trash barrels overflowing with beer cans lined the edge of the parking lot. In the four blocks of Water Street were eleven honky-tonks. When Paul was a boy, these blocks had been occupied by the bank, dry-goods stores, a hardware, and a dime store. Now all those had moved to the dusty strip mall at the edge of town, and Water Street went over to the oil-field rednecks who had moved in from the backwoods of Texas and Arkansas, bearded, longhaired welders, roaring roughnecks and roustabouts come down looking for big pay for dumb work.

The curbside door to the Black Rig was open, a dust-caked fan roaring in the door, and as he drove by on his slow inspection, he could smell cigarettes and sour beer buoyed in an aura of deodorant cakes stewing in the urinals.

Next, he drove the neighborhoods. The town's streets were humpbacked asphalt lanes draining into grassy ditches. The chief landmark of the black neighborhood across the tracks was the Club Satellite, a cinder-block slab painted with dirty handprints. Most of the houses were bleached-out low wooden rectangles propped up on concrete piers and jammed together as though hiding from the sun. Some were armored with asbestos siding; a few were brick-veneered against the daily thunderstorms. Nowhere was there a street without an engineless, abandoned truck, without wavering packs of mixed-breed dogs. Paul had never seen a purebred dog in Tiger Island. Every animal seemed to be half collie and half beagle.

At seven-thirty he stopped at the Little Palace, an old man's bar next to the auxiliary power plant, a place of unvarnished wood floors, dusty cardboard beer signs, and a pressed-tin ceiling dropping ringlets of sea-green paint. He sat at the bar, and his *grand-père* came up and asked him in French for five dollars so he could stay in a bourrée game in the back room. Monique LeBlanc, his boss's sister and bookkeeper, pestered him about a crankshaft for Ledet Towing Company. His cousin B.J. fell out of the rest-room door, fussing with the zipper on his coveralls. He asked Paul if he wanted to play pool with him and another cousin—Claude, the depressed one—but Paul waved him off, said that he was burned out from work. The stoop-shouldered bartender came up and squeezed him on the arm, beginning a joke. "You know how to make Mogan David wine?"

"No."

"You pinch him on the nuts." The old man let out a long, rattling laugh, bent down at the knees, and then crab-walked off. Paul's cousin Ted and his great-uncle Octave came into the bar, playing Alphonse and Gaston with the door. They had been drinking and were yelling. Octave spotted him and filled the bar with his voice. "Heeeey, T-Bub. I heard you whipped your wife's boyfriend's ass, yeah."

Cousin Ted picked up Paul's empty bottle and wiggled it at the bartender, but Paul got up from his seat, begging off. "I got to go now."

"Aw, come on," Ted told him. "One more won't kill you." He flashed his pearly dentures and reached for him. But Paul was too quick and had gained the door before the bartender could pry open another Dixie. At the entrance he bumped into old lady Fontenot's crazy brother, Simon, coming up the steps.

"Hey, T-Bub, let's do like the vampires walking past the funeral home," he said.

"What?"

"Let's stop in for a cold one." Simon slapped Paul on the back and brayed like a mule. Ted and Octave heard the laughter and came out to drag Simon up the steps into the bright light and crashing voices.

"T-Bub," they called through the door as he walked down the street. Their voices were hysterical and harmless. "Hey, T-Bub, you ashame of us?" Cackling laughter.

* * *

He sat in a porch rocker until the mosquitoes found him, and then he went inside, rubbing the fiery stings on his neck. In bed, images ignited in his head—drunk relatives, unusual dogs, weather-ruined houses. It seemed that the town he'd become used to like an old pair of pants no longer fit him. Now he was thinking things he didn't want to think. He closed his eyes and listened for distractions. He heard the deep and far-off steam whistle from Calumet Factory send its aspirate hum through the willows, then the sawmill watchman's muted high-pitched signal, the hoot from the bridge's long-bell air whistle, the thrum of a northbound tow-boat's Kahlenberg air trumpets, and finally, a fluting train whose approaching thousand wheels sounded over Tiger Island like a wave rolling over the moon-buffed metal roofs and into T-Bub's rising dream.

It happened on a Wednesday in early October. He was across the levee from the machine shop, lying under a steam engine on the bucket dredge *Gruenwald,* an obsolete thing the town operated to keep the channel deep near the docks. Paul was the only machinist who cared to work on the dying machinery aboard. The boat had just been run in from working a sandbar above town, where it had blown a packing gland on a piston rod. After walking from engine to engine, putting his hand on the bearings, feeling to see if any were running hot, he adjusted the gravity drip lubricators for the farsighted engineer and then tended to the broken gland. Paul lay on his side and backed out the stripped studs and put in two new ones, replacing the packing rings and drawing the gland down with new nuts. At the end of the job, he felt the boat shudder, and he rolled onto his back, feeling like the needle of a compass that had subtly turned. He realized that the boat was being towed away from the landing at the machine shop, and he remembered that LeBlanc intended for him to stay with the dredge all day to perform maintenance and then to come back at night with the crew. He lay in a slurry of hot water and steam oil, staring at the bottom of the cylinder casting, feeling trapped in a mechanism, as dead as gray iron. He tried to think of something soft and living, then he tried to think of perfume, but the valve oil, kerosene, and boiler fuel around him would let him have none of it, and he scrambled from under the drain cocks, wiping his hands with a shop cloth as he ran toward the stern, coming out between the anchor spuds and glancing once at the rolling water, which was glossy with sun and broken into a million facets in the quarter mile between him and the riverbank. *Big Rat*, the tug that tended the *Gruenwald*, was pushing it back out to the sandbar, and past it he could see the tin roof of LeBlanc's drifting, and he thought of the black phone in the storeroom and of how Colette's voice once sounded on it. Without thinking, he jumped the gap between the dredge and the bow of the tug, climbing up to the wheelhouse, where he found Etienne the giant at the controls, his huge hands covering the steering levers.

"Etienne, you got a skiff on this thing?"

"Hallo, dogmeat. *Non*, but I got a dingy in my pants you can have."

Paul sat on the deck, pulling off his boots. "Will you throw my clothes on the wharf when you tie up?"

"What? You gon' fly back to the bank?"

"Swim," he said, shucking his coveralls, emerging in striped boxer shorts.

Etienne looked through the wheelhouse door. "We a long ways from the bank, neg."

"I got to get going." He wadded up his clothes and shoved them behind the narrow door.

"All right, man. I'm gon' cut the engines until you clear the wheel wash. Okay?"

He didn't answer. He climbed down hot steel rungs to the first deck, ran aft, and sprang over the stern, his bronze chest hitting the water like a flat stone. A few strokes out from the boat, he heard the engines rev as Etienne gave them the throttle. Paul swam for the dead water above LeBlanc's landing, where the swimming would be easier, and he chopped along with steady swings, scissoring the river apart. He went a quarter mile before reaching a sandbar below where his *grand-père* tethered his cypress skiff, and he climbed out, panting, the river rolling off his back in diamonds as he jogged along the batture and up the levee to LeBlanc's. His *grand-père*, seated under the oak tree, eating half of Maurice LeBlanc's sandwich, could not swallow a big bite in time to think up a question. Paul ran into the storeroom and sat before the greasy phone, staring at it until his eyes adjusted to the darkness, then picked up the receiver and asked the operator for the number of the train station.

He wanted to ride the railroad as she had, as though taking the same trip might help him understand how she thought. At nine o'clock the station agent set the semaphore to flag the train, and when it stopped, he told his parents good-bye for the third time as the impatient conductor cupped his elbow, tempting him off the ground, the step stool floating from underfoot at the same moment he lifted his shoe from it. The coach lurched and he was moving away from Tiger Island, wagging his hand gravely from the vestibule as though returning the waves of strangers. Walking back to the diner, he sat next to the window, his face against the black glass. After the train thundered across the river, it moved along like a shimmying boat, so fast that lights flew by like pale fireworks. Crossing warnings were bloody smears; buildings and cars next to the track blew by like blasts of dust. In a few minutes the coach hit flat farmland, thousands of acres of moon-silvered sugarcane. Colette would have noticed this. She could spend an hour splitting up a big purple stalk with his pocketknife, biting the sucrose out of the woody fiber and spitting the wads of pulp off the porch.

The conductor tapped on his shoulder and asked for his ticket. He handed it over and asked, "They got any sugar plantations in California?" The young conductor punched his ticket and did not look at him.

"In California they have whatever you can pay for," he said.

Six

The next morning he woke up in a nubby coach seat and rubbed a crick out of his neck. Later, in the diner, he listened to an old lady talk about how her son's oil-field supply business was going bust, and her words were like the wheels under the train, background noise for watching east Texas unroll, mile by deadening mile—flat grazing land, tin barns, and blacktop roads melting in the sun. He went back to his seat and watched the country dry out, and over the horizon rolled little gritty towns: Rosenberg, East Bernard, Glidden, Flatonia. At Harwood he watched a biplane buzzing alongside the train like a huge fly, then sailing off, visible for ten minutes in the biggest sky he'd ever seen.

He tried all day to imagine what Colette had thought of Texas, the hamlets made of wavy galvanized iron, the kind that people had built garages and feed stores out of forty years ago. Colette would say they looked squashed and dull. A Mexican boy sat next to him and tried to bring in a radio station on his Walkman. For five minutes, accordion music spiked the air of the coach, and Paul tapped his foot.

The rocking, air-conditioned idleness of the train hurt his bones. He longed toward San Antonio, where, his pocket schedule told him, there was a fifteen-minute layover. When he dropped off the coach into the stovetop heat, the ground felt hard as iron, and he kept walking, wondering what Colette had thought of the ornate station, whether she had broken a sweat and come alive again. The whistle sounded and he turned back. In three minutes he was hurtling toward Macdona, on his way to Lacoste and Noonan, Quihi and Hondo, watching stretches of sand and an ear-shaped plant stippled with long spines, which the Mexican kid told him was prickly pear. He began to have a sense of how far Colette had gone—that her track could be plotted from a satellite. The train hurtled against space, through real rock, yucca, gorges, amber plateaus wavering in heat. At Del Rio he stuck his head out of the vestibule door into a gas furnace and decided that he needed a drink.

The lounge car was old, a welter of padded seats, oval tables, and broad windows. He sat at a table with a retired history professor, grave and gray-bearded, and soon they were playing knock rummy. The cards rattled for hours as the station signs flew by, proclaiming Langtry and Pumpville. On the horizon were city-sized humps of rock that he presumed were mountains.

The sun set between Watkins and Dryden. He and the professor ate in the diner as the train cracked around curves and thundered over bridges, sending their water glasses sloshing around the table. Old ladies walked drunkenly in the aisle while waiters flew around them as though skating on ice.

When the windows went black, there was nothing to do but talk, and Paul wondered if someone as smart as the professor could tell him why his wife had left him. "What kind of history did you used to teach?"

The professor did not look much like a teacher. He was tanned and wrinkled, straight in the back, with a flat stomach. The sleeves of his button-down shirt were rolled halfway to his elbows. "Just American survey and occasionally a course in French history." He sat back in his chair and glanced up at the ceiling as if reading words there.

"You know, I was wondering the other day, what did the early guys think when they went through a place like New Orleans for the first time—I mean, before the city was made."

The professor bobbed his head as though a circuit had connected. "De Soto didn't think much of it. Of course, he was looking for gold and rubies."

"In Louisiana? You can't find a rock no place."

"So he found out. He discovered fever, mosquitoes, impenetrable undergrowth, and cannibals, but no gold."

"So what did he do?" Paul caught a water glass about to slide over the edge of the table. The train must have been doing ninety.

"He died. No major European explorer was interested in the area until many years later." He looked at Paul. "La Salle."

"What was his thing?"

"A visionary. He would have colonized the moon." The professor looked out at a trace of lavender horizon. "Can you imagine a European coming over then? Louisiana must have seemed like another planet."

Paul followed his gaze. Even in the dark, he imagined he could see ten miles. "I know what you mean, man."

The professor got off in the middle of the night, and Paul woke to a sunrise outside of Cambray, New Mexico. He saw the rigid plants that grew out of the parched rock and wondered what they were good for. He studied coppery mountains and saw that nowhere in all those of miles of baked stone could a man grow a single stalk of sugarcane. What was Colette looking for in these towns that were forty miles apart, unconnected to the world except by the train, which streaked through them like an afterthought in a lizard's brain?

To pass the day, he taught the Mexican kid how to play bourrée, and they stayed in the club car for many hours, until Paul had lost forty dollars. The train was to arrive in Los Angeles about three in the morning, but at sunrise, porters and conductors were banging up and down the aisles, complaining about lost time, their radios squawking on their belts. The train was rollicking along at forty miles an hour, and he could see rounded hills, apartments, interstates, and palm trees. When he stepped off at the Los Angeles terminal, he was feeling drugged and crippled. He gathered his bags and endured the echoing tunnels and passageways as he hiked to the cavernous lobby to sit and think. He had gotten Colette's address from her parents, but that was all he had. She did not know he was coming. Hardly anyone in Tiger Island knew he had quit his job and left town, and now he felt like de Soto wandering uncharted territory, unsure whether around the next rock might be some last disaster.

Colette managed a rare call home the day before Paul arrived in Los Angeles, and when she heard that he was coming out with five big suitcases, she felt invaded and angry. She stalked through her small Sherman Oaks apartment, kicking at the sofa, the bed, the briefcase she'd brought from work. She was a minor loan officer at her bank, the only woman officer, and tolerated the job when she could keep the men off her back. Instead of a glamorous place full of friendly, sparkling people, she found that much of L.A. was as plain as Birmingham. She did not fit in with her fellow workers, who thought she talked funny, the way she flattened her a's. The people she longed to be like made jokes about her, called her "the swamp queen." The ones who were friendly were friendly in a way she did not understand, unlike the people in Tiger Island. And on top of these aggravations, she would now have to deal with Paul. She knew he would find her, and she dreaded the surprise of it. She made a cup of coffee and broke the cup. What would the fool do when he got off the train? He might try to rent a room in a bad section downtown and get beaten up or killed. Then for a thousand years people in Tiger Island would talk about the man who went out to California to his wife and was killed for his love. He would be a regional saint.

Nelson Orville would write a song about him and sing it in the Big Gator.

Early next morning she dialed Amtrak and found out exactly when the train would arrive. She would go to the station and create a scene. She would make him get on the next train back.

When she arrived at Union Station, she sat at the end of a long bench by the door and stared across the echoing waiting room. She saw him come in trailing a redcap with a dolly full of bags, whom he dismissed by the telephones. He began to fumble with the Yellow Pages, and Colette found herself wondering about the heft of him, the smell, and then she stood up and walked over. "What you think you're doing, Paul?"

"Hey." He smiled but did not reach for her.

"Hey yourself. What're you doing out here?"

"I just thought I'd see what someplace else looks like. Like you're doing." He put down the Yellow Pages, a volume as thick as a wholesale company's catalog. "How'd you know—"

"How you think?" She crossed her arms. "I hope you bought a round-trip ticket."

"What's that mean?"

"You know damn well what it means. I came down here to tell you that I don't want you bothering me to come back with you. I want you back home."

He crossed his own arms then. "I'm not planning on bothering you, babe. But you told me a bunch of times that one of the things that's wrong with us is we never lived nowhere but Tiger Island. That we don't know anything about someplace else. So here I am." He ducked his head for emphasis. "Someplace else."

"Damn it." She stamped a leather-soled loafer and the noise popped back from the roof. "This is *my* someplace else." It was a silly thing to say, and she knew it. "I mean, it's where I've come to make some real money, learn some new things, meet some nice folks."

He nodded. "Yeah, that's why I'm out here, too—you know, to get away from the mosquitoes and alligators, gaze at some mountains."

She looked up at him, at his dark hair, which was growing too long. "You came after me."

"You the one met me at the station."

"Paul?"

"What?"

"Go back. Get on the next train and go home." She moved out of the way of a passing redcap and leaned against the pay phone.

"Naw, I already got me a motel picked out, and then I'm gonna get a place." He pointed to an ad in the Yellow Pages, and she looked past his finger.

"You fool, that's in the middle of Watts."

"It's a Day's Inn. I can stay there cheap for a while."

She shook her head. "You can stay cheaper at your momma's house."

"I'm here and I'm staying here. How about this one?" He moved his finger to a Motel 6 listing.

"You'd have to speak Spanish to stay there," she told him. And she fell into the hunt with him, finding a safe place on the outskirts of Burbank. "There. Stay there and wander around by yourself a couple days until you go crazy for gumbo. Then you'll see you don't belong out here."

He grinned. "You belong where your heart is."

"Oh, don't give me that. Your heart is in the *Gruenwald*'s engine room."

"No, I am in love with the Larousse twins, and I came out here to forget them." He bent to pick up his heaviest suitcase.

She put a fist to her mouth. "What are you going to do out here?"

"Find me a job. Etienne the giant's second cousin works for the state downtown. He'll help me out."

She stepped away slowly, and before she turned for the entrance, she told him that he'd need all the help he could get.

She went back to her third-floor apartment and stared through the sliding doors, down into a vast cement ditch, a shallow and petrified watercourse an eighth of a mile wide, bottomed with skull-size rocks. She looked around at her living room, which was furnished with modern walnut tables and a tan leather sofa she had bought after getting her first paycheck. No one had seen it except for her. As pretty as she was, no one interesting had asked her for a date, except for a man she worked with who only wanted to sleep with her, and who made that fact as obvious as the wrinkles in his forehead. She looked at the phone and thought of calling home, but instead she got up and made a cup of instant coffee, frowning at its smell, adding sugar and cream, mixing it carefully, and then pouring it down the sink. Late that night she stood next to her bed and remembered what it was like to slow-dance with Paul. Sliding her bare feet, she closed her eyes and turned slowly. She briefly stood up on her toes.

Four days after Paul arrived, Colette was sitting at her desk in the trust management office and looked up, her thumb in someone's will, and wondered where her husband was. She felt that by now he should have made some obnoxious gesture. The following Monday she went to lunch with a coworker, but she couldn't concentrate on her grilled tuna. Then she began to wonder where he was on a daily basis, actually scanning the police reports in the paper for a story of some dumb outlander who had tried to go to a dance hall in a bad part of town. At the end of November she called home and her father answered. The old man took two minutes to recognize her, and then her mother came on the line, sharing the news, asking questions. The call lasted an hour, the first long call she had given them, and it was painful to hear their voices, because it made her want to be with them. That was why she called so seldom.

When the conversation began to slow, she was proud of not breaking down and asking about Paul. And then her mother said it. "Colette, has Paul been by to see you?"

"No, ma'am. I know he's out here somewhere, but . . ."

"Oh, then you don't know about his job? I spoke with his mother after Mass and she told me he tested out for a boiler repairman's license—I think that's what they call it—and he has a good job already."

Colette pursed her lips. "He got a good job already?"

"His mother said they need him as a specialist because he knows so much about historic machinery."

"Well, he didn't let me know anything about it." She slapped a thigh.

After hanging up the phone, Colette looked out over the tile rooftops of her neighborhood, then across the river. She kept looking for a long time, as though she might see her husband fixing something in the distance. Her mother had asked her again why she'd moved away, and she'd given the old answer: to see a better part of the world. Well, she found that California was better, but she was not used to the food, and the air made her eyes sting. Most people she'd met were into exercising, collecting, or recreational sex, and as much as she tried to forget it, at heart Colette was still a food-loving, nonmaterialistic Roman Catholic. The air was cool and dry, but poisonous; the highways were smooth and fast, but long; the people were good to look at, healthy and smart, but restless, never satisfied. Most people she had met and spoken with seemed to be waiting for something to happen to them. She looked around her and wondered what she had begun waiting for. More money? Mr. Right?

She put on an expensive pair of running shoes and headed for the street. Jogging was a new sport she'd picked up. She hooked a little can of Mace to her belt, ran down the stairs, and headed north on the sidewalk, a well-maintained sidewalk, unbuckled by tree roots, unswamped by live-oak leaves.

Paul had found a job with a machine shop and boiler-repair business in Van Nuys, and after cramming for a week in the company library, he had tested out into a position that paid double what he had made at LeBlanc's. He rented an apartment not far from Colette's in a nondescript cinder-block building. He decided to get used to Los Angeles, and his first attempt to do so was to locate a place he could eat on a daily basis, as he had in the Little Palace back home. The first time he walked into a restaurant, he asked for a poor boy, and the waitress looked at him as though he had lost his mind. She handed him a menu, which showed no red beans, gumbo, or étouffée. He looked up at the tanned waitress, feeling stupid and alien. He ordered a cup of coffee, then stared through the weak brew to the bottom of the cup, feeling naked without his food.

The next day he was driving on the beach highway south of the city when he saw a gold-lettered sign for a Cajun restaurant. He warily pulled into the parking lot, his appetite hopeful. Inside, he was seated in a dim, crowded dining room under a drooping net that held a few dried starfish, animals he had seen only in pictures. When the waiter brought the menu, Paul opened it and frowned.

"Do you need help with our selections?" The waiter was a healthy blond kid.

"What is all this stuff? I thought this was a Cajun place." Paul looked past the boy at a tank of lobsters.

"Yes, sir, we have authentic dishes from the bayou state. Today's special is blackened swordfish."

Paul stared at him blankly. "I never seen a swordfish in my whole life."

The waiter motioned to the man at the next table and bent close. "It's what the gentleman next to you is eating."

"It's all burned," he cried.

"Not burned, sir. Blackened. It's the most traditional way of cooking seafood among the Cajuns."

"Someone's been pulling your leg, man." Paul went back to the menu and read the descriptions of bayou lamb, Cajun barbecued liver, and escargot de Lafayette. He found the word *gumbo* on the back page and ordered a large bowl. A half hour later his waiter brought a small cauldron of bitter juice so hot with Tabasco that after the third spoonful, Paul broke into a sweat.

His waiter glided past and asked, "How's the gumbo?"

"Man," Paul said, "you people must have spilled Tabasco in this stuff. My tongue's been killed dead."

The waiter laughed. "It takes time to develop a true Cajun palate."

Paul pushed away the steaming bowl. "Let me tell you, it sure don't take much time to ruin one." He waited patiently for the bill, thinking of a medium-brown roux Colette had made last winter as the base for a shrimp gumbo. He closed his eyes and saw her hands cutting up onions.

After a few days, he began to experiment with Mexican food. The moderate pepper content gave him solace, though most things tasted like hot cheesy mud. Memory of Colette's food began to follow him like an aroma—creamy red beans over steaming white rice, corn soup, a chicken stew from heaven. Sometimes he would sit in his modern apartment, staring through the sliding glass door, thinking of food, wondering when Colette would call. When he got home from work at the boiler shop, he would clean up and go for a ride. After two weeks of relentless driving, he felt like a map maker or a real estate agent desperate for the feel of a big neighborhood. He went to the tourist places like Disneyland, where he rode the steam train and steamboat over and over, his face staring out of the

coach window or over the steamer railing like that of an immigrant peasant examining a rich new land. He took long drives to
the Sierras and short drives north of the city, where he frowned
through canyons choked with rich homes hiding in expensively
overgrown landscaping. Here the land pitched up or down and
the houses had to be propped up in back on stilts to keep them
from riding down the slopes. He drove the same road three
times in one afternoon, studying the bottoms of houses. He decided that California was easy on the eyes and that it was impossible to get bored here, but for someone from Tiger Island,
the place was like a movie set—too pretty, too shaped for effect.
The wealthy neighborhoods got him down and the poor neighborhoods scared the hell out of him. One day he took the tour
of Forest Lawn and was beside himself with disorientation. Back
home, visits to the graveyard were spent praying for his or Colette's family members, searching out the tombs of friends, looking for the love of amiable ghosts. He considered the rolling
billiard-table grass of Forest Lawn and wondered why dead
strangers were called on to entertain. In Tiger Island, a cemetery
was the ultimate reality, where all the bullshit of life was put
away in the face of a final fact, and a name of one's bloodline on
a cross formed not celebrity, but a remembrance of either love
or nothing, heaven or hell.

Not so in the City of Angels. A cemetery was a tourist at-
traction, the ultimate amusement park, a Disneyland of the
Dead.

Even his job as a boiler repairman at times seemed an illusion.
He was given a title, "inspector of lapsed technology," a car, and
a route of canneries, laundries, museum operations, and tourist
railroads. He would be called out for a maintenance check, stick
his head in a fire door or smoke box, make an announcement that
the boiler was either safe to operate or needed repair, then go
back to his office to make a report, figure an estimate, and, in

the case of dangerous conditions, notify the state boiler inspector. His supervisor, Mr. Mason, a mean, gray-skinned man with a face as sharp as a hatchet, bounced back half of Paul's reports, generally disagreeing with plain facts. They'd had their first argument within a week when Mason called him into a littered office and told him to sit down.

"You redlined InsCo's boiler by mistake," he said.

Paul folded his hands over his belly. "The right water-leg sheet had a bulge in it."

The supervisor lit a cigarette and seemed to ignore the remark. "I want you to tear up the blue sheet."

"Nope. State inspector's got to know about this one. That thing's got a hernia."

The supervisor's voice carried remnants of his Chicago youth. "You didn't see any bulge."

Paul shook his head. "You know what code says about bulges above the mud ring. The engineers are not blowing out sediment often enough, and the stuff is heating up inside the boiler shell and softening the iron. They're running a hundred and seventy-five psi out there at InsCo. If a water leg ruptures, they'll be able to serve the firemen on a platter like crawfish."

Mason looked at his watch. "The state guy's giving them their regular inspection at the end of the month. He'll catch it. But you, you saw no bulge."

"Why you paying me so damn much money to look for stuff if you want me to forget about it when I find it?"

"Let's just say it's a question of timing. InsCo's been very good to this business. We don't want to slow their production. You saw no bulge."

"Okay, okay." He held up his hands. "But why don't you take my car away and let me sit in my cubicle and make up fairy tales on your forms?"

Mason narrowed his eyes. "I'd fire your ass if you didn't know so much about old equipment." He threw a folder into Paul's lap. "Now rewrite this report and get it back to me in an hour."

And that was the way his job went. Paul was happiest when there were no field inspections to make and he was sent to the shop to help the welders and stay-bolt men, where he could break a sweat and smell soot. His hefty paychecks went mostly in the bank, though he did buy a set of shiny, expensive wrenches that rang like little bells when he picked them up. He also bought a used Crown Victoria, four-door, white, with low-end upholstery. He would drive it home at four, after work, check the mail, take a shower, and wait for the phone to ring. One afternoon, it did.

When he heard her voice, he leaned against the wall in his kitchen. "This is a surprise," he told her.

"So you got a job? A good job?"

"Yeah. I give advice and eat a little carbon."

"How much you make?"

When he told her, the line went silent for a long moment. "You still there?"

"Why they paying you so damned much?"

"What, you think I'm not worth it? Should I tell them I'm just a dumb coon-ass from Tiger Island and they shouldn't throw so much money away on me?"

"I'm sorry," she said. "I guess that was what I was thinking. You must have something they can't find around here."

"Old machinery, babe."

"What?"

"I know the old stuff nobody can fool with anymore. Canneries. Museums. Somebody with the state park service paid my shop a hundred and twenty-five dollars an hour to have me come over and set the valves on a Hardy-Tynes compound Corliss they have on exhibit."

"You learned about all that from those greasy old books you used to leave around the house?"

He smiled at the word *house*. It brought everything together for a moment. "Those greasy books are making money now."

"What're you doing with your paycheck? You buy another accordion?" Her voice was light, joking more than cruel.

"I bought a car."

"What kind? No, let me guess. A used Caprice."

He looked up at the ceiling. "Crown Vic."

A laugh came over the phone. "I knew it. Hey, your job got a title?"

"Yeah. Everybody's got a title out here. You know that."

"It gives you credibility," Colette said. "How you going to maintain it driving a car that looks like a taxi?"

He closed his eyes and sniffed, as though she were in the room. "You want to go for a ride in my big car?"

"Maybe."

He straightened his back. "I found an Italian place that's not too bad."

"If it's a place you like, it must have a squad of old greasers playing R&B."

"Aw, Colette."

"I'm kidding, sort of."

He picked her up and she ignored his car. At the restaurant, they didn't say much to each other. Paul let the word *credibility* roll around inside his head like an indigestible meatball. He watched Colette eat, looked at her hair, which was pulled back, tight, tight. He asked about her parents and she ignored the question, making a comment about his big Ford.

"Colette," he complained. "It gets me around. It holds my tools and coveralls in the trunk. What's the big deal?"

She wiped her mouth and put a hand palm-down on the table. "The big deal is that you are seen in that brontosaurus every day. People like your boss will form opinions about you. Your boss's boss, he'll look at that white thing and say to himself, 'blue collar.' "

"Hey, it's a four-year-old Vic, not a Gremlin with sheet plastic in the windows."

Colette took a drink of water from a stemmed glass. "Like it or not, you're in a faster lane out here. You've got to compete."

"Listen to this." He looked off to the side at nothing.

She narrowed her eyes at him. "Don't you want your boss's job one of these days?"

His head popped back. "My boss has a flat prostate from sitting in front of a phone all day."

"Don't you ever think of your future?"

"Getting rid of a white Ford is going to ensure my future?" He shoveled up a mouthful of spaghetti to avoid saying something that would make her angry.

After a few minutes she said, "You should sell it and buy a low-end Lexus, or maybe a Volvo."

He stabbed at a meatball. "I'd rather drive a Vespa in Iceland."

She sat back hard against her chair. "Why are you so damned stubborn?"

"Nobody looks at me. I'm just an immigrant to the West Coast, trying to make a buck. I like a plain, serviceable car, one that doesn't need a man in a white jacket and tie to fix it, one that can take a ding in a parking lot and not break my heart."

She put her napkin on the table. "You'll have the money soon to afford better. I mean, it's okay for Tiger Island, but . . ."

"I will not sell my big white Ford, can you understand that, babe?"

Her chair slid back an inch. "Don't call me babe."

"It means baby," he snapped.

She seemed to smile, then got up slowly, walking toward the ladies' room. After ten minutes, the busboy came to clear the table, and the smiling waiter brought his check. Paul went to the bar and drank a beer, watching the entrance to the restaurant. Then he went into the parking lot, where a Mexican sat behind the wheel of his taxi, singing in a wavering, furry falsetto.

"Have you seen a woman come out by herself?"

The young driver gave him a serious look, as though in respect for some tragedy. "Yes. A nice-looking brunette with bright skin. I took her home, just a few blocks away."

Paul looked down the dark street. "Was she mad?"

"I don't think she was happy."

Paul kept staring down the boulevard. "We had a discussion about a car," he said, mostly to himself.

The driver lit a cigarette. "It's a shame to lose such a woman over a car," he said, watching Paul carefully. In consolation, he told him, "If you stick your head in my window, you can still smell her perfume."

Seven

When Colette got back to her apartment, she kicked her new leather sofa. She was angry with herself for meeting her stubborn worm of a soon-to-be ex-husband. She was also angry with herself for leaving him at the restaurant. His dull Ford was not what had upset her. All during the meal she'd been afraid that she was going to invite him to her place. She thought of his shoulders and put a hand on the phone. Someone to talk to was what she needed. Another woman's voice. She could call Elise from Payroll, but she would tell her that her problems were merely hormonal. Everybody in California had a scientific answer for everything. Her hand left the receiver. The thought occurred to her that she could call her mother, but that would be trading with the enemy, returning to the swamp. She sat on the expensive sofa, which was hard and stiff and noisy, and tried to daydream of what she would buy with her next paycheck. She looked up to a pair of expensive abstract prints and thought of her bedroom in Tiger Island, decorated with a church calendar and a drawing of a shrimp boat. Somewhere in her future was something glittery and special. A new car maybe. Not a secondhand Ford, either. She thought about her husband's job, amazed that he could function in the city's smoky air and traffic.

Around ten o'clock she realized that he would not call, that he would wait her out again. She wondered how long that would take.

On Sunday she went to Mass and sat in the back. It was a large church, and up in front she saw what seemed to be the back of Paul's head. The next Sunday, she avoided that church, attending Mass in Glendale, where she waited out a long homily in Spanish. The following Saturday night, she was driving back from Elise's house in Canoga Park. When she got off the freeway, she passed an old lounge, a regional middle-class watering hole with a stone facade and a pink neon sign shouldered against the road. In front, three police cruisers were parked randomly, blocking traffic, their flashers on. In the parking lot, men chased one another, and a policeman raised his baton, threatening a young man who was staggering backward, his jacket knotted in the policeman's fist. The officer seemed more annoyed than angry as he hammered at the air above the young man's head, and then Colette saw that he had his hand on Paul. She pulled out of the street, then walked around two sets of men struggling on the ground to where a policeman had Paul pinned against a light standard.

Colette smiled at the officer. "Can you tell me what's going on?"

He put another hand on Paul's jacket and seemed to forget what he was doing when he saw her. "You know this man, ma'am?"

She looked at Paul, who was weaving like a reed, a little drunk and fight-tired, his denim shirt out, a hole torn in the knee of his trousers. "Yeah, you might say he's a relative. What's he done?"

"As near as I can tell, he asked the same woman to dance twice, and her husband didn't like it. Three guys got on him and then a couple boilermakers joined in."

"Colette," Paul said, a little rill of blood seeping from the corner of his mouth.

"Shut up." She turned to the policeman, who had taken his

hands off of Paul and was straightening his uniform. "Are you going to bring him in?"

"Yes, ma'am. He's not fit to drive anywhere. But it's the others who'll be charged for fighting and all the breakage."

"Can you release him to me?" She smiled wider now, and Paul turned his head away, closed his eyes in a wish.

The policeman looked over to her little sedan and shrugged. One of the other fighters got up on one elbow and cursed all the officers. "All right," he said. "Take him home and leave him there."

As they drove off, Paul gave her a one-eyed look. "Why'd you stop?"

She wouldn't return his glance. "If you get hauled in, your name might wind up in the police reports. Your boss might hold it against you."

"That the only reason?" He wiped his mouth on his jacket.

She waved him off. "What was it about?"

"Damned if I know. I found a lady who knew the bob step, and when I went back for another dance, a couple jarheads jumped on my back for a ride. Then Manuel and Jack jumped in."

"Manuel and Jack?"

"Stay-bolt setters from the boiler shop. We were out for a little fun, you know?" He touched his forehead and winced.

"So you come two thousand miles to export Tiger Island's favorite pastime?" Her mouth turned down.

Paul looked at the floor and smiled. "Colette, if you want to inflict pain on me, stop the car. I'll lie in the road and you can roll over my windpipe a few times."

"But a fistfight? Nothing's changed." She tapped the back of a hand on the steering wheel.

"You think back home is the only place in the world where people fight?"

She caught the hopeless note in his voice, as if he were saying,

She will never give me a break, and she knew that he was right about the fighting. Wherever there were fists, there would be fistfights. "Where do you live?" When he told her, her mouth fell open because the address was three blocks from her own. Carefully, she stole glances at his face in the passing streetlights to see how bruised he would be. When she stopped in front of his apartment building, a vacuum formed in the car, and to fill it, she asked him if he would like to go somewhere the following Saturday, regretting it the minute she said the words.

He seemed cautious and looked at her. "Where to?"

"A little office get-together. The people I work with."

"You mean a stand around and drink and talk kind of thing."

"Yeah."

"Okay. How do I dress?" He winced when he asked.

"I want you to buy a nice tweed coat, a pinpoint oxford white shirt and a navy tie with a subtle print in it. Shine up your best set of loafers."

"You want me to spend two hundred and fifty dollars for a little office get-together?" She gave him a look and he held up his hands. "Okay, okay. I can wear that stuff next time I go out dancing."

"Just go to a good men's store and let the clerk dress you."

He put his hand on the door handle and paused.

"What?" she asked.

"Uh, you want to pick me up or what?"

"I'm not going to ride in that white whale of yours, that's for damned sure."

The next Saturday was cool and windy and they showed up at Colette's boss's beach house an hour after the party started, looking storm-tossed and alien. The party had already broken into islands of talkers who were busy ignoring the other groups floating over an expanse of aqua carpet. Colette cut loose from Paul and told him to mingle. She wanted to watch him to see if he would pick a fistfight or throw the piano player through a sliding door. She saw her manager across the room and headed over, hoping for interesting conversation. Soon she was listening to him talk about a recent takeover of a publishing house by a railroad. It was the same drone she had heard three times in the past week, and her spirits came down a notch as she wondered if these parties would net her anything more than tired talk passed around the way children toss beanbags at recess. She listened in to the other islands on her way to the bar, hearing snippets about business or sex, which were the same thing for most of the people she worked with. She drank one whiskey sour with her boss, Dirk, then felt the need for another, lingering at the bar and looking at all the talking going on, all the nothing being said. She also watched Paul hulk around and smile, exchanging single-word greetings, subsiding against an aquarium and staring at the air pump in the tank. Other men at the party were at ease and chatting freely. Chet told a complicated joke. Clint summarized a play. Paul studied the air conditioner's thermostat as though it were abstract art.

Dirk, the vice-president for investments, came up from behind and pinched her. She brought her angry face around quickly, but when she saw who it was, she changed her expression. "Up to your old tricks with the girls?" she asked, waving a finger at him stupidly. She wanted to throw the drink in his face.

"You know I only have eyes for you, beautiful," he told her, handing her a martini. She took a drink and looked at the wrinkles around his eyes. She tried to guess his age, but he was like a facade at Disneyland—new and old at the same time. "Say," he said, "why don't we go for a walk on the beach and discuss the Pendleton portfolio?"

"We could do that right here." She kept her voice soft, the way the other women talked when they were around him.

"But we could have the discussion in better style." He winked.

"Uh-huh. See me Monday at the office." She gave him a

careful smile, confident that she could fend him off yet again. She was experienced with him already.

"Who'd you come with?" He motioned toward Paul, spilling a little of his own martini.

"Just a friend from home," she said a little too loudly. "I'd better check on him." She walked over and sat next to her husband, who was talking with the pretty blonde from programming. She was telling him about her grandfather who had been a blacksmith. At the end of the story, when the woman got up for a drink, Colette caught his eye. "You making friends?"

"Not like you, babe." He made a pinching motion with his hand.

She blushed and swallowed twice, then took a drink. "And you didn't mash his head with the piano lid?"

"Hey, I got a tweed jacket. People with tweed jackets don't get upset about a little butt-feeling, even if the butt that got felt does belong to their wife."

"Hush up." She looked away. "I see you still like blondes."

"I know you don't believe that crap Clarisse told you."

"You're a man," she said, as though that explained all the evil in the world.

"It would take more than a big-ass dummy like Clarisse to make me cheat."

Colette crossed her legs. "You didn't even kiss her?"

"I been out with drunk women before and I can tell when they're fixing to blow."

She laughed. "So the only reason you didn't kiss her was you were afraid of getting a mouthful of puke?"

"Not the only reason."

She seemed to think about this a long time. "What about the programmer you were just talking to? What if she hit on you?"

"Don't worry, babe. These are nicer people than you think. The little blonde just wanted to talk about anvils, and that bald dude who makes life miserable for the tellers has a '49 Chevy he takes apart every weekend."

"Well"—she snagged a martini for each of them from a tray that was going around the room—"I guess you think you fit in pretty well."

He took a sip and made a face. "Hell, I can talk to a Jehovah's Witness and enjoy it."

"You're not scared of making a faux pas?"

He gave the room a quick sweep with his eyes. "I'm not related to any of these quarter-rolling fools. They can think what they want."

Colette took a long swallow of her drink. "You don't have to call them names."

"I can't call the guy who felt you up anything? In Tiger Island you'd have given him a high heel in the throat." He shook his head and looked at the floor. "I guess you're playing by California rules now."

She said nothing because she could only have praised him for holding back.

The party began to thin out after midnight, and Colette was getting sleepy from the drinks and bloated from the cocktail sausages that languished in bowls of tomato sauce around the room. She became angry with a male teller who made fun of her Cajun accent, and Paul had to put a finger in the belt loop of her linen trousers to pull her away from behind. He said good-bye to her boss and got her out into the night air.

"Beach boy bastard," she said. "At least I didn't learn to talk from a television."

Paul took her home and steered her up to her apartment. He waited until she unlocked her door. "You all right?"

"Yes, I'm all right. I just had one too many." She looked him in the eye. "And you're not coming inside."

"It would ruin your reputation for your husband to come in your place, that right?"

She put a hand against the door frame. "No. I just don't feel well right now."

"You still get heartburn?"

"I got it now." She put a hand on her stomach.

"Me, too. Can you get me a couple of your chewables? I don't have anything at my place."

"Here," she said, "I've got some in my purse. Oh, man, those little weenies are about to kill me."

He took the roll from her and peeled out two tablets. "And those damned drinks. What'd they put in them?"

"Vermouth."

"Tastes like lacquer thinner," he said. "We used to thin gasket compound with something like vermouth down at LeBlanc's."

She looked into her apartment. "I hope you don't expect a good-night kiss."

"Not on your life. You look like you're ready to throw up all over my tweed jacket."

She went in and closed the door but for a crack, watching him through it. "I don't know if this date was a good idea."

He turned his head sideways. "I enjoyed it. I felt like a dollar sparkler." Then he turned and left.

She went in and ate three antacid tablets, drank a glass of water filled with finely crushed ice, and slowly chewed four soda crackers. She looked at her reflection in the black sliding glass door and thought about three things: her next paycheck, a promotion already looming, and the eroded landscape of her boss's face.

For Paul, the weeks passed like loaded oyster luggers going against the current. He fell into the rhythm of inspecting tourist-railroad steam locomotives and obsolete laundry boilers, going through the drill of checking for leaking flues, bulged water legs, cracks in the shell plates. At dawn, he would get up with no boat whistles to listen to, hearing only the muted breath of the central air conditioning. He began to write letters, wanting to touch someone back home with his words, even writing to Etienne the giant, telling him about the money, the lacquered and tanned people.

Every ten days or so, his boss would throw a report back on his little desk and he would reshape a few facts. One morning, he was sent out to check a problem with one of the company's customers, Wu's, Inc., a small industrial laundry in midcity. He met Mr. Wu at the front desk. He was large for an Asian man, and unusually gray.

"Let me show you this old baby." His accent, Paul guessed, was from New York. "We've had it forty years and it was secondhand when we got it." They went through a door and down a creaking set of unvarnished stairs and then through a room the size of a hangar, filled with pressing machines and sweating Asian women. The heat and the bang of the pressing pedals was dizzying. On the other side of a brick wall was the boiler, an ordinary locomotive type set in masonry.

"What's the problem?" Paul noticed a bad steam leak on the boiler's far side.

"No, you got it wrong. I'm supposed to ask that question." Mr. Wu poked him with a long finger and smiled.

Paul turned on his halogen light and found a leak in a pipe union outside the boiler. "Hey, it's just a fitting. I've got an inch and a half like this on the truck. Has this been leaking long?"

"I called two weeks ago, and it leaked some before that."

"The steam probably cut the seat. Cheapest thing to do is change it out."

Mr. Wu nodded. "Since I finally got you here, give the thing the once-over. We got steam on number-one boiler, if you want to take this one off-line for a while. I can put some pressers on packing jobs." The old man opened a petcock on the water glass to blow it down. "We take care of this thing. It got us through some rough times, you know?"

Paul turned off the natural-gas burner. "How long have we been doing the maintenance?"

"Two years, maybe. Some Germans used to keep it up for us, but they retired. Check it out good. I'll bring you an ultrasound from last time that was done."

Paul had the union changed out in twenty minutes. He beat open the latches on the smoke box and checked the front flue sheet, then he walked around and checked the firebox. Everything was flat, no bulges or leaks. The honeycomb of flues looked new, as though each pipe end had been hand-rolled and beaded over by a watchmaker. He closed the firebox door and went over the rest of the boiler as best he could, then sat on his toolbox to wipe sweat. Mr. Wu came through an iron door and held out a cold beer, then popped one for himself. "How's she doing?"

"No problem I can see. That old thing's built."

"Yeah. It's shaped like my wife nowadays." They laughed and Mr. Wu handed over an ultrasound report done by the state boiler inspector. "Can you make heads or tails of that?"

"It's all right," Paul said after a while. "There's some flame erosion on that back sheet, but it's within tolerances. Should last at least another three years of daily use."

Mr. Wu took a long draw on his beer can and smiled, the silver bristle on his skull moving back.

At three o'clock Paul got called into his boss's office. Mason's face, usually thin and olive-colored, was as dark as old iron. "What's the story on Wu's boiler?"

Paul did not sit down. "It's in the report."

"Come on. That thing's old as the hills. There's got to be a possible crack or bulge somewhere."

"Nope. I didn't see a thing. What's a possible crack, anyway?"

His boss ignored him. "I want you to file a request for the boiler inspector to X-ray the thing. Say you suspect a crack."

"I don't suspect no crack."

"Just do what I tell you."

Paul put a work shoe on the padded chair next to him. "You want state government to send one of their assholes down and condemn the unit so you can sell Wu a new one. He can't afford it."

"We can put a package boiler in there for a hundred and fifty thousand."

"It's an old plant. If we take his main boiler, the business might fold. To pull the bastard out, he'll have to pay to demolish an exterior wall."

"Get your damned foot off that chair and go file the request."

He didn't move. "There's nothing wrong with the boiler. He has the ultrasound to show it."

"I don't want to hear that shit. The owner of this business is on my back to pick up earnings." He stood and put a finger in Paul's face. "Since you have such great morals, I'll make the damned request myself. And when the state knocks that unit down, I'll send you to install the new one so you can comfort your Chink friend."

Paul straightened up. "Hey, the old guy only keeps ninety pounds on that thing for his pressing machines."

But his boss was already digging through his desk for a blue form. "Thibodeaux, if you keep whining, I'm gonna fire your ass, you hear that?" He slammed a drawer. "I might do that anyway."

"I got one word to say about that."

"What?"

"Disneyland."

His boss crushed the form in his hand, and when he saw what he had done, he began searching for another one, perhaps remembering that the Magic Kingdom had heard about Paul and requested him to consult on their steamboat and locomotives. "You're a lucky bastard, remember that."

Paul turned for the door. "You the same as me, just not lucky."

"Hey, where the hell do you come from with your funny accent and noble attitudes? What'd you leave Louisiana for, anyway? Just to make my life miserable?"

"No," he said, "to make my life miserable."

"Oh yeah? Well, read the newspapers. The oil and gas industry is going in the toilet and they're laying off in droves down there. You better make sure you value the job you got here, jack. You can't make money down on the old bayou anymore." He pulled a rubber stamp from his desk and slammed it down on the blue form. "Wu's boiler is going to the junkyard."

"Maybe," Paul said as he closed the door behind him.

Eight

After Christmas Colette was promoted at her bank, her office moved down the hall to a private suite of walnut-paneled rooms next to Dirk, who began to bother her for luncheon dates. In the afternoons, he would slide into her office, sit on her desk, look down on her, and talk, while from her chair she examined his caps and bridgework. Dirk confessed that he was the bank gossip, that he knew "who was doing whom." Colette asked if he knew about anything other than sex and money and he laughed loudly, showing two caps and a Maryland bridge.

In the evenings she began to cook for herself, making shrimp gumbo, sometimes white beans and pork roast, eating her one serving and freezing the rest. She invited Elise over, but she would eat only salads and dried fruit. Colette missed people to eat with and discovered that eating alone was only half a meal. She would stare at a bowl of gumbo and remember her brother, mother, and father gathered with her in the old high-ceiled kitchen back home with the square plastic clock nailed to the wall over the iron sink, its plastic hands slicing thin circles off their lives. She thought of her little Formica kitchen in the rent house she shared with Paul, how even there they had company once a week, talking through steam rising from the food.

* * *

Colette became a trust officer and endured the hounding of fast-living beneficiaries who tried everything to get advances from the sum left by a well-meaning relative for their maintenance. Some tried to bribe her; young men tried to entice her; some whined like the children they were. All of them seemed spoiled and filled with contempt for her. When she was working with the lawyers to set up the trusts, she had to explain terms up to eight times when the clients were very old. As a woman, she was expected to be understanding, tolerant, and patient. The manager of the bank told her this when she was promoted, and at that time Colette thought of her raise and agreed, jumping into the job with a forced smile for the many old people, retirees from every part of the country.

The senior officers in the bank treated her with a friendly disdain, admiring her jewel-like fingernails or the way she moved her arms while explaining terms to a client, and she saw their condescending smiles when they heard her diminishing Acadian accent. They considered her to be above average, but not exceptional, not expertly ambitious for one with her kind of looks. She also knew they had hired her because the company employed few women holding a rank above teller and needed to up the quota.

She couldn't remember anybody's name. In twenty years she might know some of these tanned or aged Californians, but they still would not be cousins she'd grown up with or oldsters who had seen her in a kindergarten skit or remembered her from looking through the glass in the hospital on the day she was born. Each day, she came home from work feeling that she had dragged Dirk and all the strangers around on her back for hours.

One afternoon in February, after dealing with a sixteen-year-old imbecile who wanted delivery of all his trust money immediately, and after plucking the hand of her boss from her buttocks again, she drove downtown and bought a new Mercedes diesel sedan. She needed the car the way she needed painkiller for a storming headache. Idling at the edge of the parking lot, a little wave of panic swept over her as she wondered who would like to see her new machine. Who might be impressed? She drove to Paul's apartment for the first time since the cocktail party.

He answered the door, his finger in a small leather-bound copy of *Locomotive Catechism*. He was unshaven and still in his work clothes.

"What you been doing, Paul?" She pushed in past him and looked around at the plain room.

"Watching TV and counting my money. What's your big news?"

"I got a new car. Come see." Her hair bounced against her shoulders. It had been a long time since he had seen her excited.

When he saw the silver sedan, he said, "Ah."

"Isn't it gorgeous? Let's go for a ride." The sparkle of enamel danced in her dark eyes.

"Sure," he said, opening a door and leaning inside, wrinkling his nose at the smell of the leather. "But first I have to change my clothes. I can't ride in this thing dressed in coveralls."

Soon she was twirling through Griffith Park, speeding, testing the brakes and the cornering. Shrubbery flew past the window in a green blur. At one point she charged a stop sign and Paul stomped the floor and yelled out something in French. Colette panic-stopped the car just past the sign, a puff of rubber smoke blowing ahead. "What the hell are you trying to do?" he said.

She smiled and his neck hit the headrest as the car squealed through the intersection and up the mountain, Colette trying her best to drive like the helmeted men in the commercials. On the outsides of curves, the tires droned like cellos, and when she arrived at the observatory, she saw that Paul was sweating.

She threw her right arm on the back of his seat and pulled off her sunglasses. "Well, what do you think?"

He swallowed. "Is this how you have to drive to own one of these things?"

"I'm just testing it out."

"Babe, if you tried to drive like this back home on our roads, you'd wind up wrapped around a live oak for sure."

She drew back her arm, but her smile stayed. "In California the roads don't have potholes big enough to flip you into the woods."

Paul looked around at the instrumentation, felt the dash as though it were a museum piece. "How much did this thing cost?"

"A lot." She stared at him hard.

"Nice machine," he said. "Nice color, silver." He looked at the emblem that rose from the hood like a gun sight. "This is the kind of car that people point at and say things like 'Hey, look at that!'"

She leaned over and gave him a wet kiss, then mashed the accelerator, the car bounding away from the curb in a puff of brown smoke and squealing into the first curve. Paul was oblivious to the velocity and the noise, able to feel only a cool spot on his lips as they drove all the way to the foot of the observatory road, where the electric yawp of a siren rose behind them and a state patrolman pulled Colette over. He was a motorcycle officer in pants so tight, he looked like a ballet dancer. He took off his mirrored sunglasses, looked at Colette and then at the automobile, seeming to focus on the hood ornament, bobbing his head as though amused at some private joke. Then he wrote her a ticket for $206.

Colette took the paper without a word, raised her window, and smiled, driving off in a wispy clatter of valves.

Paul looked at her and forced a smile. After a while he said, "Rides smooth."

"Just as smooth as your Ford?" She made a turn.

He wanted to say, Just as smooth, but he caught himself in time. "No comparison" was what he said.

"I won't have to buy another car for twenty years."

Paul frowned at the thought of having to ride in the same car that long. "Is that how long the payments last?"

She smiled back thinly, willing to take it as a joke this time. Nothing, nothing at all, was going to ruin her afternoon.

The next week she picked up Paul every day after work and they took the car everywhere, down to the beach, up to the mountains, spinning around curves as though pursued by bandits. Paul was the only person she knew who had the time to ride around like a dash ornament and look at scenery. Most of the time he was silent, like a man waiting for something to happen. Sometimes he and Colette would argue and he would let himself lose. A forbidden topic was their relationship. A sore topic was her parents.

"It wouldn't kill you to call them more, maybe go home for a quick visit," he said, watching the huge tires of an oil truck slide by his window as she passed it on a two-lane road.

"I call them once every two weeks."

"Your mom's not well. Your dad's got that old-timer's disease."

"Alzheeimer's, you fool."

"I knew that. I used to know that, I think."

"Be quiet."

"They probably think you're too poor to call."

"Come on, spare me the guilt," she said, zipping around a small pickup.

"I write five letters home a week and my phone bill comes in a box," he said. "Don't you like them anymore?"

"I don't want to talk about this." Her knuckles turned white on the wheel.

"You better. You're hurting their feelings." He leaned with the car into the next curve and looked down a mountainside strewn with loose shale.

Colette picked up a hand and let it drop. "It hurts to talk to them, so I don't do it. When they've got me on the phone, it's like a big suction forms, drawing me back down there."

"Does it hurt not to talk to them?"

"Yes, that, too."

This was enough. He could have said something more, but he knew her limit. It was enough to know she hurt when she *didn't* talk to them. If she wouldn't hurt then, he would have nothing to do with her.

Colette drove even without Paul. Using the car proved that she needed it. Watching people as she drove past them, she checked to see if they saw her, then willed herself not to see them. The tension of trying not to see pedestrians got on her nerves.

When she drove the car to a shopping center, she parked it on the lot's fringe, never next to another car, and when she would return on her long trek from the store, she would walk around it to check for dings. The day she found the first one, in a Sears parking lot, she felt violated and cried like a schoolgirl.

One Saturday, when her car was in for maintenance, she borrowed Paul's Crown Victoria to run her errands. She was self-conscious, as though she had gone shopping in hair rollers. She noticed, however, that no one looked at her. The car was a rolling cliché, unnoticeable and matched by yeoman Fords everywhere. After one day of riding in the plodding sedan, which smelled slightly of oil, she became used to it, the aroma, the tintinnabulation of loose tools in the trunk.

She had to pay to have the Mercedes hand-washed and -waxed because she didn't trust the two-dollar car washes anymore. She fretted about oil-change intervals, types of fuel. She had to protect her investment, her commitment to twenty years of driving the same vehicle. At the bank she never parked under a tree where birds might congregate, and daily she chipped her nails by scraping dried bugs off the grille. She maintained her pride in the vehicle, since it and glittering things like it were what she had come to California for.

One day Dirk stopped her in the hall next to the vault. "Hey, you look a little steamed, gal." He put a palm on the wall by her head. She guessed he had seen this move in an old cowboy film.

"I have been fighting for two days with a lounge-lizard trust recipient who wants a ten-thousand-dollar advance to pay his bar tabs. He has insulted me in every way he can think of, including an offer to sleep with me as a bribe."

"Well, his heart's in the right place."

She narrowed her eyes at him. "That's not funny."

"Take it easy." He put his arm down. "Tell you what. Just go down the hall to room six and deal with old man Schaeffer and help him disinherit his grandson. I'll take care of the lizard." He smiled, his face running with wrinkles. "Come into my office and get the Schaeffer file."

She followed him to his desk, where he sat down and pulled her onto his lap, all in one motion. "Now, let's talk about your lounge-lizard friend."

"What?" She wiggled to stand, but he held her.

"His name is Dalton. He's upset because you won't let him have a few thousand."

She turned to look at the washed-out eyes. "He's run up a liquor bill he can't pay. You want me to fund that under the emergency medical provision or something?"

"Yes."

She was so startled that she forgot where she was. "I was joking."

Dirk smiled patiently, as though he were dealing with a child. "Dalton's family has been doing business with this bank for a long time. He's worth bending the rules for."

She watched his eyes. "Are you ordering me to give him the money?"

"Oh, don't phrase it so harshly. Just do it."

She tried to get up, but he cinched her hard around the waist. "Let me up, Dirk."

"Not yet. I have what might be some good news for you. I'm being transferred, if I decide to take the bump upstairs."

She stopped struggling and turned a cool but interested expression on him. "Now, what does that mean?"

"When I go, everybody here goes up a notch. Or maybe two."

"Well." Colette's eyes grew wide.

"Yes." Dirk's smile slid open and cracks and wrinkles ran from his mouth. "Of course, we'll have to get together over at my place and discuss your career plans."

Her face went dark, and she sprang from his lap. "I think you know how I feel about private discussions by now."

"Come on, Colette. I could help your career a lot if you'd just be a bit friendlier. I know you're not crazy about me, but there isn't a girl in this building who wouldn't crawl in the sack with me for a six-figure income." He smiled broadly and she saw a silver clip in back of his twelve-year molars. She looked at his hair, and the gold seemed like silky polyester on a doll's skull. She closed her eyes a moment as though something hurt, then walked toward the door. When she opened it, she said, just loudly enough for the secretaries to hear, "I'd rather go back to wrapping pennies than get promoted for that."

His smile did not decrease in power, and she knew he held all the cards. "Well, if you change your mind, let me know. Meanwhile, run the paperwork to me so I can give Mr. Lizard his medical advance."

As she left, she looked at the two young secretaries for some sign, but their faces were deliberately without light.

As the day wore on, she tried to put Dirk out of her mind, but she found herself slamming drawers and balling trash paper until the sheets were like wooden balls. She went down to talk to her friend Elise, who listened patiently and then suggested that she might be overreacting. It was then that she realized big blond Elise had worked at the bank a very long time, and was also ambitious.

At quitting time Colette's silver car sailed out onto the boulevard on a quest of someone to talk to. She dialed her neighbor on her car phone, a retired woman from Nebraska, but she wasn't in. Colette began to understand why several of her coworkers went to analysts. She stopped at a traffic light, and when it turned green, she did not press the accelerator. The amplified insect beep of the car behind chased her through the intersection and then she drove around the same block twice, not knowing where to go. She took a cross street and began to wander, taking rights and lefts at random, in and out of residential and commercial neighborhoods, palm trees and stucco, granite and glass. The steering wheel turned as though over a Ouija board, and eventually she parked in front of an apartment building. When he answered the door, he still had his coveralls on and smelled like Liquid Wrench.

"Babe, what's up?" He did not look especially happy to see her.

She walked past him and into his little kitchen. "I got to talk to you a minute about work." Looking up, she saw that he had a bump high over his temple. "You bang your head on a milling machine again?"

"Smoke-box door fell off its hinges. Son of a bitch weighed a hundred pounds."

"You have something to drink?"

He opened a cabinet and looked. "I might have some beer. Manuel left some tequila when we were playing poker the other night."

"Tequila's fine. You have some mixer?"

"No. All I got's Sprite."

"That'll do." She fixed herself a drink and took a long swallow, then leaned back against a counter.

"You drink hard stuff every day?" He looked at her glass.

"No. And don't start getting on me about drinking. I came by to tell you something and get some feedback." She told him about her job and about the troubles with Dirk. Her hands were trembling, but he knew better than to take them.

He folded his arms and looked down at the checkered tile, listening. When she finished, he looked up. "Why you telling me this? You want me to go down to the bank and press his suit with him in it?"

"You can't do that in Los Angeles."

"What you want from me, then? Advice?" He laughed. "Get a lawyer and sue him for wanting to have sex with you. But you'll have to sue every straight man in the state who's got eyeballs." He pulled open the refrigerator, grabbed a beer, and turned for the living room.

"This is different. He's my boss and he's trying to make it a condition of my employment." She sat in a folding chair next to his sliding glass door. "I just need to talk about this."

"This burns my ass, Colette."

"What?"

"I feel like I'm your girlfriend. A man makes a pass at you and you don't want me to be upset, you want advice. A girlfriend gives advice. A husband would go down and put that slug's dick in a pipe threader. But I can't do that. All I can do is ride around with you like a pet hound with his tongue hanging out."

She pouted up at him. "You smell like coal oil, you know that?"

He jumped up and unzipped his coveralls, heading for the bathroom. "Jeez, I got to smell like a rose to give advice."

She called after him. "I didn't mean you had to take a bath. You just don't want to sit on furniture smelling like that. It'll stay in the fabric forever." When she heard him slam the door, she got up and fixed herself a double with cracked ice in a tall tumbler. A letter was open on the counter and she saw that it was from Paul's father. Scanning it greedily, she saw that the oil industry was drying up in Louisiana. Most of the fabrication yards in Tiger Island, the tool suppliers, the mud-boat operations, they'd closed up and sent their workers packing. It was a long letter telling of many little disasters, ending with the fact that LeBlanc's had closed down when the *Gruenwald* turned turtle at the machine shop's landing, pulling the dock apart when she went down. There were news clippings with the letter and she read these, too, until she had drained her glass. Paul came in, barefoot, in jeans and a denim shirt. He got himself a beer and fixed her another drink. "You figure out what to do about your boss?" he asked.

She went into the living room and sat on the sofa, sniffing it. "I'll just have to dance around him like I've been doing. I'll just tell myself that everyone else wants to have sex with me, so he's normal."

Paul sat next to her. "I don't want to have sex with you."

"It's a good thing." She took a drink.

"I want to make love with you."

Colette drew in a deep breath and leaned slowly into him. "You bastard, you've still got some good timing left."

He touched her hair with an open palm. "I've been out here for months, Colette. I've given up my life to follow you here. I've stayed away from you when it wasn't easy to."

"It's good that you stayed away." She looked around the room. "You've learned to keep house living by yourself. I bet you learned a lot."

"Safe bet. If I had a lawn, I'd cut it."

Colette emptied her glass and muted a burp. "You miss me at night?"

"Do you?" He put an arm lightly on her shoulder.

"Man," she said, "oh, man."

"You still on the pill?"

"Yeah. They're like using snow tires in the desert." She put her head back on his shoulder and looked at him. "But you never can tell."

"Ah, Colette, let's tell."

They kissed and five minutes later they were in his bedroom. For both of them it was like dancing to silky-good soft music, using all the moves and steps they'd learned by heart. And after a long time, at sundown, they went out on his little terrace and watched the sun disappear into the smoggy hills on the west of the tile-roofed neighborhood. They drank strong coffee and ate aspirin, deliberately not talking, not knowing what to say, both of them amazed at what had happened.

Finally, Colette asked, "Is California a funny place or what?"

Paul watched the orange sky and shrugged. "Remember in history class we heard about those English explorers who brought an Indian to London?"

"Yeah."

"Well, sometimes I feel like that Indian."

Colette nodded. "You're one of a kind all right." She looked into her coffee cup until she could see a clear image. She blinked. "Wow, that tequila's still got me."

"Colette."

"What?"

"If you come back, I'll never go dancing without you."

She giggled. "And what about your accordion?"

"It's in the pawnshop on River Street right now."

She looked at him, her eyes wide. "You sold it?" She pictured the inlaid, chrome-buttoned windstorm sitting on a shelf with used televisions, a price tag on one of its stop knobs. "I can't believe that. Do you miss it?"

His coffee had turned cold, so he threw it over the rail. "No."

"Do you miss anything?"

"Yeah," he admitted, because he knew she could smell a lie from half a parish away. "Mammas and daddys. Aunts and uncles."

She got up and sat on his hard thighs. "You miss hearing the whistles."

He could not believe the touch of her, and he stared at a patch of skin under her throat. "Don't miss the mosquitoes, though."

She put her nose in his ear and he could smell the hot snap of tequila. "How about the red bugs?" she asked.

"Pas du tout."

"Et les écrevisses?"

He sighed. *"Tout le temps."*

"Et Nelson Orville et son accordion?"

"Un 'tit peu. Et toi?"

"A little. But I wish he could sing better."

They talked until past dark, argued a little, kissed, then Colette told him she was going to her apartment. At the door she told him that they were now officially dating.

"Dating," Paul repeated. "You want my high school ring?"

"Hey, don't start."

"You want me to ask your daddy if we can stay out past twelve?" He put his hands in his pockets and rocked on his bare feet.

"Hey, man, between boilers, give me a ring."

The next morning she noticed that the Mercedes's silver paint was dusty, coated with a smoggy road film. She started it and it clattered and stank in the closed-in parking area. On her way to the bank she wondered how long twenty years lasted. The following evening, she sat down to write a letter to her mother, tearing up five different beginning pages. She called Paul and asked him how to begin.

"This is the first real letter home and it'll be a long one," she told him. "You write someone back home every day. How do I start?"

"Well, first there's the inside address."

"Come on."

"Just do it like a phone call. Like when you call home."

"It's not the same."

"Colette, why are you writing, anyway?"

"I feel enough distance. I can bear to write to them." She put a palm up to her eyes. "And I know what you're thinking. They're the ones doing the bearing, right?"

"Damn straight."

"You know what's hardest, though? Reading their letters and finding not one shred of meanness, anything that would cause me pain. Nothing between the lines." She grabbed a handful of her hair and gathered it into a fist. "I've got to be grateful for that."

"Tell them that in your letter. You know, how much you enjoy what they tell you."

"What?"

"Maybe they think you left because they weren't good enough."

"I don't want to hear you say that again. You can't make me feel guilty."

There was a long breath on the other end of the line. "Other people can't make you feel guilty."

Colette bit her lip for a long time. "How do I start this thing?"

"How about 'I'm sorry I haven't written sooner'?"

"There you go again."

"Well, say what you want, then. Tell them you're not sorry one damn bit you haven't made them happy with a letter."

"You don't have to be mean."

"Okay. I'll try. Just tell them how busy you've been, then explain what that means. The news will come out while you're trying to give it. You going to tell them about us?"

She made a face. "Us," she said, "is still under construction."

"Later," he said, hanging up.

She fixed herself a pot of coffee and sat down at the kitchen table to stare at the little tablet on which she had written an address and salutation. "I'm sorry . . ." she began.

Nine

Early in May Paul was reading the *Los Angeles Times* and saw an ad for reduced airfares to New Orleans. He bought a ticket over the phone and then for the first time in his life flew on an airplane. From a window seat of the DC-9, he regarded the thrumming engines with great suspicion. His father met him and took him to Tiger Island.

"T-Bub, you won't believe how everything's gone down in the little bit of time you been away." Paul had heard. He watched the traffic and noticed what he didn't see: pipe trucks carrying oil-well drill column, blue Schlumberger x-ray trucks, red-and-gray Halliburton cement trucks. They rode over a hundred miles, seeing only lumber, dry goods, and mail hauled over the road.

Tiger Island had changed for the worse. The movie house was padlocked and the Silver Bayou Drive-In was overrun with brambles. Only two of the town's fifteen oil-field businesses were still open. Cut-grass and thistle had taken over the abandoned pipe yards, and slow-stepping herons hunted minnows in the rain-cratered parking lots. "Damn," Paul said, looking from one side of the highway to the other as they came into town. He found his mother to be a little heavier. She fed him étouffés and gumbos, and he ate like a man who had not seen food for a lifetime.

Twice he had long visits with Colette's parents, explaining how busy she was with her job, how well she was doing, how happy she was. Once, Mr. Jeansomme got up to retrieve a bottle of wine, but he came back five minutes later empty-handed, having forgotten why he had left the room. Mrs. Jeansomme talked about Colette as though she had not left, not filed for a divorce still pending. The three of them pretended it didn't matter that she was not there.

On his third and last night home, Paul and his father walked down to the Little Palace for a beer, taking the table by the door, under the yellowed Regal beer clock. A crowd of bragging firemen lined the bar, flicking ashes on the shoe-polished cypress floor.

His father scratched an elbow. "T-Bub, it was good to see you. We got your sister and brother here, but you the baby. When you here, your mamma and me don't feel so old."

"Let me get used to those damned airplanes, and I'll come back before too long."

"Man, I hope I never have to get on one of those things." His father waved at a cousin. "You better try to get that girl down here pretty quick. Her folks ain't getting any younger, you know."

"Since when has anybody been able to tell Colette what to do?" He took a long, cold swallow of Dixie.

His father leaned forward against the table, his shoulders rounding. "Old man Jeansomme ain't gonna last forever. His mind's in terrible shape." He also took a long pull on his beer. "Loisel down at the clinic says Colette's mamma's blood pressure is sky-high. You gonna tell that to Colette?"

"If I get a chance to."

"You make the chance." He waved to Mr. Lodrigue, the station agent, who was at the bar. "So. You got a pretty good job." He said this as though it was an accusation.

"Yeah. I like the pay."

His father sniffed. "LeBlanc closed up. I was down there the other day and LeBlanc and *Grand-père* was just sitting on the bench, staring at the levee, cussing the Arabs."

"Arabs?"

"T-Bub, the Arabs are pumping so much oil that nobody around the Gulf wants to bother to look for it anymore. The rig count is next to nothing."

"Etienne wrote me about it, but I didn't half-believe what he said."

"Etienne who?"

"Etienne the giant."

"You mean the big Partian?"

"That's the one."

"Lord, you must know everybody in the parish." His father straightened up and waved for another round. The little bartender dipped into a cooler and two caps spat off in the opener. "You know lots of people in Los Angeles yet?"

"One or two."

"I hear that. The more people in a town, the less of them you know." The beers arrived along with cousin Sidney with a joke about a priest and a hamper of crabs.

The next night Paul's father and *grand-père* rode with him to New Orleans to catch his plane. The black snake that was Highway 90 wound narrow and uneven through little swampy settlements, a slow road, poorly lined. Paul's father let him drive, preferring to stare out the window. The grandfather sat in back and talked enough for everybody.

"Hey, T-Bub. You daddy here told me you think Tiger Island's ugly. It wasn't always like that, no." He coughed. "It used to be a lot worse. But it was okay because there was always work. I used to pull lumber in the big mill and at night trapped muskrat." He folded his arms slowly, as though they wouldn't bend. "I worked from can't see to can't see, and still I didn't make no money. Everybody was pretty much the same way, so it didn't matter. Not many could afford a nice house, no. The streets was made out of dust and we had to burn our garbage in the backyard. After the war things got to where you could make a little money, but most people in Tiger Island, they were set in their ways. We was happy in our ugly little house."

"That's right," Paul's father said.

Grand-père Abadie continued. "A nice brick house is okay, but if you had one, you couldn't take your car apart in the side yard. That wouldn't look right."

Paul laughed and steered around a pothole. "I guess not."

"That's a damned fact," *Grand-père* told him. "Now you and Colette, you gonna be able to buy what you want. Everything's gonna work out all right if what you buy is really what you want. Now you mama told me Colette bought herself one of those Adolf Hitler cars."

"What? You mean the Mercedes?"

"Yas. That thing cost a skiffload of money, I bet."

"Lots of people drive them out in Los Angeles. It's not an Adolf Hitler car."

"Well, what kind did Mr. Hitler drive, Mr. Smarts? A Dodge?"

Paul's father turned his head. "Hitler wouldn't drive no Dodge, Daddy."

"That's my point. He had to drive the best, like a big shot. I remember the newsreels. He had bigger nuts than the governor of Louisiana."

"Colette told me that car will last twenty years."

The grandfather sat up and talked into Paul's ear. "I had me a Ford Maverick lasted longer than that. I'd still be driving it if they hadn't stopped giving me my damned license."

Around Paradis his *grand-père* fell asleep. Paul could think of nothing to say for miles. An unnatural darkness rested between him and his father, and Paul could not fool himself into forgetting that he was leaving again; the youngest was going away, taking along his parents' image of youth, removing from them his un-lined face, the noise of him in the house.

At the airport he hugged the two men, and through his father's cotton shirt, he smelled Aqua Velva and felt his bones.

"Ask Colette to please write" was the last thing his father said. Paul boarded the flight with the dry, husky feel of the men tingling on the ends of his fingers.

Ten

Something was happening to Colette. Shopping for dried flower arrangements and framed prints began to bore her. She couldn't tolerate more than a few pages of *Victoria* magazine. The novelty of her car waned. She had driven the length of California, from the Oregon border to Tijuana, and knew that she had been too greedy with the landscape, had eaten it up too quickly. Every night she began to get out of bed and go to the sliding glass doors to stare into the grave vault of the Los Angeles River, rubbing the air-conditioned chill from her satiny arms.

On a Saturday, she went to a shopping center and parked out back in the employees' lot; when she returned, she found that the car would not start. She had not called Paul since his visit to Tiger Island, afraid of being weakened by news from home, but her car was in trouble. He came in a few minutes, unshaven, his work shirt out.

"Pop the hood and let's see."

She gave him a suspicious look. "What are you going to do?"

He looked at her steadily, detecting something new in the air between them. "Jeez, if you don't trust me to look at the damn thing, why'd you call me out?"

She went into the car and pulled the hood latch. Paul came to her side of the car.

"What is it?"

"I'm glad you're sitting down."

"What?"

"Somebody went up under this thing and stole the starter."

Colette's anger whizzed off like a rocket. She yelled about security at the mall, she yelled at him for not knowing where to buy a starter, she yelled until all her straight white teeth showed. And when Paul told her he guessed a new starter would be about eight hundred dollars, she started over. Finally, he looked around the parking lot and interrupted her. "Colette, it's just a car, babe."

"Just a car! Do you know what the note on this 'just a car' is?"

"Why you yelling at me? I'm not the one pouring money down a snake hole for this egomobile. Somebody like you ought to stick with a Toyota." He regretted the words as soon as they came out.

"What you mean, somebody like me? You think I'm not supposed to own a car like this because I'm a young bayou girl from a trashy town in Louisiana?"

He braced himself, set his jaw. "You said it, I didn't."

Colette exploded into a crying fit, resting her fists on his chest and bawling into them. Paul's mouth fell open and his arms wobbled at his sides. Then he tried to touch her, and she cried, "Keep your hands away" as she burrowed against his chest. He had never seen Colette cry like this in his life, and she hid her face from him. "Don't look at me," she squealed. "Turn your head. Don't look at me. I don't do this."

"I got to admit," he said at last, "it's like watching a bird jump rope."

The next day, when Paul came home from church, he saw Colette's Mercedes in his parking lot, obvious among the little Chevys and Isuzus. She got out of it and came to sit with him in the Ford, moving his copy of *Appleton's Cyclopedia of Steam Mechanics for 1898* to the backseat. "Let's take a drive up to Mount Shasta and look at the forest," she told him.

He lounged back in the creaking seat and watched her suspiciously. She was cheerful. "If I look at another big pine tree, I'll turn into Bambi," he told her.

"You can't be serious. You'd rather sit in town with your nose in that book than ride with me to the mountains?"

"I guess so. You won't let me read it on the way, I know that."

"Come on. I don't want to drive up there by myself. You can't tell me you're used to these big California forests already."

He focused his large brown eyes carefully on her. "No. I could camp out in them twice a year and be happy. I like nature as well as the next fellow, but I'm not Smokey the Bear, babe. I get my fill."

"How could you ever get your fill of one of these mountains?" Her voice accused him, suddenly on the verge of anger.

Paul touched a finger to his forehead and pulled it away. "Colette, you could build a house on the rim of the freaking Grand Canyon with picture windows overlooking the view, and in six weeks all you'd be doing is watching old black-and-white movies on a portable TV in the bedroom, and you'd be throwing your garbage down the cliffs."

She crossed her hands in her lap. "You don't like living out here, is that it?"

"I love living out here. It's a permanent vacation."

She crinkled her straight white nose. "Permanent vacation. That sounds like death."

He looked at her intensely, her eyes, the sheen of her hair. "You feeling all right?"

"What do you mean?"

"You never say things like you just said." He blinked. "You sure you're all right?"

"There's nothing wrong with me. You're the one would rather stick his nose in a steam engine's butt than visit a national park." She got out of his car, then, remembering something, leaned back in. "As we speak, there are people driving all the way from Louisiana just to visit these mountains."

He looked over the long white hood of his car. "Also as we speak, a bunch of California people are driving to Barataria to take a ride on Boudreaux's Swamp Tours. You sure you feel okay?"

"Yes," she yelled, slamming the door so hard the sedan shivered like a horse.

By the end of May, Colette knew she was not all right. Each day brought a second or two of vertigo, accompanied by a taste of brass at the back of her throat. One morning her feet were swollen. Another day it hurt to put on her brassiere. And then one night she got up and rummaged through the pantry, desperate for a tin of sardines in tomato sauce. Sardines! Her head snapped up from the neatly arranged cabinet and she ran to her desk calendar in the living room. When she saw that her period was two weeks late, she sat quietly on the sofa and stared at the numbers, trying to make them add up differently. She knew that once or twice a year, she was not regular, so she did not panic. A week later, however, she gave in to her fear, drove to the drugstore, and bought a home pregnancy test. Back at the apartment, she looked at the result and began to tremble, deciding to will that this would not make a difference in her life. The sliding glass door gave back her reflection until false dawn as she thought about what she would do if she was indeed pregnant.

Because it was not an emergency, it was two weeks before she could get an appointment with a gynecologist, who told her that she was about two months pregnant. During that two weeks she did not answer Paul's messages, and the people working under her at the bank were scalded by her hottest words at the least provocation. On a Tuesday when she had come home from work,

Paul was waiting for her in the hall. He saw how she looked at him, and he whistled.

"You mad, or what?" He put his hands into a new pair of tan slacks.

"Does it show?" She opened the door and stood in it, facing him.

"Is this about going to the forest again? Okay, I'll go."

"It's not about the damned forest."

He cocked his head at an angle. "What did I do now?"

"Oh, you did the big thing."

"What?"

She put a hand over her eyes. "You knocked me up. You satisfied?"

He tried to touch her arms, but she backed up a step. "This is great," he told her.

Colette looked at the beige carpet. "I'd like to know why it's so great."

"We can get together again."

"Yeah. Because I'm pregnant. Everybody will say, 'She had to go back to him.' Even we'll say that, down the line. That's not a reason to be together."

"I think it's a damned good reason."

She looked up at him and pushed her hair back over her shoulders. "If only you hadn't gotten me drunk."

He put up a hand like a cop. "Wait a minute. You the one who went after the tequila like a Mexican bandit."

"You saw the condition I was in and took advantage of me," she said.

Her words stung like wasps and he backed up into the hall. It was several moments before he could think of something to say. "You been reading too many of those women's magazines."

"What's that supposed to mean?"

"I see 'em on your table there. *Cosmopolitan* and those others.

You read those articles that say every time a man touches you, he drains you, like you're a flashlight battery or something. That's bullshit. I didn't take advantage of you and you know it." He punched the door frame and Colette saw the blood rise through his neck. "You probably missed a pill or something and won't admit it."

"Why would I miss a pill?" she shouted.

"Because the only reason you were taking them was that you were trying to keep from having cramps." Now *he* was shouting. "It's for damned sure you weren't taking them to protect yourself from me."

"That's a fact. But you knocked me up anyway."

"Colette, a husband does not 'knock up' his wife. Let's get the terms straight here. We're still married." A door opened down the hall and a middle-aged man looked out, a newspaper pinched in his fingers.

"Keep your voice down," she told him.

Paul threw a look at the man, who backed in and closed his door. "What are you gonna do?"

"I don't know."

"What do you mean, 'I don't know'? What's the maternity rules for your job?"

"I don't know, I don't know," she said, slamming the door in his face and putting her back against it. She did not hear him walk away. Her name came through the wood and she closed her eyes. He called again, softly, "Colette Thibodeaux," and she said to herself, "*I don't know.*"

The next day, Colette was walking briskly though a suite of offices during the lunch hour, her mind buzzing, making plans, canceling them with the next thought. The building was nearly empty, most of the employees down the street eating, except for a few tellers up front. She clutched a Masonite clipboard against her right side, a new one with a shiny steel clamp at the top that she had just drawn out of supply. She wore a loose-fitting full skirt, a delicate material that floated at her knees. As she turned into her office door, Dirk stepped out and slid his hand up between her thighs. "Baby, he said to her opened mouth, "are you ready to be head of the trust department?" She did not think about what he said, just as she would not think about swatting a hornet that had landed on her sleeve. She brought the clipboard up with both hands and swung its edge at his face. Dirk let out a yowl and fell back against a desk, a long cut above his left eye. Colette felt her heart leap, and then words came to her.

"You slimy son of a bitch," she yelled, raising the clipboard and swinging again, putting a dent in the top of his head.

Dirk put up an arm and yelled, "Help!" She dropped her hands and glared at him, wanting to hit him again, and then doing it, letting him have the board in a broadside pop. A teller walked in, froze, then turned and left slowly, as though she had seen nothing.

Dirk fished a handkerchief from his coat and held it to his eyebrow, which was pouring blood. He seemed about to cry, and then, to her amazement, he did. "It's not that much of a hit," she told him. "A man shouldn't cry over a hurt like that." An image of Etienne the giant came to mind, fighting roughnecks with his arm broken in two places.

Dirk said nothing and walked off toward his offices, his head tilted up and to the right, as though afraid his brains would pour out. She sat at her desk, trembling with anger, and when that began to subside, it was replaced with fear. She had never understood Dirk's type of passion, which was not about lust. Maybe it's about power, she thought. Something went by the window, and she turned her head and saw a Lincoln fly toward the street. The blood in the carpet came up with cold water and tissue. When she went up front to check with the young teller, the woman told her with a bland face that business was slow, that nothing unusual had happened.

The next day Colette spotted an envelope on her desk. She

held it a long time before carefully slitting it open and finding that she had been fired. As though on cue, the telephone rang, and Dirk told her in a flat voice that she'd better not waste her time trying to get a job at another financial institution in California. She could, of course, expect no recommendations.

She went to see the bank president and told him what her boss had done to her. He informed her that such behavior was irrelevant. Dirk was being promoted, and two people with similar training were being brought in to replace him, and her as well. No, there was no other position for her. No, only Dirk would be the proper person to write her a recommendation. She should count herself lucky that he hadn't filed charges for aggravated assault. The president was a blocky, cold man with white hair, obviously once blond. In his eye was a dying glimmer of something like Dirk's want for her.

She went to her desk for the last time, biting the inside of her cheek until she tasted blood. All the good work she'd done for this bank counted for nothing, and she was being put out like a janitor caught drinking on the job. The thought of suing crossed her mind, but what would she win? And what if Dirk decided to sue for bodily injury? She thought about how he had touched her; she thought about what she had lost, and she knew without a doubt that she would hit the bastard again.

She cleaned out her desk and carried two large boxes to the Mercedes, discovering that they wouldn't fit in the trunk. She tied the lid down with a piece of twine and stepped back to look at the car. When she started it, it jittered and snarled. She looked around at the expensive leather, then drove straight to the dealership and gave her car back, taking for her equity a five-year-old yellow Caprice sitting at the rear of the dealership's lot. She drove home trying not to cry, and no one looked at her car.

*　*　*

The day after Colette told him she was pregnant, Paul was sent to the northern part of the state to work on a boiler system at a lumber mill. He was deep in the woods for a week. When he returned, he got her answering machine every time he called. He sat out on his balcony and tried to think what it would be like to have a child, but he could not imagine anything. He remembered holding nieces and nephews, but they were not his. The feeling would not be the same. He figured Colette would call again. It was always better to wait for her. If he did phone, she would call him a stalker. But after two more days he was hungry for the sight and sound of her and he called again. A recording told him the number had been disconnected. His white Ford screamed up the street and soon he was standing outside her apartment, looking through an open door, watching a young black couple put up drapes. She had moved, they told him. No, they didn't know where. He phoned her bank and listened to the few polite words a woman in Personnel told him.

He had not called home in several days and did so now. His father answered the phone.

"Hey, T-Bub, how's it going?" His father sounded sleepy.

"All right. Any big news down home?"

There was a moment of silence and he pictured his father staring down at the linoleum, trying to count the countless splotches of meaningless design. "What kind of big news you got in mind?"

"She's there, right?"

"I saw her up at the hardware. She moved back in with her parents maybe three days ago."

"She's not renting a place?"

"I don't know. I guess she got to find a job first. That'll be a trick around here nowadays, let me tell you. The economy's plumb busted."

"How does she look?" He was not going to ask if she appeared pregnant.

"What you mean?"

Paul sat down on a stool in his kitchen. "Nothing."

"I got laid off."

"What?"

"Yeah. The tool company folded up like a Kmart card table and took down my retirement with it."

"Aw no."

"Me and Mamma are living off savings right now. It's rough. We can't even afford to turn on a window unit."

The phone call was a long catalog of men moving out, more companies going under. For the rest of the evening Paul thought of Tiger Island, wondering what Colette was doing, if she was still pregnant. He went for a walk at dusk, up the tree-lined street toward Glendale, where a warm breeze steamed the sweet ground-hugging smell of apricots and nectarines from backyard fruit trees. Passing into a neighborhood of tile-roofed bungalows, he heard salsa music coming from kitchen doors, and after a few blocks of this, he turned right, found the Los Angeles River, and walked the concrete apron toward the railroad yards. He thought about whether his shortcomings had earned him the grief Colette had given during their marriage—her sarcasm, her baleful over-the-shoulder looks. He wondered if he was a little stupid for putting up with her meanness and then chasing her down to get more of it. But then he remembered why he wanted her, other than her cooking and her looks. She was the smartest woman he had ever known, and, like him, she had stuck with being Catholic as best she could. Even though he believed that she might divorce him in a legal sense, he knew that being married in the church meant something to her, something more than a judge could put a finish to. He was sure his wife was not a bad person, just bad-tempered sometimes when things didn't go her way. He knew plenty of women who were bad but sweet-natured, and he wanted nothing to do with them. For all of Colette's anger and ambition, he suspected that she knew right from wrong and one day might manage to grow up. And, of course, she could really dance.

He stopped and looked across the river to the hissing interstate and thought about traveling home to hard times and humidity. In California was money, no boredom, and anything you wanted under the smog. He understood why Colette had wanted to try a life here.

Paul called Manuel, the stay-bolt specialist, a profane, sleek dancer who was too good at making women laugh. They went out and hit the bars in the neighborhood. Manuel was like an open drain to which women flowed. But the women Paul met looked into his eyes and saw he wasn't really there. When he danced, he insulted them with his movements, showing his back, bending their fingers.

The next week, the men went out again and met two jitter-bugging female Realtors. They were intelligent, handsome, and Catholic. Manuel was delighted. Catholic women who cruised were rarities. Paul thought they were too kind, and both lacked a gritty style on the dance floor, no snap, no courage in the turns. They swung on his arm, heavy as skiffs. A woman had to be tough to jitterbug right. She had to have a mean foot.

His boss sent him up to the state transportation museum in Sacramento to do estimates and consulting, plus a little welding on steam-locomotive boilers. He came back late in July with blisters on his arms and lungs full of carbon. When he stepped from his Ford in the parking lot, an elderly Asian man got out of a car in the next row. It was Mr. Wu from the laundry.

"Hello," he called.

"Hey," Paul said. "The laundryman."

"That's right. Look, I got a question for you."

"What's that?"

"Did you call the state and tell them my boiler was ready to blow up? That I carried a hundred and fifty pounds on it?"

Paul looked over the man's head, as though the answer might be hanging in the air. "Did a state inspector come by?"

"Yeah. The bastard who checks blue sheets. He condemned the boiler. Says I got to buy a new one, and hey, you saw my operation. I can't afford that." Mr. Wu ran a hand over his bristly gray hair.

"What's the alternative?"

Mr. Wu tilted his head slightly. "I'll close down for good. Send the girls home to draw welfare."

Paul couldn't look at the man. "I'm sorry things didn't work out for your business." He thought of his sullen boss first, then his paycheck, and he began to move away.

Mr. Wu stepped subtly into his path. "Did you tell the state my boiler was no good? Did you excite those ninnies and tell them to come down on inspection?"

"I can't help you." The tawny face slid out of his peripheral vision and Paul saw nothing until he put the key in his lock. Inside, he tried to make coffee, but he forgot to put the grounds in the dripolator. He decided to mix a drink instead, but he could find only remnants of a fifth of tequila, which he held and stared at for five minutes. Picking up the phone, he called his parents' house. His mother answered, and he knew by her voice that some part in the universe of Tiger Island had fallen out of orbit. In five minutes she told him that Colette had gained a lot of weight. He held the receiver to his head with both hands.

"You mean she looks like she's pregnant?"

"Oh, I never said that. My God."

"But you mean, Mamma, that her belly is sticking out in front."

"Well, you could say that," his mother whined.

He took a deep breath. "Don't tell anyone, but it's mine."

"Oh, Paul," she squealed, a grandmother's noise.

"Mamma. Colette is divorcing me still, I'm sure. So calm down and keep quiet."

The line fell silent for a moment. "When it's born, she'll let you see it, won't she? What are you going to do about it out there?" He had no answers for her questions, and when he hung up, he found that all he had were questions.

After a sleepless night, he went in to work and gave Manuel instructions for a firebox repair. When he entered the office area, he ran into Mr. Wu, his boss, and Bradley Scott, a troubleshooter for the state boiler inspector's office.

Scott turned a clipboard toward Paul's face. "Is this your signature?"

Paul looked at the handwriting on the blue form, then glanced over at his boss's glowering expression. "Why you want to know?"

"Because this report says Wu's laundry was operating an old boiler at a hundred and fifty psi. That's way over his allowed pressure. It also states that the crown sheet was glowing when you inspected the firebox."

Mr. Wu put his hand on Paul's arm. "Did you say this, buddy?"

Paul's boss cursed. "Yes, he said it. It's right there under his signature. The guy needs a new boiler, that's all there is to it."

"I don't have a hundred and forty thousand dollars," Wu told him. His dark eyes became primitive, showed betrayal.

Scott moved in closer, like a policeman trying to threaten. "Look, I love to jerk the boiler tickets on old stuff. But if I shut this guy down on a false report, that'll leave my ass in a cast."

Paul looked down at a wrench in his hand, one of the expensive ones he had bought with his first paycheck, and took a breath. "It's not my signature," he said. "The boss made up the report." Cursing rolled around in the little office like a thunderstorm until Wu and Scott slammed the door behind them on the way to the parking lot. Paul turned to look at his boss, who held up a hand.

"Save it. Get your shit out of your locker and get the fuck out of here. I don't ever want to see you again."

"You're firing me because I wouldn't let you screw that old man?"

"No. You're history because you don't appreciate what you have to do to be worth a big paycheck."

Paul sucked on his bottom lip a moment. He looked out a window and watched Mr. Wu walking fast to keep up with the state inspector, banging his fist into an open palm. "I can live with that," he said.

Eleven

The big Crown Victoria ate up desert for two days. As he backtracked through the cactus and stone, Paul felt like a broken-down pioneer who couldn't take the frontier anymore. Coming out of the burned stone facade of New Mexico, he stopped the car on the side of the road and walked out into the oven. Standing behind a saguaro, he urinated and watched a tarantula bustle over a rock. He looked over the cholla and prickly pear at the trillion-thorned desert, every plant armed, every rock blistering hot, then turned back to the car, which waited at the edge of the melting asphalt like a cool white mint.

Two days later he crossed the border into Louisiana, and the humidity began to mix with nose-itching emissions from the chemical plants. Isolated clots of black cloud hung in the sky, and as he drove, the day became ugly, rain crashing down on him in Lafayette like gravel. But at least everything was green and nothing was thorned. The rice fields were green, the fallow fields were roaring with willow, marsh alder, and honeysuckle, the sugarcane fields spread out as endless mesas of green, and even on truck-haunted Highway 90, a slender fuzz of grass stood up in cracks against the mowing traffic.

By the time the smokestack of the first sugar mill poked out of the vapor, the sun broke through, pulling wraiths of steam from the fields. He turned on the radio and the reedy complaint of a diatonic accordion buzzed into him, the sound of homeland. The music made him think of food and loss.

Many kinds of loss showed at the side of the highway. Oilfield offices sat empty, their parking lots blowing with weeds. Pipe yards showed only empty racks; hangarlike equipment buildings were padlocked and chained. On the outskirts of Tiger Island, one of the biggest offshore fabrication yards in the world was now a moonscape of white clamshells, crows racketing about the empty construction bays. Two barrooms were burned-out hulks, erect thistles mocking the parking lots. When he crossed the bridge into town, he looked down the Chieftan River and saw rafts of tugs and offshore supply boats tied side by side in the willows.

There was no traffic on River Street, and the only person at his parents' house was his *grand-père* Abadie, rocking on the front porch and drinking a Schlitz in the heat. Paul gave the old man a hug.

Abadie looked up at him carefully with his coffee-colored eyes. "You ain't heard the bad news."

"What?" He sat down in a ladder-back chair and turned toward the old man.

"Vera, she's dead."

Paul leaned forward. "What? When?"

"Two days. That's where your daddy and mamma is, the burial. They should be back anytime."

"But what did it?"

The old man looked at the back of a hand. "Stroke. Colette brought her mamma a cup of coffee and found her on the floor in the dining room, already gone." He shook his head once. "You maybe better clean up and get over to her house."

"Yeah." He ran both hands through his hair. "But I don't look forward to this."

"You don't think Colette wants to see you?"

Paul stood up. "She'll probably blame this on me. She'll probably think that if she'd never married me in the first place, she'd never of left town. You watch. She'll peg me for her losing these last months with her mama." He closed his eyes. He imagined her feelings coming at him like radio waves from across town.

His grandfather took another drink of beer. "If she thinks like that, you in trouble, yeah. That girl got a lot of sense, but she still got to grow up."

"What about me?" He put his hand in the mailbox out of habit.

"If you ain't growed yet, stick around," the old man told him.

At three o'clock the town had a near miss from a thunderstorm, and things cooled down under a damp wind. Paul set his teeth together and walked up onto the wide porch at Colette's parents' house. Inside were relatives, people with Jeansomme foreheads and noses and Comeaux ears, standing around and talking or eating from little plates of food brought by neighbors. He shook a dozen hands, saw Colette across the living room, and the house closed in on him like a warm fist. He went to her and wondered what he could say.

She looked up, saw him, and said, "I'm glad you wore a tie."

"I'm sorry. I just got in."

"Your mother told me you quit your job." She raised her head in a way that made him angry.

"No. I was fired."

She made a motion with the corner of her mouth, which suggested it was what she'd expected to hear. "So why'd you come home?"

He looked over to where her father sat on the sofa between two ancient aunts. The old man opened his mouth to say something, pointed, and then his lips closed on the broken thought. "I guess I figured there was more here for me than there was out there, you know?" He looked down. "When are you due?"

"I don't want to talk about it with you." Just then a cousin from Napoleonville came up to talk, and Paul stepped back. He looked at his father-in-law, who was speaking to a young boy dressed in the smallest suit Paul had ever seen. The boy stared at his great-uncle, uncomprehending.

Colette's brother came up with his pallbearer's boutonniere still pinned to his navy coat. "Paul." He put out his hand.

"I'm sorry to meet you like this."

"I know." He put up a hand as though to say, Enough.

"It was all at once, right?"

"Not really. She'd had several little strokes over the past four months. She didn't want us to tell Colette, you know?" He arched his left eyebrow.

"Aw, man."

"That's right." He came in close, bobbed his head to the side. "What's up with you and Colette? That your loaf in the oven?"

"Yeah. I want to patch it up. But . . ." He shrugged.

"T-Bub. Colette is my sister and I don't pretend to understand her. She can't let herself be satisfied with anything. At least most of the time." He leaned in closer, almost whispering in his ear. "If she wasn't pregnant, I'd tell you to get out of it. Just walk. But now, I got no idea."

Paul made a face, but before he could reply, his uncle Simon grabbed his arm and pulled him out to the porch, where he plied him with questions about his skiff engine. A half hour later he went in, talked, drank coffee, ate sandwiches, and waited for Colette to come into the room. He thought how her dissatisfaction would become general, more complex, because of her mother's death. He waited until sunset, but she had gone and left her brother to shake the last hands, to say the last good-byes.

The next morning he visited his sister and her husband, Nan and Raymond, and let her children climb over him like puppies. He stopped by his brother's house. His brother was now out of a job and running crawfish traps. Driving by LeBlanc's, he tried not to look at the weeds and the rust. All day he looked for a job, but the places that were still open had on skeleton crews and weren't hiring. He tried at Ramosville and across the river in Beewick, but he could tell by the thin traffic and the many FOR SALE signs in front of houses that luck would be scarce. The welders had all moved away or were running trotlines. The machinists were at home on welfare, watching television, listening for the phone. At sundown, he dropped in at the empty Little Palace, and the bald, stubby bartender stopped wiping the counter and said, "Here comes the rush."

That same morning Colette went out onto the front porch and sat in her father's glider, looking up at the beaded-board ceiling and the little bit of millwork between the roof supports. She closed her eyes and imagined she could feel her hair kink up in the humid air. From across Perrilloux Street she heard the scuff of shoes and looked to see Mrs. Fontenot, Paul's neighbor, coming toward the house. She shuffled up to the steps and called out, "Ey, Colette, I just walked over to say I'm sorry to hear you mamma passed."

Colette went to her and looked down the tunnel of her sunbonnet. She was the last woman in Tiger Island who still wore one. "Thank you, Mrs. Fontenot."

"You mamma was a nice lady. She taught my two boys what one plus one was." She pointed at nothing with her short forefinger. "You remember Claude and Ray?"

Colette nodded, thinking about the silent, thin boys who now worked in the oil field. "How are they doing?"

Mrs. Fontenot wagged her bonnet. "Aw, *chère*, it's too sad. I'm all by myself in town now. Each of them lost his job and they living up north somewhere. Way up north in Arkansas, one of 'em is. And Alabama. It's sad when children leave the town where they mamma lives, let me tell you."

Colette looked back up on the porch and said nothing.

Mrs. Fontenot shook her bonnet and turned toward the street. "How'm I gonna keep my shovels sharp without no boy to run a file on 'em?"

Every half hour someone would come by, spend five minutes or so, then move on like intermittent puffs of wind, relief from her stifling sorrow. A young girl cousin from the next block visited, then a lady from across the street walked over carrying a Tupperware container of potato salad. Family friends from Bayou Oeuf and Sorrel Pass telephoned, and she became worn-out from everyone's care. Late in the afternoon, when a thunderstorm in the next parish pushed away the heat and weighted the air with the smell of rain, she went out onto the porch again. A short, blocky old man was coming up the street, rocking his shoulders from side to side, his palms facing backward. It was Paul's *grand-père* Abadie, looking all of his eighty-five years as he pulled himself up the steps.

"*Alors, Monsieur Abadie, tu veux un peu de café?*" Colette did not speak much French. It was a politeness for the old man.

He held up a hand and shook his head, sitting in a chair opposite her. "I come down to tell you I'm sorry about Vera," he said, putting the accent on the last syllable of her mother's name.

"Thank you," she said flatly, for the twentieth time that day. She studied the old fisherman. He had not spoken to her ten times in her life.

And then he touched his forehead and began a little story. "Forty, fifty years ago, me, I was setting a trotline in high-water time up north of town. The current pulled the boat and I caught a hook in my wrist right there." He held up a wrist to show a white scar shaped like a teardrop, between two dark veins. "I went overboard quick, yas, hooked like a big catfish, and that old iron—what you call a bow brace—caught me on top the head and knocked me out." He popped his white hair with the heel of his hand to demonstrate. "When I came back to, I thought I'd be dead and somewhere else, but I was in you mamma's daddy's big new cypress skiff. He saw me go over and crossed the channel, pulled up the trotline and me on it, cut me loose, and pulled me in his boat. You mamma, she was just a girl, maybe twelve, but she held my busted head in her lap and put a rag over where it was cut." Abadie turned his face and looked over his shoulder a moment, as if preparing to tell a secret. "I tried to sit up, and she told me, 'Be still, else you gonna get blood all over my daddy's new skiff.'" He straightened up and began laughing a wet and raspy laugh: "*Ha-haaaa.*" Colette looked over the rail at her mother's lilies. "It was a long time ago, that's for sure. She took care of me. I got dizzy, and they had to carry me up the levee on a board. She stayed with me until my brother came and cut the hook out, and when he did that, she poured the whiskey on the hole." He looked at his hand, flexed it. "Some fella, they lost they hand when they got a hook in that deep."

Colette took the hand, studying the scar. "Now I know why you came."

He shrugged. "Some people's born good and some got to learn it the way they learn to ride a bicycle. Even from the start, you mamma was a good lady, yeah." He stood up, put his scaly hands in his pockets, and looked around his feet as if he had misplaced a cane. "I can't see too good. Sometimes I think I'm walking up the street and I'm walking down the street. *Ha-haaaaa.*" He took the porch steps suspiciously, as if each were a waterborne plank. She walked behind, her hands under his elbows, but not touching his khaki shirt.

She stayed in the narrow front yard to pick up sticks that had fallen from the two monster pecan trees near the sidewalk. The long black hood of a Lincoln floated past in her peripheral vision, then stopped and backed up to where her walkway touched the street. Bucky Tyler got out from behind the wheel and took off his sunglasses. Colette saw his gray sport coat, which had slanted western breast pockets. She noticed a heavy ring as he walked up. He looked like east Texas money.

"I thought you went off somewheres. Arizona?"

"California," she said, putting down a bundle of sticks. "I decided to come back."

"Why's that?"

She looked him in the eye. "I got fired and I got pregnant."

He cocked his head back and seemed to think about this. "It's your husband's, ain't it?"

"That's a kind guess, and you're right." She was impressed that he had said that.

"If I recall, you were going to divorce him."

"Still am."

"What about the baby?"

"Maybe that's why I'm divorcing him. I can take care of only one baby at a time."

Tyler laughed. "He deserves that."

"You still mad about that fight you had with him?"

His smile capsized as quickly as it had come. "I didn't know you'd heard about that." He raised up a hand, forced a new smile, changed the subject. "You seen the town since you been home? All the damage?"

She shook her head. "What damage?"

He bobbed his head toward his car. "Let's go for a ride."

Her eyes caressed the long car. Her father was napping, and no one else was coming up the street to visit. "Okay. But just for a minute." She slid onto the white leather as he held the door for her. And then they were moving and she was enjoying the big soft seats, the new smell. "What you doing nowadays?"

"Like the man says: Somebody gives you lemons, time to make lemonade. When the oil company laid me off, I took my severance, sold everything I had, borrowed a little, and went into business." She did not like the way he said "bidness" but let it pass. "I bought the old pogy plant. Five acres of tanks and machinery, and they just about gave it to me."

"The stink plant? What for?" She bunched up her nose.

Bucky put his hand on top of the steering wheel and turned up River Street. "I'm kind of a trash man. We burn some in the old boiler system and reduce some with the steam in what used to be fish cookers. It's dirty work, but somebody's got to do it, gal."

She watched Paul's house go by on the left, almost hoping someone would be on the porch to see her. "Must pay well."

"You might say I'm in the black nowadays."

They rode past the cypress-weatherboard shotgun houses and their postcard vegetable gardens, rode to where the blacktop ended and the shell road began. Colette could not believe what she saw. Where the Big Gator had stood was a freshly graded plain a quarter mile long. A bulldozer squatted where the dance floor had been. Farther down, where there had been other clubs, the roadside was bare.

"It's all gone," Colette said. "It's really all gone."

"You ought to be glad."

"What happened?"

Bucky pushed a button and a tinted window rolled down. "The guy who owned the Big Gator couldn't make it. People in town think he burned the place. Those bars farther down folded up when that trailer town full of welders and boat builders moved away." He looked at her and arched an eyebrow. She liked the movement. "There ain't a lot of beer and barmaid money left in south Louisiana these days."

Colette squinted one eye, remembering the hot boiled crabs soaked in red pepper and bay leaf, the buckets of angry red crawfish, smoking like little devils, heaped high on the table. She thought of the chattering music, the two-steps, Paul's arms arching over her hair during the waltz turns.

Next they rode out to the main highway on the other side of town, a place where at one time, day and night, shell dust hung in the air above the movement of flatbeds, mobile cranes, and hotshot trucks. Colette studied a succession of empty construction bays and boat slips, sheds as big as aircraft hangars behind weed-woven chain link, a mud boat turned turtle at the dock because no one was left to pump her out.

Back in town, he showed her stores that had died on the vine. Gagliano's meat market was empty, its porcelain display case on the sidewalk, the building's windows dull like the eyes of a dead fish. She had worked there one summer when she was fifteen, trimming fat from the chops, cutting up chickens.

The Rexall had burned; the King Hotel could afford only one drunk out front; the liquor store kept only a few bottles in the windows. Colette felt as if she had been away for ten years. "You just didn't know how far the oil money went," she said.

Bucky snorted. "Half the sons a bitches left in town are think-ing about all the green stuff they had and pissed away."

She didn't look at him. "You did your share."

"That's a very fact," he said. "You want to find a place and get a drink?"

She put a hand on her stomach and looked at him.

"Oh yeah."

"I better get home. My father is starting to wander nowa-days." As the car rolled through the streets like a big drop of black oil, she stored its motions in her, remembering her Mer-cedes, her mahogany desk at the bank in California.

"You need anything, you call me out at the plant. I'll probably be in the yard working with the dagos and coon-asses, but I'll get back to you." He smiled, showing a rack of straight teeth.

Colette watched her reflection in a glossy strip of wood grain on the dash. She knew he'd get back to her.

* * *

The next month, the divorce was finalized, and when she held the papers in her hand, she didn't feel anything, and this worried her. She yearned for the clean break, a feeling like cool air and sunshine as she walked down the street. She felt nothing of the sort. She was unemployed, with a senile father to tend. Had she been employed and fatherless, she would have to deal with pests at work and loneliness at home. She saw that freedom was a thin fantasy touted by TV commercials: freedom from sleeplessness, freedom from wetness. On the way home from city hall, she passed the church and remembered that she was Catholic and couldn't remarry. This prohibition gave her a cynical joy, an excuse not to get tied down to another man.

Every day when her father's mind was clear enough for her to leave him for a few hours, she'd put on a loose dress and go to the neighboring towns; there were two poor, stagnant hamlets that could offer her no work at all. She'd given up on Tiger Island after one day. Her old bank job had been cut, and her supervisor suggested glibly that she might go back out west. A man in the hardware who knew her looked at the floor and said her that the Holiday Inn needed a maid. She tried to get on as a bookkeeper at one of the local grocery stores, but the grocers were employing their daughters and cousins. In early August Colette got out a notebook, went over her finances, and saw that she would have to budget to get prenatal care. She had a nest egg from California, her Caprice, and her father had a pitiful retirement from his years as a principal. His Chrysler had gone to glory in a cloud of blue smoke a month before Vera died. Her mother had left behind almost nothing other than her burial policy. Within two weeks, Colette began to feel the pinch. She had to order maternity clothes from a catalog. In the market, she began choosing cheaper cuts of meat. The first time she put a T-bone back in the cooler, the pain was physical. Her hand ached and shook.

Poverty invaded her dreams. One night she was stealing food

from the back of a truck. On another night she dreamed she was shooting rabbits with her father's .22 pump rifle and then cleaning the animals in her kitchen. She woke up expecting to see the gun gleaming in a corner, but she realized she had not seen it in years, since the days of shooting matches across the river with her cousins, boy cousins she outshot.

One day when she was walking uptown, a sudden thunderstorm generated out of the August heat and the downpour chased her under the hardware store's awning just as Paul stepped through the door. He looked away, looked back. "Well, well," he said.

"What's that mean?"

He shook his head. "I saw you the other day, riding with John Wayne." He waited for her to blush, timed his next statement. "The day after you buried your mamma."

"Why would you want to say something like that to me?" She looked into the rain as though she wanted to bolt into it. "It was just a little ride," she said after a while.

"Where to?"

"None of your business." She folded her arms. "Just looking at all the closed-up shops."

He bobbed his head and stepped back against the building, for the rain was blasting down, the wind out of the south, whipping it against their shoes. "You find a job yet?"

"You?"

He laughed. "Shit no. Mamma just sits around and bitches because she can't afford to go to bingo anymore, and daddy reads and walks around town." He looked at a shoe, shook off the rain. "The cable man disconnected us last week."

"Now there's a tragedy."

"All I can get is fuzz on the set with rabbit ears." He seemed genuinely sorry about the lack of television.

"I can't believe a machinist can't find work."

He sighed. "I better find something. Daddy started drawing

a little pissant Social Security check, but that won't even pay the lights. Mamma's going into savings already to buy high-blood-pressure medicine."

"Don't let her get behind in that. She'll get sick and then you'll really have problems."

"I got problems now."

"You always had problems," she told him, going into the store, slipping behind a tall rack. She pretended to look at wood screws, worrying a dozen tiny boxes. She heard the customer bell jingle on the door and soon felt him standing behind her. "What?" she said without turning around.

"Uh, how's your stomach?"

"My stomach," she said stiffly, "is doing fine."

"Well, if you, you know, need anything . . ."

"What can you do? You're broke."

"I have a little saved up from the job. You going to the doctor?"

"I'm not stupid." She turned and faced him.

"Yes you are. That's why I'm asking you if you went to the doctor."

She pinched a Phillips-head screw until the point popped her skin. A store clerk walked up and asked if he could help her find something, and when she finished talking to him, she turned and confronted an empty aisle. The bell rattled above the door and she walked to the window to watch him plod toward home, head-up in the downpour.

Bucky Tyler called, came over with a half dozen roses, and drove her all the way to Lafayette to eat in a fine restaurant. She looked down at her eggplant stuffed with shrimp and crabmeat and felt briefly prosperous. Next to them on a room divider was a giant stuffed alligator purporting to creep through a patch of plastic swamp growth. On the way down, Bucky had acted like a high school senior on a big date. He told Cajun jokes while she looked out the window. He talked about what he'd done all week down at his little disposal plant. Here in the restaurant, she watched him eat. He was a good-looking man with a reddish tan and nice moves at the dinner table. The restaurant had a dance floor adjoining the table area, and they got up and moved through a two-step to the geriatric house band's music. She decided she liked his cowboy version well enough, though he had a little too much hop in his step.

Back at the table, he stared at her over dessert.

"What you thinking about?" she asked.

"Nothin'. I'm just glad you got shut of that night-owl husband of yours."

She looked down at her bread pudding. "He's gone, all right. No more bull to put up with."

"Yeah. The barmaids can worry about him now."

Colette rolled her eyes. "I don't know. He's a Catholic boy. Probably thinks he's still married in the eyes of the church and won't fool around."

Bucky lit up a cigarette. "You Catholic?"

"Yes."

"You gonna get married someday?"

Colette suddenly felt as if she were a business deal looming in Bucky's future. "I just got rid of one man. Why I want another?" She laughed, then took a big bite of bread pudding before she could say something else.

"I like you Catholics," Bucky said, leaning back in his chair. "Y'all really stick to your guns."

"Yeah. Paul would have to die of old age before I could get married again."

Bucky laughed. "That might work both ways. That'd be good revenge."

"What?"

"Live a long life, gal, and keep the poor bastard horny till the day he dies."

She pursed her lips in thought, then pointed her spoon at him. "I don't think you understand religion," she told him.

He tilted his head to the side. "What you talking about? My folks were east Texas Church of God."

Colette nodded and smiled a closed-lip smile, her mouth full of pudding. She wondered if he really thought religion was hereditary.

"Hey, I bet you was a cheerleader in high school."

She shook her head and made a face. "I was on the dance team for a couple years. It was hard to cheer for football because we hardly ever won a game. Who could win a game when their name's the St. Mary Blue Gators?"

Bucky talked out a lungful of smoke. "Yeah, when I played football, we used to smash those little private schools into the dirt. What else did you do when you was growing up? Wrassle any snapping turtles?"

"No, but I fished with my brother, and I was president of Four-H. The school had a lot of dances, and when I got to be seventeen, the lounge owners would let us in to jitterbug to the old stuff."

"Did your old man find out about that?"

"Hell no."

Bucky stubbed out his cigarette. "Yeah, I know what you mean. My daddy used to think I went to Bible study every Wednesday night."

"Where were you?"

He picked up the check and looked at it. "I forget," he told her.

Twelve

For two weeks she looked for work with the desperation of a newly landed immigrant. The only business in town that was hiring was Trosclair's U-Haul franchise, which was hooking up the departing welders and pipe fitters as fast as trailers could be deadheaded into town from other parts of the country. One afternoon, she was ironing her father's shirts, wondering if a lounge would hire a pregnant barmaid, when the phone rang. Bucky Tyler's voice drawled out of the receiver, telling her that his bookkeeper had run off to Atlanta with his stationary engineer. He wanted to know if she would work for him. Her last bank statement flashed in front of her eyes, and then she considered Bucky's sandy hair and horsey grin. "Yes," she said too quickly, surprising herself.

"Now, it don't pay more'n eight dollars a hour," he told her. "But it's better'n welfare."

The next morning, she went down the blacktop south of town, turned off onto a wide weed-haunted road topped with powdery clamshells, and drove the two miles to what used to be a factory that processed trash fish into fertilizer, but which now simmered and stank behind a plywood sign proclaiming TYLER INDUSTRIES, INDUSTRIAL SANITATION. The man at the guard shack motioned her in as though he'd been told to expect her, and she drove to the office, a building covered with asbestos siding next to a murky canal full of listing barges. Inside she found a jaundiced Bucky Tyler sitting in a folding chair with his head nearly between his knees.

"You okay?" she asked.

He looked up at her, his eyes runny and hurt. "I'll be all right. One of our shippers just sent us a little surprise is all." He got up slowly and began to show her what the previous bookkeeper had been doing, told her about logging in shipments and billing at the various rates for waste incinerated. "You can turn on the computer and figure out how she ran things. I don't know a damned thing about those machines." Just then a tall man covered in yellow dust opened the rear door of the building and yelled for him. Colette was left alone in a paneled closet of an office. Everything was gritty and smelled like a child's chemistry set. Her typewriter was smudged and twenty years old. The floor was a crusty cement painted gray. She booted the computer, which buzzed and hooted, taking a full minute to light up its screen.

For two weeks she recorded truck shipments and deliveries from the occasional small corroded barge, and when her first paycheck came in, she held it like a cool drink of water. The work hadn't been bad. However, the business was strange: An occasional bargeload of liquid would come in from Ghana or Italy, and sometimes the whole region smelled like toilet-bowl cleaner for two days, but she got the hang of the record-keeping software, and the hangdog employees treated her well.

At the market on payday, she bought two small sirloins, grilled them, and cooked snap beans and new potatoes. Her father sat at the dark oak table and looked around carefully before beginning to eat, as though trying to remember who was supposed to be there. He smiled and asked about her new job. Sometimes his mind ran straight as a railroad for miles. She would have a real conversation with him, and he would be living in the present. But then his wobbly memory would jump the track, and Colette would be in the room with a younger father, or worse, a stranger looking at her for a moment—nowadays just a moment—seeming to think, Who is this in my house? Who let this person in? But at this meal, at least, he enjoyed his sirloin and nodded as he listened. Then he picked up his white head as if he'd heard a noise and he asked, "Why isn't Paul home yet?"

Colette straightened her back and put a hand on her jeans. "Paul and I aren't married anymore," she told him for the tenth time.

Her father continued chewing carefully. "How did this happen?"

"He never thought of my feelings," she said. Each time she answered this question, she said something different.

"How do you mean?"

"He has no ambition. Fifty years from now he'll still be knee-deep in machine oil."

"He was dirty?" He scooped up a forkful of green beans.

"Oh, no. He kept his hands cleaner and softer than a baby's. But he was happy doing stupid things like dancing with women I didn't like, and reading stupid hundred-year-old manuals until sunrise. He wouldn't grow up and plan for the future." She shrugged, as though not understanding her own explanation.

"Where is he?"

"I left him, Daddy."

"You left him because he was happy," the old man said, closing his mouth on a luminous potato.

She dropped her fork on her plate. "I left him because *I* was unhappy," she said, feeling childish. If her father had been whole of mind, he would have asked if Paul was the source of her unhappiness—but instead he asked again when Paul was coming in, his old mind derailing and bumping along through a pathless field.

* * *

Driving home after work one day, Colette counted FOR SALE signs fading in the yards of empty houses. The last oil-field pipe yard had closed up and a local tugboat line had auctioned everything off. Automobile traffic was down so much in Tiger Island that the two traffic signals on River Street were reset as blinking caution lights. She parked down from the hardware and got out in front of City Pawn's crumbly brick facade. A little glimmer of gold foil caught her eye, and she turned to see Paul's accordion in the window, its ebony stop knobs gray with dust. It made her angry to see it on public display, like some secret part of her past put out for everyone in town to view. She went in and a cowbell over the door clanked twice. Ray-Ray LeBoeuf sat up behind a glass case full of yellowed Nintendo games.

"Hey, Miss America come to the pawnshop," he said.

She looked at his hard, bony shoulders and long, thin hair. "You're Teeny's big brother that was in jail."

"That's right. What can I do you for?"

"That Paul's buzz box in the window?"

"That's the one. You want him a anniversary present?" He put his palms down on the glass and looked her over.

"I was just wondering what you were asking for it."

Ray-Ray touched his thin face. "We askin' nine hundred."

Her eyebrows formed little hoops. "For that thing?" she said, too loudly.

"Hey, that ain't no piece of junk Hohner or a Regal. That old boy in Eunice made that thing from scratch. We paid Paul a bucket of change for it, let me tell you. It's a piece of art, you know."

"That?"

"You ever look at the inlay on that thing?"

"No," she said. "Do you have to keep it in the window?"

He looked at the black accordion. "You scared it's gonna get sunburn?"

Colette turned for the door and frowned at the copper-plated cowbell. "Never mind."

"Hey, if you can't use that, we got some of Paul's other stuff, too."

That stopped her. "What other stuff?"

Ray-Ray motioned to the counter. "He been comin' in with like his high school ring, his good fishing rod. I think I got his watch around here somewhere. His mamma come in yesterday with some rings, and his old man the day before with his World War Two souvenirs, some German stuff."

She looked into the display case and saw an opal pin Paul's mother wore on Sundays. "None of them's found a job?"

"They ain't no job for nobody to find. The old man's car broke down and they had to sell my boss some stuff so they could try and fix it." Ray-Ray shook his head. "They in Spam-eatin' shape right now."

She stood a long time looking into the counter. "Is that high school ring the only ring he sold you?"

Ray-Ray nodded. "That's the onliest one so far. But if he got another one, I guess we'll see it before too long."

She bit the corner of her mouth. "That bad?"

"Hey, I saw him at the Little Palace the other night, and he bummed money for a beer offa *me*. How's that for a switch?" Ray-Ray did a little dance and turned around. "He told me he tried to get a job holding the flag with a road gang, but they hired the mayor's nephew instead."

"He actually said he'd work holding the flag?"

"That's a fact."

"In public, where everybody in town could see?"

Ray-Ray tilted his head and looked Colette up and down. "I think the idea is to get everybody to look at that flag, yeah."

* * *

Bucky Tyler dated Colette two weekends in a row, and when he called and asked a third time, she told him that her belly was too big and she felt awkward going out in public with a man she wasn't married to. He told her they could do something about that, and she laughed him off and hung up, feeling that she'd just dodged a speeding truck. She liked Bucky Tyler's moves; she liked the way he could squeeze money out of anything through hard work, but there was something behind his amber eyes that she was not sure of. It was not clear what he wanted from her.

During October business picked up at Tyler's plant. Trucks of damp ash began to show up after dark, and she had to stay late to key in the scale records and product routing. She also had to endure the stench of the place, the snarling trucks and forklifts, the noisy, complaining workers who would slam into the office building cursing and stamping a nose-burning blue dust off their boots. The steam plant kept breaking down and Tyler fired a series of three men for not running the boilers correctly. He came into the office one day with the yard foreman, who was drenched in used dry-cleaning fluid. Bucky spiked his hard hat on the floor. She pretended not to notice and kept counting her scale tickets for the week.

"Son of a bitch."

The other man shook his head as if to clear it. "I told you he didn't know shit."

"He killed all the steam." Bucky waved a freckled arm toward the door. "What we gonna do with all that soppy crap?"

"Put an ad in the New Orleans paper for somebody can run that boiler house, or shut the plant down," the foreman told him.

Bucky sat down and pushed a hand through his brassy hair. "We'd have to look in a fucking nursing home to find someone old enough to know that setup."

His foreman ran a finger along the bottom of his mustache. He was another Texan, big, Germanic. "You can always buy a new package boiler for a million dollars."

Tyler looked through a dusty window as another truckload of wet ash came through the plant gate. Below the window, Colette was counting one more handful of scale tickets in her office, not looking at the slips of paper, but at her boss.

"What's going on, darlin'?" he called out.

She kept counting, peeling each slip back with a buffed fingernail. "The boiler house. How bad you need a new man?"

"I need him like Custer needed a machine gun." He got up and stood in her doorway. "You got somebody in mind?"

"You not gonna want to hear this."

"What?"

She thought of the pawnshop, Paul's mother's jewelry under the glass counter. "Paul Thibodeaux has a stationary engineer's license," she told him.

"The hell you say," Bucky hooted.

"That's right."

"I'd piss on a live wire before I hired that son of a bitch."

She snapped a rubber band onto the scale tickets and picked up another pile. "Raise steam yourself."

The yard foreman tapped Bucky on the shoulder. "If the boiler plant's not straightened out by tomorrow afternoon, we'll have to start laying off shifts and putting all that perchloroethylene on the ground. Those people need their trucks."

Bucky kicked the doorjamb and looked hard at Colette, and she returned the stare, watching his eyes. She was trying to tell what he was thinking. "I'm not trying to do *him* a favor, if that's what you're wondering about," she said.

Bucky let out a little growl. "Is he working somewheres?" He was staring into the middle distance now, figuring.

She shook her head. "Probably swatting mosquitoes on the porch."

"Give him a call, then."

"Uh-uh. Not me."

"Well now, you don't expect me to personally offer a job to

the bastard that kicked my ass through a shithouse floor, do you?"

"You have to talk to him sometime or other."

"Aw hell," the foreman said, "give me his number and I'll call him."

The next morning Paul was trying to repair his father's rusted-through lawn mower when his mother called into the yard that he was wanted on the phone. When the foreman told him who wanted to hire him, he laughed out loud.

"This is a joke maybe, right? You down at the Little Palace and Uncle Simon put you up to this?"

"No joke. If you can repair injectors and got any kind of stationary license, you can start work in an hour from now," the foreman said.

"Wait a minute." He stared down at the linoleum. "My ex-wife works out there. Did she have anything to do with this?"

"I'll tell you what's got to do with this. This boiler room was put together out of secondhand machinery fifty years ago by chuckleheads, and they's nobody in the parish can make it put out the volume we need. I know you and Bucky had differences in the past, but if you can stay out of his face and put up with a little of his bullshit, we'll pay you fifteen dollars an hour."

Paul looked through the screen door to where his father was beating on the rusty lawn mower with a wrench. "I'm just curious about who gave you my name."

There was a bit of static in the phone. Maybe the foreman was changing hands in desperation. "She did."

"Oh yeah?"

"But let me tell you something. She's trying to save her job by keeping this place open. They ain't no romance in that gal."

"I wonder why not?" Paul said to himself. The foreman heard the comment and became angry.

"Look, damn it, you want to work or not?"

"Well, hell yeah."

"Then get your ass down here."

"I'll be there when you see me." He went out and stood on the edge of the front porch, bouncing on the balls of his feet. A job, he thought. A job where Colette works. How the hell was this going to play out?

The foreman showed him the boiler house, a big corrugated tin shed with three iron smokestacks rising fifty feet into the fetid air of the plant. "Here you go. T-Bub, is that what they call you?"

"That's a fact," Paul said, zipping up his coveralls.

"You got three two-hundred-horsepower boilers here, two Eries, and that old Babcox we ain't used."

Paul looked at a tarnished brass steam gauge and shook his head. "What you burning in 'em?"

"Whatever the oil companies send us to get rid of. We mix that with number-two oil to get the flame fairly clean."

"What you do with the steam?" He looked up at the shed roof where a spritz of hot vapor showed a leak in the main supply line.

"Some goes to cookers and reducer vessels full of the bad shit they send us from Italy. Some goes to a kiln where we're sterilizing soil and drying out dry cleaner's sludge."

"Damn." Paul crinkled his nose.

"This ain't no bakery, that's for sure."

Paul put on a glove, bent down, and jerked open a fire door, looking into the combustion chamber and the honeycomb of fire tubes beyond. "Shit."

"You gonna need a fireman?"

"Hell yeah. These flues need scraping bad. Send me somebody big and stupid. Somebody who can stand a lot of heat."

"I got just the man," the foreman told him, heading out into the sunlight, wiping sweat.

Paul studied the injectors, which were piped wrong, the auxiliary boiler feed pumps, which were corroded and stuck, and the gauge cocks, which were limed shut. He heard a pair of boots coming along the cement firing apron and stepped from between two boilers to meet Bucky Tyler, who was wearing a shiny new hard hat and sunglasses.

"Hello, coon-ass," Tyler said.

"What's going on, Texas?"

Bucky looked away a moment, then swung an expressionless face back. "I hear you can keep up steam." He gave Paul a slow, nasty smile, little strings of spit hanging off his eyeteeth.

"If you can sign a paycheck, I can keep up steam."

Bucky looked up at the main gauge, which read a paltry fifty pounds. "What's wrong with these things, anyway?"

"Nothing and everything. They just gonna take a lot of babying along. I'll have to change out a few pipes on the water supply. The main problem was, your last engineer had his head three miles up his asshole."

"Let's not make that a tradition around here."

He ignored the statement, thinking of the money. "I'll lower the safeties to one sixty."

Bucky shook his head. "We need the extra heat and pressure for faster turnaround."

"Somebody's got 'em set at one eighty per square inch. That's over your state ticket, and if you keep running over pressure, these things will cause you big problems."

"Let me worry about that," Bucky said, louder than he had to.

Paul put up his hands. "All right, Hoss. You the boss."

"You just stay out here and keep these things rumbling."

"You got it," he said, turning around.

"How soon can I get a hundred and eighty pounds?"

"Foreman's gone to get me a man. We'll scrape the flues, adjust the atomizer, put a bigger pipe on the injector, and shoot in whatever crap you got for fuel. Me and the fireman'll say Hail Marys until the safety valve goes off."

The fireman showed up, and it was LeBlanc's redneck, Gatlin. He was skinny and seemed lost in his old overalls. He nodded at Paul and said only, "Things been rough," then picked up a scraper rod. They cut off the fuel supply, beat open the smoke box doors, put on wet caps and goggles, and began to scale corrosion and soot out of the hot flue pipes. In three and a half hours, the two of them brought the plant back to life, and the tin sheds and outbuildings were spouting clouds of silver vapor. Paul and the rusty-faced Gatlin sat on a two-by-twelve propped up on cinder blocks and drank tin cup after tin cup of ice water from a galvanized Igloo cooler.

"Man," Gatlin said, shaking his head like a retriever. "Even the water tastes like cleaning fluid."

Paul was too sweated-out to talk. He looked past the overhang toward the office, where Colette came out of the back door with Bucky Tyler. They stopped and talked, Colette smiling like a plump schoolgirl. Bucky patted her stomach, then slid his hand around to her backside. She pushed him away, laughed, and got into her car.

Gatlin shook his head, grabbed Paul's cup, drew another charge of ice water, and put it under his nose.

For two months, Paul nursed the steam plant, and the company site began to pile up with mountains of green rock sitting in pools of gelatinous slop. Instead of being satisfied with his modest though profitable recycling business, Bucky sought out more and more dangerous items to deal with, some of which he had no idea how to process. Paul watched as a small tank farm sprang up, soon to be filled with insecticide from Italy, orange oil from Arizona. One day the boiler fuel was laced with a potent liquid that nearly exploded in the firebox when Paul opened the atomizers in the morning. All day, his stack smoke was green.

One stormy December noon during a cloudburst, Paul and Gatlin sat eating lunch, their backs against the fire doors, their faces wincing at a cold blast of air coming off the swamped yard, where puddles linked to form one sheet of chocolate sludge.

Paul washed down a bite of ham poor boy with a swallow of root beer. "This place has got to be breaking some kind of law."

Gatlin nodded glumly. "I heard he's got the sheriff in his pocket, but even so . . ." He looked over to a tanker lurching off the scale, its hatches steaming in the rain. "If the bastard didn't try to rake up all the bad shit in the universe, I don't think nobody would of noticed us." He folded a soggy french fry into his mouth. "The government shuts this place down, we'll go back to eating out those little cans with keys stuck on the back."

The rain kept up, and by three o'clock the trucks were sending wheel wash rolling up into the boiler room's floor. Paul put on a slicker and waded over to the office. The only one in the building was Colette, who was looking out her window, a hand on her stomach. The rain hammered the metal roof like gravel as they looked at each other the way strangers do. Paul had talked to her about supplies at least once a week, but about nothing else. He had seen her three times in town while she was out with Bucky Tyler, and each time he had turned his head as though he'd been slapped. He'd tried to put her out of his mind and was getting good at doing that. Catholic boys had often been told about how to avoid dwelling on sexual thoughts, and Paul found the discipline worked well on other types of thinking as well. He tried to forget her by dating another woman, a divorcée from Labadieville with two pale, sweet-faced children, but though she was his age, she seemed a generation older. She had been someone else's, and it occurred to him that she might have the same feeling about him, that he was like a used car that smelled of its previous owner. He tried to give himself to this woman and discovered that he was not his own to give to her.

He walked up to Colette's doorway and knocked on the frame. "You seen Bucky?"

She looked at him with a coolly interested stare. "He rode the hotshot truck over to Patterson to get a pump. What do you need?"

"I need him to tell the worms over by the ditch to get a few sandbags to the south side of the boiler house. I don't want the ash pits to fill up with water."

"You could ask the yard foreman for his crew."

"He won't listen to me. He's got his own problems trying to contain that green rock. What is that stuff, anyway?"

She sat back in her chair. "You don't want to know what half the crap is back there."

"You feeling all right?"

"I'm slowing down, if that's what you're asking."

"How's your daddy?"

She shook her head. "Aunt Nellie watches him during the day. He hardly knows anyone anymore. He's not who he is." She straightened up and hit ten strokes on her computer. "I'll tell Bucky about the sandbags when he gets back."

"Colette." He pulled off his slicker cap and twisted it like a washcloth.

"Yeah?"

"When it comes, you gonna let me visit it?"

She kept her face turned to the computer, which further brightened her white skin. "I couldn't keep you away if I tried, Paul. I've got to drive in front of your house every day. You could sit on your porch and see it. You could walk in front of my house and see it on the porch, or in a sitter's yard."

"You've been thinking about this?"

"I've faced the fact that it's yours as well as mine." An invoice popped onto the screen and she frowned at it, changing numbers in the little voids. "Part of you is in me, and I'm learning to deal with that."

He wanted to put a wrench through her computer screen. "You really know how to make a guy feel great." He fastened his slicker's top button and twisted it off in his hand.

She looked at him quickly. "I was not put on earth to make you feel great," she said.

He wanted to say something like "That's a fact," but he held back, thinking about what she'd said, about what it meant. He turned for the boiler house, wondering where Colette got her ideas. Was she born with them? Did she get them from those women's magazines she subscribed to, the ones with the foxlike big-hair gals in low-cut red lamé dresses on the covers, the magazines that tried to make women into world conquerors who raced German cars through life looking like movie goddesses, dressing like millionaires, having better and better sex with every issue?

At the boiler house he checked the gauges and pulled on the injector levers.

"You all right?" Gatlin asked. "You got a funny look on your face."

"I'm thinking," Paul said.

Gatlin walked over, pulled off the slicker cap, and looked at him closely. "Damn," he said.

The next night Colette and Bucky were on her front porch. She was staring over the rail at her car, worrying about a transmission noise she'd heard for the first time that afternoon. Bucky was droning on about an upcoming deal with ordinary sewer sludge. She was trying to be patient with him, but the baby was kicking, patting its foot on her bladder as if keeping time to music.

"If you're making so much money, how about a raise?"

He had the bright, toothy laugh of an actor, as if he'd been trained to laugh. "All you do is press buttons, baby."

"Come on. You pay Paul more than you do me. A lot more."

His smile disappeared. "I know. But the bastard keeps things running. If I could find somebody cheaper, believe me, I would."

"If you could find someone to do my job cheaper, I guess you would," she said, her voice filled with pretend hurt.

He kissed her, then sat back and looked her in the eyes. She thought he had feelings for her that were genuine and intense. Sometimes in their relationship she felt that she was a prize Bucky Tyler was pursuing, and she understood that most women would value this. But his arm at her back was furry with reddish hair. Through his aftershave, she could smell a trace of phosphoric acid. "Darlin', I'd never replace you," he sang, like a line from a country song.

"Bucky, don't talk like that. I'm just a friend. Not a girlfriend. Women who are eight months pregnant are not girlfriends."

"But you could be. And I know I'll like that kid, when it comes." He looked down at a hand-tooled boot. "And it'll need a daddy."

"This again."

"It could be where we're goin', darlin'."

She looked into the street at his new car, pursed her lips. He would be such a dreadful husband with all his east Texas backwoods views of women and how they should have big hair, look good, and shut up. "I can't get married because of Paul. It's against my religion," she said at last.

Bucky got up and turned to her, running a forefinger along her brows and down her full cheek. "Now, we can't have you running against your religion," he said.

On a Friday, Paul stood in a firing bay, his hand above his head, clutching a loop of cable. He was looking at his watch. When the second hand covered the twelve, he pulled the cable, listening to the quitting whistle cough up condensate and build into a hoarse, rising chord, gradually clarifying into a unison of three notes flooding out of the factory toward town. After thirty seconds he let go and saw Gatlin clear the overhang, his empty lunch box banging his thigh. Paul heard a noise behind him and turned to see Bucky Tyler come through the back door of the boiler house wearing a sport coat and shined boots.

"Hey, coon-ass, can you write?"

"What you want, Bucky?"

"I'm thinking of having this third boiler rebuilt. You know, so we can bring it on-line when one of the others is getting worked on." He pointed to the idle boiler sitting in the shadows, against the far wall. "I need a write-up to send out for some ballpark figures."

"You want a written evaluation for repairs, call a boiler shop. They'll send out their own inspector."

Bucky shook his head. "Nah. I want you to do an inspection so I'll know if they're making stuff up, trying to rip me off."

"I don't have time." He bent down and cut the atomizers back to a pilot flame.

"You mean you want extra pay, damn you. All right. You give me a complete inspection report by morning, day after tomorrow, and I'll give you two hundred. If you can write, that is."

Paul walked over and threw a wall switch and one incandescent light bloomed over the old leviathan of a fire-tube boiler—a giant drum, seven feet in diameter and twenty feet long, lying in a brick cradle and run through end to end with two-inch-diameter flue pipes, hundreds of tubes to carry the fire's heat through the water. "That means I'll have to go to work now."

"That's right."

Paul put on a tool belt, climbed up to the doors of the smoke box, and beat on the handle with a ball-peen hammer. He swung the doors wide, rust flakes falling like brown snow from the inside surface. He turned on a flashlight and saw a dozen lower tubes corroded shut. Lime deposits from old leaks formed stalactites at the ends of higher tubes, and all surfaces were wet with condensation. The breaching had rusted through over the firebox. He climbed back down. "This is a piece of junk. It hasn't been fired in twenty years at least."

"Anything can be fixed." Bucky put his hands in his pockets and smiled.

Paul looked at him a moment longer than he should have, shrugged, and got a clipboard off a nail above the workbench. "It's your money," he said. Bucky left, dragging his cloud of aftershave with him, and Paul slithered into the fire door to inspect underneath the boiler. Next he climbed into the smoke box. It took him one hour to count all the leaking tubes and locate eroded sections of the tube sheet, testing for thin metal with careful taps of the hammer. After exploring the rear sheet, he mounted the top of the boiler shell, which was covered with two inches of fish-meal dust and asbestos powder. Under the sooty wooden roof beams, he struggled to get the manhole nut off its stem with a two-foot pipe wrench so he could climb down into the boiler. It wouldn't budge. He climbed down to the floor to get a can of penetrating oil and a pipe to slip over the end of his wrench for more leverage. While he was slicing the plastic spout of the oil can, he thought he heard someone walking under the overhang. He listened, thinking that the watchman was beginning his rounds. Walking to the big sliding tin door, he looked to the parking lot, where the last worker's car skidded away in a cloud of white dust. Paul turned around and went back through the boiler house and stared toward the buildings at the rear of the plant. Somewhere a loose piece of roofing banged in the wind, but he heard nothing else. He climbed back onto the boiler and wrestled the manhole cover open. A moist metallic breath rose from the hole, and he waited ten minutes for fresh air to flow inside. The blood rushed to his head as he slid through into the darkness, and he immediately became disoriented. He wound up kneeling on the top row of flue pipes, bending his head to clear the arching boiler shell. The chamber was dank and smelled of corrosion and calcium scale. Putting on his gloves, he reached out and pulled his tool belt through the manhole. He was now a doctor inside a body. Something about the rarity of what he was doing excited him, this getting into a machine, fitting inside the mechanism itself. He turned on his flashlight and crawled twenty feet over the flaky pipes to the forward tube sheet, where the flues would be thin from heat and rust. With his hammer, he tapped a flue where it joined the sheet, and it dented like a cheap pot. For the pipes to be weak this high in the boiler meant the whole apparatus was probably worn out. Paul grinned at the thought of Bucky wasting two hundred dollars for the inspection. He should have known better. Even from the outside, a fool could tell that the boiler was no good. Paul began to make notes on his clipboard. He banged an angle brace with a hammer and wrote again.

His knees slid between the rough flue pipes and ached. As he turned to crawl back to the manhole, he heard a noise above him, a metallic rattle, as though someone wearing a tool belt was crawling along the outside of the boiler. Before he could move all the way to the rear, he heard the manhole cover toll shut and the sound of the three-inch nut being hurried onto the single bolt that held the cover in place. When he got to the closed hole, he stared at the iron in disbelief, giving the head of the bolt a playful tap with his hammer as if to prove that it was real. The manhole cover was an oval plate that pressed against the inside of the boiler shell, held in place by a large bolt that ran through it to an exterior arch bar that pressed against the rim of the hole. The bolt was held fast by its nut, which was screwed against the arch bar.

Paul thought that someone must have made an innocent mistake. He banged on the boiler shell with a hammer to signal to whoever had shut him up. In response, hands and feet scuffled down to the forward end. Then nothing. It occurred to him that he had not been shut up by mistake, and he lay back on the rank of pipes, trying to think, trembling slightly when he realized that his first problem would be oxygen. Turning off his light to conserve the battery, he felt his tool belt and found four chisels, a heavy screwdriver, a twelve-inch crescent wrench, a small wire brush, and a foot-long scraping tool. He closed his eyes. The location of all the boiler fixtures appeared in his mind like a diagram: the water-supply pipe, the blow-off pipe, the water-level gauge. Sitting up, he felt along the arched top of the boiler for the opening to the spring-loaded safety valve, sliding his hand along the gritty steel until his fingers entered a cavity above his head. Turning on his light, he saw the three-inch-wide bronze valve seat. He drove the scraper against it, jamming it open. That would allow a thread of air to flow in, if he could find another opening. He scurried to the face of the boiler and pulled out his long-nose chisel, shining his light around until he found where two pipe nipples entered the side of the shell, probably coming from a water-level indicator. With the chisel he beat out the nipples in ten minutes, hearing a muffled racket as some device fell from the exterior and hit the floor of the boiler room. Putting his eye to the holes, he saw no light, so he pressed his mouth to the higher one and breathed. He found fresh air.

Back in the rear of the boiler, he examined the single huge bolt that held him captive. It would take forty minutes to shear off its head with his chisel if the tool would stay sharp. He straightened his back and began hammering, stopping every twenty blows to examine the slowly growing cut between the bolt head and the manhole plate. In only a few minutes he was dripping with sweat and his heart was bouncing like an unbalanced tire. He crawled over to the safety valve and gulped breaths of air directly from the opening, feeding his heart, making it idle down.

It was during this break that he first thought about dying. He imagined his cement grave covering in the bright cemetery next to the railroad track, and he saw his parents on their porch, alone for the rest of their lives. He closed his eyes again and imagined the volumes of air moving around the working space of LeBlanc's Machine Shop. He wondered if in the next life he would be a machinist. His heart misfired once, and he said an Act of Contrition on his knees.

Then from below came the sound of water running, soon accompanied by a gurgling like that of a commode flushing, and Paul sprang to all fours like a surprised cat. Someone had turned on the pumps and was filling the boiler. He turned off his light, as though darkness would accelerate his thinking. Numbers ran through his head as he remembered the size of the feed pumps and estimated the time it would take to drown him. He fished around in his belt and grabbed a thick, short chisel and shuffled to the rear of the boiler, hammering the tool against a flue where it entered the rear tube sheet. After a few blows, it penetrated, and with more strikes he had opened up a two-inch hole through which the water would pass out of the chamber. For once in his life, he was grateful for weak flues, and he set about cutting through the entire top row. When he finished, he was ready to pass out from lack of oxygen, so he dragged himself to the front of the boiler to breathe directly through the punched-out nipples. His mouth filled with scale, and he fell back coughing, gasping like a dying fish.

He listened to the water rise like terror, coming up until it reached the level of tubes on which he lay. It soaked his work shirt and he waited to see if it would creep above the level of the drain holes he had cut. A bubbling noise reverberated in the shell, the water stopped rising, and Paul allowed himself a little smile. He had outsmarted the bastard, whoever he was. Paul skidded back to the manhole and started to pound on the bolt. After twenty minutes, his blows had grown too weak, and sweat beaded off him like drops of mercury. He lay back and shined the light toward the drain holes he'd cut, which gasped and rattled, barely keeping up with the water. The boiler shell arched above him like a coffin lid, a rash of white-and-red scale blistering its surface.

With idleness came fear. He shook himself and tried to realize that he was almost through the bolt head. He thought of what the old people said about God never sending more than you can bear, and this made him feel, for a moment, safe.

He was resting, but he continued to sweat. Then he sensed the pipes slowly heat up on his back like electrodes, and with a pang he knew that someone had lit the fuel-oil atomizers. He began for a minute to cry great, slow machinist's tears, becoming angry because he was betrayed by one of his machines. He sat up and found the safety-valve hole, his anger building a shout through the opening. Shucking his coveralls, he crawled to the rear of the boiler, stuffed them over the drain holes and waited for the water to rise over his shoe tops. He took out his short chisel and hammer and waded to the front tube sheet, where he would be closest to the fire, and he began cutting tubes open furiously, water pouring out of them and into the firebox, cooling the flame. Steaming water rose from each hammer blow until he cut open ten flue pipes. A hot spot raised a blister on one knee, and he started a dance motion to keep from getting burned. He reached the point at which the same amount of water was pouring out onto the fire as was being pumped in. He went back to the manhole bolt and worked as hard as he was able. After ten minutes of banging, he was nearly through, but he became completely winded, his arms falling to his sides like limp plants. The flashlight floated away, and all he could do was to lie back in the rusty water and look after it. He took what he thought would be his last rest, one way or the other.

A cloud of heat seemed to pass through the chamber, and at first he thought he was flushing with exhaustion or panic, but when he heard the water falling in a diminishing rattle through the holes he had cut, he knew that someone had turned off the pumps. Now the fire would rage, and the remaining water would steam him like a crab. He got up on his knees, knowing that he had one minute left. He whammed the chisel into the bolt, and it flew out of his hand and disappeared below among hundreds of flues. Somewhere under him, a rank of pipes began to hiss. He gathered his coveralls and put then beneath his knees, then, fumbling in his tool belt, he found a shorter chisel he'd forgotten, a sharper one. He sought the cut in the manhole bolt with his fingers and inserted the edge of the tool. The hammer, a two-pound maul, he found under his shin, and he took a steamy breath and hit, willing the tools together repeatedly, knowing that a missed blow might break his hand, or, worse, cause him to drop the chisel. He stopped thinking and concentrated only on the purposeful movement of his arms. After thirty lessening blows, the bolt head flew off, and the thick manhole gouged down on his shoulder and flattened him against the pipes, which whispered on his back like branding irons. He sprang up and into the opening, propelled by a freshet of live steam out into the world, his red skin smoking and puckered, his head roaring and building pressure. When his feet cleared the hole, he tumbled backward, his head slamming a catwalk and skidding over. He sensed a brief airy fall, ended by a head butt onto a cast-iron duplex pump. He opened his eyes but could see nothing through the unbelievable pain in his skull, and after a while, he gave up trying to see, hoping only for something to stop the hurt. He tried to yell but could make no sound. His legs seemed to be on the other side of the room. Because his mind was the only thing that was working, he tried to use it to kill the pain, and he attempted to think of his parents, who loved him, or his friends at the machine shop, who would sell their clothes to buy him a beer on a hot day, but no faces came to him at all, and when he closed his blind eyes and prayed for something to appear, he could picture only Colette, her minty skin, the nighttime in her hair, the balm of her restless eyes.

Thirteen

Colette had put her father in his bedroom, found a flickering black-and-white movie for him on his television, and came out onto the porch to wait. She scowled at the empty space in the street where Bucky Tyler's car should have been. He had invited himself over for supper and now was late. Walking into the kitchen, she stirred a pot of red beans and sausage, banged the spoon or the pot much too hard, and returned to the porch to sit and tap her foot. When he did show up, he did not apologize. His sport coat had a rusty smudge on it, and he smelled of fuel oil. They ate under the dim brass light fixture in the dining room, and everything she swallowed, the baby kicked at. Bucky seemed preoccupied with his food, saying one thing during the meal: "Did you ever learn to make chili?"

They watched television in the front room while one block over on River Street an ambulance screamed east out into the woods. With a slow turn of her head, Colette followed the sound like radar.

The next day was Saturday and the phone got her out of bed a half hour after sunrise. Her aunt Nellie was on the line.

"Colette, *chère*, I don't know how interested you gonna be, but I got some bad news for you."

The baby tumbled once in her stomach. "What? What is it?" she said, blinking the burning morning out of her eyes.

"There was a accident down at the stink plant last night and

Paul's almost dead. They brought him over to Lafayette to that hospital they bring blowed-up oid field people to."

She grabbed her hair and pulled it back out of her eyes, as though she needed to see better. "What happened?"

"I don't know—he just got burnt up is what I heard. You want me to come look after your daddy?" Colette heard the clink of Nellie Arnaud's Zippo lighter as she fired up the first cigarette of the day. A long pause followed, and then the cough. "Colette?"

She sat on the edge of her bed, thinking that the baby might never see its father, and she didn't know how she felt about that. "Yes," she said, "come right over."

At one point she looked down at the speedometer and was surprised to see how fast she was driving. At the hospital an intern stopped her and told her obstetrics was in the other direction, and she realized how big she looked, her belly swaying as she navigated the halls. She found Paul's family gathered outside intensive care. No one was smiling, and Father Clemmons was coming through the swinging doors, folding a vestment. They all greeted her as though they'd gathered on her account.

She took a breath. "Well, what happened?"

Paul's father shook his head and pulled her down the hall a few feet, motioning his wife away with his free hand. "The watchman found him on the floor in the boiler room when he made nine o'clock rounds. He was scalded bad, yeah, and he hit his head." He stopped and looked into her eyes to gauge how she was taking the news. "You all right?"

She made a motion with her head. "How bad is he? Aunt Nellie said . . ."

Here the old man's voice became low and soft. "Colette, baby, the doctor said he's been overheated. He's got some bad kind of heatstroke—plus his skull is fractured." He looked at his shoes. "They say he might not last through today." He stepped back, trembling at his own words, and she reached out to put her hand on the side of his neck. A tuft of shaving cream hung behind his earlobe and she made it disappear between a thumb and forefinger, just as she had done to Paul when they were first married. At the touch of the old man, she thought of the son lying in ICU, and how young she and Paul were.

In fifteen minutes they let her see him, but he was inert, ruddy, and swollen, his skull shaved and stippled with sutures. She was overcome with a terrible fear she couldn't name, and she began to cry, dabbing at her eyes with a handkerchief as though to force the tears back in. The tubes and tape overwhelmed him; the monitors, drips, and drains kept him separate. Only his feet seemed uninjured, and she looked at them, white and tender, remembering he never went barefoot unless he was swimming.

After, she drove back to Tiger Island, ignoring the cane trucks, the drizzly road flying with mud. She stopped at the old brick church to pray, kneeling in the sweet waxy light until Altar Society ladies began to appear like ghosts, changing the flowers, dusting the pulpit.

At home she relieved Aunt Nellie and put her father down for a nap. Every hour Paul's mother called, saying there was no change, and around eleven o'clock she picked up the phone after the first ring and said, "Hello, Mrs. Thibodeaux," only to be met by a male voice with a Cajun accent she recognized.

"No, baby. This is Lester St. Pierre."

She put a hand on her forehead. "I'm sorry, Sheriff. What can I do for you?"

There was a long silence on the line. The sheriff was sometimes slow to speak, a careful thinker. "We down here at the factory, trying to figure out what happened to Paul, you know?"

She sat down slowly next to the old phone table in the hall. The sheriff was crooked, of course, but he was not dumb. "It was a terrible accident. I don't know what to think."

"When did you see Paul last?"

"I saw him right at five o'clock when I was leaving the office.

He was in the doorway of the boiler house, talking to that blond guy, LeBlanc's redneck."

"We talked to Gatlin," the sheriff said, almost under his breath. "He's got a good alibi."

"Alibi?"

Again, a silence on the line. "Colette, somebody locked Paul up in a boiler and turned on the water and the fire. He had to cut his way out with a damned chisel."

She sat down on the floor in the hall, letting her dark hair fall into her lap. "Somebody tried to kill him?"

"It's the damnedest thing. We trying to figure what's going on down here. Did Paul piss somebody off real bad?"

Now the silence was on her end of the line.

"Colette?"

"No. Nobody but me," she told him.

The sheriff gave a little laugh. "Look out."

"Have you seen him?" she asked.

"Yeah. I seen him."

"You see a lot of bad accidents. How does he compare?"

"I'm not sure what you want me to tell you."

"Just make a comparison. I need an opinion right now." She looked up at the cypress crown molding in the high hall, trying not to cry.

The sheriff stammered around for a minute, then said, "For a live man, he looks pretty bad."

"Yep," she said quietly. "That's what I thought, too."

At noon, Paul's sister, Nan, called. She said Paul was going into convulsions and that Colette shouldn't drive back to Lafayette.

Colette twisted the phone cord as if trying to choke bad news in the line. "Can't they give him something?"

"If they give him anything else, they'll kill him. I've never seen nothing like this. I was going to bring the kids in to visit him just in case, you know. But I didn't want them to see this. Colette, some bastard cooked him like a crawfish."

"I saw," she said.

"Did the sheriff talk to you?"

"He called and told me it wasn't an accident."

"What the hell? Who would do that to him?"

"I don't know," she said softly, looking out toward the street.

Colette woke her father at three and led him out to the porch, where she had the usual cups of coffee waiting for them on a tray.

"Ah," he said, as though three o'clock coffee was a surprise.

"How are you feeling today, Daddy?" She pushed his hair out of his eyes and straightened his wing collar.

"Fine, baby," he told her, blowing easily on his coffee, then taking a slow, hissing sip.

"Is the coffee sweet enough?"

He nodded. "Just like Mamma fixed it for me."

Colette was never sure when her father was in the present. His mind was like a little boat in a rolling ocean of time, gaining sight of the horizon on each wave crest, then losing it down between disorienting walls of water.

"Do you miss her?"

"Yes," he said, taking another gulp. "Now and always." A look of alarm crossed his face for a moment like the shadow of a crow's wing, and he put the cup down on the porch floor. "I wish she'd hurry back."

Just then Bucky Tyler's long car pulled up in front of the porch. He got out, dressed in a white shirt and white jeans, wearing sunglasses, and came up on the porch. The old man stared at him blankly. Bucky swatted him on the knee, then looked at Colette.

"I guess you heard about your ex?"

She nodded, trying to look through the glasses. She saw he was close to panic, his smile a sick grimace. "He's nearly dead." She said it like the cold fact it was.

He shook his head and leaned against a porch column. "That coon-ass sheriff thinks somebody tried to kill him."

She got up and went into the kitchen, hearing him follow over the creaking floorboards. At the range, she poured another cup of coffee into an ironstone mug, and he came up behind her. She wanted some sort of sign that would tell her what she needed to know. He looked out of the kitchen window, and she could tell it was a hollow act. "Did that sheriff call here?" he asked casually, the way he might ask whether she'd put gas in her car that morning.

"No."

"If he does, and he asks you what time I got here last night, what will you tell him?"

She looked at Bucky Tyler, at his hard shoulders and wavy blond hair. He was close enough for her to smell the heat of him, and he was washed and flavored with a touch of cologne. Nice clothes, nice, worried mouth, empty eyes. "I'll tell him you got here on time," she said, waiting.

He looked at her long, a slow smile sliding across his teeth, and then came what she was waiting for. He put a hand on her buttock and squeezed slowly. She smiled back and handed him the cup of coffee before walking toward the porch. And now she knew.

Paul lived past suppertime, and the doctor said that that was something, at least. In the morning, Colette was feeling really big and slow, but after early Mass, she still drove to the hospital, an hour away in Lafayette. Paul's father was asleep in the hall when she got there, his legs straight out from the chair, and she stepped into ICU with the permission of a drowsy nurse who was just going off night shift. Paul was still unconscious. His head was a monster's, swollen and covered with a terrible violet bruise mixed in with the red-and-white scald. The nurse had told her that they could manage the exterior burns, but that the problem was inside, with the brain. They just didn't know yet.

Colette looked at the tubes and knew that Bucky had done this because he believed that once Paul was dead, she would marry him. In a way, she had led him to think this. She'd put Paul like a strong fence between herself and Tyler. Now here was her ex-husband, dying maybe, because of something she'd said. This suffering was her fault, she realized. She thought of Bucky Tyler, how he spoke, the way he smelled, his creaking boots. She was at a crossroads where she could marry a man who stood a chance of becoming powerful and rich one day, or she could do something else—she didn't know what, just that it could involve hard times, bad food, and cheap clothes.

Paul gasped and one eye opened wide, showing only white, and she came close, pulling the lid down with a thumb. "You're going to get better," she said into his swollen ear. "Come on, you."

He cried out low, as though someone were working a knife through him in a dream, and Colette's teeth slid together and closed. "Son of a bitch," she said slowly, balling a fist.

In the parking lot she met the sheriff, a short man wearing a curled-up tan cowboy hat with a gold badge on the crown. He made her sit in her car before he would talk to her. "Colette, you're big as a house. You better get someone to start riding with you."

She gave him an ugly look, leaden-eyed. "You got any suspects?"

He made a clown face and rocked his head back and forth. "Well, we looking at the leads we got from a few interviews."

"Please, no bullshit. You know Bucky Tyler did it."

The sheriff looked around at the parking lot, at the live oaks seining a light north wind. "I know Paul got in a fight with him a long time back. But Tyler hired him. What kind of man would hire someone he wanted to kill?"

"You gonna check for fingerprints?"

"Colette, he owns the damned place. He crawls all over it."

She set her jaw. "He was supposed to be at my house at six. He didn't show up until after seven."

"You see him on the factory yard after five o'clock?"

She looked over her hood. "No."

The sheriff put one hand on her open door and the other on the roof and hung his hound's face above her. "How's Paul?"

"When I was walking out, the doctor said his kidneys and heart were working adequately." She flicked her eyes up at him. "I think he's got a chance."

"Bucky's just started making some real money with that place he's got. He can hire a good lawyer. Unless we got a eyewitness, he'll never do time. I ran his record, and he's clean."

"What if Paul can tell us he did it?"

The sheriff took off his hat and wiped sweat from his bald head. "How's he gonna know? He was in the damned boiler."

"Maybe he was forced in at gunpoint."

"No, baby. He had all his tools in there with him. A lot of people will say it was an accident. This kind of thing happens. A man's inside a machine and someone comes along, sees an access hole open after quitting time, and closes it up."

She put a hand out and lightly touched his uniform shirt. "When Bucky came to my house, he smelled like boiler fuel."

The sheriff gave her a coy expression. "How you know what boiler fuel smells like?"

"I lived with a man who came home covered with it. I washed his clothes." She put her face in her hands. "I made love with him."

He put a thick palm on her back and patted her. "I'm sorry. But someone like Tyler will never do time on an attempted-murder charge." He leaned in and put his face close to hers. She could see what looked like cracker paste in his bottom teeth. "But federal pollution violations are another matter."

"What?" She put her ear to his mouth as if she wanted him to kiss it. She remembered that he was the young patrolman who, the day she was born, had taken her mother to the hospital.

"I got a phone call two weeks ago—a question from a Washington man. People up there are interested. That's all I'm going to say. You a smart girl. You can figure what to do."

"Wait a minute. Who've you been talking to?" But he put his hat back on and straightened up, looking around again, waving to a middle-aged couple walking into the lot from the hospital.

"See you later, baby," he said. "I got to check on Paul and his family."

At midnight the baby was kicking like a swimmer and her insides bulged and groaned low down. She sat on the sofa and leaned on the arm, panting. Paul's mother called and said that he was stable, though he had not said a word.

For a long time, Colette had been on the phone, getting numbers from various operators. Monday she drove home on her lunch hour but did not eat, spending the whole time talking to a DEQ man in Baton Rouge and then a friend of his in Washington. Her calls threaded through the bureaucracy of several government agencies until she found a voice that she could trust.

At quitting time, Bucky disappeared with an oil man in a bad suit, driving off toward New Orleans and a boozy meal. Colette stayed on until the watchman visited at five-fifteen, and then she put a new toner cartridge in the Xerox machine and began making copies of invoices and scale tickets that showed contents of shipments and points of origin. She made sure to copy current inventory of everything in vats, tarp-covered storage heaps, barges, and "the well," an abandoned dry hole that was on the property when the fish plant was first built. Bucky pumped the most aromatic items down into this rusty nub of pipe, which never seemed to fill up. Pulling the list of chemicals mixed for burning in the boilers, she stared at the pages, finding it difficult to keep her mind on what she was doing. At seven-fifteen the watchman came in again, as he did again at nine-fifteen when she was finishing up with Bucky Tyler's illiterate personal business letters, which she had pulled from the safe. One of them bore this colorful sentence: "You gennelmen from Planetoil can send me dead babies floating in sianide and I'll charge you ten dollars a gallon, bury it, and tell the dumbass feds its green Jell-O. They believe any fucking thing you tell them." She made five copies of that one.

She drove to Beewick and woke up her uncle Lester, who was a notary, making him read her cover letter and then affix his seal to it over her signature. The next morning before work, she mailed off two boxes of papers, one to Baton Rouge, one to Washington. Her phone rang three days later. Certain agencies had been watching Tyler's plant already, she learned. She imagined the Washington boys to be like old ladies praying for things in church instead of going out and making what they want to happen happen.

It was like waiting for justice to come in the mail, and come it did. Certain chemicals and pesticides that were on her list caused a great deal of excitement from the Potomac to the Mississippi, and three weeks after Colette mailed her boxes, she was in her little office when the front door flew wide, showing a procession of eleven state and federal agents and as many Louisiana state troopers, carrying arrest warrants for Bucky Tyler and his foreman. All day she watched men in respirators wander the plant yard taking samples from drums, piles of black slag, storage tanks, trucks, and bunkers. Lawyers ransacked the office and tried to get into the old third-hand safe. Bucky was served with court orders and subpoenas, then taken away in handcuffs, red-faced and cursing, and all workers were told to go home. The gate was padlocked, and that was it for the stink plant.

Late at night, Colette's phone rang, and it was Bucky Tyler. "Yes?" she said coolly.

His voice was a whisper. "Colette, if you care for me at all, you got to go out to the plant and get inside the safe and burn them records. They got a lot of shit on me, but I don't think they got it all—not the real bad stuff in my letters."

"Don't let them scare you, stud."

"Oh, lady, I'm plenty scared. They got me in this old jail in New Orleans that feels like the big house. They found out about that dieldrin that came in from Ecuador, and they think I'm Charles Manson. Hell, I'm under a million-dollar bond and I'm on the evening news. If they get aholt of my letters they won't let me store piss in my own toilet. Darlin', I could do real time. I never seen the pollution boys move on somebody like this. You got to get those letters out my safe. They don't have the combination yet."

"They've got the letters."

A gasping silence filled the line. "How?"

"Why, I mailed those letters to them, along with all the other evidence against you, darlin'."

"You turned me in? You shut down the company? Why?"

She picked up her head. "Because, you east Texas corn-shitting white trash, you tried to kill a good man just so you could get to me," she screamed. "No one gets to me like that, you turd with eyes." She slammed down the receiver on the word *whoa* and crossed her arms above her belly. Then her water broke in a cascade over her white canvas shoes.

Fourteen

S he was back from the hospital in two days with an eight-pound boy, Matthew, and the company of nearly every female relative in the parish. Only her brother and old white-shoed uncle Lester, the insurance salesman/notary public, represented the men. Colette fussed at the women, trying to run them off with mock ill will. The truth was that she missed having her mother with her, and in the rare times when she was alone with the baby, she felt the lack like a newly missing tooth, a painful void of blood. Aunt Nellie, with freshly bleached hair, managed the company, showing up with baby things and fighting her sister Margaret and two other neighborhood women for the right to fool with the child. Colette would sit on the porch in the afternoons, looking down into the baby's face, picking out her own features, her mother's features, ignoring Paul's chin. She liked the smell of her baby, the squiggle of his skin against hers. When his eyes would open like arched gates and look at her, she knew she was finally at the center of somebody's world. Matthew stuck out his tongue at her. He looked as if he could eat her up, and this scared Colette: It occurred to her that she wasn't sure what to feed him for the rest of his life.

After Christmas, not many days after the baby was born, she rode to Lafayette with Paul's sister, Nan, a fairly tall brunette who lived in jogging shorts and talked like a tugboat captain. Paul's capsized mind was coming back, and he knew everyone again. Much of the swelling had gone out of his face, and the doctors had managed to do careful skin grafts on his neck, cheeks, chest, and hands. Most of the burns had not left scarring. His speech was a beat too slow, and his left arm was not functioning correctly. When he wanted it to go forward, it would go back. He remembered nothing of the accident. She showed him the baby, and he didn't seem to understand fully what it was. She told him that Tyler was in Texas, paying a lawyer every cent he owned to fight ninety-seven federal and state charges. Paul fell asleep while she was talking to him, and she was left with a deep sense of how ruined he was.

She ate at a McDonald's with Paul's parents and watched them dig through their clothes for money for the meal. On the drive home Colette studied idle tugboats and supply vessels listing at their landings in roadside canals and thought of the times she'd walked into an upscale restaurant and ordered whatever she wanted without looking at the prices on the menu.

January was colder than usual. She now had two babies to look after, her father and Matthew, but with the help of her aunts, she found time to shop at places like Al's Dollar Store, looking at thin, coarsely made baby clothes, loose threads hanging from the seams as though somebody in Albania had given up in mid-stitch. Soon she ran out of makeup and merely washed her face each morning, making do with that. She clipped coupons out of the throwaway newspaper, and moneyless weeks passed, seeming like little lifetimes. Paul came home from the hospital and was trying to rehabilitate himself with some exercises the hospital staff had taught him.

One night when the baby and her father were asleep, she took a long bath and thought of her mother's advice—how she should always remember God, become educated, choose a good man and a good job that would allow her to live comfortably. She wondered what she'd meant by the word *comfortably*. She knew rich folks who were uncomfortable with everything. Closing her eyes in the tub, she tried to see her mother again, a thin lady who preferred dresses to pants, who moved with delicate patience through life, good-humored and kind, a schoolteacher. What else had she said? Something about nothing wrong with being poor but that poverty sometimes bred a hardness toward others, a suspicion in the blood that colored the way one looked at things. She remembered now. Her mother had sat up with her, talking to her on the porch in the rare coolness of a spring night, before the bugs got bad. She'd said merely that hard work and education got you good food and a good roof for your whole life. It also made people look up to you, which made you look up to yourself. It made her feel strange to realize that she would have to say the same things to Matthew one day.

What bothered Colette in the stores were the glances from people who knew her, expressions of pity for a tragic figure, the smart, pretty girl who went west to make her fortune, only to come back busted, divorced, and living at home. It embarrassed her to shop for anything, because she could afford nothing of the best anymore. It also embarrassed her to realize how much she liked money, thought about money, yearned after shiny things in general. She began to feel guilty when she wanted things. When she thought of the Mercedes, she winced at the sum she'd wasted and wondered whether she could ever handle good fortune again. She hoped she'd achieved a sort of wisdom by having it and then losing it.

Early in March she loaded Matthew in her Caprice for a trip to visit an ailing aunt in the next town. A few seconds after she turned the key, the engine convulsed once and died in a cloud of gassy smoke. The baby made a noise and shook his fist toward the dashboard. It was a Sunday, so she couldn't call Barrilleaux's filling station for advice, and no one else would come out for free. Going into the house, she put a hand on the phone, noting that the motion felt inevitable. She called Paul, and he said that he'd walk over, that he needed the exercise. In twenty minutes she went out to wait by the car and saw him walking up, his left hand turned backward, his hair short and wayward.

He asked to hold the baby and she gave it over, hovering close, watching Paul for steadiness. "He's a keeper," he said, putting the baby's face against his neck. He had been with Matthew only a few times. "Now that I can get up, maybe I can see him some more."

She looked at Paul's face as he studied the baby's features, and she bit the inside of her cheeks, afraid he was wanting the boy too much.

"Give me a call when you need to," she told him. "Now, let me have him back, and I'll get in the car and try to start it so you can listen."

Paul opened the hood and thrust it up with his right hand while Colette turned the key. After a while, he let the hood drop.

"Well?" she said, getting out.

"If we had three dollars, we could have a Mass said for it."

She sat against the hood and put the baby over her shoulder, patting it. "Oh no."

"Yeah. It's a timing belt. Two hundred dollars at least. I'd try to fix it, but I pawned most of my tools." He looked behind him down the street. "I can't hardly hold a wrench, much less turn it."

"You're walking straight. That's better."

His head drifted on his neck a bit. "I got to concentrate on it, make that left leg go. Sometimes I forget, and I'll step in a circle. It's the damnedest thing."

"I'm sorry you had to walk over. I forgot your daddy's car isn't running, either."

"Might as well walk," he said. "Can't dance anymore." He gave her a half smile. "Can't get in any trouble."

She changed shoulders with the baby. "You want to come in for a cup of coffee?"

He looked up at her porch. "I don't feel so good. I'm gonna head on back."

"It's a bitch, taking so long for you to get straight."

He sat down on the hood of the dead sedan. "In the mornings, I walk about a block to Abadie's, and by the time I get there, I'm sweating and out of breath. One time, I made it down to LeBlanc's and sat on the bench under the tree and like to died."

"It's dizziness or what?"

"Doc says my liver's not right. I guess it got cooked."

"How's *Grand-père* doing?" she asked, trying not to remember what Paul looked like in the hospital. His skin was gray, but changing for the better.

He stared down at the curb. "I go by his house and he's down in his little yard, fussing at his chickens, throwing feed and talking French, like *'Mangez les, alors. Ça me coûte vingt-cinq sous.'* I tell myself he's eighty-five years old and has more strength than I do, and it pisses me off so bad, I feel like going drown myself." He slid off the hood and turned his back on her. "Later."

She put a hand over her mouth as she watched him cross the asphalt and step up to the far sidewalk, raising his leg like an old man. She wondered if he would ever get his steps back, his jitterbug timing. When she was again inside the house, she remembered his dance leads, the twirling logic of his arms, and she swayed with the baby in her arms. She had caused Paul to lose more than she'd realized, and she decided it was her job to help him get something back.

That night Matthew woke up crying out from the grasp of a 103-degree fever. She sponged him with water and put him facedown on a cool sheet, patting the pain out of him. Later she called Aunt Nellie, but no one answered, and she remembered that her aunt took the phone off the hook some nights. She walked ten blocks over the town's broken sidewalks to the little Tiger Island hospital, and the nurse on duty, who had gone to high school with Colette, argued with her, refusing to believe that she couldn't afford to pay up front. Colette was treated like a transient brought in after a knifing, and when the doctor showed up to see the baby, she heard him down the hall saying, "Okay, let's see this poor little white child."

When she woke up, a pattern of window lights was on the plaster wall of her room, so she knew it was early. She put her hand in the crib and found that the baby was no longer feverish. On her way to the kitchen, she saw that the front door was open, and, checking, she found her father in the swing, drinking a glass of milk, his uncombed hair hooking out in silver curls. She looked at his purple feet.

"Hello," he said, raising his glass.

"You're up early," she said, watching him.

"The sun." He put out his empty hand.

She walked over and kissed him, sitting down.

"Dad."

"Huh?"

"Do you remember the Winchester pump rifle I used to shoot with when I was little?"

"Did you ever shoot it?"

She put her lips close to his ear and spoke in a low voice. "I'd like to have it. Where did you put it?"

Her father took a long swallow of the cold milk and squinted down the street, which was flowing with yellow dawn light filtered through the bare hackberry branches. "My brother gave it to me when I was a young man. I never used it, but he told me to keep it oiled. It was a nice gun."

"Where is the rifle?" she murmured.

He looked across the street and his mouth briefly became an O. "I killed a mad dog with it right over there after the '47 hurricane. I hated to do it. Took three shots."

She put an arm on his shoulder. "Do you think we could find it?"

"It's not lost. I know just where it is."

She looked down. Perhaps he did. "Where's that?"

"The winter place."

"What?"

His head turned, not a willed action, but a malfunction. "Send Mama out when you go to the kitchen." He pushed her hands away and leaned his cheek against the swing chains.

When she walked into the creaking upstairs hall, she could see her mother everywhere. She expected her to walk around every corner, through every door, pacing the routes of her children's lives. The upstairs wainscoting and ceiling were made of beaded board painted an old glossy cream color nobody had used in decades. Her grandfather had painted the upstairs with it in the forties. The floor was darkened pine and it cracked like a spine as she walked into her father's office, a little room where his books and records gathered dust. On his desk was a photograph of her mother, and she reached out, her hands balking before the glass. Next to the desk was a narrow door leading under the eaves, a storage place for quilts—the winter place, named by her own baby talk. She pulled on the porcelain knob and reached into the dark space to the right. Her palm closed on the sharp angles of the rifle's octagonal barrel, and she pulled it into the light. It was still gleaming and rustless, its barrel and magazine tube retaining all the original factory blue, the receiver and hammer showing the fiery yellow, red, and azure swirls of case-hardened color. She slid the walnut forearm down, listening to the pop and sing of well-tempered springs, the glide of hand-fitted steel. Putting her thumb on the hammer, she lowered it, going downstairs with the gun in the crook of her arm to call Aunt Nellie.

It was not unusual to see people walking the streets of Tiger Island carrying shotguns, because the town was locked in by woods on two sides. Men would sometimes walk from their porches right into the trees, going after a fat stew rabbit. But to see an attractive young woman carrying a rifle into town was exceptional. A porch full of old women looked her over carefully, wondering aloud where she was bound, sure that for such a nice girl to do such a thing, there must be an explanation. For every head she turned, Colette flushed, feeling trashy and desperate. She walked to the hardware and got the oldest clerk, Buster Lirette, to wait on her.

"Hello there, girl. You going shoot pigeons out a window fan with that thing?"

She held the gun out to him. "What kind of bullets will shoot best in this?"

Buster took the gun from her and turned it over in his hands two or three times. "This is a pretty old one, but it's in good shape, you know? Don't shoot no souped-up twenty-two trash they sell nowadays. All that high-velocity stuff does is foul up the barrel with lead. Not accurate worth a damn."

She looked around the old sporting-goods section at the corks, rusty fish hooks bleeding into cardboard racks, dusty Remington automatics, and the beveled glass case where ammunition was kept. "What do I use, then?"

"Standard-velocity long rifles. The bullets this gun was made for."

"How much do they cost?"

"One dollar sixty-nine cents for a box of fifty."

She dug change out of her slacks for a full minute. "I guess I can spring for one."

Lester looked back and forth between her hand and her face several times. "You want me to charge it to your daddy? They ain't much on the old account we been carrying on him. A couple dollars."

She had forgotten that her family had an account with the hardware. It was something from another time, another life. She charged four boxes, and felt guilty, as though she was pretending to be someone she was not. When she wrote *Colette* on the charge ticket, the word seemed like the name of a ghost. She left the store without even a smile at the amiable Buster, quickly crossed

River Street, walked along the moldering wall of the ice plant, and crossed the levee behind it, following the batture for a mile toward the Gulf and away from any houses. After wading through fifty feet of willow brake, she stopped at the river's edge and loaded the tubular magazine under the gun's barrel. Seventy-five feet downriver was a mud flat, and on it, a small jam jar and a beer can. She pumped the hammer back and took aim, pulling the trigger and smiling at the familiar crack of the bullet. The shot gored the mud two inches below the can. She pumped the empty out and fired again, missing three inches to the left. She took a breath, put the gun stock on her shoe, and tried to remember what her uncle Lester had told her about shooting. She spread her feet and made her shoulders almost parallel to the barrel, fired again, and missed the can by two feet. She concentrated hard and the next shot whacked a sapling a hundred yards off.

She cursed, gave the gun an angry look, then jerked it around to her shoulder and fired in anger. The shot spun the can, and she fired again quickly, offhand, and the can jumped into the air. A third shot flipped it off into the water. Colette found a dry spot on the bank and sat down to reload. Her uncle more than once had said that she owned a born talent for shooting. She wondered if talent required that much concentration. As she let the glossy bullets slip into the Winchester, she resolved to relax and fire from a still mood, not a still body.

On the first shot, the jam jar shattered to diamonds on the mud flat. The base was still intact, facing her, and the next bullet pulverized it. She looked hard and thought she saw the lid standing edgeways, but she could not find it in the rear V-notch sight. The old gun also had a tang sight, a flip-up peephole device behind the hammer, useful mainly for long-distance work. She adjusted it, taking five minutes to figure out how it worked, lowering the rear V-notch just out of the tang sight's line of vision. When she brought the rifle up and looked through the peephole, the lid was easy to see. She squeezed the trigger and the disk of metal flew off like a butterfly.

She scoured the mud flat and found cans to set up, backing off a hundred feet and aiming for the rims, sending each target into an acrobatic spin. She fired and set up cans until she ran out of shells and the ground around her was jeweled with spent casings. Back at the house, she did not start cooking supper's plain beans until she had cleaned and oiled the rifle. And late that night she sat on the porch in the cool air and listened to the bridge tender blow a come-ahead signal for a tug, wondering if Paul still had his sensitive ears, if he could at least still listen to the voices of machines he couldn't work on anymore.

The next morning she made a few phone calls, the last one going to Paul. "Can you walk over here?"

"Aw," he said, then a long pause. "I don't think so."

"You got to keep yourself exercised, fool."

"Yeah, I guess." Then he said nothing, and that silence came on her like a great weight.

"Then I'm coming over," she said.

"Here?"

"Yes."

"I need a bath. Don't come over."

"I'm not going to get close," she said stiffly. She hung up, checked on her father, who was watching a soap opera, picked up the baby, and began walking.

He was sitting on the peeling porch when she came up, and he did not look good, physically or otherwise. Colette thought her mother would say that a lot was missing from his eyes. His skin was yellow, his cheeks puffy, and he lay back in a wicker chair like a limp house plant. She knew what was wrong; she could see it in the angle of his arms and legs. She believed he needed to be put to work. She handed him the baby, and he kissed him on top of his head while he regarded him suspiciously, but did not cry. Matthew settled in the crook of his arm and looked at his mother.

"I came over here because I'm starving to death, and I know you can work."

He regarded her over the baby's dark fuzz. "Me and my folks are living on government cheese, and you're gonna ask me for alimony and child support?" He put a hand up and let it fall.

She looked around at all the failing paint on the porch. "That's not what I mean."

"What, then?"

She took a long breath, as if sliding underwater. "Who will loan us a good skiff?"

He tilted his head to the side. "Crawfishing's hard work. You think I'm up to it? I can't hardly climb out of a bathtub."

She shook her dark hair, which was beginning to frizz in the humidity. "I wasn't thinking of crawfish. I can't afford the traps and bait."

"What you need a skiff for, then?"

"Nutria."

He laughed, and the baby looked up at the sound. "You been inhaling too many fumes out at the stink plant."

"No, listen, hardhead. Oudry's is buying them unskinned again. I saw a new sign. Two dollars each."

"Ah," he said. "Dog food plant's buying again." He smoothed down the baby's hair and let a finger trail along its cheek. "You'd need a good skiff. Those rats weigh thirty pounds, some of them. All the good skiffs are out after the mud bugs. Nan's husband had to scrounge all over the parish to rig up his."

"What's a good skiff?"

"An eighteen-footer with a broad belly to take the weight. A boat what won't roll, with enough sheer in the front so it won't tugboat with a load of rats."

"Tugboat?"

"Dig its nose in the water."

She took back the baby, who was starting to arch his back and whimper. "If we had a good boat, we could make some money at least. Oudry's is buying channel cat and even water snakes for the laboratory in Schriever."

He looked at her hard, as though trying to get at her meaning. "What's this 'we' business?"

"T-Bub, all I'm interested in is being able to buy clothes and food and pay the light bill, is that clear?"

"No surprise to me," he said, long used to the anvil-hard way she said things.

"So don't start having any fantasies, all right?"

"That's hard to do with you around."

She smiled a little at that. "Listen to this. I called the conservation department's office this morning. The swamps west of here are overrun because nobody's hunted them for the past two years. There are three no-limit days next week that mostly the old swamp trappers know about. If we could get a boat, we might be able to make a couple days' good money."

He yawned. "*Grand-père* Abadie could tell us where there's plenty nutria, but I don't know how to trap 'em."

She tried not to be brought down by the defeat in his voice, telling herself that it came from inside his pained bones. "When I was a little girl, I saw the trappers come in with boatloads of them shot through the head. Back when there was no regulation at all."

"You're not a trapper."

She looked down at his leather shoes, which were wrinkled like an old man's face. His shirt was a washed-out button-down, limp as dishrag. She did not know how to tell him that maybe you had to become what you weren't, sometimes. Paul's mother banged out onto the porch, saw the baby, and Colette passed him off and told her that yes, she could take him in the house and show him to his grandfather.

Alone again, she told Paul to get up and walk with her to the levee. He waved her off, but she persisted. "You sitting here feeling sorry for yourself."

"I'm sitting here feeling ready to die," he told her.

"Come on." She grabbed his bad arm and pulled it, and he came out of the chair yowling in pain. She led him through the house, over the crackling linoleum of the kitchen, off the back porch, and up the levee. She let him get his breath at the top, then started off toward LeBlanc's Machine Shop. "You got to keep moving to get back your strength. It's going to hurt. Come on." They skirted the roiling Chieftan River, brown as coffee and moving under a lace of vapor as it played along the trunks of the numberless willows. Between the cut-over levee slope and the tree line was a skirt of brambles and pigweed that the water had risen into, and they saw a five-foot water moccasin exploring a stem of blackberries. She pulled Paul down the slope and up again, feeling his neck for pulse when they were back at the top.

He shook when she touched him, but he acted as though the vibration meant nothing. "What's the diagnosis, doc?" he rasped.

She made a face. "Feels like a motorboat. You got to build yourself up."

They walked until they were at the rear of *Grand-père* Abadie's house, stopping to stare at the paintless honesty of its cypress planks. "You know," Paul began, "Abadie never had any more than he has right now. He's poor and doesn't know it. We used to have some money. That's what hurts."

Colette looked in the other direction and saw the old man's tarp-covered skiff as it swung in the shallows, twenty feet from the bank, tethered to a trimmed sapling. Unlike the house, it was painted. "What's that, his old skiff?"

Paul looked where she pointed. "He hasn't been out in it in fifteen years, but he turns it over once a season, scrapes the bottom, hammers cotton into all the seams, and paints it gray. It's got to stay in the water so the seams stay swelled shut."

Colette walked down toward the boat, which was flat-nosed and twenty feet long, made of narrow, tapering planks. It did not have much of a belly, but a five-inch-wide rail board ran along the hull opening. A bump under the tarpaulin was the inboard engine.

She took off her shoes and waded out next to it. "What kind of motor's this thing have?"

"An antique. A Ferro, I think. Made in the twenties. He's had it in four other boats. One cylinder with a front flywheel you turn by hand to start."

She pushed down on the rail and saw that it was fairly stable. "Why's he keep it?"

Paul shrugged. "One time he told me that as long as he had a boat, he was still a fisherman. Without it, he would just be an old man."

"Can you run it?"

He closed his eyes and shook his head. "No."

"A machine you can't make work. I've found one at last."

He shifted his weight. "I mean it's cranky. I haven't ridden in it since I was a kid."

She came up out of the water and slipped her white feet into her shoes. "You think he'll let us use it?"

He pursed his lips and stared at the tarp. After a long silence he said, "We could ask. He could tell us if the bottom's too soft to trust."

"The engine's a real cast-iron antique, huh?" she asked, watching him. "What about it? Tell me."

"Nicely made," he said without looking at her. "Lots of brass fittings. Low compression. Not too hard to start."

"It'd be fun to run, wouldn't it?"

Across the levee they let themselves into Abadie's chicken yard, coming through the cypress picket gate into a pungent square of ground, barren and dark. They walked up to his house, a narrow shotgun on brick piers, and mounted the gray steps to knock, but he had seen them, and he opened the door as Paul reached out to touch it.

"*Comment ça va?*" he called. "*Vous voulez du café?*"

"*Mais* yeah," Paul said, looking into the kitchen, where Father Clemmons was seated at the porcelain table, out on one of his morning visits.

"Don't mind me," the priest said in his big preaching voice.

Abadie jerked a thumb toward him. "He thinks he gonna save my soul. I told him I didn't think I was losing it." The old man's hair was uncombed, but his T-shirt was tucked into his khaki pants, which pooled over his veined feet. He sat and leaned back against the cypress boards of the kitchen. "What you babies up to now?" He rubbed his nose and gave Colette a half-smile, waving for them to sit.

She flipped her hair behind her shoulders. "I'm trying to get Paul to come out with me after a boatload of nutria."

Abadie looked at the priest, who shrugged. "Little girl, all you know is fancy pants and pretty perfume. How you gonna mess with them big orange-tooth rat?"

"I can shoot."

"Oh yah. So that's why you come around. So you can borrow my rifle, hanh?"

"No, your boat."

He raised his white eyebrows and looked out through the window again, as though something of great interest was in the chicken yard, as if thinking of how to say no. But then he turned to Paul. "T-Bub there, he knows how to make the little engine fire. He knew how to crank a Ferro when he was ten years old, yeah."

Colette put sugar in her coffee. "We won't tear it up if you let us use it."

"Hell yas, you can use it. I want to hear it go downriver again, with that exhaust poppin' slow out that pipe." He turned to Paul. "You know who built that boat? My daddy. Last thing he did."

"I didn't know him," Paul said. "He died before I was born, but I thought he was an engineer in a sugar mill."

Abadie's face caved in a little when he brought his lips together. He hadn't put in his teeth yet. "When Belle Terre mill close up, he sat around in his yard back behind you house and made maybe two, three skiff a year. Maybe he made six before he passed, bored to death because he couldn't run them big Corliss engines in the mill." He turned his head in the direction of Belle Terre mill, now a weedy hackberry grove studded with brick engine foundations. "He learned to build boats from you great-great *grand-père.*"

Paul sat up straight. "I never knew anybody who met him."

"What you talk? Right here, me myself, I knew him. He ran a farm on that elbow by the river above town. But you young people, you don't care about that. Once somebody's dead, you turn on that television and forget their name."

"Tell me his name," Colette said. "I won't forget it."

Abadie opened a hand toward her. "It was August Théodore, and he was a damned good cane farmer. And his daddy was Viléor, the blacksmith.

"Born in 1826," Father Clemmons added. "He made the lightning rods for the first church. And his father was Zefirin Marcelian, who was, as I remember from the church records, born in 1799 and thrown out of church because he wouldn't snuff his pipe in Mass. He lived in the swamp behind town, had eleven children, and outlived three wives."

Paul took a long swallow of coffee, thinking about the old names. He looked at Colette. "In high school you looked up your family tree."

"We're drifters," she told him. "Been here only a hundred and forty years or so."

Father Clemmons nodded. "Came over from the Lafourche region. The first Jeansomme started a tavern about where Le-

Blanc's Machine Shop is today. They were prolific, and many are in the old graveyard that was closed forty or so years ago."

"A lot of ghosts," Colette said, looking at an expired calendar hanging on the kitchen wall.

"Was that Zefirin guy the first one in my family around here?"

The priest shook his head. "Abadie made me look them all up."

"That's right," the old man said. "Before Zefirin was Arsène, and before that was François, who was thrown out of Nova Scotia by those damned English. The what—the Spanish gave him some land that one time covered half of downtown. It's in the records," Abadie said, pointing in the direction of the church.

"Arsène made fiddles in the winter and fished in the summer," the priest said. "The aristocratic priest kept notes on his congregation in Spanish, which I happen to read."

Colette sat against the wall and let the town spread out in her imagination two hundred years back, the mud-and-moss farmhouses, the hand-ditched fields, a log chapel, a *bal de maison* with couples dancing in the yard, fiddlers on the porch scraping a tune from Arsène Abadie's instruments, their music like wasps in a drainpipe. She shuddered, feeling the spirits of fishermen and farmers gathering in this little room made of narrow boards patterned like mattress ticking.

Abadie had gone into his bedroom and they heard him bumping around in an armoire. He returned with a yellowed navigation map, which he unrolled on the kitchen table, placing their coffee cups on the corners. Running a thick finger down the blue vein of the Chieftan, he showed them where to go with the boat.

"*Là*," he said, tapping his finger on the paper, "the old diversion canal. They's gonna be plenty nutria going over to eat in the cane field that runs all along the levee on the north side." Without looking up, he told them what time of day the animals would be in the water, and how they would swim. He studied the map as though it were the breathing marshland itself, his face filling with so much memory that he forgot anyone was in the room with him, and he began to speak to himself. "Nutria can't be shot in the water, no. He might sink right where you shoot him. When he hits the edge of the bank, pee-yow, you let him have it in the back of the head, and that's where he'll stay."

"You could come with us," Paul said.

The old man laughed. "I'm gon' be eighty-four or -six next month. I got no business out there." He rolled up the map. "I don't know if you gonna do any good. You got to have the sense in you bones when you go out there," he told them.

Colette stood and put the cups in the sink. "You have to be hungry for something better than what you have," she said.

Paul shook his head. "She feels better than I do."

"She's a Jeansomme all right," the priest said. "They want to get paid for their misery." Father Clemmons turned to Abadie. "Now put in your teeth and tell me your confession."

The old man smiled, jerking a thumb over his shoulder as he walked Colette to the door. "That priest is a *couillon*. I'm too old to even make a sin."

Colette pulled Paul up the levee and walked him home. "I'll get the licenses and we'll go tomorrow."

He shook his head. "No. This is a bad idea."

"Damn it, you'll feel better if you work."

"If I fall overboard, I'll be too weak to swim."

She stepped in front of him and put a fingernail into his sternum, not the first time she had done this. "If you're not ready when I come tomorrow, I'll drown you myself in your own lavatory."

Fifteen

By three o'clock the next afternoon, they were ready to go. The baby cried when Colette gave him over to Aunt Nellie's flabby arms. For two blocks, Colette imagined she could hear him squalling after her. Borrowing money for gasoline from Paul's brother, Larry, fees for a license from his sister, Nan, and a handheld spotlight from Colette's uncle Lester, they were already in debt. Paul was afraid of setting off in the wide river and fighting the wheel wash of big tugs with his *grand-père*'s antique boat. He waded gingerly out to the skiff, stopping when the water threatened to boil into his knee boots. Colette sloshed along behind him, put the shiny Winchester in the bow, and slung herself in. They had decided to make an evening run and come back after dark.

Colette pushed them out of the shallows with an oar while Paul set the spark on the engine so the flywheel wouldn't kick back and break his arm. He opened the hinged door of a cypress box next to the engine and checked the lantern battery and buzz coil, opening the knife-blade switch that fed spark to the plug. Into a priming cup on the engine's domed head he poured a sip of gasoline, opened a valve, and rolled the flywheel back and forth to suck the fuel into the cylinder and mix it with a good charge of air. Closing the knife switch, he cranked the engine up past dead center. It sneezed, banged once like a pistol, and spewed a bar of blue smoke from the two-inch exhaust pipe, which ran straight back over the stern. It started to run with a slow throb like an iron heart, and he advanced the spark and pushed the steering stick over, aiming for midchannel, remembering the engine's sound like a song heard in childhood and not since, four beats a second, pounding out toward town over the broad plain of river, turning the heads of all the old fishermen in Tiger Island.

He adjusted the drip oilers and turned down the grease cups on the crankshaft, then played with the spark and carburetor until he had the skiff pushing downstream at a good fifteen miles an hour. Colette sat in the bow and looked ahead. He noticed that she had trimmed her hair up to her shoulders, as though long hair was a luxury she could no longer afford. She turned, feeling his eyes on her. "You sick yet?"

"I'm alive—that's all," he yelled over the engine noise. He glanced astern at a crew boat gaining and his heart skipped. He put the skiff into the dead water next to the bank and the big vessel sliced by, several oil workers waving their hard hats and pointing at Abadie's boat.

Paul and Colette chugged under the railroad bridge and rounded the point below town on the west bank, passing a raft of tied-up tugs and mud boats. The water was as brown as café au lait, heavy with silt from the previous week's rains. Paul cut around an abandoned rig boat listing away from its moorings; two miles up the channel, they passed a few trappers' shacks, abandoned plywood hulls dotted with nests of paper wasps. Another mile and there were only willows on the bank, and later, not even a bank, but a deep raft of hyacinth-filled swamp and a brake of second-growth cypress.

About five o'clock Colette moved into the bow and loaded the rifle. "Time to make money," she called.

Paul cut the engine speed to an idle, watching her scan the edge of the channel, which had narrowed to one hundred yards. She knelt down and drew back the hammer, aiming at something on the bank Paul could not see. The gun spat, and she put its butt down and pointed for Paul to nose into the bank. She put on a canvas glove and reached over the bow, drawing up into the boat a brown twenty-pound rat, its arms and legs splayed out, two-inch orange fangs flashing once in the sunlight. A small red hole shone behind the rodent's eye, and the animal was still, as though it had been dead for hours. "Two dollars," she said, poking the webbed feet and thick coat with the gun barrel. With the oar, she shoved the boat away from the bank and Paul started the engine and ran it dead slow, keeping thirty feet off the tree line, looking for the cane field diversion canal Abadie had sent them to find.

A fat aluminum skiff approached from behind and flew by, the fisherman aboard waving broadly, on his way to the outer marshes on the Gulf's fringe. As the other boat disappeared around a bend, Paul reached back to check the lubricators. He watched the wake rolling sleepily out from the stern until he heard the gun pop again. Colette motioned him to the bank as before, and she looked over the bow, pumped the gun, and fired again. It was a big sow rat, and she could hardly lug it over the rail. "Two dollars," she said, rubbing a spot of blood on her patched jeans.

"We rich," he said, spitting over the side.

She turned to glare at him, then looked over his head. "Bend down," she said, and as he did, she fired over his back and across the stream. "Number three is over there by that stump." She pumped the empty shell into the boat.

He ran the engine backward toward a mound of fur. He watched her pull the carcass in and throw it on the others. "If you say two dollars, I'm turning back," he said.

"Come on, get this thing moving. They're really coming out."

She was right. The overbred swamp was teeming with animals. As the light lessened, they could hear their cries, like babies, human and unnerving.

"Sounds like we're hunting kids," he said.

"The darker it gets, the more they cry out, Abadie says. It'll help us find them."

In a mile or so they saw a cut in the bank and knew they had reached the mouth of the old diversion canal. Leaving the main channel, they entered a narrow thread of black water. Paul steered close to the bank, and the rudder glanced off a stump, so he put them in the middle and slowed the engine. On the left was marsh grass, on the right a weedy bank sloping up to a ten-foot-high levee built to protect cane fields on the other side. He could see paths cut in the weeds where the rats made their nightly runs. It was after six o'clock. Reaching down to the duckboards he picked up the handheld spotlight and tested it. He saw a little water in the bilge, so he grabbed a Luzianne coffee can and bailed.

Colette shot a rat right in front of the boat and had him up dripping and dying before they could run over him. "Kill the engine. You got to paddle for a while."

He stood up, wobbly in the knees, and grabbed the long oar, stirring it through the water on one side, then the other. Two animals began crossing the canal at the same time, one fifty feet ahead, one twice that distance. He could see only a vague movement where the farther animal swam, but she shot it first, as soon as it reached the bank, before lining the nearer animal in her sights and blowing a hole through the top of its skull.

"You didn't get the one down there a ways."

She squinted ahead in the long shadows. "Yes I did. It's on the bank."

And when he poled down there, it was.

They worked the sluggish canal for three miles, up to where crooked black oaks grew low and near the water, their limbs strung with Spanish moss shining silver in the reflection of the black swamp runoff. Forty-seven nutria lay heaped on the duckboards, and the bilge ran red. Between shots she sat in the bow and thought of easy California, wondering what she would be doing if Dirk had not taken her job away. She saw the yellow fangs of a rat flash five feet away and she imagined it was her former boss as her slug slapped it dead between the eyes.

In the oak grove they drifted through wiry garden spiderwebs spanning the overhang from both banks, and several of the big spiders fell into the boat. She watched one crawl up to her knee-cap, its orange-and-black legs and irridescent green body moving deliberately, before she backhanded it overboard. "Let's turn around," she said. "The boat's crawling with these things."

He poled the skiff into a wide spot and turned them. It was seven-thirty then, and nearly dark. "The spiders don't bother me much. I'm scared we'll hit a hornet's nest in these branches." He checked every low-hanging limb carefully with the light. On one was a black snake, which he ignored. On another was a small cone of yellow jackets, and he wondered how he had missed seeing them on the way up. Colette raised her rifle to shoot a nutria that had shown its eyes in Paul's beam, and she let out a yell.

"What's wrong?"

"A spider big as your hand. Right on top of the barrel." She shook it off into the water.

"Hey," he yelled. "Don't point that thing at me." He held up an arm.

"I didn't point it at you."

"Bullshit, you swung it past my face."

"I wouldn't shoot you. You're not worth two dollars."

He didn't say anything, and she sat down to replenish the gun's magazine. When she looked over, he was staring into the bilge, reaching for the bailing can. "I'm sorry," she said.

"Colette, you got a tongue on you like a fillet knife." His voice was bone-tired and made her walk the rail around the mound of carcasses and sit on the rear bench with him. She lit a rusty lantern and hung it on the steering stick. "Where are you hurting?"

"Sometimes the scalding feeling comes back across my chest and stomach. My heart speeds up and I feel like I got mono and the flu at the same time."

"You need a sandwich." She bent behind the engine and picked up a little plastic cooler. "Ham or egg salad?"

"You ought to know the answer to that one."

She opened cans of soda and they chewed their food slowly in the lamplight, not knowing what to say to each other. Finally he told her, "This is the first time I've been around you when I didn't smell your perfume."

"Ran out. What do I smell like?"

"Nutria blood."

"Yeah, well, you smell like gas." She looked up and saw the sky weakening to lavender, the clouds pale ghosts of themselves.

"Colette."

"What?"

"You ever, you know, miss me in bed?"

She threw her sandwich bag overboard. "Aw, hell, what kind of question is that to ask me here in this little boat where I can't slap you and run off?"

"Can you answer it?"

"Hell no." She crossed her legs, then uncrossed them. What about you?"

He took a long pull on his soda can. "Lotta nights I had to sleep on my back, you know? Before the accident, anyway."

"Hey, you can't mess around. You might make somebody a good husband."

"Ow. Colette."

She ducked her head. "Okay, I'm sorry again. But just don't ask me whether or not I get horny, because you know the answer. Here." She handed him a bottle. "The mosquitoes are getting worse. Put this on yourself."

They doped themselves with repellent, for the mosquitoes

were now humming all at once above the canal in droves, as if in response to a signal. "Kill the lamp," he said. "It's letting them find us."

She leaned over and turned down the flame. For several minutes everywhere she looked, she saw the yellow tongue of the wick. "You feeling better?"

"Yeah. I was hungry and disgusted."

"Now?"

"Just disgusted." By the flashlight he refilled the lubricators on the engine. The deep *rum-rum* of the bullfrogs barreled up and down the canal, and the high-pitched squalls of nutrias arched over the boat in the tones of frightened children. These sounds meshed in with a fabric of trilling spiders and the rasp and saw of giant black grasshoppers. Colette clicked on the spotlight and set it in the bow. A pair of eyes swam toward her, and she grabbed the rifle.

"Don't shoot it."

"Why not?"

"Look at how far apart the eyes are."

She put the gun down and watched the twin marbles poised on the surface of the dark canal. "He must be over twelve feet long."

"Makes you think twice about sticking your hand in the water."

She took the oar and shoved them clear of a hyacinth raft, moving the skiff quietly, letting the light play on the surface fifty feet ahead. An animal swam into the beam and she dropped the oar, picking up the gun.

"Damn it, I lost sight of that rat." She handed him the spotlight. "Shine it up for me."

He swung the beam over to the levee side, on the left, and as soon as he touched the nutria with the light, she fired. The shot missed the brain and the animal tumbled wildly into the shallows. She ripped off three shots as fast as she could pump.

"Let's go get it," she said, resting the crescent butt plate on her thigh.

The animals were not easy to find with the light, but once their eyes fired up in its beam, she would pump a round between them. After an hour they had piled twenty new animals inside. The skiff was wallowing low in the water, loaded with a hill of bodies so high Colette could no longer walk to the stern. Paul bailed what he knew was mostly blood from the bilge with his coffee can. He was done in; his muscles felt separated from the bones and lay like dead fish under his skin. He gritted his teeth and waited for her to give up first, to ask him how he felt, so he could say "All right," but in such a way that would make her say she'd had enough. But she kept shooting and reaching down, bailing in the carcasses, not wearing a glove now, heedless of the knifelike carroty incisors. He put his fingers over the side, surprised at how near the water was to his hand.

"Colette, we don't have much freeboard left." He wasn't going to ask to go. He would let facts decide the issue. He watched her head move around toward him, and he tried to guess her expression.

"Start the engine, then." Her voice came like a cool note of music. "I'll hold the light."

Soon they were throbbing over the dark cut of water between the islands of hyacinth, a boil and squash of water sounding around the low-riding boat. The engine labored, its heavy exhausts rebounding like shots off the invisible levee. Colette stood in the bow, holding the light straight ahead, watching for stumps. There was no moon, and the skiff cut through oil-black water. Near the mouth, the canal widened out, the channel becoming indefinite. A cypress grew in the middle of the stream. At the moment they passed the cypress, she leaned left and shone the light down on the bow swell, then back along the rail to see if they were taking water over the sides. It was then that the right side of the hull skidded up on what felt like a sunken log, and she went over, her light illuminating an instant of lacy splash, then going out. Paul was in darkness, listening to a gasp of water come over the left side. The hull slid off whatever it had struck, and he grabbed the plug wire from the engine, killing it, taking three sharp pulses of electricity from the buzz coil. Lost in the sudden blackness of the overgrown canal, not knowing if the boat was still moving or not, he shouted her name. Thrusting his arms over the side, he felt for her, leaning until he heard water lazing into the nearly sunken boat. He listened with his sensitive ears for her struggle in the water but heard only the hiss of the hot engine. He jerked off his boots, feeling the water in the boat up to the middle of his rubbery calves. Not knowing if he could still swim, he fell off the stern, out of blackness into blackness, swallowing a gulp of brackish water and coughing it back up. He started to swim like an old water spider on the water, clearing his lungs so he could cry out for her again, not knowing if he was swimming up or down the canal. One high overhand stroke caught his hand in a branch, and he let down his legs to the mud bottom, sensing the left bank and at the same time yearning to climb into the shallows and breathe. A terrible weariness flowed like poison through his arms and chest, but he turned and swam back away from the bank. He gasped and went under, splaying his arms like a gull's wings and flying through the terrible water after her. He came up for air, blowing like a whale, and then sounded again. On the second long trip under, he could feel himself blacking out, and when he tried to get to the air, he came up beneath the slick broad hull. When his head broke water, he hung on to the rudder brace, took several breaths, and then swam west, back up the canal. Taking the middle, he pulled his flaccid arms through the surrounding night, calling her name, hearing nothing but the crash of water in his ears and the rush of his own breath coming fast and desperate. He swam until he felt sure that he was going to drown. Then he swam through that feeling and out of the other side of it, because he knew he would never stop spending the swaying, reaching strokes, would swim out of this life and into the next looking for her in the long canal, her black hair, her dark frowns. There was nothing else he could do.

He stroked into a bed of water lilies and became disoriented among the pulpy tubers, chopping at them lamely. His right foot touched bottom, and that instant the image of Matthew came into his mind, a bright face ringed with the dark silk of her hair. Paul was dying, caught between pushing off for the middle of the canal again and leaning into the shallows his body yearned for. He began thrashing both ways at once, afraid he was going to cry. His left hand reached out and grasped the hairy root system of hyacinth, and he listened to his breath explode from him in hoarse spasms, his foot still caught in the tempting mud of the levee side of the canal, hyacinth all around, on his head, scraping the back of his neck. The root system in his hand seemed to have unusual texture, and he pulled that way, opening and closing his fingers on something finer than plant root, as fine as hair. He dropped under and found her, as still and limp as if she had been growing there for years, waiting for him to come. He grappled for her tough denim shirt, his fingers numb in the cloth.

Now his feet scrambled for the mud until he found himself within his depth and able to stand, bringing her head into the dark night with him. He stopped and gulped air to fuel his fight to gain the sloping bank. Rising until the cut-grass rattled at his ears, he fell backward into the shallows, backpedaling up the bank, pulling Colette out, turning her on her stomach and pressing her back. He stuck his finger into her mouth and felt water run from her in a gush. Turning her over, he tried to bring her back, dreading to feel for a pulse, not wanting to waste time, even for that. He breathed into her several times, but she remained limp and still. On the last breath, he thought he smelled copper. Running his hands over her face, he felt that she was sticky with blood. The thought that she might have been hit by the propeller struck him like a stone, but there was no time for panic. He began compressions on her chest, interspersed with breaths, praying while he was doing this, without even realizing it, as though prayer was an element of rescue, as necessary as effort and fear. Giddy with exhaustion, he worked on feebly for a long time, until his arms started to fail. He straightened up from the waist and spread his hands to the weeds, feeling a catbrier behind him and running his forearm along it to wake himself, the thorns grating like saw teeth over his skin. He put his arms down again into the dark, unable to find her face for a long moment. He breathed into the rubbery mouth, compressed her chest, rolled her over, grabbed her belt and raised it taut, then struck her back with an open palm, determined to keep trying as long as he could stay conscious, thankful that he was blind and could not be distracted by the sight of her.

Colette was unyielding and dead in his hands. Again, he breathed into her, but her mouth was a limber slit, and feeling her slack lips under his made him pray again. He pressed her until he thought her ribs would crack and breathed until there was no more air left in him. He heard only a little catching noise in her throat, and he stopped to listen as he would to a far-off steam whistle. A narrow hiss ran from her mouth, his own breath coming out to mock him. Then he imagined he heard a little air go in. He bent down and gave her a gentle breath, and she returned one watery sigh of her own making.

Turning her over at once, he heard a blast of water come up. She heaved, began gasping, started to move under his fingers, and he listened to all of it, the sounds of her coming back. In five minutes she was in the world, and he found her twisting hands and held them. "I'm here," he said. "I'm here." He felt her pull her hands away, then grope openhanded, as though playing the piano. Touching her face, he found that her eyes were open, and he asked if she could hear him. In a tiny, croaking voice, she told him yes. Feeling carefully above her hairline, he found a three-inch-long cut slick with blood. He guessed she had struck her head on the bottom of the boat, maybe on the iron rudder.

"I feel awful," she said. "Where am I?"

"On the bank. Be quiet."

She turned her head and spat. "Have I been sick?" She began coughing violently, the spasms scouring her lungs.

"Yeah," he said, falling back in the weeds, suddenly too weak to tend her. He listened to her move around, and he savored her motion.

"How did you fish me out? Did I come up by the boat?"

"I swam."

Her voice was reedy, and she coughed again. "How long?"

"As long as I had to."

He imagined that she was next to him, holding her head. "Jeez, how did you find me in the dark?"

"I swam as long as I had to."

"How could you?" She put a hand on his arm to locate him, then took it back.

To Paul, the touch was like a live wire. "Don't worry about it." He turned on his side, ignoring a catbrier burning around his biceps.

In an hour they moved to the top of the levee, where the grass was short. Paul looked across what he imagined to be cane fields, but could see nothing, so they lay down again, endured the mosquitoes, and slept on and on toward sunrise. He awoke at the cry of an egret and sat up to find himself drenched with dew, the hair of his arms glistening like frost. The tops of cypresses were backlighted across the canal, and gradually daylight filled in the details of branches and leaves, the woods and marsh developing like a photograph in a tray. He looked down at Colette's face, which was frowning through a smudge of blood and dirt. Examining the wound on the top of her head, he saw that it was a propeller cut. He wiped her face with the tail of his shirt, and she stirred and began to wake up slowly. He flexed his sore arms, wondering if he could pull her upright, out of the wet grass, then decided not to.

There was nothing to do but walk east along the canal and look for the skiff. He listened, thinking for an instant that he heard an engine, wondering how far south of Highway 9 they were. It would be a long walk through the fields, maybe five miles.

He put his hand on her shoulder, and she opened her eyes, focusing on him slowly, but sitting up at once, looking around with jerky head movements to the coarse grass, the muddy bank below, palmettos on the opposite side.

"Welcome back to the world," he said.

She sniffed. "It sure ain't California."

"Is that a plus or a minus?"

"Please." She put a wrist to her forehead, remembering. "Where's the skiff?"

He shrugged. "Could be a few hundred yards off. Could be sunk."

"What'd you hit anyway? Smack a log?" She put her head between her knees. "Some navigator you are."

He looked at her a long time. "How's your head?"

"How you think it is?" she snapped.

"I think it's up your ass."

She looked at him carefully then. "What?"

"I mean, I pull your bitchy butt out of the canal and next thing I know, you blame me for putting it *in* the canal." He turned away.

She grabbed his arm and pulled him back. "Who hit the log?"

"What, I got X-ray vision so I can see a canal bottom at midnight?"

"Aggg, I'm too sick to argue." She lay back in the grass and put a forearm over her eyes.

He looked down the canal. "Come on, let's walk the bank."

"I can't. I feel like I might throw up."

He put his hand on her back and leered into her face, "You'll never get your strength back if you don't work."

"You bastard," she said, with the slightest sign of a smile.

He stood up as quickly as he was able and cocked his head like a spaniel. "You hear that?"

"What is it?"

"Shhh." The thin thread of an outboard's hum came to him over the water. "It's a boat, and it's running slow." They made their way down to the water's edge and Paul leaned out.

"Can you see anything?"

"Yeah. It's a big aluminum hull, one of those homemade jobs the Partians build." In five minutes the boat came abreast, shoved by a smoking outboard running without a cowl, and Paul shouted out, "Hey!"

The old man leaning on the steering wheel saw him at once. It was his silly uncle, Octave. He steered into the bank and cut the engine. "What the hell you doing out here in them bushes?" He squinted at them over his cigarette. "You been playin' in the mud?" He handed Colette into the boat.

"Did someone send you out to get us?" Paul grunted as he swung a leg into the bow.

"*Mais non.* I'm going out check my trap when I see Abadie's skiff hung up in a willow tree and loaded down with rat. I don't know what to think, because it don't make sense for him to go shoot no rat with that old boat." He pointed a denim-covered arm toward the mouth of the canal. "So me, I come up to see the body, 'cause when you find a skiff like that, most times ain't someone left to tell the tale." He pushed back his hat. "Ey-yi-yi, Colette, baby, you caught a propeller in the head." He examined the cut while Paul explained what had happened. Octave reached into his baggy pants and pulled out a bottle of aspirin and told

Paul to retrieve the thermos from the bow. He dipped his handkerchief into the canal and cleaned her face with downward strokes, as though she were a little girl who'd gotten muddy in the yard. He rinsed out the cloth and told her to press it against the seeping wound, all the while shaking his head. "You babies don't know nothing about taking rat." He gave them a scolding look, then reached to pull the starting cord on his faded Evinrude.

They found the skiff near the mouth of the canal, barely afloat. "Careful," Uncle Octave called as Paul reached out to grab the stern. "That thing's like a teacup floating in the sink." He handed his nephew his own bailing can and Paul began to empty Abadie's boat a quart at a time. It took a half hour before he could step inside, planting a foot in the center of the rear bench and bailing with a bait bucket until the water was down to the duckboards.

The first thing Colette had done when they drifted close was to grab her gun, which was riding dry across the bow, where she had dropped it. She wiped it down, glad she had coated it with gun grease before they came out. Paul blew on the electrical contacts and wiped down the buzz coil, then drained the water from the crankcase of the engine. After several turns of the flywheel, the Ferro thudded to life, the noise and smoke driving off some of the flies from the mound of nutria.

"You ought to let me tow you back," the old man shouted.

"No," Colette told him. "Your aspirins are starting to kick in. We'll be all right if Columbus here can keep us on the route."

Soon the boat was popping along the middle of the canal, and in five minutes they were back in the main channel of the Chieftan, veering north. The smooth whine of Octave's motor overtook them as it arced to the south through a broad, smooth turn of river, leaving them in the rainbowed spray of his prop.

Around the first bend they faced a tugboat and fought its wake. Paul put them in easy water against the bank, where they could bail a few gallons that had slid in over the rail. Before long they were approached by a low aluminum flat propelled like a bullet by an overmatched Mercury. A chunky man with a black mustache raised his hand. It was Paul's older brother, Larry, and he curled around their stern, pulling alongside.

Paul leaned over carefully and slapped his hand. "Did they send you out looking for us?"

"Hell yes. Got me out of bed before daylight and told me you was all eaten up by alligators." Larry pushed back his cap and shoved his black hair from his eyes. "I told mamma that this old junk rig of *Grand-père*'s broke down and you were waiting for daylight to come out, but she wouldn't listen."

"We're all right now," Colette told him. She had cleaned her arms off, but her clothes were muddy and puckered.

Larry gave her an appraising stare. "Babe, I don't think chasing rats agrees with you. You ought to come crawfishing with me."

"I'll take my chances with the dead rats," she said, not smiling.

"Ow." He held his hands over his heart as though shot.

"Tell Mamma that we'll be in at the fish dock about ten-thirty," Paul said.

"Okay, man, but don't get in no races with that speedboat you got." Larry pushed the throttle lever and the enormous Mercury put the flat up over the water like a kite.

Throughout the morning they dealt patiently with the sluggish trip, fighting swells of passing skiffs and trawlers. A young fisherman, a Guidry distantly related to Colette, pulled alongside and studied their load, asking if they needed help. Then three miles below the railroad bridge, a sheriff's helicopter swooped down low and hovered over them, Joe Trosclair asking over a bullhorn if they were all right.

When they cut the engine and glided to the fish dock, Paul's mother, father, sister, and brother and Colette's brother were waiting as though he and Colette were floating back from another world, which, Paul figured, they were.

The load of rats went for $134, and then Nan drove Colette to the hospital for stitches. She insisted that she could not afford to pay, and she would not stay overnight to have her lungs monitored. After a long argument, the head nurse yelled down the hall that they would have to write off the sutures as charity, and even the poor, damaged people in the waiting area of the emergency room looked at her with traces of contempt. Colette was angry down to her soggy boots, but on the way home she looked at the crumpled money from her labor and could not believe that it could all have been taken for a few inches of thread and a squirt of medicine. She remembered the salary she had earned in California and could not begin to imagine what she had done with it all.

Paul's sister drove her to the Thibodeauxs' so she could give Paul his share. There, she found that ten people had shown up to see him, but he was still cleaning out the skiff, so they lighted on her for the story. Someone passed her a plate of white beans and rice with a gravy steak nestled on top, and as she ate, she told what happened, and then later retold it with more detail to Mrs. Fontenot, who had tottered in late in the telling. Those who had loaned her money for the venture were there, and she offered to pay them back, but they refused loudly and with much waving of hands.

Eventually she got free and walked over the levee, where she saw Abadie and Paul down in the willows, working on the skiff.

"Getting ready for this afternoon?" she called out.

Paul gave her a frightened look. "What's happening this afternoon?"

"We're going back after more nutria."

After a while he stepped around the old man into the bow and then nearly fell out into the shallows. "You need a bigger bandage on your head. Some of your brains are leaking out."

"Gas up at the landing and I'll make sandwiches and buy another light."

"Hell no. I'm about to drop."

"Look," she said, pointing at the water. "Look at all the work you're doing. You're feeling better already. Go home, get your mamma to rub you down with a whole tube of Deep Heat, and take a nap."

"Why today, already?"

She showed him the little wad of bills. "This is why. Come on. We'll wear life jackets this time and tow that little aluminum johnboat that's under your daddy's house. We'll put some of the nutria in it and make better time that way."

He took her by the arm and led her up the levee a few feet to a cypress drift log and sat her down. "How's your head? Did they shave the cut?"

"I've got a little white alley up there. I took four aspirin for the headache."

"How much of the money did they take at the hospital?"

She laughed. "You should have seen Gladys Fontenot's face when I told her I couldn't pay. I thought she was gonna shit on herself."

"You got it all?"

"Yeah. And we gonna get some more, because there're two days left to this free season."

He looked at her left eye, which was bloodshot, then at her dry skin. "Why you doing this?"

She widened her eyes and looked straight into his. "This is the only way to make decent money. I'm surprised that you, of all people, should have to ask. You love hard work. Even though you're sick, you love it."

"Are you paying me a compliment?"

Her mouth fell open, but nothing came out. In the skiff, Abadie was laughing as he poured gas into the fuel tank.

* * *

At quarter to four Colette poled the skiff away from the shallows, the featherlight johnboat drifting behind like an afterthought. Abadie stood on the spongy bank, hands cupped around his mouth, shouting to Paul how to coax more speed out of the engine, the flat *a*'s of his words spangling the water as he called, "Take the gas out another notch, yeah, and make Colette sit in the middle bench so the *bateau* runs flat." He pulled off his khaki cap and waved it. Paul turned the flywheel and the engine popped alive. Soon Abadie was a small stooped figure picking his way back up the levee.

They did make better time. Soon he was listening to the crack of Colette's rifle fill the canal as she fired over and over from the front seat, and the bilge rolled with the brassy gravel of her spent casings. By nine-fifteen they were crossing the river back to town with a skiffload of seventy-four carcasses.

The next afternoon, they had competition on the canal from a young trapper, but they still managed to take seventy animals, including one albino, for which the fish dock paid a bonus. Overall, they cleared right at four hundred dollars.

After unloading the rats, Paul had run the skiff back to Abadie's while Colette settled up with the buyer. She walked the batture to Paul's house and saw that the old boat was not tied in the shallows but run up all the way to the water's edge. It was still filthy inside. She plucked her rifle out of the bow and crossed the levee in time to see an ambulance pull out of the Thibodeauxs' driveway with its flashers going. Paul's mother met her at the back door.

"Nan's coming to bring us to the hospital."

She put the gun inside the door frame. "What happened?"

His mother had tied a dishrag in a knot. "Paul fell down as soon as he got into the kitchen. He was talking, but we couldn't get him to stand up, and then he started shaking and sweating, so we called the ambulance. Let's go out front."

In a minute Paul's sister pulled up in her dusty truck and they rode to the hospital, pacing the emergency room for an hour before a doctor came out, a Lester Cox, the same doctor that had sewn her up.

"I called the doctor in Lafayette," he told them. "Mr. Thibodeaux is still suffering from that trauma of a few months ago." He watched them carefully through his wire-rim glasses, looking as though he was about to tell them something important. "You can't expect a man who's had his brain cooked to work like a new man. When he came around, he told me he's been working three days straight." The little doctor shook his head. "He can't handle that yet. His heart rate's high, his liver counts are all screwed up, and we'll have to keep him overnight at least to straighten out his electrolytes and run a few more blood tests."

Colette picked up an arm and let it slap against her leg as though punishing herself. She had pushed him too hard and would have to make it up to him. But even as she thought this, she wanted to go home and think up another way for them to prosper—a crawfishing venture, maybe, now that they had some money for traps and bait and sacks. "Can I see him?"

"One at a time. Just a little while. He's in one eighty-six."

When she went in, he tried to smile. "Lo."

She walked up to the bed and looked at him, at the two drips in his arm. "I got the money from Oudry's," she said. He didn't respond, though he kept looking at her.

"What you looking at?"

"I don't know," he said.

"You too sick to look at me like that."

He closed one eye. "How's this?"

She walked to the window and pulled the blinds. "I got this idea. If we took the whole sum and put it into a used motor for that little twelve-foot johnboat, Abadie could show me where to set crab traps and a route of trotlines for catfish. Oudry's buys from two other women who fish, and he tells me they clear a hundred dollars a day when they can go out." She had the wad of bills held out to him like a folded green tongue. "Since I'd be using your boat and your half of the money, I'd split the profits with you."

He looked at the money, then back at her face. "You can string line and pick up crabs, but you don't know a damned thing about buying a used outboard."

She sat on the bed next to him, conscious that she smelled like mud. "You can tell me right now."

One hand rolled on the bed, palm-up. "I'm tired. I know you can't understand that, but I'm tired past the bone."

She put a cool finger lightly on the back of a flushed hand bearing a needle. "What horsepower?"

Sixteen

Old lady Fontenot came by complaining of cutworms in her tomatoes and Colette snagged her to watch her father and Matthew for an hour or so. She walked up River Street, noticing that the clock in the brick tower of city hall read seven o'clock. She was on her way to see Nelson Shapley, an old Yankee who worked on outboard motors. In spite of the fact that he had moved down from Cleveland to Tiger Island forty years before, he was still known as "the Yankee." He lived in a boxy house covered with greasy asbestos shingles. In the front yard was a thirty-foot Lafitte skiff turned upside down over several dismantled inboard engines. Not a blade of grass grew from the oil-soaked yard.

She knocked and had to wait five minutes, listening to grunts, cans being knocked over, a television being turned off. He appeared behind his screen door like a foul cloud. She saw his huge bare feet, his dirt-colored T-shirt and smudged khakis.

"Yeah?"

"Do you have any rebuilt outboards for sale? Around a twenty horse?"

He opened the door a crack and flicked an ash from his cigarette at her shoes. "I got a nice big seventy-five back there in the shed. Got a nine-nine."

"Too big and too small," she said, staring him in the eye.

"Well, you know those middle-sized engines don't burn much

gas. I can't keep 'em on the place. Have to charge a good price for one like that." He blinked something out of his eyes and looked her over slowly.

"Let's see a middle-sized one, as you call them."

"I didn't say I had one."

"So long, then. I'll go see Bobby Lodrigue."

He stepped out into his carport and scratched a tattoo of a spiderweb on his left bicep. "Wait a minute. Lodrigue just sells junk. I guarantee my engines."

"You got one like I need?" She had a foot turned away, ready to follow.

Shapely flicked his cigarette onto his bald lawn and reached into his pocket for a ring of keys. In a tin shed was an array of used outboards mounted in fifty-five-gallon drums full of orange water. He walked up to a Johnson twenty. "This here's a damn good engine. Overbuilt and heavy. Got more power than a modern twenty."

"Start it."

He looked at her and rubbed his caterpillar stubble. "You that gal threw T-Bub Thibodeaux out on his ass."

"I guess I'm famous. Start the engine." Just like that, she said it, as if it were an easy thing to say.

"That was a good boy."

She ignored the past tense of the statement. "Good for what?"

He picked up a gas line from a six-gallon tank and plugged it into the engine, squeezing a rubber bulb built into the hose. Pulling out the choke, he motioned with a mocking bow to Colette to give the starting cord a pull, grinning around his cigarette as though she wasn't strong enough. She saw that she was dealing with someone who had never sold a woman anything. She wanted to get him off balance.

Colette put her back and shoulder into the pull, and the engine stuttered alive at once. She listened to it for a minute, shifted it into forward and reverse, watched it throw water, and then cut it off. The little shed filled with choking blue smoke, and she walked outside. "You guarantee it?"

"You know I do."

"How much?"

"Five hundred."

She spun around. "That's too much. It may be in good shape, but that engine's twenty years old at least."

"That's what it's worth," Shapley said, reaching for another cigarette, eyeing her carefully.

"Does it have transistorized ignition?" Paul had told her to ask this.

"Uh, no. It's got points."

"That's a pain in the ass to fix when you break down out on the water."

He looked back at the shed. "I guess I could take a little off."

"The paint's all faded and the mixture knob is broken off."

"How much you got to spend?"

"I've got cash."

"You got four fifty?"

"Hey," she reached out and thumped Shapley on the shoulder with her middle finger. "It's not worth four fifty. Lodrigue will let me have one for three hundred in that size."

Nelson Shapley laughed nervously. "But it won't last you but a year."

"Maybe that's all I need out of it," she said, backing up two steps toward the street, putting her hands in her back pockets.

Shapley's eyes disappeared for a moment in cigarette smoke. "That's a real desirable engine, that twenty."

"Aw, bullshit. It's not big enough for a commercial fisherman."

"How much money you got?" He took a long drag, eyeing her jeans.

"Now if I told you that, I'd be plenty stupid." She turned from him and cocked her hips but did not walk away.

Shapley ran his dark fingers through his graying hair. "You know, everybody's got to make money. I've got to eat."

Something in his voice made her smile and she turned around. "I'll give you three fifty for your old Johnson. You ought to be able to eat on that for a while."

"Naw, I can't take that." He waved her off.

She looked down at the ground, at the imbedded spark plugs and piston rings paving his drive. What had Paul told her to say? "Has that engine got the old shear-pin system?"

"Yes. It's got the old pain-in-the-ass shear pin."

"Cash money. Three hundred and fifty. No 'I'll pay you next week,' no 'Twenty dollars a week,' no 'I'll pay you when I fish.' Right now, Mr. Shapley."

He took an interminable drag. Colette imagined that his lungs were going to catch fire. She backed away another two steps. "Can't do it," he finally said.

She took the money from her front pocket slowly, three crisp hundreds and a fifty. She held the bills up so he could see the way the number 100 curled around the corners. "Take this and put the engine in your truck and bring it and me up a few blocks on River Street."

"No. No, I . . . I don't think so," he stammered.

"That's fine," she said, turning and walking down his lumpy driveway.

When she put her foot in the street, she heard Shapley's smoky voice rising behind her. "Three sixty-five," he shouted. She put on a nasty face and turned around.

"What would you say to three sixty?"

He nodded, throwing his cigarette down in the drive. "I'd say Paul Thibodeaux's luckier than I thought."

*　*　*

Colette put her motor on the aluminum johnboat and tooled around the banks of the Chieftan above town while Abadie hung on to the middle seat and showed her the best place to rig trotlines and drop her crab traps. "Colette," he called over the noise of the engine. "Not so fast. This t'ing's so light, I feel like I'm riding in a pie pan." Each day for a week she sat in his chicken yard while Abadie showed her how to bait the traps, how to tie them off to empty Clorox jugs, how to tie the knots for the trotlines. He went with her one morning when the sky was only a beaten sheet of lead. They put out the first lines, sank the first traps, but by eleven o'clock Paul's *grand-père* had a spell and she brought him in and helped him across the levee, his spotted hands held over his heart.

She established her rhythm, baiting traps and lines, running them twice a day, continually repairing the twine, then delivering the catch to Oudry's for the payoff. When she saw herself actually clearing fifty dollars a day, she made more wire traps, put out more lines. Meanwhile, the last machine shop in that little corner of the oil patch closed up, and Paul despaired of working any-where. Even though he lay on the floor of the porch and did his prescribed exercises every morning, his strength returned only in tiny amounts. Once a week he kept the baby when Aunt Nellie couldn't come. On a different day, he would watch Colette's father, following him around the yard, keeping him from standing in the street. Once a week Colette would come by his house for a few minutes and share with him half of her earnings. She would hand him an envelope, ask him one question about his health, and then leave, the payoff just another beat in her new rhythm. Paul's mother got a job picking crabmeat at Oudry's and Paul's father wandered the town, attending Little League games or bumming a beer down at the Little Palace, anything to keep busy.

When Colette was tempted to buy herself something that was unnecessary, she thought of how many catfish she'd had to fight into the skiff to make what the item cost. In her economy, a cheap blouse might be twenty-eight catfish, a scarf two dozen crabs.

She began to fish much harder and smarter than anyone else. Asking questions, studying tides, moving locations daily, she brought in as much as the middle-aged men who'd fished all their lives. Through the steaming rhythms of August and September, she began to make good money, but the heat was like a hammer on her back. Even though she wore a straw hat, her skin browned like bread dough, and thick pink spots formed on her long fingers where she struggled with the twine. She dressed in loose long-sleeved shirts from the war-surplus store because they held the cooling sweat against her as she hauled up fish under the skin-searing sun. Every night she would shower and in the foxed bathroom mirror look for an expanding matrix of wrinkles forming in the corners of her eyes. She would see how the sun was burning the dark gloss from her hair. The harder she worked, the more she trimmed back her hair, until by the beginning of October the inward turns of her locks rose under her jawbone like iron hooks. She saved money, gave Paul much less than half her earnings, and she told him this the first time she did it.

"It's okay," he told her. "You need to buy some new pants."

"What?" she asked. "What's wrong with my pants?"

"I don't see how you can get around in a skiff in them. They're too tight."

She had turned around once, trying to look at her own rear end, and knew that it was true: She was gaining weight. She thought of a couple of girlfriends from the bank who visited, how they were filling out toward thirty years old, and she suddenly hated the noodles and chili she was forced to eat, the cold cuts, the cheap hot dogs.

When the weather turned briefly cool in November, she still went out early, and when she had to break ice out of the bilge in late December, she still went out over the pot-metal whitecaps to pull up whatever pitiful catch she could. Even when the old fishermen stayed inside their drafty houses and trailers, huddled next to gas heaters smiling with heat, Colette was running her lines. One blustery afternoon she pulled up a trotline that stirred with five-pound catfish on every hook. She used a three-fingered grip on the big fellows the way Abadie had taught her. On the last hook was a small hardhead, and because her hands were cold, she hurried it off the line, but not before it finned her with a poisonous dorsal spike. She pouted at the dark well of blood in her palm. The wound burned all afternoon, and by the next morning her hand was swollen and throbbing. She would not throw away sixty dollars to see the doctor, so instead, she walked to Abadie's house and showed him the hole.

"What would you do?" she asked, standing in his kitchen.

He put on his glasses and looked. "I'd go to the doc and get a shot, me."

"No. What did you do in the old days, before you went to a doctor? I know you've been finned a hundred times."

He ran a hand over two days of white whiskers. "Colette. What's wrong with you, baby? You've got enough money to take care of this." He sat at his little kitchen table, and she took a chair next to him.

"I've got to save my money."

"For what?"

She held her aching hand and looked out the window toward an old chicken, ragged as cotton against the fence. "Someday Matthew and I will get some kind of break. I don't know what. Something good will come up, and I'll need my money. You don't know what it's like when I'm rocking my baby and wondering how I'm going to afford to send him to school, buy him a bicycle and clothes the other kids won't laugh at."

The old man scratched his white head. "Ey, you and Paul."

Her eyes shifted to his. "What about Paul?"

"He won't even buy himself a plate lunch down at the Little Palace."

"He's not spending his money?"

"Some goes to his mama, but most of it he's got in the bank."

"Paul? I thought he'd be buying his accordion out of hock by now."

The old man shook his head.

"What?"

"You think you know it all. He thinks he knows it all." He made a motion, as though he was chasing a fly off an ear, and then went into his bedroom, coming back with a faded bottle of Dr. Tichenor's antiseptic. "Let me see that hand." He poured the amber liquid into her palm and her feet drummed his wooden floor. Wiping the wound clean with a paper towel soaked in the antiseptic, he pressed it open. Then he went to the bottom drawer in his refrigerator and rummaged around with a steak knife in one hand, returning with a silver-dollar-sized cut of salt meat. He tied this into her palm with a strand of gauze. "Now, don't take this off—no matter how much it hurts—for twenty-four hours, no."

She was doubtful, and by that afternoon the place in her palm burned like fire. It felt as though the salt meat was sucking at the opening, and as she tried to watch television with her father that night, the salt meat seemed to move in her hand like a mouse. At bedtime she took a bath, her hand hanging out of the tub, thrumming like a radio. She slept soundly, then got up and tended to Matthew and her father, doing everything one-handed until the twenty-four hours was up. The hand had not hurt when she woke, and when she took the bandage and the meat away, she saw a whitened wound, clean of infection, though the disk of salt pork had absorbed a dark blue blot of poison or bad blood, something hurtful from her flesh. Another day, she thought, and I can go back out in the channel.

227

But with a scowling black sky and a fusillade of pecans on the tin roof, the weather turned cold enough to keep even her inside. The fish seemed to abandon the river, and in January she could work only nine days, and in February, four. In March, as usual in Louisiana, warm weather came with a two-footed jump out of the south, and she began working harder than before, coming in with skiffloads of supple catfish bound for the restaurants of New Orleans. She added new lines at Sugarhouse Bend, moved a set of traps down by Terrapin Light and Poor Man's Chute, worked longer days, getting home at six, in time to relieve whoever was taking care of Matthew and her father, throwing together a quick supper, washing the fish slime off of her in time to put the baby and the old man to sleep, hoping that they would indeed sleep all night.

Her lack of spare time was an anesthesia; the work gave her no time to think of what she was doing. But Matthew began to walk and to understand what it meant when she put on her washed-out work clothes. He followed her down the hall in the mornings, yowling. She heard him sometimes until she got over the levee. Whenever she had a close call on the river, she thought of him, wondered who would read to him, teach him about music. And there had been several close calls. Twice she had almost been run down by crew boats. Many times, she had nearly tipped over while working a line in a stiff current or alongside a driftwood raft. One time, a twelve-foot alligator followed a big catfish she was drawing in on her line. She was tired, paying attention only to the fish until a long crown of fangs flashed at her hand, and then the suitcase-size head came up for her. The animal had one scaly leg in the listing boat before she pulled the starter rope and skidded away, a big claw riding the rail and raking out a crab trap before slipping off the stern.

That was not as scary as the big snake. The river had been pooling after a sudden rise, and she had to run the skiff up into a patch of pigweed at the levee near Paul's house. When she stepped out of the boat, her foot caught in a root under the cover, and she went over, spreading her arms to break her fall, her hands smashing into the mud. An instant later she felt movement under her right palm. A mass of coils wrapped like a current around her upper arm, and without thought, she closed her hand on the snake's head, knowing its shape to be a moccasin's, knowing that if she let it go, it would strike. She pulled up into a crouch, thrashing her boot to free it, amazed as she lifted foot after foot of the snake from the weeds under her. The dull black skin told her it was a cottonmouth, and she screamed in her biggest voice for help. The head turned in her palm, and she gripped it tighter, standing up, yelling again, holding her arm out from her body, turning her face away. The snake coiled tighter on her arm, trying to push its head free, and she yelled again, her voice sailing along the green batture like a whistle note. She looked down the levee toward town, saw no one, and she yelled again in a loud, fractured voice. Colette stepped over a log and out of the mud, her left hand now over her right, increasing the pressure on the spade head. The mass of arrowy scales piled onto her arm, six feet of cold, live meat, and she was afraid she might pass out, losing control of the poisonous skull rotating in her palm. "Help," she screamed again, the snake now jerking at its head, its coils gyrating fiercely, its tail spanking her face and forcing her head back, eyes looking at clouds. "Help!"

"Hey, ya," a voice yelped from up on the levee.

She looked and saw a little man shuffle down toward her. He was dressed in jeans and wore no shirt. It was Gilbert Gravois, one of the trashy Gravoises from the edge of town. "Help," she pleaded.

"Hol' on there, beb. What you doin' to that snake?"

"I've got his head and can't let go," she cried, trying to keep the flickering tail from her face.

"*Mais*, that thing's a mile long." He ran his hand back through his oily hair to clear his eyes. "I ain't brought my knife."

"In the skiff," she grunted. "On the front bench."

Gilbert sloshed into the weeds and came back with her long fillet knife. He grabbed the snake close to her hand and cut it in two with one swipe, peeling the still-moving loops from her arm. Colette stood still as a tombstone, the head clasped in her hands, imagining it still moved. Gilbert wiped dark blood on his jeans and watched her.

"You can drop the head, yeah."

"I can't believe it's dead," she said through her teeth.

Gilbert motioned with his free hand. "Oh, yeah, it's dead, beb. You just relax and chunk that old snake head in them bushes."

She looked at Gilbert's squirrely eyes and the dusty stubble on his face and saw that he was trying to be kind, him a trashy Gravois, whose parents had lived in an abandoned school bus before they moved up to an abandoned trailer. He smiled at her, and she saw thousands of wrinkles and not many teeth. She remembered that he had been one grade ahead of her in school.

"Oh," she sang, pulling her left hand away and giving a baseball pitch with the right, knocking down a big thistle with the oozing head.

"Hey, you okay? You want me to go over and roust T-Bub?"

She bent down and washed her hand off. "No, that's okay. I owe you one, though."

He handed her the fillet knife handle first. "How'd you get that thing in you hand anyway?"

"I fell on it." She shook her head and looked down, slightly giddy.

He looked at the head and whistled. "If that had been me, I'd been bit ten or eight times, yeah."

She waved him off. He was paying her a compliment.

* * *

She worked into the new heat of April, noticing that when she talked to Paul, he hardly looked at her. One day when she handed him a share of her fishing, he grabbed hold of her fingers and turned up her palm.

"What," she said, letting him look at her hand.

"Your skin looks worried. It's even got a nap to it," he said. "You better work some lotion into those things." He pointed out the white, husky calluses under her fingers.

She took back her hand. "Some people work for a living."

"I'm getting better. Last week I did a little plumbing on the boiler down at Oudry's. I'm finally getting some strength back. And look." He held up his left arm. "It's rotated back like it was."

"Fine. You're getting younger and I'm drying out like a prune."

He tried to touch her hair, but she moved her head. "You gonna fish forever?"

"No. Something'll happen. The economy's got to turn around sometime." She stole a look at him, noting an improved color, an old saucy look in the eyes. "You tried to dance lately?"

"No place around here can afford to hire a band. You know me, I don't like a jukebox. I got to have it loud."

"Yeah, well, speaking of loud, Matthew's going to be yelling for his supper."

"You leaving him with me tomorrow?"

"Yeah, the usual time." She stepped off his porch and headed for the street. A few yards down the sidewalk, she turned, knowing that he was looking after her, but all she saw was an empty rocker swaying.

The next day around lunch she became overheated and tied up in a narrow pipeline canal. She had been bitten three times by big lake crabs, and her thumb ached from another finning. She poured ice water on her head and sat watching a pair of nutria cross in an arrowy wake. There was an explosion of white water and one of the rats disappeared in a cage of teeth as an alligator brought him under the black surface. Against the bank a blue heron stepped out to surprise a minnow with its fate. She felt alone and misplaced, waiting for something bad to happen. Colette thought of her mother, who should be with her and feeling the sun on her living back.

She looked down the tunnel-like canal and could see across the big Chieftan the bent, ugly tin steeple of the Pentecostal church jutting up from behind the levee. She imagined that all towns had a hell of a lot of ugliness in them and that people still chose to stay there, listen to the wind in the trees at night, sit on the porch in the dark and wonder at the empty street. Maybe Paul had been right about California and it was only a place for a vacation, a place that kept you away from blood kin if you moved out to stay. At that thought, Colette felt that her mother was in the skiff with her, and she turned around to confront nothing. Looking down at her sunburned arms, she began to cry. After a minute she became angry with herself for losing control and she ripped at the starting cord and, as if fleeing a ghost, twisted the throttle, charging her skiff down the brush-lined canal. She shot from under an arched willow into the main channel and instantly the sun went out in a rusty blur. Over her head loomed the Nashville bow of an empty oil barge making ten knots, and the skiff's engine cowl hung on a bow raker and stopped her at once. Colette flew over her boat's side and hit the water like a falling skier, skidding out into the open channel as the oil barge rolled over her rig. She stayed under, stunned, for ten seconds, coming up near the tug, waiting for someone to spot her. But the pilot had not seen the splash, and no crew were in sight as she floated and bobbed in the little tugboat's wheel wash. She yelled, but no one came out on deck, and when she tried to yell again, she got a mouthful of water and began to cough.

She treaded water until she spotted a twenty-foot open aluminum boat streaking toward her, and she put up her arms. As the boat slowed to keep from swamping her, she recognized the La-rousse twins. Their engine, a 115-horsepower Mercury with no cowling, smoked and spat as they came alongside and hauled her up.

"Hey, *bébé*," Victor said, his hands holding her upper arms as he made her sit on the deck. "You all right?"

"I guess so," she said, blinking water from her eyes.

"We seen that freaking *cou rouge* run you down. You want us to go jump on his stern and make grind meat out that wheel-man's ass?"

"No," she croaked, coughing up a cup of river water. "It was my fault."

Vincent cast a dark look after the tugboat where it slid around a bend, hugging the bank. "If T-Bub was fit, we three could catch that sombitch where he drinks and put his nose in his pocket to bring home and show his mamma."

She wiped her face with a hand. "What you doing out here?"

"We fixin' this skiff for Max Tinney," Vincent said. "We in the fixin' business nowadays."

She looked at their tattoos and blinked again. "I'm glad you were out here. Any chance of fishing up my skiff?"

Victor spat in the water over his nattering engine. "We saw it happen. That poor little Johnson knocked his brains out on that bow rake."

"Colette, you know you got thirty-five feet of water here at least," Vincent said. "And a bottom current to boot. I don't think the sheriff could find it with his body boat."

Colette sat on the wide skiff's front bench and put her head in her hands. "Oh shit."

"Yah." Victor nodded. "We gonna bring you by Oudry's and give you a ride home."

Vincent gave his twin a look. "What gonna happen if Brenda sees us with a woman?"

Colette squinted up at them. "Didn't you boys get married last year to the Thibaut sisters?"

"Yeah," Victor said. "Ain't been in jail since." He shook out his oiled-down curls.

Vincent looked upriver at an approaching clamshell tow and put the engine in gear. "They nice girls, but they don't make money like you, no."

Victor spat over the bow twice. "If Lucinda ever get off the sofa and away from the damned soap opera, maybe she could work some."

"Yah." Vincent nodded and put up one finger for emphasis. "Brenda lives at Wal-Mart. Every time I see that woman she going to buy polka-dotted toilet paper or mirrors framed in plastic bamboo." He gave Colette a worried look. "We can bring you to the dock, but if we ride with a good-looking woman through town in our truck, they'll bitch at us for a month."

"That's silly."

"That's Lucinda and Brenda," they shouted together over the engine.

"They know me," she protested.

Vincent and Victor looked at each other, then back to her. "Colette, when Paul brought your cousin home in his truck, you walked away from him like he was a Yugo with a cracked block." The engine cut off and they coasted into a tire lashed against Oudry's dock.

"It wasn't the same thing," she told them weakly. She didn't want to ask Aunt Nellie to have to load up Matthew and her father to come get her, so she called her uncle Lester down at his office, but there was no answer. Next, she called Paul, and he drove down in his father's car, which he had patched up.

When she got into the front seat, she realized she was shaking.

"What's wrong?" Paul looked at her shirt. "You're all wet."

She told him what had happened, that it was her fault. He convinced her that they should pick up her father and Matthew and eat over at his mother's for supper.

"You need a break. Mamma's got a big pot of red beans on."

"I got a *big* break coming. I'm out of work." Leaning her head against the window, she turned the air conditioning vent onto her face. "I'm almost glad. It's so damned hot out there."

"You could buy another boat and motor with what you've got saved up." He turned around in the clamshell lot of the fish dock, sending a cloud of white dust drifting north.

She held up her hands and looked at them. "I don't know." She knew he was looking at her. "Paul, am I still good-looking?"

"In a wet kind of way."

"Don't take this wrong, but do you find me desirable, like, you know, when we were married?"

He let out a long sigh.

"What's wrong?"

"I wish you were desirable to me."

"What? Oh no."

He patted her on the knee like a brother. "Relax, babe. You still good-looking. But that desirable business caught me off guard a little bit. You know, I ain't had a hard-on since the accident."

She frowned. "You don't want women anymore?"

"The doc said it would come back."

She stared straight over the hood. "Do you still want to dance with women?"

He smiled, the first real smile she'd seen in a long time. "I dream about that," he said. "Day and night."

In the middle of the meal, Colette's face snapped up. "Where's Toot's Sweet Lounge?"

Paul's father ducked his head. "That's a dump on the back swamp road to Cayenne."

She swallowed a forkful of beans and chewed thoughtfully. "Last month, I was running lines by Sugarhouse Bend and Mr. Guillot was down at the end of his lines by me and he paddled up and asked if I was planning to shoot nutria when the season reopened. He said he heard that I was a good shot. He also told me that there's a rifle match with a five-hundred-dollar jackpot the first Saturday of every month at that lounge."

"That's day after tomorrow," Paul said.

"Mr. Guillot asked me to keep it under my hat because the betting's illegal."

"Hah." Paul's father cleared his throat, then reached for a round of French bread. "There ain't no law around Toots. It's ten miles from the nearest house, and there's a cable ferry on either side of it. If someone wanted a cop, they'd have to write a letter."

"How do they do any business?" Colette spooned a second helping of beans onto her father's plate.

"Mostly fishermen and a few trappers. They got a landing across the road on the bayou, and a wharf in back of the building on a logging canal." Paul gave the old man a slice of bread, put it into his fingers. Colette watched this and pursed her lips.

No one said anything for several minutes, then Colette stood up. "I'm going to enter that shooting match."

Except for Matthew, everyone stopped chewing at once. Paul cleared his throat. "Uh, Toots makes Scadlock's Boiler Room look like a gay bar. I stopped there once coming back from Verrett Landing and like to never got out alive."

She sat down. "How can they be worse than we've seen around here?"

"Etienne and the Larousse twins don't hold a candle to them. Some are half-Indian and half-redneck with maybe a little Cajun and Spaniard thrown in."

Colette drew her lips into a thin line. "Do you think there will be a fight?"

"Does a three-legged dog swim in a circle?"

"Saturday, too," Paul's father said. "The Partians and folks from Cayenne will be there rubbing shoulders with the swamp rats."

Paul put his fork down. "It isn't safe. When I was there, I didn't see one woman."

"Let's bring someone with us to get me out if things get rough."

"Who's that big?"

"The Larousses would go."

He shook his head. "Brenda and Lucinda."

"Oh yeah." Colette sat back from the table and looked up at the crucifix over the kitchen door. "How about your brother? He used to be a good scrapper."

"No, ma'am." Paul's mother shook her heat-tightened curls. "You not getting him in any trouble."

Colette put a hand on her arm. "I don't mean he'll get in a fight. He'll just help me get away from the place if trouble breaks out."

"No." She shook her head until the curls jittered like springs.

Colette turned to Paul. "Well, I guess we can't go if I can't have a couple big fellows to protect me," she said, putting out her lower lip and giving Paul her darkest, sweetest smile for the first time in years. He saw it and got a chest pain. It was such a mean thing for her to do that he was delighted beyond all measure.

Saturday afternoon at one o'clock they were on the serpentine road that ran through Pierre Part, on their way to Toot's Sweet Lounge. To their left a glimmering bayou merged with the unlined highway, water pooling up onto the asphalt. Paul was feeling good. He was piloting his brother's pickup, the first vehicle he had driven out of the parish in months, and Colette was with him, her rifle between her knees. He told her not to put on perfume, that she must be as unnoticeable as possible. She wore loose-fitting work jeans, a baggy lavender cotton blouse, and no jewelry, her hair straight and trimmed to the jaw.

He hit the brakes to slow down, scanning the low wooden houses passing on their right. In one yard an old cast-iron bathtub was sunk vertically, half its length into the ground, facing the road. Inside its shelter stood a carefully painted statue of the Blessed Virgin. Behind the shrine, a Lafitte trawler rested on oil drums, a venerable plank boat named *Crazy Ass*. Paul stopped, bumped the horn once, and almost immediately Etienne the giant mounted into the cab like a big cumulus, wearing a white knit shirt and a ton of cologne.

"Allo, dogmeat," he said, smiling widely. "You right on time. What's this about you buying me free beer?" He turned the rearview to comb his thick sandy hair.

"We're going to a rifle match at Toot's. Colette is going to shoot for money. If there's a fight, I want you to help pull her out."

Etienne banged the dash lightly with a huge fist. "Damn. If I'd knowed we was going to that hole, I would have wore a oyster sack. You sure you don't want to go over by Paincourt-ville? The cane farmers gonna have a peaceful little dance with a jitterbug band."

"Not unless they're going to have a shoot," Colette said.

Etienne brought his eyelids low and gave her a narrow smile, showing only his big bottom teeth. "You still pretty, even though you been fishing awhile."

"Etienne, I have a rifle."

They drove ten miles past Pierre Part through Molineaux's swamp. Second-growth cypress trees arrowed out of two feet of duckweed-covered water. Snapping turtles and water moccasins sunned in patches of hyacinth. At a turnoff, Paul steered the truck onto a one-lane shell road that cut into a more savage section of swamp where the water stank and the snakes coiled at the road-side, building courage to cross the hot surface. After a few miles, they reached the cable ferry at Stump Bayou and rode across with one other car, an old Dodge idling in a bullfroggy rumble of smoke. Down the road was Toot's, a sixty-by-thirty-foot tin-roofed box set behind a parking lot paved with bottle tops and flattened cans. The outside was painted brown, but over that grew a thick layer of bright green mildew, thicker near the bottom, where the rain splash fed it. The front wall of the building was chewed by the bumpers of customers' trucks, and the perimeter of the front door was one greasy smudge. The bar's name was painted in green on a metal rectangle propped on the roof, nearly illegible from rust. Next to the door was a warning written on a flattened Kotex shipping box: NO MINNOR ALOW.

Etienne the giant bent down so he could see under the folded-up visor in the truck. "Hey, man. Last time I was in here, some-one tried to hit me with a slot machine. This place is a toilet without a handle."

A bowlegged trapper walked into the bar carrying a Browning automatic .22 rifle. "Let's go in with the gun," Colette said. "No sense in leaving it out here to get stolen."

Inside, the bar had dusty pine floors, scratched and gouged plywood walls, and a drooping, water-stained Sheetrock ceiling. To the left was a long bar backed with a forest of liquor bottles. To the right were a few bare wooden tables, a blank expanse of dance floor, and a cracked and faded Rockola jukebox with strap-ping tape holding its glass bubble together. Several middle-aged trappers sulked at their tables, dressed for Saturday night in un-tucked thin plaid shirts, sharing long-necked beers with two sun-burned women. "See," Colette said. "There are women here. It's not gonna be so bad."

Standing near the bar were twenty or so younger fellows, stout and shaggy, many in rubber knee boots and short-sleeved denim shirts. They compared rifles and waved money around for side bets and entry fees. One fat, dark man held a long-necked bottle in his right hand and poked another big fisherman with his right forefinger, sloshing beer down the other fellow's shirt. The man with the wet shirt grabbed the bottle and turned it upside down in the fat man's belt. This caused a momentary reshuffling of the room, but no punches were thrown, and the fat man ordered another beer, waddling out to the spindly wharf at the rear of the building to dry in the sun.

When Colette walked into the bar, she drew many stares, and when she paid the entry fee, everyone who noticed her either smiled bitterly or glowered. Paul looked about at the smelly crowd and bent down to her. "Let's go back home. It's not worth it."

She waved him off. "Do you know how hard I have to work to get five hundred dollars?"

Paul made a face and turned to Etienne, who was already back from the bar with three foaming cans of beer. "Here's your change, dogmeat," Etienne said.

"I don't think Colette wants a beer."

"I know. These two's for me."

The jukebox came alive and several couples stood up to dance. A Sabine Indian, his face the color of burgundy, came up to Etienne and poked him in the ribs. "My wife says she wants to dance with you," he said, his expression unreadable. Etienne glanced at the man's sheathed hunting knife and followed him through the crowd.

Paul turned toward Colette in time to see a gray-eyed young man say something to her under his breath. She flashed around, her rifle upright, and pumped a shell into the chamber. The young man turned quietly to the bar as she backed out of his reach. She looked at Paul and said, "Save your strength." He took a long pull on his beer and watched her lower the hammer on the Winchester.

A man wearing waders and carrying a Ruger carbine walked up to Colette and smiled, showing two huge incisors, a hole rotted out between them the size of a cigarette burn. "*Bébé*, you wanna bet you ain't gonna win?"

"I don't bet unless the odds are good," she said, looking away from his brown eyes, in one of which a cast floated like a fingernail clipping.

He snorted. "You want odds? Ten to one you don't win," he said.

"Here's my ten," she said, waving a bill at him.

"Easy money," he leered.

The bartender, hearing the exchange, went in for another ten dollars, as did a freshly slicked-back Partian who had just come in the door. Two others bet before she ran out of money.

The bartender yelled that the match was going to start and that the shooters would fire from two double windows in the rear of the building at a target rail set up above the L-shaped wharf. Only .22s could be used, no scopes allowed. Men began thumbing rounds into clips, filling tubes, checking their sights. Colette looked to the wharf, a narrow rotting structure running out into the shallow swamp. A dozen pirogues were tied up on the left, away from the target area. The shooters would be given a series of progressively harder targets. Each shooter would have to knock down ten small tomato juice cans out of ten to qualify. Colette judged the distance to be seventy-five feet. No problem. Just a heat to get the drunks out of the way. She turned to Paul. "I was hoping there would be more time for everybody to drink before things started."

"You better spit on your sights," he said. "There're a couple good rifles here."

"I've got a good rifle, too," she snapped. "You want to bet against me, go ahead." She gave him a mean look.

"Not me," he said. "I've seen you shoot the gnats off a rat's ass."

"That's a little better," she said, still scowling. Just then the crack of a rifle broke through the barroom and the sweet, dusty smell of gunpowder blew back through the window. The match had begun.

Etienne cleared a path to the rear door and leaned out. The fat trapper with the wet pants cranked the bolt of his old Mossberg ten times and knocked down ten cans, most of them falling into a skiff five feet below the two-by-four rail. A balding, bony kid picked them up and reset them, an unpunctured side facing the building. Cans blown off into the water were replaced with fresh ones. As the kid scampered into a pirogue on the left, another rifle popped. Colette looked behind her. Nearly forty men had entered the contest. She watched the tall, clean-shaven fisherman with the new Browning automatic knock all the cans down in fifteen seconds, and someone behind her cursed. The next man missed the first can and was disqualified. The next missed on his last shot, began screaming, and threw his rifle like a spear at the tenth can. The kid sullenly watched it arc and hit the water but did not try to retrieve it. In a general cry of "Asshole," four men grabbed the shooter and threw him into the parking lot, where he landed on his butt in a cloud of shell dust.

Over the next hour, shooter after shooter qualified. One of the experts was a dark, skinny man who said he was from Cayenne but who had an exotic northern accent. He wore a Marine Corps camouflage cap and shot a heavy-barreled bolt-action military training rifle. He took his time with the cans, ticking them off the board with neatly placed center shots. An old Partian everyone called Gris-Gris shot all ten while seated in a chair pumping an octagon-barreled Remington, a cold beer held in his crotch. More men came in through the front door. A gang of oilfield workers pulled up outside in their red cement-pumping truck.

Colette made the qualifying round, but at the end of the cut, only seven shooters had been eliminated. The next stage of competition involved hitting ten tomato sauce cans that were lying down, their bottoms toward the shooter. An entire skiffload of small cans floated alongside the wharf, saved from a month of Bloody Marys from three bars. This new set of targets gave more shooters trouble. Colette took her time and tried to relax, all her shots finding the targets, though one bullet struck a rim. At the end of the round, twenty shooters remained. Those who fell out of competition drifted back to the bar to drink and tell lies, and the overall commotion level increased, voices racketing off the plain wood walls. Colette watched the boy place a slotted four-foot-long flat bar of steel on the target rail.

Behind her she heard Etienne guffaw. "Heeey, girl, that's your pretty little ass. I know what that thing is." She watched as the kid carefully lined up ten bottle caps in the slot. Colette put her head down and rested her eyes, trying to figure how many catfish made up five hundred dollars.

One shooter squinted out the window. "Shit, what's them things?" he asked. Another only whistled.

"Come on, podnuhs," the bartender shouted. "Bottle tops at seventy-five feet." He was bald and little, with a big droopy mustache, and seemed to be the only man in the room having a good time.

The first shooter, a youngster with a Winchester single shot, got six down. The next man got six. The third knocked down seven, sending the first two contestants cursing to the bar. For a while no one could top that, then the old man called Gris-Gris raked the gray hair out of his eyes and shot eight. Colette shot next and missed the first cap. A beery laughter rose behind her, making the tops of her cheeks burn. She pumped her rifle, knocked down seven, missed another, and drilled the last. No one could do better until the last shooter, the man with the marine camouflage cap. He went through eight straight without a miss, and some shooters turned away for the bar, figuring the match was over. He was shooting smoothly and with increasing rapidity. Colette hoped that he would get carried away with himself, become overconfident. He smiled broadly when the eighth cap spun like a quarter over the dark swamp, worked the bolt on his rifle, and fired as soon as his finger touched the trigger. He missed. The double windows in the bar suddenly filled with faces. The man in the cap blinked, worked the action of his rifle slowly, and listened to the hush mount behind him as he lined the last cap up in his sights.

At this point Colette had a religious experience. A dragonfly lighted on the end of the man's barrel the instant he pulled the trigger, and he missed. She didn't hear the roar of cursing and the rattle of chairs and beer cans that cascaded out into the swampy air. She watched the emerald dragonfly flitter off above the duckweed like a little lace-winged angel sent down to make sure she did well in the match. A surge of confidence rose up in her as she turned around to look at her competition: four men, clear-eyed and hungry for money. It was time to reload.

This time the bottle caps were laid flat. The first shooter was Gris-Gris, who hugged down on his Remington as he sat in a ragged vinyl chair. Behind him the men made noise, creating excuses for themselves, turning over long-necks, dragging tables around and rattling money into the jukebox. Gris-Gris became still as a stone and fired his ten shots, hitting four of the caps. Two men followed, shooting only three caps each. Colette watched them all, deliberately not thinking of the money at stake, focusing on the idea of God-given talent. That was the only thing that gave her a chance, an ability to put technique out of her mind and handle the gun like a dance partner, mining grace out of herself by instinct. This time, when it was her turn, she sat resting her elbow on the windowsill, lining up her sights on the target until sights and target seemed one object. Then she breathed comfortably and one muscle in her whole body moved, the one in her finger, and that as slowly as a minute hand. Her rifle spat and the first cap spun off into the water. She hit the next one and was so surprised that her heart began to race, sending little pulses down the length of the rifle. She missed four straight shots before calming down and nipping two more caps off the iron. The marine shot last, standing, and also knocked off four.

For the three remaining shooters, the bartender walked out on the wharf and set up the targets himself. He swung a two-foot piece of cedar with five kitchen matches sticking up from it out over the water. He nailed one end of the board to a piling top thirty feet from the window and told the kid to get off the wharf. As he walked back, he grinned at the three stern-faced shooters, twirling a hammer in his hand.

Paul sidled up to Colette, leaning into her. "You all right?"

"Just fine," she said, not really noticing him, already lining up the sights in her mind.

This time the marine went first. He became so still for the first shot, Colette thought he had gone asleep. Then the sound broke through the window. It was a miss. He raised his head and inspected the targets, lowered it, pulled the trigger, and missed again. Taking his hat and jacket off, he wound the rifle sling around his left arm and sat down in a chair. He hit two matches and missed the last. Colette studied his face and saw that he was not really as old as she had thought, more like twenty-one, just out of the service. He seemed not so much confident as shy. She tried hard not to like him.

Gris-Gris, she noticed, was older than she had first thought, close to sixty, a thick-skinned Frenchman, sunburned and wrinkled, bright of eye. But he shot down only one match, pounding his fist hard on the wall when he knew he was out. Enduring the taunts of the other shooters in the room, he thrust his Remington into its gun bag and walked into the simmering parking lot, saying nothing. Colette sat down and discovered that the matches disappeared when she sighted on them. The white shafts melted into her nickel sight bead. She rubbed her eyes and tried again. She was afraid to switch to the tang sight at this point. Holding her breath, she squeezed off a shot and cut a match in half. A hubbub rose at her back. She fired again and knocked down another. A smile snaked across her lips as she realized she would win the match. There was no way that she could miss three straight. Coarse shouts rose at her back as a wave of betting swept the bar. Men pulled bills from their hats and out of their socks and a babble of bad English and worse French filled the boxy room. Some sort of new reality was dawning on Toot's Sweet Lounge, and the men were betting on a woman's serious success.

She missed the next three shots. There was no way to catalog the anguish in the room. A fistfight broke out between two Partians, and several men began to dig through their dungarees for folding money. One man was in the parking lot, pulling the floor mats out of his truck, looking for a lost stash. The bartender sweated and cursed, handing out four or five long-necks at a time, gathering handfuls of bills from the crowd as though picking cotton.

The kid showed up with a cleaning rod and gun oil for Colette and the marine to use. "It's okay, yeah," he told them. "You better clean you barrels before the next round."

The two shooters looked at each other. "Ladies first," the marine said, smiling for the first time.

"Sure thing." She wished he hadn't smiled. She wished she hated his guts. She had been shooting standard-velocity ammunition, and her bore wasn't leaded up, so she just ran a tight swab through it, twice with oil, twice to dry. He scrubbed his vigorously with a wire brush, then they both loaded and waited for the next test.

The bartender shouted at them. "You take a break. You gonna need it."

Paul and Etienne came over from the bar with fresh beers, and she grabbed a bottle from the giant and took a swig.

"Ey, Miss America, it took me five minutes to get that one."

Paul put his hand on her shoulder. "You want me to get you a mixed drink?"

"No, this is fine," she said, stifling a burp. "I need something to calm my nerves. It's time for this."

"Your competition isn't following suit." He motioned over to the marine, who was leaning on the window frame, waiting for the next set of targets.

"Let him stay dry. I'd just as soon he drank a cup of coffee about now. Might make him shake." Within five minutes she drank half the beer, several bettors watching her with worried faces. She picked up her rifle, and it felt solid and comforting in her hand, the edges of the octagonal barrel precise and logical against her skin. She held it close to her and read the lettering on the metal, the patent dates and serial number. She wondered who in her family had fired it first, who had lifted it from its wooden box when it arrived from New Haven, Connecticut.

The bartender hurried out to the wharf in a rocking canter, stopped at a piling only twenty feet from the window, and nailed up another board with five matches rising from it. He came back in out of the sun and put his hands on the marine's shoulder, but he looked at Colette, a smile sliding from under his mustache.

Colette motioned with her beer bottle. "You're taking it easy on us," she said. "We're going to knock down matches again, but closer?"

The bartender shook his head.

"What's up?" the marine asked, glancing at the kitchen matches.

"You ain't gonna knock 'em down," the bartender said. "You gonna light 'em."

An outburst of guffaws came from the crowd. Etienne doubled over. Everyone liked the perverseness of the round, especially those who had bet against Colette, because unless she won the round outright, without a tie, she would lose her side bets, and everyone knew how hard it was to light a match with a rifle bullet. A new flurry of betting started, delaying the shooting for five minutes. During the course of the match, men were drifting in and getting caught up in the action. Nearly one hundred drank, danced, and jostled in the steamy bar, and yellow flies began to come in after the gathered meat.

The marine sat down, wrapped his left arm tightly in his leather rifle sling, and sighted. He missed once, twice, then stood up and blinked, stretched. He sat down and a yellow fly bit him on the neck just as he pulled the trigger, and he missed a third time. A Partian behind him remarked that no one could light a match with a bullet. He poked the man next to him and said that he might as well pay off. The match was going to be a tie. The marine fired a fourth time and Colette imagined she saw a fine dust fly off a match tip, but there was no flame. A fifth shot rang, and the shooter removed the remaining bullets from his rifle, left the bolt open, and shouldered his way to the bar. Colette smiled at the many unshaven and creased faces around her and took the vacant chair. The bartender retrieved a new target from behind the bar and set it up. "New shooter, new target," he announced from the wharf, spitting into someone's pirogue.

She lined up her sights on the first match but could not see the white phosphorous tip. She imagined where it was, eclipsed it with the front sight bead, realizing that even though it was behind the bead, she could miss it. Again, she had to shoot by instinct, what her mind could see, not her eyes. She squeezed off a shot and the match wiggled but did not light. A hush came over the room. One trapper who was watching with field glasses said, "What the fuck." She fired again and bit the head off the second match. Three men whistled. Pumping her rifle, she exercised her eyes, focusing on the window ledge and then the straight cypresses beyond the wharf, the blurs of moss hanging down to the water. Her next two shots were misses. She leaned next to the man who had the binoculars, smelling his sour shirt.

"Let me see your glasses." He handed them over slowly, and she studied the matches a long time. Biting her lip, she stood up and stretched as the marine had done, handed back the glasses, looked over the bar at the mildewed Dixie beer clock and then at all the wilted work shirts around her. "I have to go to the bathroom," she announced. Some men laughed and some yelled at her to shoot now and pee later, but she charmed a path through them as she made her way to the women's toilet through a narrow unpainted door next to the jukebox. Paul held her rifle and looked around the room. Etienne inched close, the hair on his forearms bristling against Paul's skin like steel wool. "Something's up, seems like."

Paul looked out into the sunshine at the matches, scanned the swamp, looked back at Etienne, and shrugged. They waited five full minutes, and then the bartender began to yell.

"What the hell's taking her so long?"

"Keep your drawers on," someone called.

"Get her out here so she can miss and I can collect," the man with the wet pants shouted. The men were amusing themselves with their yells and a dozen obscene suggestions about what she was doing in the bathroom, carping back and forth and watching the narrow door at the end of the hot dance floor until some voices grew truly angry. At this point the door of the ladies' room opened and Colette stood in it, holding the knob demurely, taking her time. She did not walk to the window, but went instead to the bar and ordered a Coke. When the bartender pushed a sweating bottle toward her, she shook her head.

"What's wrong?"

"I want it with ice, in a glass." She smiled politely, as though she was at the Hilton in New Orleans, facing a well-groomed bar back instead of a smelly little man wrapped in a spattered canvas apron. He found a tall glass on a pine shelf, put some ice cubes in it, and shoved it at her. "There," he said between his teeth.

"I want it," she said delicately, straightening her back like a fashion model, "with finely crushed ice." She dragged out the word *finely*. Several men hooted like mill whistles.

"She can bitch as good as she can shoot," a voice yelled.

The bartender looked quickly out the window toward the matches and began to say something, but didn't. He found a clean bar towel and beat the ice cubes into fine powder with a rusty claw hammer, then poured them into her glass. "Here you go," he said stiffly. "Swig it and shoot." Paul and Etienne looked at each other with narrowed eyes. Colette took her time with the drink, walked over to the window, and asked for the field glasses, studying the matches for a full thirty seconds.

"Get on with it," someone yelled.

She gave the glasses back to their owner, a ruddy, whiskered man who had a bite out of his left ear. "These are pretty good," she told him. "Where did you get them?"

"Found them on a dead man," he said, looking at her hard.

She sat down, took her rifle from Paul, pumped a shell into the chamber, rubbed a gleam of spit on the front bead, and aimed long, putting everything out of her mind and waiting for the sweet feeling of perfect alignment to form in her shoulders and chest, a feeling that the shot has been made before the trigger has been pulled, a knowing that the bullet will graze the top of the match. Letting the front bead sink like a pearl into the pocket of the rear sight, she waited for the sun to come from behind a cloud, and then she fired. A small dusty luminescence burst above the match into a gold flare as the sulfur ignited. A full second of perfect silence was blasted by a crash of recognition in Toot's Sweet Lounge, a hundred voices saying something different all at once. The marine came over and shook her hand, but before she let go of it, someone came up and pushed him in the chest, yelling that the marine nearest him had cost him a hundred dollars because he couldn't outshoot a damned woman. With an open hand, the marine swatted him like a fly, and three or four men began a grabbing, mixed-up shuffle. Colette quickly found the men she had bet with, and Paul snapped his fingers at the bartender for the five hundred. Etienne was across the room, arguing with someone over a side bet, and Colette gestured wildly to him to come on.

"I hope we clear this place before they find out, if they do," she said.

"What you talking about?" Paul wadded up all the money and shoved it deep into his gray work pants.

"I can't say," she whispered. Then her eyes grew wide. The man who owned the field glasses was out on the wharf examining the matches, touching them. "We've got to grab Etienne and get out of here, now."

The man with the field glasses charged into the room with the target in his hand. "How many of you bet with Thibaut"—he jerked his thumb at the bartender—"saying the match wasn't gonna be no tie?"

About twenty men yelled and began to move toward the bar, the impending fight subsiding for the moment. "Well, the matches he gave the girl to shoot at was wet. Look at how the color was running down the sticks." He held up the board to the room. "He tried to rig a tie."

The trappers and barflies were too drunk and angry to figure out exactly what was going on, but a misdirected, incoherent anger began to spread like propeller wash through the room; the scuffle around the marine boiled up into a six-member war, Etienne began to beat up the Indian and two men from Cayenne, and a dozen men jumped the bar, taking the bartender's clothes off, tying him to a chair, and pouring his best bar brands on his head. "Get the bastard's register," someone yelled, and a mad flurry of bills got handed around the room. The Indian's wife and two other women leapt out of a window into the parking lot, Colette matching their timing by hurtling through the door with her Winchester. A rooster of a man with long, greasy hair trailing down his back pulled out of the crowd and started after her. "Hey, bitch," he yelled, putting a claw on her shoulder and jerking her back in. Paul grabbed his hand and hit him twice in the face, but he didn't go down. The little man threw a stomach punch, and then both of them were rolling on the floor.

Colette stood outside, listening to the crash of tables and the thud of bodies, worrying that there were so many guns in the room. Standing on tiptoe, she looked through a window, hoping for a glimpse of Paul, but she saw only Etienne rolling the jukebox across the room like a boulder. She ran to the truck and started the engine, revving it hard, hearing it pop like a rifle when she let off the gas.

At this point a lone state trooper on his weekly road check rolled into the parking lot. He saw the fight spill out of the door of Toot's Sweet Lounge, and he pulled his nightstick. But as soon as he walked up to the building, half the crowd fell on him like a wave, took away his gun and gas, dragged him across the road to the bayou, and handcuffed him hugging a cypress. The man with the wet pants started the flashers on the cruiser and put it in neutral before a gang pushed it into the bayou. For a while it looked as though the brawl might end, but then some men wanted to take the policeman's clothes off. "If you want to do that, you got to be queer," an Indian shouted, and another fight kindled in the road between the Indian's relatives and neighbors and a band of Halliburton cementers from the Smoke Bend oil field. Some men ran back inside, where fighters were still bumping about like maniac children in an oversized cardboard box. Two young men wearing white shrimper boots fell out of a window and began limping up the road toward the north. Etienne, his white shirt looking as if it had been chewed by tigers, appeared in the doorway, Paul slung over one shoulder. He jogged for the truck and got in as Colette gunned the engine, heading south for the ferry.

Etienne looked back over the truck bed. "Let's get the hell out of here before they eat the fuckin' truck. I never seen people so hard to knock out."

She looked at Paul. Blood streamed from a cut in the middle

of his forehead, and his lower lip was split. "He was right," she said. "It wasn't worth it."

Etienne wiped the blood from his big nose with a handkerchief. "Oh yas, it was." He pulled a cabbage wad of bills from his pants. I made nine hundred thirty, and I don't know how much dogmeat got."

"Eleven hundred twenty-five," Paul mumbled, a rill of blood running from the corner of his mouth.

Colette watched her rearview as she sang around a curve. She saw the ferryboat guard with his hand on the gate and gunned the engine, blowing the old truck's sour horn. The guard backed away when she hit the brakes and skidded through the loose bed of shells on the landing, over the steel ramp, and onto the ferry's deck, where the truck bottomed out, bounced once, and subsided against the safety chains on the boat's starboard side.

Once she was off the ferry, Colette kept the truck humming along the asphalt at twenty miles above the limit. Paul wiped his face and fell asleep. A mile from his house, Etienne the giant's huge cow face broke into a grin. "Hey, Miss America. You sorry you moved back from California?"

She thought a moment, looking out at a pink trawler capsized in the roadside bayou, an egret clasping a propeller blade. "No," she yelled over the roaring air vents. "Things down here make more sense."

Seventeen

A unt Nellie Arnaud was sitting on the sofa, a highball on her fat right knee, when Colette came in. Matthew was in a playpen, bombarding her with plastic blocks. He acted surprised when his mother bent down to pick him up, as if she were a stranger.

Aunt Nellie looked the worse for wear. "Colette, I got to talk to you, *chère*."

"What?" She put the boy on the floor and he began to play with the laces on her brogans.

"Me and Florence and Misres Fontenot been talking."

Colette put up a hand to stop her. She knew what she was going to say, that she'd not been spending enough time with her father and Matthew, that the women had their own lives to deal with. "Say no more. I'll be spending more time at home, especially since I don't have a boat anymore."

"We can keep on helping, baby, but we can't be your husband, you know?"

Her eyes flashed at her aunt. "You think I should get married again? Boy, like *that's* gonna solve my problems."

Aunt Nellie drained her glass and put it on a side table. "I never thought I'd say this, but maybe you should take Paul back."

"You, of all people." She turned Matthew on his back and checked his diaper, and he lay there raising his arms to the brass light fixture hanging from the plaster ceiling.

"Look at the way he's been acting the past year."

"He's sick—that's why he's behaving."

Aunt Nellie finished her drink and rattled the ice. "Colette, you're as mean as a snake." She got her purse and jacked herself up off the couch. "He hasn't been dancing in a beer hall since he got back from California."

"They're all closed up," she said, her feelings hurt. Her aunt had never said such a thing to her. "When he gets his health back and things turn around so he can start making money again, then we'll see."

Aunt Nellie was heading for the front door, but she stopped and swung around. " 'We'll see'? Aha. Where there's 'we'll see,' there's a way."

"Yeah, well, like I said, we'll see."

Aunt Nellie walked out then, letting the screen slam quickly to cut off the mosquitoes. "He's grown up a lot, baby," she said, her mouth pressed against the screen. "How about you?" She slapped a bug on her neck and was gone.

Colette put the baby on her lap and thought about Bucky Tyler for a while, and then she remembered the sight of Paul in the hospital. Downriver a big tugboat whistled for a starboard crossing, and the baby raised his face to the sound. Colette watched Matthew and thought, her knee bouncing under him.

The next day was Sunday and she and the old man and Matthew went to seven o'clock Mass. Her father was clear and said the responses in the proper places. Sometimes he was mostly there, and she would let him walk the few blocks to church to say his rosary in the mornings. Other times Aunt Nellie would walk with him, let him go inside while she sat on the church steps and smoked, her dress pulled over her knees, the rolled-down tops of her stockings visible from the street. This Sunday morning he even sang the right melodies, and Colette basked in what was left of him.

Monday she wanted to visit a girlfriend in Beewick to show

off Matthew, and she called Paul to come sit with her father. He came over, still bruised in the face, and he knocked on the screen.

"Hello, Annie Oakley," he said, not smiling.

She gave him a close look, as though he were a machine she was considering buying. "How do you feel?"

"Not bad, considering all the footprints on my ass." He needed a haircut and a shave, but she saw that his color was good.

"I'm going across the river for a couple hours."

"I'll visit with him." Leaving her, he went inside and found the old man trying to make coffee with a drip pot. "Mr. Jeansomme."

"Hey, boy. You come to cut the grass?"

"Something like that." He found the kettle, filled it, and put it on a back burner. Then he loaded dark-roast coffee in the dripolator's basket.

"You doing all right in school?"

"Yes, sir." He got out the cream and sugar, sat down at the kitchen table, and waited for the water to boil. "You enjoy having Matthew in the house?"

"Who? Who do you mean? That little boy?" He sat down and his eyes moved as if they were watching mice run across the table. "He's good-looking and noisy."

"He's got strong lungs like his mamma." The kettle whistled and he made them coffee, hot and sweet, strong and full of cream. After a while, the old man stood up, ran a fist over his silver wad of hair, and walked down the back steps into the yard. "Oh Lordy," Paul said to himself, getting up and following.

They went alongside the tall house, through the front yard, and across the street toward the river. Mr. Jeansomme topped the levee and headed south, mounting the railroad embankment and toddling down the other side, stopping before a raft of idle boats: tugs, offshore supply vessels, and one fat-bellied shrimper, listing slightly, the nail heads in the hull streaking rust. There were no docks here and the boats were cinched off to willows. "Why are they all tied up?"

Paul had lagged behind, wanting to be invisible, just to see what he would do. Now he stepped up behind him. "There's no more work for these boats."

"That shrimper belongs to Lester Serpas. Why's he letting it run down like that?"

Paul looked down the slope. "It's an old wood boat. Maybe the bottom's gone." A trio of crows set up a racket high in a sycamore tree growing at the edge of an abandoned shipyard. Paul watched to see what they were fussing about, if there was a nest they were raiding. When he turned around, his breath caught. The old man was in the middle of a twelve-inch-wide gangplank that led from the bank to the shrimper. "Hold on, Pop." He ran to catch up, but Colette's father stepped on board and was waiting for him.

Mr. Jeansomme put his hand behind him on the blistered wood. "This is Serpas's boat. He built it himself on the batture behind his house. Look at the sheer in this thing." Mr. Jeansomme nodded to the deck and looked from bow to stern. He broke off a dirt dauber nest from the cabin overhang and sidearmed it into the river, where it skipped once.

"We better get off now," Paul told him. "Come on."

"This thing has hauled a lot of shrimp in its day." He pushed open the cabin door and stepped into the varnished air, standing behind the wheel and looking through the cloudy windows. Paul looked around himself, opened a door, stepped down through the bunk room and into the engine room.

"The engine is still on her," he said. He could see almost nothing and came back up out of the oily air. "Water's not over the planks yet."

Colette's father was humming something, turning the wheel gently one way, then the other, taking a voyage in another lifetime. Then he spun it quickly hand over hand to port, going around some log in his memory. Paul looked astern and saw a watery comma drift away from the rudder.

He wanted to say something, but the old man's eyes were vacant, and things had gone beyond words. Only touch was left, so he grabbed both shoulders and pushed him ahead deliberately, the way a little boat would shove a barge on a foggy night.

Not long after that, on a hot Wednesday afternoon, Paul had come in after working as a flagman on a resurfacing job at the edge of town, and he was treating himself to an icy Schlitz on the porch swing. He looked down River Street, down the sidewalk that humped over the roots of China ball trees and sycamores, down to the first crumbly brick buildings of the town. Colette was walking up, on the other side of the street, and he guessed she had come to talk about the boat she'd lost or some other money matter. Maybe she needed him to watch Matthew. She was wearing a faded pair of blue dress pants and a white cotton blouse. He squinted. A thin gold necklace spangled her bodice, and he sat upright. Directly across the street she stopped and looked at him a long time, as if she were a salesman rehearsing a spiel. A dump truck loaded with clam shells passed, then an empty pipe truck, and she stepped into the street, her eyes on him. He wondered what he had done wrong as he watched his ex-wife come on, giving off vibrations like a friendly Judgment Day.

"Hey, babe," he said.

She sat next to him on the swing, and he gave her room, putting a hand up on the chains on his side. She was wearing perfume, and at first the smell scared him to death. He counted up how much money he had in savings.

"How've you been feeling?" She actually looked at him.

"All right. I worked the road gang today. I feel all right." He made a muscle and put his arm back down.

"That's good."

"How's Matthew and your daddy?"

She nodded. "Matt's fine. Dad's the same, I guess."

"You, uh, want me to watch one of them for you or something?"

"No. Aunt Flo is over there for a little bit. I just wanted to get out."

He felt awkward, the way he'd felt when he was fifteen and out on a date, trying to figure what the girl was thinking. It had to come sooner or later, the sarcastic verbal slap, the complaint. He started to tell her she smelled good. He wondered if she was going on a date with someone. "You on your way somewhere?"

"No. Just out for a bit. I wanted to talk to you." She leaned back and looked into the side yard. "You still haven't fixed your car."

"No."

"Saving your money?"

"That's a fact."

She put an arm in back of him on the swing, not touching his shirt. "I came over to talk to you about something, and it's hard to do."

He emptied his beer and put the can on the porch rail. Mrs. Fontenot's old yellow pot hound walked slowly across the lawn and disappeared around the corner of the house. "You need some money for a new skiff?" He looked at her in the eyes then.

"No, it's like this." She put her palms up on the backs of her knees and began to explain things—what she wanted in the next five years or so for herself and Matthew. She didn't want to go out fishing again. She didn't want to live like a pauper in her parents' old house for the rest of her life. She explained things in an uncharacteristic calm, her voice thin but clear. "What do you think?" she asked when she had finished.

"That's good," he said quickly. "Who wouldn't want that?"

"I haven't thanked you for helping with Matthew and Dad."

"Hell."

"Thank you."

"Colette, one of 'em's my son and the other used to be my daddy-in-law."

She thought about this and nodded. "Okay."

"Why you telling me this?"

She frowned a little. "You're suspicious of something?"

"You're wearing that perfume I gave you three years ago."

"You remembered?" Her red mouth fell open.

"Yas, your big dumb-ass machinist ex-husband who uses coal oil as aftershave can recognize Adolpho." He moved his head toward the street.

She pulled on his arm, but he didn't turn to her. "I'm thinking of taking you back."

He felt a little rush go to his head, then spread downward to his heels. Her touch was what he imagined dope to be like. "What?"

"I don't mean right now." She began talking with her hands. "I mean if you can figure something out where we can put our money together, maybe a business or a service, something that could grow, something that would support us so we could buy decent clothes, a car that runs, a meal out once a week." She moved close and looked at his eyes. "We could try it again."

He had questions, but none of them seemed to matter in the damp cloud of perfume that captured him. "You telling me if I can start a business, get some money coming in, you'll marry me again?"

"I've thought about it a lot the past few days. You're different."

He shook his head. "You said it. I'm not a hundred percent. Sometimes I don't feel like a man, you know? I'm not making a joke when I say I might not be man enough for you anymore."

She tilted her head back, parted her lips. "You still don't get it up?"

He shook his head sadly.

"Not when you think of me?" She touched his ear and he made a face, pulling away slightly.

"I try not to think of you for a bunch of reasons. When you lose something, you got to forget it."

She put the swing in motion with a little kick. "Even when you wake up with a full bladder in the night, it's not up?"

"No, I told you. The doctor said he can't help."

She leaned into him and slid a hand around his waist. "Look at me."

He did—at her skin, which was like tan milk nowadays, at her powdery lipstick. He breathed her in. "Why?"

"Because I know you," she said. "I didn't before, but I'm beginning to."

His heart rate rose, and he felt he might be blushing. "Don't jerk me around, now."

"Remember the second time I kissed you? In high school?"

"Colette."

"Close your eyes." He did, feeling her sweet breath on his face, pouring over his nose and chin, and then something touched his lips like a butterfly's wingtips dipped in confectioner's sugar, causing his mouth to open slightly to a hot swipe of tongue. She did it again, and he sat up and opened his eyes wide. He was panting.

"You cured?" she asked.

He threw one leg out in front of him. "Well, I'll be damned."

Eighteen

He stayed up all night working over a yellow tablet, figuring, figuring. He called the whole region the next few days, looking for machinist jobs, but the nearest one was a hundred miles away in New Orleans, downtown, and didn't pay enough to justify the daily trip over.

A few days later, Colette called and asked if he knew where her father might be. The old man had seemed alert when he got up, so she let him walk to church by himself to say his rosary.

"I don't know, unless he went back to the shrimp boat." He heard scuffling noises on the line.

"Never mind, he just dragged up on the porch. What shrimp boat?"

"The other day he got away from me for half a minute and boarded the old boat Serpas's got snubbed off in the willows below the railroad."

"Why's a shrimper tied up there?"

"It's the old *Saxon*. Something must be wrong with it."

"Is it on the bottom or what?"

"No, it's afloat yet."

The phone fell silent for half a minute. Then she told him to meet her by the boat the next morning. She wanted to look it over with him. She called Lester Serpas, who had leased the boat three seasons before to old man LaBat. Serpas said the boat was made of cypress planks and was forty years old. It had been good for open-water shrimping out in the Gulf, but he was worried that the bottom was too soft to trust in the deep water any longer. He'd decided to retire the boat and let it sink. "It's okay yet, but I wouldn't want to get caught in a big storm with that old boat," he told her.

Colette called until she had a page full of figures before her: fuel estimates, the price of shrimp, ice, labor, batteries, licenses. She called Paul at home and made him contact Serpas again and question him closely about the engine.

They clambered all over the boat after daylight. Paul watched her poke at boards, bend over and free up the hoist. He had worked on a shrimper a few times as a teenager and remembered only a sore back and cut-up hands.

At lunch they sat down next to the pinball machines in the Little Palace and talked everything out. "It will take all our savings to rig that boat," she said, "and it might sink if we're not careful with it." She took a bite of French bread, chasing mustard off her lip with her thin tongue.

"We can have it pulled up on the ways for two hundred and fifty dollars just for a check. But Serpas had it up two years ago and coated the hull with fiberglass."

"We can't afford to pull it out. Do you think it's too far gone for deepwater work?"

He took a bite and chewed the question again and again. "I checked the bottom from the bilge, and the redneck who works down at the shipyard says it was patched up pretty good last time they had it out of the water."

They ate on in silence, Colette shifting in her chair, thinking. After a while, she began to cry, putting down her sandwich on its ironstone platter and looking around for a tissue.

Paul slid next to her and gave her a paper napkin from a dispenser. "What's wrong, babe?"

She leaned against his shoulder and let her tears run on him. The men at the bar looked quickly, turned back. One got up and put a quarter in the jukebox. "It's so scary," she said. "We could lose everything on that boat. Serpas practically wants to give us the thing, but it'll cost so much before we drop a trawl." Flashing through her mind were images of the rifle match, the hot days of fishing, hauling aboard thirty-pound rats in the dark.

"But we have to do something," she said finally. "There're just no good jobs anymore in this state. We can't even move away. I've got the house, and Daddy."

"I'd be just as unemployable somewhere else as here," he said. "I don't think many company docs would pass me yet." He watched her blow her nose into the napkin and pick up her head.

"I want some money for Matthew, damn it. I brought in some for a while and I didn't complain about what I had to do, but let me tell you, it's hard work catfishing for a living."

"You took your share of sun," he said.

"I look so damn awful. Have you looked at me?"

He put a hand on her knee. "You still good-looking."

"Still?" she almost shouted. "Did you hear what you said? You're talking about me as though I'm a ten-year-old sedan that someone has kept waxed and 'still' looks nice." She crossed her legs, calming herself. "My hair is all paint bristle. I have no nails, and I go around smelling like starch."

"I could find a boat and take over your fishing." He said this as he looked across the room toward an old whiskered man sitting alone at a table in the corner.

"Your heart wouldn't be in that. You dream of working on machines, not skinning catfish. The shrimp boat is a machine."

"How you know what I dream about?" He cocked his head and took a drink from a plastic cup of water.

"You used to talk in your sleep."

"No." He put the glass down.

"Yes."

"You never told me that."

She wiped her eyes and then her mouth, picked up her little purse, and put it on her lap. "That's right."

The next day they put their money together and bought the boat. As she signed the check, Colette's face contorted as though she were in labor. Immediately, Paul went down to the water and began recharging the *Saxon*'s batteries, blowing out the fuel tanks and lines, freeing up the winches, cleaning every electrical connection of their green complexions. A patched trawl was in the hold and they bought new rope for it, then hired Etienne as wheelman and Nan's husband, Raymond, as help. They fired off the old diesel engine and brought the boat at half speed up the river to the fuel dock and topped off the tanks. Paul noted that the engine ran evenly, but a worrying rope of blue smoke hung onto the exhaust stack.

Three days later, both families went to six o'clock Mass and prayed for shrimp. Barely an hour after dismissal, the *Saxon* floated under the discharge pipe at the ice plant and took on a half ton. When Colette paid the clerk in the ice-plant office, her eyes followed her money as it disappeared into the cash drawer.

On the dock she waved the first trip off bravely, managing to smile at the men. Paul cranked up the engine while his brother-in-law slipped the lines. Etienne turned the wheel for midchannel, already blowing three longs for the railroad bridge to open. Paul looked back at the dock, where his mother waved, holding Mr. Jeansomme's hand because he was close to the edge. His father, Nan and her kids, Colette and Matthew looked downriver ahead of the *Saxon* as though they were all trying to see into the future.

Paul stepped into the engine room when the boat was a mile below town. He checked gauges, looked for leaks; he listened like a physician.

Etienne called down the engine room's stairs, "Hey, Captain Dogmeat, you want me to hook this old tub up?"

"No. Take it easy with this engine."

Raymond came through a little door in the rear of the engine room. "Man, this thing's a antique. I'm glad to see you got us a skiff tied on the roof." He walked through and went up the steps to the wheelhouse.

After two hours Paul walked to the stern to see where they were. The boat rounded Derniere Chute, and the land began to fall away from him on both sides. He looked ahead at the watery belly that was the Gulf. A breeze sprang alive and the old shrimper heeled down into broad valleys of swells. To the southwest, the sky looked like the underside of a skillet with flames of lightning licking along its bottom.

Within an hour the broad, low waves turned to four-foot rollers, and a peppering rain forced the men into the wheelhouse to watch the heaving water through the boat's misted windows. Etienne kept the bow into the waves. Raymond mounted the wheelhouse bunk, a ledge over the companionway leading to the engine room. A lightning bolt struck fire from the flinty waves.

Paul whistled and slapped Etienne on the back of the head. "Be careful with my boat, it's the only one I got."

"Hey. Soon's I run out the back of this thunderstorm, I'll let you play with the wheel."

Etienne's face was set against the weather as if he were fighting the storm in a barroom brawl. Paul knew that Etienne could pilot a dredge through a hurricane, so he walked down the steps, opened the door to the engine room, and stooped in to listen. He saw the dark wink of water sliding under the deck boards and he threw a knife-blade switch to run the pump. All their money was here, he thought, every cent and then some. Colette's uncle Lester had helped to buy the ice. There in the shuddering compartment, he tried to imagine what it would be like to lose the *Saxon*, somehow survive, and then be brought under the eyes of the most beautiful woman in town, who had roughened her fine skin in fish guts and dead rats to buy the boat. If that happened, he thought, everything would be over for them.

He checked the bilge level again, then climbed into the wheel-house, catching Etienne in midstory. "And when we pulled that net up, we had shrimp running four to the pound."

"Damn," Raymond said. "You musta kept 'em on a leash."

"That's a fact. And the crabs in that trawl was big around as the steering wheel on a dump truck."

"No shit. They had four claws each, too, huh?"

Etienne turned and looked at him hard. "Hey, I was there pulling 'em in."

"You musta been dragging the Lake Charles canal where that nuclear power plant has its discharge pipe."

"Yeah, man. They glow in the dark. One night a running light burnt out and we just climbed the boom and hung a Lake Charles crab on the end."

Paul went out in the rain, checking nets and hatch covers. The wind was stiff from the south, but ahead the clouds were like pulled-apart cotton. By eleven they were in light seas and the thunderstorm was a black gilded racket off the stern. Paul and Raymond fed out the net, threw over the trawl boards, fought the corroded machinery and booms. They made a pass, drew in the net, and dumped the catch into a sorting platform on deck. Raymond turned the bill of his polka-dotted cap to the rear and waded into the catch, tossing out trash fish and crabs, cursing his tight welder's jeans.

Paul bent down and tossed menhaden and spot over the side. The shrimp haul was only forty pounds. Before the trip would cover fuel and salaries, they would have to make many such hauls. They put the shrimp on ice, saved two redfish to fillet for supper, and paid out their patched net once more. This time they brought up a shark, five stingrays, a sea turtle that didn't make it through the turtle excluder device, and thirty pounds of shrimp.

Etienne spotted a flock of pelicans and steered for them on the third pass, but when the net came up, there was a waterlogged timber and a ton of trash fish. A trawl board jammed Raymond's hand against the rail and he jumped around the deck in a circle as if strumming a banjo.

That night, they rode out another squall, not as rough as the first. In the varnished plank cabin, they watched the lightning and talked in low voices about fishing and women. Paul asked Raymond about his hand.

"Hell yeah, it hurts, man. You lucky you some kind of left-hand relation or I'd sue your ass for mental cruelty."

Etienne the giant reached over and pulled Raymond's cap off. "You got no mental to be cruel to."

The next day brought better luck, and by dusk they were tied up in Tiger Island, swinging off baskets of shrimp. Colette was in the office, tallying expenses on a Big Chief tablet and waiting for the payoff, which Nerby Billiot, the manager, handed to her. Paul saw her walk onto the dock and then stand next to a piling, trying to decide whether or not to jump down to the boat. He came out and stood on a hatch. "Did we make anything?"

She looked down at him with a little smile.

"I can tell it's not much, but we're not in the hole, right?"

"You cleared ninety-eight dollars, and that's after I deducted fuel, ice, and labor for the next trip out." She put the check for the catch in a pocket of her white cotton blouse.

"We can pay some on the light bill at your house," he said.

"Nope. Replace that gear on the hoisting winch." She crossed her arms and looked at the *Saxon*, running a red tongue back and forth over her front teeth.

Raymond asked her to take him home to Nan. He was dead tired and sunburned. Paul and Etienne rode the trawler down to the public wharf and tied up below LeBlanc's Machine Shop, where they washed down and locked the cabin.

Over the next few weeks the old boat brought up enough

shrimp to make ends meet and then some. The more money they made, the more amiable Colette became. Paul asked her once if he could come over late one evening and spend the night. She bit a fingernail playfully and told him not yet, and he was not discouraged. He went out that night to the Little Palace, drank several rounds, and kidded with the old men. But when Ray-Ray showed up and asked him to go over to a dance in New Iberia, he thought a long time about a tight accordion band and hot two-stepping on a waxed floor before saying no.

On the boat he endured the rocking squalls, snagged nets that took a day to repair, and endless hot days when the Gulf, spread out like a mirror, would yield only seaweed and old tires. Even so, most of the out-of-work men in Tiger Island envied Paul and his crew; though they worked hard for no great profit, at least they had something to do. The front porches and backyards of town were burdened with young men either waiting for their jobs to come back in like a sluggish tide or daydreaming about moving to Texas or Florida, anyplace that would get them away from their yards, where they puttered daylight away cleaning awnings, touching up peeled paint, repairing lawn mowers, expending any effort so they could look in the bathroom mirror in the mornings and see a working man.

For three days Etienne couldn't work, so Paul called down his list of friends until he got to Vincent Larousse, a fair wheel-man. Some trips, Paul's father would come along, though the next day he'd have sore shoulders and see spots before his eyes. One time Colette's uncle Lester volunteered. Paul watched the old insurance salesman warily as he waded into a fresh catch to cull out stingrays and crabs, wearing his antique two-tone wing tips. He was by far the best cook among all of them and wore a red embroidered apron with pride when he stirred his own pot above the little propane stove in the wheelhouse. Gradually the *Saxon* became a project of relatives and friends. One day Uncle Octave came aboard and the crew had to endure two days of jokes about goats and testicles. Paul's brother, Larry, came on as wheelman when Vincent got called out on a temporary welding job. Colette's brother, Mark, came out and complained for two days about the politicians and how they'd turned the state into a wasteland by courting only one industry for fifty years: big oil. Even *Grand-père* Abadie rode on one trip and cooked, but the heat was too much for him. Paul watched him trying to help with a catch, playing with a crab, trying to grab it and flip it over the side. *"Ah, tu veux manger mon doigt?"* he asked, teasing the snapping claws. When Paul was eight years old, riding in the cypress skiff, he had heard Abadie ask the same question of a stray crab raising its claws from the muddy bilge. Abadie probably still thought of Paul as a child, someone who needed all the help he could get. The old ones never admit that you grow up, he thought, looking over at Colette's uncle Lester, short, overweight, dressed in worn polyester pants and a fifties-era fedora. Only Lester's memory of Colette as a sweet-faced girl-child could bring him into the boiling waters of the Gulf to fold up his arthritic knees and pick out from the shrimp the stinging hardheads and finger-killing oyster fish. Only in a place where people had known them as children could he assemble such a crew.

The fish dock began asking him for crabs, so he saved them in moss-covered hampers and brought in more money that way. Paul wondered when Colette would say to him that they were on their way: that they could keep doing this, or buy another boat, or put a new bottom on this one, and then get married. He didn't speak to her about it because only she would know when he would prove himself. His illness had taught him that patience pays off, because his strength was coming back, slowly, the way a bone grows.

In the next three weeks he made ten trips. The boat began to shed its old paint, and heavy seas worked caulking out if its seams. The nail heads in the hull showed red daggers of rust, but he made money and everybody in town knew it. He took his father and Colette down to the Little Palace one night, drank six rounds with them, and felt damned good. His luck seemed to be turning; Colette's hair was growing longer, and her skin was losing the sun, taking on soft tones they had both forgotten. The Caprice was running again, and she could visit friends, shop a bit. One morning, taking the newspaper on her walk, she read that Bucky Tyler had been sent up for nine years. When Paul untied the boat that night to move it down to the fish dock, Colette leaned out from the wharf and gave him a long, drifting kiss, which he drank down like ice water on a hot day.

She watched the current catch the *Saxon* and drift it south like a tainted cloud, then called out, "I have to take Matt to the pediatrician in Beewick for free shots and checkup real early. What time are you heading out with the boat?"

He stepped into the wheelhouse and started the engine. "Late," he yelled. "I have to wait for Etienne. It'll be eight-thirty maybe."

"Can you stay with Daddy until then? Mrs. Fontenot is supposed to be there by eight. I hope to be back by nine—earlier than that if everything goes quick."

"I'll come over."

She walked to her car and opened the door, but before she got in, she looked at his face in the open window of the wheelhouse. "Catch a ton of shrimp" is what she called. "When you figure it's time to come in, make one more pass. Then we'll get your car fixed." He waved and turned the boat into the channel.

The next morning at seven he walked up onto the long porch of Colette's father's house and knocked. This was just a habit. Even if the old man was ten feet from the door, he wouldn't answer. Paul walked in and called, but he heard only the buzz of a wasp trapped against a windowpane. One by one he looked through the high-ceilinged rooms downstairs—the echoing kitchen, the spare bedroom, the music room, where Colette's old George Steck gleamed in the corner. He was tempted to press a key, but he pulled his hand back.

The kitchen door was open, so he went down into the yard, which was fragrant with gardenias, and called for him. He checked the old workshop and the leaning garage, finding only the smells of rust and kerosene. He walked back inside and upstairs, passing through the bedrooms and the little office. They were all empty. He sat among his father-in-law's tangled sheets and used the phone on the night table to call Aunt Nellie.

"Hello?" she said in the middle of a fit of coughing.

"You better quit those cigarettes."

"What you want, Paul?"

"I'm supposed to watch Mr. Jeansomme, but I can't find him anywhere."

"Did you look in his workshop?" She did not sound worried.

"Yes."

"Well, what's today? Friday?" There was a long silence on the other end of the line as she inventoried the old man's habits. She coughed fiercely and then gasped. "Open the top drawer to his chest and see if his rosary's there."

He did what she asked and found an old Sunday missal, a Way of the Cross booklet, a novena book, several holy cards, and a dozen handkerchiefs. "No rosary," he reported. "What's this about?"

"Nothing. Friday at six-fifteen, the Ladies' Altar Society has a Mass and says the rosary. That's why his rosary's gone. Remember? When you were a little bitty, you used to serve that Mass. Swing by the church and pick him up, honey."

He walked four blocks, turned a corner, and saw the rosy brick church, a Gothic design built before the Civil War. He pulled open a twelve-foot-high door and saw that the east windows were blazing with sun, Adam and Eve being driven out of the garden, St. Blaise healing a throat. Mrs. Adele Foret was coming down the aisle, a pixie smile painted on her powdered face.

"Paul, baby, he's sound asleep," she told him, motioning to the middle of the long church. "He's been that way forty-five minutes. We just went on without him, you know?" She reached up and straightened the collar on his work shirt, then moved off toward the door.

He saw the old man slumped against the end of a pew, over by the wall. Paul walked up and went sideways down the pew and put his hand on a shoulder to wake him. Shaking him a little, he bent over and said to him, "Mr. Jeansomme, it's time to go home." The old face showed no sleep, just a complete vacancy, and when Paul placed the back of his hand against it, it was cold. At the touch, he felt a thrill of fear, and he thought at once of Colette. He sat next to him and said things, but when he pulled his arm, his ex-father-in-law went over slow and heavy like a sack of oysters. Paul called to him again. "Hey," he said, and again "Hey," but Mr. Jeansomme was beyond all voices. He felt the hand for a pulse and saw the thumb and forefinger pinched on the third bead of the first decade of the rosary. The old man had prayed off into the sorrowful mystery of death, and Paul sat back, looking up at the dark-haired Virgin, her heart bound by thorns and floating on a broken gulf of blazing glass.

Nineteen

First things first. He went up the aisle to find the priest, and then he called the ambulance from the rectory. While Father Clemmons was anointing Mr. Jeansomme, Paul went outside the church and leaned against its sun-warmed brick, listening to a siren rise across town. He felt weak and ashamed for not following the paramedics in, for letting the priest give Last Rites alone. He did not want to see Mr. Jeansomme handled onto a stretcher, the dead limbs swinging like a killed animal's. A sheriff's deputy drove up and went inside, taking off his hat at the door and hanging it on the handle of his pistol. Whatever they were doing was taking a long time, and he walked back over to the cypress rectory and let himself in to use the phone. He heard Colette pick up while she was talking to Mrs. Fontenot, and when he began to speak, he knew for the first time how life changes in midsentence; one second the brain deals with an old lady cooking greens and the next with the death of a father, the words coming as unstoppable and random as bullets.

He walked up in front of the church and watched her come running down the street, jogging under the oaks and sycamores. He guessed she didn't want to spend the time to find the keys, start the car, drive it, and find a place to park. She passed him as though he was not there, swinging through the Gothic doors in an instant, and he did not follow, because worse than seeing the body would be seeing her look at the body, then turn inward and blame herself for leaving him both this morning and the other time.

Something important had happened, not only for Colette but for Tiger Island. Looking up the hot concrete of River Street, past the tin roofs, crape myrtles, and hackberry trees, he thought of people who considered themselves children again when they were around Principal Jeansomme. Now the man who gave them that youth was dead, and the old students in town were older still. Paul felt he'd aged in the past hour, and when he heard a huge door behind him swing open on a vast, incensed emptiness, he put a hand over his eyes, hiding from everyone's loss.

Two days later, Colette's sorrow was distracted by the number of people who came to the wake, the funeral Mass, the burial, the house. Her mother's funeral had been large, but a high school principal's contacts over the years expand like a family. Dozens of people she had never heard of attended the wake, squeezing her hand, telling her who they were. The funeral home was overflowing with strangers and their flowers. Her father's six brothers and sisters and their families came out from Napoleonville and Bunkie, Paincourtville and Mamou. These were people with bits and pieces of her father in their faces and in the way they spoke and in how they scratched themselves and turned their heads and held their lips. The crowding at the funeral Mass reached the level of spectacle when her father's chapter of the Knights of Columbus, old men dressed in feathered hats and bearing nickel-plated swords, rattled through a ritual of good-bye. Paul watched her weather the flurry of condolences, the storm of visitations. As they were leaving the Mass, he pulled her away from the stream of mourners for the first time in days.

"Oh, I'm okay," she said, looking around her. "Can you believe this? It's like he's not completely gone." She smiled at him.

But that night, after the last relative had gone down the steps, and after the last lady had dealt with the last bowl of potato salad or gumbo, and after Matthew had gone off to sleep, the house became the real tomb.

The phone rang in the middle of the night at Paul's and he stumbled through the dark to pick it up, knowing who was on the line. "Colette," he said.

She was crying fiercely. "I've got to move away from here. There are too many ghosts. I've got to get out."

He listened without interrupting to the things she told him and did not try to stop her crying. Finally, he told her, "There's no ghosts over there, babe."

"Everywhere I look, I see him. I see her."

"Think of something else."

"What?"

"Think of the *Saxon*. Of all the people working on her, for us."

She sobbed. "I'm in this house, not the boat."

"That's what it is—a house. Your house."

"I can't live here."

He sat in a scratchy, overstuffed chair in his parents' living room. "The house is empty. It's wood and glass, old furniture, a piano, and hundreds of pictures of you and your ugly brother." He listened. She seemed to be quieting down. "You want me to come over?"

She thought a moment. "No. I want to go somewhere."

"No, you don't."

"Yes, I do, damn it."

He closed his eyes and thought of what to say next. Out in the river, a trawler questioned the drawbridge with a tinny horn. "Colette, what would your mother want you to do?"

"That's not fair," she cried. "You're using my ghosts against me."

He let out a pent-up breath. "Go to sleep."

"I can't. I'm lying in bed with the windows open because I don't want to run the air conditioner. I expect the door to swing in and—"

"Shhh. Listen."

"To what?"

"Did you hear?"

The line was silent. "A boat whistle? What do—"

"Shhhh. Picture a big trawler, Barrileaux's new boat."

She was quiet for a moment. "It's southbound."

"Here comes the bridge."

"Four shorts. Why won't it open?"

"You know."

Again the line went silent. "A train."

"That's right," he said. Sure enough, at the edge of the parish came a freight whistle, barely audible, like music across water, a diminished chord, rising and falling, two longs, a short, and a long. "Greenwood crossing," he told her.

Another signal drifted in a minute later, and she said, "That's the junkyard road."

He waited until the next sound rode into town on an east wind. "Now, Grizzaffi's shipyard. Listen to that whistle cut up. Must be some drunk taking the crossing too slow."

After a full minute, another signal. "Now that's the grave-yard," she said, her voice going hollow for a moment.

"Here," he said quickly, "Tell me what's next?"

"The box factory." And he heard the whistle in the phone now as well. Along Railroad Avenue washed the coming thunder of a thousand wheels polishing the midnight iron through town.

The whistle was quiet for two minutes, then tore down River Street from the depot, the locomotive thumping out onto the bridge, the river quadrupling the rumble for ten minutes as the hotshot freight shone its light for Texas, blew its air trumpets for Beewick and beyond, little places announced by the two of them in turn.

"Cotton Road," she said, yawning.

"Bayou Vista," he told her, turning his head toward the open back door.

"Shadyside mill." Her voice was small and drifting, like the distant chant of the train whistle, which maybe she only imagined she heard, figuring the train's progress through the swamps and cane fields, guessing at the crossings.

"Patterson cut?" he whispered.

After a minute she murmured, "Bayou Triste," and hung up, the train whistling off into the silent west of her dream.

Paul brought the *Saxon* out and trawled off Point au Fer and came back the same day with a moderate catch. As he was approaching the dock, he saw Colette standing next to the red diesel pump, wearing a housedress and balancing the baby on her hip. As soon as the boat shouldered into the old tires hanging against the dock, he jumped off.

"What's the matter?"

Her face was hard to read, and she wouldn't look him in the eye. Matt yelled and pointed at a gull. "I'm still having a hard time, you know?" He could see that she was trying not to be specific in front of Matthew.

Paul touched her elbow and she shifted the boy to that arm. He put his hand in his pocket. "Like you were the other night?"

"Yeah. Like that." Her eyes were wide and full of ghosts.

"Okay," he said, looking at the roofline of the fish dock. "Here's what we gonna do tomorrow."

* * *

Colette and Matthew slept at her brother's, and the next morning at first light she met Paul at the steps to her father's house. Deliberately, like hired movers, they went inside, intent on not stopping to look at things, for Paul knew that if they did that, they would wind up sitting on spindle-back chairs in the hall, staring at a photograph or a package of letters. Colette headed straight for the kitchen and threw out her father's tins of sardines, mason jars of blackberries he had put up himself, a bottle of whiskey and a bottle of strong, bitter mints. Paul went upstairs to Mr. Jeansomme's bedroom. First, he put the old man's underwear and handkerchiefs in paper bags, then he dumped his shirts, pants, and few coats and ties in suitcases he found in a closet. He piled up shoes, socks, and hats, then stripped the bed, bundling the bedclothes to wash the smell of memory out. When Paul looked for the next job, he realized that he was working away from the old man's body, dealing first with the things closest to the skin. He went through drawers for belts and pocket change, prayer books, broken wristwatches, scratched eyeglasses, a few bottles of pills, unframed black-and-white photographs of Colette and her brother, a half box of corroded .22-caliber bullets.

The dresser was a forest of framed photographs, and these he left. The room had already been emptied of Colette's mother's things. Some images had to remain. He scanned the plaster walls and took down a picture of Mr. Jeansomme's brother holding a fish. He left a crucifix next to a window. Leaning into the hall, he dropped the suitcases on the floor, ready for the Goodwill people. Other things—a shoe-shine kit, a pump shotgun—he put upstairs in the attic. Next he took on the bathroom and its jungle of pill bottles, razors from the past twenty years, colognes, soaps, a bottle of hair oil plugged with a twist of paper. He tried not to think of what he was doing, and he disposed of things as if they had belonged to a stranger. After the bathroom, he was further from the body, and he took up to the attic fishing gear, books, carpenter's tools, a collection of brass buttons from the Civil War, Victrola records by Gene Austin and Vernon Dalhart, and all the lifetime of things stuck in closets or leaning against walls. He couldn't move everything. Just in terms of objects, the old man would be with Colette for years. But he thought that if they could diminish his presence for a while, Colette could begin to let the house be her own.

Up the dark oak stairs came the clink of bottles as Colette threw things from the refrigerator and freezer into garbage cans. He went down and helped her go deep into cabinets, where they found older quarts of faded blackberry preserves made from fruit they had picked together the spring they were fifteen years old. They cleaned as if cleaning were an athletic event, without mercy, without thinking about what anything meant. They pulled appliances from the walls and attacked the dust, sweeping Mr. Jeansomme's buttons and matchsticks out of the dark. They threw dented pots and broken coffeemakers and popcorn poppers down the back steps. Colette did not speak, touched nothing in a slow, fond manner, just grabbed and threw like a hireling, the way Paul had told her to act.

By two o'clock they were through with what they had planned. Mr. Jeansomme had placed forty-watt bulbs in all the house fixtures because that's what his eyes were used to, he'd said. Paul had bought twenty hundred-watt bulbs, and the last thing they did was to place them in the ceiling fixtures and lamps, washing the house down with light. Then they left at once, walking briskly off the front porch, through the low gate, breathing deeply when they reached the street, as though they had just escaped a building about to burst into flames. Paul put his hand in the small of her back and kept it there while they walked north, made a five-block circuit, and came back to the house from the south. He stayed on the sidewalk while she walked up the steps to a place she'd never been, unlocked the door, and stepped through all the bright rooms. Two minutes later she came out and sat in the swing.

"Colette."

She looked at him quickly. "It smells good in there. The cleaner, the mop water." She smiled. "The light."

He leaned on the picket fence. "Anything else you need me for?"

She looked at him as though she had just then allowed herself to notice things again. "You can go down and make arrangements to take ice at dawn."

He nodded. "We making pretty good money lately."

She put her head back and looked at the porch ceiling. "I'll need some for paint," she told him. A paper wasp had built a little nest on the porch ceiling fan, and she counted one, two, three insects hanging upside down, tending their house. She thought of something, smiled, and opened her mouth to tell Paul, but when she looked at the fence, he was gone, and she stared down the street at his straight back moving away, words lodged in her open lips like an undelivered kiss.

The next morning the dawn air was a hot blanket of mist. The hoisting machinery and the black enamel on the booms dripped with condensation. Paul read the weather column in the paper, and the little drawing showed some sort of front flying off the plains and sweeping down into Texas and Louisiana. He looked from the back deck of the *Saxon* while the ice was rumbling into the hold and saw a few cottage-cheese clouds to the south, their sooty bottoms skidding across the sky. Raymond turned his cap around and went below to fire off the engine. Before the diesel was warm, Etienne pulled onto the dock in his souped-up, thundering Impala. Paul's father looked into the hold, raised an arm to stop the flow of ice, then replaced a hutch cover. They cast off before the sun came over the trees.

The trawler sliced down the Chieftan, Etienne hanging on the whistle cord as he came up to the railroad bridge, the boat's electric trumpets asking for an opening. Once through, the boat heeled to starboard down the main channel. Etienne watched the bank to judge the water level, and, seeing that he had an extra foot, he turned down Bayou Courage and headed toward old Lirette Pass, a narrow ditch cut through the woods a hundred years earlier. Later that morning, as the boat floated out of the mouth of the pass, escaping the saw grass and lily pads, the seamless expanse of the Gulf opened before it like the biggest dance floor in the world. Etienne watched the shore behind him until he knew where he was in the openness and shouted for the men to drop the net. After they finished paying over the trawl boards, he headed straight out, pulling hard. Paul heard the engine straining and headed for the wheelhouse.

"How long we gonna pull?" he asked.

Etienne turned to look at him, an eyebrow cocked high. "You been griping about how much money you and Miss America got to make. You want to bring in shrimp, you got to pull like hell."

Paul looked back at the straining ropes, then up at the smoky exhaust. "That old Cummings don't have real good bearings."

The wheelman waved a hand in the air as if to brush away a fly. "I just got her a few rpms over the usual. Don't be a old lady. Just get back and be ready to pull up the net and count your money." He looked back. "Go on. I got too much of a hangover to mess with dogmeat."

Paul went out onto the stern and listened to the exhaust. If the engine burned out, repairs would cost several thousand dollars, and they might as well sink the trawler where she stopped and paddle back to town in the skiff. Colette would be so depressed, she would want to move to the moon.

He worked all day, imagining his ex-wife's eyes on his back. He dragged in haul after haul, some brimming with shrimp, some choked with mud and trash fish. The farther they churned into the Gulf, the more worked up the water became, the sawtooth chop turning into rollers by three o'clock. Etienne ran his huge hand over the dials of their old shortwave set and got a weather report. A low-pressure system, which had been sitting dormant in the Gulf for three days like a cranky swamp bear, had awakened and was moving north. A possibility of a squall line, the announcer said. The voice was a woman's, speaking in a drawl, her words overlaid with whistling static that sounded like a storm. Etienne took a swallow of coffee from an ironware mug and set it on the windowsill, staring across the waves to the horizon, studying the dark swirls at the edge of the world. The phrase "possibility of generating a squall line" perhaps ran through his mind, but if it did, he shrugged it off. A squall was a baby crying. Nothing to be scared about. He put his woolly head out the door and looked back. It was time to pull up the last drag. Then maybe they would hightail it north.

The final pass brought up pure pearly hills of jumbo shirmp, twelve to the pound, more than they imagined the trawl could hold.

"Whoa, baby," Raymond sang, doing a bowlegged jig, flipping up shrimp with his white rubber boots. "Looka this. Money in the bank. We done hit on some serious shrimp here." He held up half a dozen jumbos by their whiskers.

Paul's father woke up at the noise, and Etienne gave him the wheel and walked back to check the catch. He asked Paul if he wanted to make another pass.

"Why the hell not? We got some daylight left."

"The radio said they might be some squalls coming up."

"Might? They mention anything showing on radar?" He looked up, not wanting to believe. "What's 'might' mean?"

"Dunno. The weather people said a front might form some roughness up ahead." He gestured with his right hand over the water, then ran it deep into his pants pocket.

Paul looked to the horizon and saw what appeared to be light rain about ten miles off, but no lightning. "We'll try once more, at least," he said. "Man, look at these shrimp."

They paid out the net again and pulled a little harder this time as the old boat struggled through a rolling sea, a cloud of gulls scissoring along behind. A light rain came up, a dusty drizzle of wind-whipped particles, and with it a few whitecaps began to form.

Paul's father gave up the wheel and went aft to squirt the hoisting winch with a heavy oil, going inside the engine room when he'd finished to refill the oil can. When he stepped down on the floor, a single drop of water jumped up through a crack. He saw that the bilge was running eight inches high, so he turned on the pump and called up to Paul. "Hey, T-Bub, come down here a minute."

"What's up?" he called from the wheelhouse.

"Get in here."

Paul ran down the steps and stopped to listen to the engine for a moment. Then he saw the bilge. "You got the pump on?"

"I just cut it in, but we pumped out when we left home. You gonna have to get this thing pulled out and recaulked when we get back." He went over to a rusty hand pump bolted on the port bulkhead and tried it. After a few squeals it began to move freely and sucked up water. "I'll stay on this awhile till she's dry."

Paul went up into the wheelhouse and looked out at Raymond, who was working the catch, throwing trash fish into the wind. After a while, Raymond closed a hatch and came in, looking carefully into Paul's face. "What's up, T-Bub?"

"Daddy found a good bit of water in the bilge. I guess the caulking is beginning to give out on this thing."

"I ain't surprised one bit," Etienne said.

"What you mean, caulking?" Raymond shook water from his hair like a spaniel.

"Cotton," Etienne said. "Rag, oakum, whatever. In case you

ain't noticed, this tub is made of boards, and between each board is caulking."

"Ain't no overgrowed Partian has to tell me how a shrimp boat is made," Raymond snapped. "I want to know why *this* one's leaking."

"Hey, nothing lasts forever." Etienne gave him a sissy smile.

"I mean, is the weather gonna make it worse?"

"What you think, baby? If I stuff Kleenex up your ass and throw you overboard in a hurricane, how long before you leak, huh?"

Paul looked down into the engine room. "Daddy's got the water on the run."

Raymond screwed up his face. "Is that supposed to be funny or what?"

A flicker of lightning lit up on the edge of the world, and the men looked out and said nothing. A puff of spray floated over the bow. The gulls flew ahead, wheeled, and winged north.

At four-thirty they pulled the net in and cleaned the catch. It was as good a haul as the last one, and the crew scampered about in a steady rain, getting the shrimp on ice. A steady south wind began to rattle the loose panes in the wheelhouse; a few minutes later, a thunderstorm banged away over the boat. The wooden decks were slippery with trash fish and mud, so the young men made Paul's father go inside before he was pitched overboard by the rocking seas. When the sky got black, everyone crowded behind Etienne at the wheel. Raymond fought with the short-wave, dialing up a report that told them they were in an intensifying system of low pressure. Etienne tuned the boat due north and notched the engine up to full speed. A phosphorescent lightning strike flooded the windows, the thunderclap following at once. "Hail Mary, full of grace," Etienne sang.

Raymond frowned. "Looks bad when the wheelman starts saying the rosary."

Another bolt hit and every man jumped. Paul sniffed and

turned around in time to see a funnel of smoke come from the radio cabinet. "Hey, this thing just fried like an egg."

Then the rain came on firehose fashion, and the boat pitched and creaked like an old rocking chair under a fat man. Waves broke like plate glass over the bow. The squalling wind heeled the boat over on one side, then the other. Paul's father opened the door that led down to the engine and saw an inch of water over the boards. He passed a hand over his hair. "Ain't no kind of money worth this," he said.

The two-inch bilge pump was doing all it could. Raymond got on the hand pump, and Paul pulled up a section of decking to work on the bilge with a bucket, throwing the water out on the side deck through a sliding port. They worked until past dark, and when the wind did not die down and the rain did not let up, they figured they were hung in something larger than a line of thunderstorms. By eight o'clock the sea was made of valleys of gray water. Etienne kept the wheelhouse spotlight trained ahead and was running at half speed. He was not sure of their location and was trying to keep from smacking into an oil platform. The three men below were holding their own with the leaks, though the heavy seas were working the hull planks like slide rules. "You know," Raymond began, resettling his polka-dotted cap, "this storm ain't really that bad."

"Yeah," Paul's father agreed. "I guess it's gusting about fifty out there, but it's been holding steady for the past hour. That's as bad as it's going to get." He looked down and took a deep breath. "Our problem is, the bottom's gone out this tub. Maybe a seam opened in the stern." The boat pitched forward and a surge of water touched the engine's flywheel and sprayed around the hold like a pinwheel of sparks.

Paul worked as quickly as he could, trying not to think about what was happening. His arms shook as he heaved the buckets into darkness. He could control many things, but all the water inside and out made him feel helpless and small. He caught himself worrying about how much he had invested in the boat and frowned at his own foolish thought. At the moment, staying alive should be the only consideration, but the dominant feeling he owned was a fear of facing Colette if he let the boat go down.

Twenty

Colette sat out on the porch swing with Matthew lazing in her lap as she watched the drizzle left over from last night's storm. It had been a bad one, crawling up out of the Gulf on silver legs of lightning, banging the shutters and pelting the roof with pecans for hours. A big limb was down in the side yard, and she took the boy down to explore it. She thought of the big stories the men would have about the weather when they came in, and she smiled, anticipating Etienne's version. Matthew straddled the limb, pointed to the sky with one hand and made a fist with the other.

After lunch Colette read him a story about a child who won a horse in a contest. She read it with enthusiasm, though the boy was unimpressed with the tale and dozed off, his glossy black curls washing over her lap. She could not believe he was not interested, and she finished the story herself, looking back and forth between the baby and the book. She thought about last night's lightning and wondered if boats could be struck.

At four o'clock she walked down to the fish dock to see if Paul had come in. Nothing was tied up but a squatty lugger that rolled back and forth as men threw burlap sacks of oysters from the deck to a conveyor. She could see an ascending towboat downriver, and beyond that, the green bulk of the dredge *R. C. Canterbury* cleaning out the channel below Beewick. The air was a damp shawl, so she walked home, holding Matthew's hand carefully down the incline of the levee, noticing how the wind was still stirring the weeds.

At five she called the fish dock and talked to old man Nerby Billiot. "Hold on, *chère*," he told her. "I'm goin' take me a look down the river to see if they cleared the bend."

She imagined the short man waddling out to the edge of the wharf, grabbing a piling, and swinging out as far as he could to look downriver. Soon she could hear him fumbling with the phone. He told her that he didn't see them. "Have you heard them on the radio?" she asked. "Maybe you could try them with a call."

"Okay, baby. Hold on while I go fuss with the set." He was gone five minutes. Colette stared at the kitchen clock and at the pot of gumbo on the stove, wondering if she should add water. She was going to meet them and invite the crew to dinner, another attempt to chase the old ghosts from the house. Nerby came back on. "I tried to raise them, but they didn't come back on me. Seem like they shoulda been here by now."

"How powerful's your set?"

"Aw, it ain't too good, no, but it gets out ten mile."

She patted her foot and looked at the floor tile. "They should be in that range. They've got to get in before you shut down at seven."

"We'll take them if they come in after that," he said.

She fed Matthew, ate a bowl of gumbo, and by that time it was dark. She looked toward the rear screen door. Etienne didn't like to run the Chieftan in the dark because the boat had a weak spotlight. At seven-thirty she called the fish dock and got Nerby again. He told her not to worry, that he would get up with the Coast Guard and have them call out on their powerful radio. She hung up and immediately the phone rang. It was Paul's mother wanting to know how big the catch was.

Colette took a breath before answering. "They aren't in yet," she said. There was a long silence on the other end of the line.

"But baby, it's after dark."

"I know, Mamma. They probably had engine trouble. When they went out, I watched it smoke and smoke."

"You know, the weather was real bad last night."

"Mr. Billiot said he'd have the Coast Guard raise them. As soon as they get up with the boat, I'll call you." She tried to sound comforting, but at the same time she wondered who would comfort her.

"Please. I'm so worried I can't eat."

Colette hung up and thought of what she had heard in Mrs. Thibodeaux's voice. She imagined what it would mean for the woman to lose Paul's father. She had married him when they were both seventeen.

Colette walked over to the stairs and thought about going up and taking a shower, but if the phone rang, she'd never hear it. She patted her stomach through her slacks and decided to do a few sit-ups. Getting down on the floor, she put her feet under the sofa and exercised until she was winded. She lay on her back listening, and she heard a trawler horn north of town, ascending empty, a disembodied, cold sound. She tried to dream of what it would be like to ride out last night's storm in a shrimp boat— the rocking hull, the wind, the platinum flash of the bolts. She closed her eyes, listened, and the fine hair on the back of her neck rose up. Why would anyone risk running in such a storm? They must have had warning of some sort. What would force him to stay out longer than he should have? And then the answer occurred to her, and she opened her eyes out of her willed dream and was ashamed.

She got up and straightened the room, stood back and looked at it. Then she went to her piano in the little room at the end of the hall and played out of a generic songbook her mother had ordered through the mail. She dug into the piano bench and took out some of her childhood recital pieces, "Palomino on the Street-car," and "Frog in a Shoebox Polka." She remembered that when

Paul was sixteen, he had laughed out loud when he heard her play the last one. Frowning at its deliberately off-time rhythm, she pounded the keys and wondered what he'd thought was so funny about it. Suddenly she was afraid that she knew much less about him than she thought she did. She played the ugly piece again, and then once more, trying to find the laugh, the telephone sympathizing with the final chord.

A man was calling from the Coast Guard station down on the river. She had noticed the squat metal government building hanging over the Chieftan all her life and had never seen anyone come out or go in, though once or twice a year someone ran gale flags up the flagpole when a storm approached, and once a week a crewman started the venerable cutter tied up next to the building or greased the big machine gun bolted to the bow.

"Ma'am, we've tried to contact your boat by shortwave and can't seem to raise him. Have you any idea where the crew was going to shrimp?" The voice did not sound at all alarmed when she said that she didn't know. It was a professional voice, frightening because it sounded schooled in calmness. "Could you give me the names of the crew so I can get in touch with their families on the chance that some of them might know?" She told him who was on board. "I'll contact their homes," the voice said. "When we locate the boat, I'll let you know."

She hung up, telling herself that everything would be all right now. She walked out on the porch and noticed that there was more lightning to the south, signaling another fiery batch of coastal thundershowers. If their engine finally died out in rough seas, they would be in for a terrible ride. She tried to remember if they had the new heavy life jackets on board. Running an inventory of the boat over and over through her mind, she became unnerved, so she sat back and listened for boat whistles. A wind came up, rattling the hackberry tree across the street in Mr. LeDoux's yard, but there were no whistles, only the bass mourning of the Blanchard's pet bloodhound alarmed by a wandering smell, and farther down the side street, in the next neighborhood, the yowl of a tomcat fanging his love.

At ten, she went in and turned on the news, half-listening to the accounts of political squabbles and assaults in New Orleans. The weatherman announced that a storm was stalled in the central Gulf, sending out one squall line after another. That explained the lack of Gulf-bound whistles. Outside, the wind mounted and the rain rattled on the cypress siding. Once in a while the house would crack like static as a gust shoved against it. Colette checked on the boy, then sat by the phone in the hall, staring at a scuffed area of the oak floor, thinking how the dark wood should be refinished some day, though she could not imagine how. She would have to ask Paul about it. A man's raincoat hung from a hook near her, and she reached out to touch it, pulling her white hand back when she felt the empty sleeve.

Suddenly, a whopping roar built above the house, and she was startled out of her chair. She ran to the front door, fearing a tornado, and saw, above the trees across the road, the blinking lights and white bottom of a huge Coast Guard helicopter headed south. She telephoned Nerby down at the fish dock as fast as she could dial.

"Hallo."

"Nerby, this is Colette. Please get your field glasses and look upriver to check if the cutter is still tied up."

"All right, baby," he said, throwing down the receiver. He was back on the line in a minute. "It ain't there no more. What's going on?"

She put a palm on her forehead. "They've got to be going out to look for the boat."

"Maybe so. But don't you worry none. The best thing for you to do is go to sleep."

"Is that what you tell people when their friends' boats don't show up?"

"Believe me," Nerby told her, "I've talked to a many of 'em."

She was one among many, then, a typical silly, worried woman. Going upstairs, she again checked on Matthew, who was snorting gently on his stomach, a little plastic wrench from his play tool set grasped in a sticky hand. To the south, thunder rumbled, almost out of hearing, like someone walking on the porch. Matthew started, the little blue wrench darting into the air. "Shush now." She put a hand on his back. "It's all right. In the morning, things will be all right. They have to be."

At first light, the phone rang, and she rolled over and answered it half-asleep. The Coast Guardsman sounded sleepy also, but he still spoke in his official voice, telling her that Paul's boat had been seen by another shrimper pulling out of old Lirette Pass two days before. As she listened, she saw through her window the treetops across the street pitching like masts. "But where are they?" she broke in.

"We sent out a helicopter last night, ma'am, to look for lights, and the cutter is still out trying to guess where they went."

She put her head down and began listening more carefully to what was behind the voice. "What else are you going to do?"

"We'll get a plane up now that it's daylight, another cutter will deploy, and we'll notify any rigs and shipping in the area to keep a lookout. We have a hunch they're far out."

"Do you have any idea how long it will take to locate them?"

An unofficial sigh came through the line. "There're lots of low clouds out there," the voice said. "It's a big Gulf."

She went into the kitchen to make coffee, trying to ignore the pecan limbs sailing around in the backyard. She missed the basket of the dripolator with the first scoop of coffee. As soon as she finished sweeping up the mess, the phone rang. Paul's mother was crying. She had been on the phone with Nerby's wife, Zola, since five-thirty. She was so upset that it took Colette ten minutes to calm her down. Finally, Colette hung up and held on to the kitchen counter, wishing there was someone to do the same for her. She finished making the pot of coffee and went up to check on Matthew. A branch hit a gable and she looked out of her father's bedroom window over the town's tin roofs to the south, where a thunderstorm sighed in the marshes, its strikes of lightning scarring the mask of sky. She felt the wind lean on the house like a giant's hand, the screens popping in their frames on the Gulf side. Thunder trembled south of Isle aux Chiens, and Matthew called to her out of a dream. She went in to him as a lightning strike came down half a mile away and the wind rose, banging the porch swing against the wall. Sitting next to the sleeping child, she heard the house's timbers crack like the ribs in a boat and she started to cry. If she was frightened in a big cypress house on land, then what must it be like for all of them, crashing through the waves in a worm-eaten ghost of a boat?

She prayed for the men, woke up Matthew for breakfast, and then prayed for herself.

At eight o'clock the trees were still loud with wind. The local radio station told again of the batch of disturbed weather in the Gulf. She called the Coast Guard and then Paul's mother, but there was no news. Three planes and a cutter were running their search patterns, and the Ladies' Altar Society was saying a rosary in church for the men. Through the morning she tended to Matthew, playing with him until he seemed worn out by her attention and wandered off to plunk the keys on her piano. At a quarter to twelve Mrs. Fontenot showed up on the front porch carrying two pots.

"Come on get these pot," she said through the screen door, unsmiling under her kerchief. "They hot as hell." She swept through the house to the kitchen, banged them down on the range, and let out a breath. "Here's some gumbo and rice. I know you ain't cooked today."

Colette stared at the food and thought of her father's funeral. "Thanks."

Mrs. Fontenot sniffed. "You got to eat, not worry. What the Coast Guard say?" Her gray head bobbed above the pots as she inspected the controls and tried buttons on the stove.

"They're still looking."

She turned her wrinkled face to the window and regarded a patch of angry sky. "Them Coast Guard boys, they not from here."

Colette picked up the note of doubt in the old woman's voice and ran with it. The Coast Guard boys were not looking for friends or relatives, after all, just blips on radar or motes swimming in the vast, indifferent Gulf. She sat down hard in a kitchen chair and put her knuckles against her lips. No one will look for you like someone who's known you all your life. Nothing fosters a rescue like ties in the blood.

"Ey," Mrs. Fontenot said.

"What?" Colette looked at the old woman's long coat, the kerchief tied down over her ears.

"You worried about the boat or them men on it?" She pointed toward the door with a ladle.

"The men, of course. If you think I'm that hard-hearted, you been listening too much to Paul."

The old woman shook her head. "He never said nothing bad about you, baby."

"I bet."

"Know what I think?" she asked, putting the ladle into the pot of gumbo and moving it in a circle. "He'd do anything for you."

Colette stood up quickly and turned off the range. "What he or I would do is none of your business."

"Oh-ho," Mrs. Fontenot mocked. "You think this old lady don't know nothing about romance, hanh? You think T-Bub, who I had in my lap the night he come home from the hospital, ain't none of my business?" She turned the burner back on and banged the ladle once on the pot, hard.

Colette sat down. "I'm sorry, but how do you know what he feels about me?"

"Me, I'm ninety years old and you think I'm always look like this." She spread her arms and bobbed her head to glance at herself. "What you think I looked like at fifty, when my husband was makin' good money and the boys was out of the house and I had a new car and the wrinkles hadn't took over my face? What about when I was forty and we'd go dancin' on Saturday night and the men would watch me and Lawrence moving like hot stuff? What about when I was thirty, with my hair dark like yours, and fat little babies, and how about seventeen, when my skin hadn't seen no sun and my ears hadn't heard no babies cry all night, and my eyes hadn't seen no bills, and Lawrence would look at me like I was cream for his coffee?" Mrs. Fontenot gave Colette a triumphant little smile. "That was when I lived in Beewick. They wasn't no bridge. One day we had a date and the ferry broke its paddle wheel on a log. Lawrence put his clothes in wax paper on his head and swam the t'ousand-foot channel through the eddies so he could dance with me and look at my face." She put the ladle in the sink and sat down in a kitchen chair, putting her spotted hand on Colette's. "You think I don't know nothin', like love wasn't around in the old times, like romance ain't been invented and nobody was good-lookin'. That's your trouble, baby. You think you the only one knows anything. And anybody in town knows what you don't know."

Colette looked at the floor, sensing what was coming. "What's that?"

"That you throwed out the best boy in Tiger Island. No lie." She poked Colette's arm with a bony finger.

"I'm sorry, Mrs. Fontenot. I didn't want to make you mad." She patted a knobby knee sticking out of the housecoat.

"A t'ousand-foot-wide river he swam for me during high-water time. They's some that drowned trying it."

Colette put her face in her hands.

"You got to pay attention when somebody takes a risk for you," the old woman said, pulling out a pack of Picayunes and lighting one with a box match.

She shared a meal with Mrs. Fontenot, who offered to stay with Matthew for the day. Colette decided to go to Paul's mother's and wait. Before she left the house, the phone rang. It was a Coast Guard radio operator saying that the cutter came back in because of engine trouble. The planes were still out, but they couldn't see much because the clouds were so low.

On the way through the door, she caught a glimpse of herself in the hall mirror. She looked awful, her color as washed out as Mrs. Fontenot's. She pulled herself upstairs, brushed her hair, splashed on cologne, and smoothed on some waterproof makeup.

Rushing through the front door, she ran straight into the Larousse twins, who were standing shoulder-to-shoulder on her porch. She had to stare at them a moment before she realized who they were. Victor had had his teeth pulled and sported a shiny upper plate, and Vincent had lost his blackest incisor, which softened his appearance.

Vincent rolled his eyes. "Hey, baby, me and Plastic Face here just comin' by. You want us to gas up and go look for T-Bub, just give us the word."

Her mouth dropped a bit. "What can you do that the Coast Guard can't?"

Vincent sniggered, not at all insulted. "Colette." He looked at his brother. "The Coast Guard is a bunch a nearsighted weenies from the city."

"They wimpos," Victor added.

She glanced at the women tattooed on their forearms and walked down the steps, hoisting an umbrella. "They're trying hard. They're keeping me informed."

"They from New Orleans. If the streetcars would stop runnin', they couldn't find downtown." Victor opened her door.

Before she got in she studied their faces, their broken noses, trying to remember when she hated them and why. "Let me call around," she said. "You gonna be home?"

"Yas. We in the garage putting new fiberglass on Nonc's Lafitte." Vincent shook back a wet strand of hair from his forehead.

"The planes are out," she said from behind the wheel. Then she looked into their dark eyes. "But you know Paul. You know the channels."

Vincent tilted his head and nodded, then closed the door for her. She watched them in her rearview mirror, their ropy arms and V-shaped heads.

She found Paul's mother seated in the kitchen, her fingers pinched on a rosary. Their eyes met, but neither of them smiled.

"Ah. I don't know what to think. Mrs. Latiolais from across the street brought some potato salad over already."

Colette opened the refrigerator and eyed the big Tupperware bowl. "I guess word is getting around." She walked over and put a hand on the prickling skin of Mrs. Thibodeaux's upper arm.

"You want some lunch, Colette?"

"No thanks. Mrs. Fontenot already brought me some gumbo." They looked at each other and laughed against the odds, feeling guilty and sad.

Colette sat at the oak table and spread out her hands on its surface, feeling the humidity on the varnish, the signs of the coming storm even here. The square plastic clock over the plywood cabinets said one o'clock. "You know, the crazy Larousse twins came by a minute ago saying they would go out and search. They said the Coast Guard wouldn't look as hard as friends would."

Mrs. Thibodeaux shook her head. "I met their momma in the store last week. She told me Vincent and Victor got in a fight over how to season a rabbit spaghetti, and one of them knocked the other's front teeth out. I forgot which did which." She stared

298

through a window into the misting rain slanting across the back-yard. "But they might be right," she murmured.

During the afternoon, six ladies, Colette's uncle Lester, and *Grand-père* Abadie came by to visit. Into the refrigerator went another bowl of potato salad, a platter of stuffed crabs, and a pot of shrimp stew. A sick feeling of danger and loss built in her along with the food, and she stepped out into the yard more than once to stare at the clouds coming low over the levee like way-ward dirigibles. She touched her hair and felt the ponderous, uncaring sky on her like an inverted sea.

At five-thirty the Coast Guard called, telling her they were suspending the search until the morning, and she fought the urge in her throat to scream at the voice on the phone. If the rescue attempt would be as large as her fear had grown that afternoon, dozens of boats would be combing the waves day and night. But what could she tell the voice? To fly their slow, blind airplanes in the dark through the moppy clouds? She hung up. The search-ers could do no better than they had done, and though they were professionals, they could operate only through science, not kin-ship.

She kicked open the screen door and went out again. In the backyard, staring up at clouds, Colette knew she was going to do something important, though she had no idea what, but she felt it coming, the way she knew the next step was coming up in a dance, the music propelling her toward that inevitable motion. She felt her will swell up and move the flesh along her back, because everything she had sensed and thought about Paul in her life came funneling down to this moment, this dot in time, and at once she knew what she was going to do. In that instant, she knew she loved him. It was the knowing what to do that told her.

She ran into the house, saw the kitchen telephone, and took the next step in the dance, dialing information for Pierre Part, getting Etienne the giant's father on the line.

Twenty-one

"Mr. Benoit, this is Colette Thibodeaux," she began. "I own half of the *Saxon*—"

Emile Benoit cut her off. "Hot damn, ain't this a hell of a mess?" Colette had never seen Emile, but he sounded as big as a lion. "The Coast Guard just called here," he said. "They call you?"

"They gave up for the night."

"They say they got no idea where them boys is at. I told them where Etienne was gonna pull the trawl."

Colette heard another visitor come into the front room and a corresponding rise in exclamations, lamentations. She pulled the phone closer to her mouth. "Mr. Benoit . . ."

"Call me Emile, baby."

"Do you want to go to the Gulf and look?"

There was no pause. "Well, hell yas."

"You know anybody with a boat large and fast enough that you could borrow?"

"My brother, Lucien, he got a t'irty-five-foot crew boat he don't use since the oil business went flat. Hey, you got to know I been thinking about this already. Everybody at my house thinks it's crazy."

"I knew it." She socked her thigh with a fist. "Will it get us out there?"

"*Mais,* let me make a phone call, then I get you right back."

She gave her number, hung up, and listened to the voices in the front, faint and worried. The image of Paul struggling in the water tried to form in her mind, but she shook this off. She straightened her back and prayed for the phone to ring. A few moments later it did, and Emile growled directions for her to meet him at first light on the levee road twelve miles above town.

"You got field glasses?" he asked.

"Yes."

"Bring 'em. Bring some baloney sandwiches and soda pop."

"Okay."

"Bring a good life jacket and a rosary," he said, and hung up.

At her own house she found Mrs. Fontenot watching early reruns of *Gunsmoke* that had been dubbed over in Cajun French. "*Lâche ton fusil, toi*," Marshal Dillon told an outlaw as Colette came into the living room. Matthew was playing on the floor. She offered to pay Mrs. Fontenot to spend the night.

"Hell, this baby ain't nothing to look after. My grandson would of had me all skint up and tied to a tree in the yard by now. And I brought my sleepin' gear already 'cause I know how these things go." She pushed herself off the sofa and walked, bent over, into the hall. "Just let me go call my sister and tell her where I'm at." Colette picked up Matthew and looked at his hair, at his jaw. She thought of the nutria hunt, when Paul had fished her out of the canal in the dark when he could barely save himself. A thunderclap sounded a long way off, and Mrs. Fontenot came into the room dressed in a faded purple housecoat with LAS VEGAS embroidered in orange across the back. "Rain, rain, rain," she complained. "My greens gon' rot in the ground."

Before dawn, Colette showered, pulled on a pair of jeans and a denim shirt, gathered a few things into a picnic basket, then drove out the shell road north of town. Under the new sun the single lane ran like a silver snake along the grassy levee's back, and a skewed forest of second-growth cypress and crippled gum trees came up on the right, a fluffy bar of willows next to the stream on the left. She saw in the distance a big man at the base of the levee. He was dressed in khaki, leaning against a Ford pickup. She slowed her car and looked. Emile appeared to be about sixty years old. His felt fedora sat back on a bald head and framed a face as oblong as an eggplant. Colette tipped her sedan over the edge of the road and stood on the brakes as the wheels did a slow, drunken slide, and she came down seventy yards at an angle, stopping in the mud next to the truck. She got out and a smile formed briefly on the man's small wrinkled mouth. "I see you know how to drive around here." He walked over and she noticed that his stomach moved from side to side. His eyes were small and tired, but not mean. She thought of raising children like Etienne and wondered what Emile would look like if he had never married.

"You a little late; it's getting light. But come on, let's get your gear and take off." He let her load him up with two shopping bags, and they walked alongside a brick-paper camp and out on its spindly dock to where a dented-up boat sat low in the water, a gray aluminum crew boat lined with old tires. The inboard engine was grumbling, and wreaths of vapor rose from the gargling exhaust. Emile planted a rubber boot on the side rail and stepped in. "If you want to come, I guess you can untie us and jump over without getting drownded?" He talked like his son.

She slipped the lines and jumped, following him into the cabin. The windows were cloudy, the ceiling studded with dirt dauber nests. "How long did you say this boat's been laid up?"

"Don't worry. I rebuilt this thing myself five years ago. It'll haul ass." He shoved the throttle forward, and the boat surged away from the dock. Soon they were in the broad canal and the willow trees were flying by like fence pickets. The bow hammered the flint-colored water and Colette hung on to a window handle.

Emile lit a Camel, clamped it between his lips, and squinted ahead. "The Guard call you this morning?"

"No." She sat on a gray stool on the left side of the low cabin. Everything was painted flat gray. The stools were plywood and their chalky paint came off on her hands.

Emile snorted like a mule. "They told me they sending two boats way out, maybe sixty mile. They think they gone to Cuba or something." He took a long drag and talked out the smoke. "We gonna find those boys close in, or ain't nobody gonna find them at all." He turned to Colette briefly, the way a doctor might when breaking bad news. "Alfred LeBlanc came in with his big trawler two nights ago, and one of his booms was tore loose, two windows broke out, and all his buckets and boots gone overboard. He told me he thinks he came through the same squall line Etienne steered into. I'm hoping they made a run for a platform or an island."

She looked at a bass boat coming at them, whizzing past without a wave. "How long can we stay out?"

Emile took another long drag and thought a minute. "How long you want to stay out?"

"Until we can't," she said. "Would Etienne want you to do less?"

He passed her a long, surprised look, as though he had noticed her for the first time. "Well, no, I guess not."

She looked at a paper bag behind her on the floor. "You like Vienna sausage, peanut butter and jelly?"

"I've eat worse."

"Then we can last as long as the fuel."

"Girl, you as hardheaded as you pretty." He slid back a window and flicked his cigarette out. "You know, the boys up at the fuel dock said I was crazy going out like this."

"I guess we are," she said, holding on as they rolled up behind a large tugboat. Emile ran right up the white tunnel of propeller wake before cutting to port, missing the hemp fender on the stern by four feet, humming past the tug and alongside the barges. Colette watched the rusty smudge in the window on Emile's side and figured the crew boat was making around thirty miles an hour. They would be in open water by half past seven.

Down past Boogalee Island, the canal dumped into the Chieftan, and when they broke into the big river, Colette caught sight of something white streaking across the water on her left like a giant Styrofoam ice chest. It was an open boat with a broad nose, a twenty-five-footer, shooting out from the bank straight for them. She got the field glasses and saw that it was the Larousse twins in a dirty fiberglass hull with the name *Unsinkabelle* painted in bright red script on the sides of the bow. Victor was flashing his new smile and waving his arms over his head like giant pincers. She went out onto the open deck in the rear of the boat as Emile slowed down to meet them.

"Hey, *bébé*," Vincent called, "we got word what you up to an' we been waiting on the bank for you to come down. We coming along." He pointed downriver with a bent cigarette.

"Can you keep up?" she asked.

Vincent bowed his back and pulled in his pointy chin. "*Mais,* we got two Black Max's on the back of this thing and can cover more water than a freakin F-14." Emile turned with the Larousses toward dead water against the bank. They were all stopped not very far above Paul's house. Etienne's father came out of the cabin and looked down at the big speed hull.

"You get that thing out in big waves, it'll stick like a dart in a big roller and sink."

"Aw, no, man." Victor seemed insulted. "You talk like this thing's one of them little boats they serve a banana split in." He shook his head. "This here's one of them Bostom Whaling boats. You can cut it up with a chain saw and walk home on the sawdust, yeah."

"Bullshit."

"Oh yah," Vincent said, idling down his engines. "What

about that torpedo boat you running there? It got so many dents in it, it look like my *tante* Lizette's thighs. Excuse me, Colette."

"You're excused."

"Hot damn, you good-lookin'," Victor said.

"Like your teeth," she told him.

Victor tilted his head back and smiled broadly at the sun.

"Hey," Emile called. "We going straight out and turning west along the marsh. You could go east and search the south side of the big island. It's all shoals there and you draw less water than me."

"Awright," the twins said in one voice. Vincent looked downriver and stuffed his T-shirt into his dungarees. "It'll be high tide in two hours, so we can cover that pretty much."

Emile looked over at the twin Mercurys as they trembled and jerked. "Them engine pretty fast?" Colette tried to say something, but it was too late. The outboards dug into the river like steam shovels, pushing the *Unsinkabelle*'s bow up to forty-five degrees. By the time the boat planed off, the Larousses were half a mile away, the tips of the propellers dusting the water.

Emile shook his head. "Damn, they already there."

They got under way once more, rounding the bend into town. In the distance they saw the diminishing ball of spray from the Larousses' boat. To their left, over the levee, the iron roofs of the old houses and three slate-covered steeples threw back the morning sun. When they got opposite the overgrown landing at LeBlanc's Machine Shop, a blast from a three-chime air horn caught their attention. Colette watched a sizable red-and-gray tugboat angle from the landing, and she would have looked away again except for something odd about a crewman standing at the railing on the third deck. He was wearing white bucks. She picked up the field glasses and saw that it was her uncle Lester, waving with as much energy as he had. She reached over and grabbed Emile's arm. "Turn back," she yelled over the noise. "Someone on that tug is flagging us." The crew boat looped and sped to the shore side of the tug, sending a big wave lapping against its hemp fenders.

"What do they want?" Emile cut the engine to drift alongside. He and Colette went out again. Watching them from the wheelhouse was the owner of LeBlanc's Machine Shop. He pulled a wet cigar from his mouth and yelled down at them.

"We been drifting around for a bit, waiting for y'all. We coming along." He pointed the cigar south.

Colette looked at all the fresh red and gray enamel. "Where'd you get the tug?"

LeBlanc hitched his pleated slacks up over his paunch. "The Lirette Towing Company owes me for some work. Hell, everybody owes me for some work." He waved his cigar at the town. In the engine room's door was Larry, Paul's brother; on the main towing bitts sat LeBlanc's redneck, wearing a new set of overalls. They waved but did not smile. Colette's brother came out of the galley, stared at her, and shook his head.

"Oh, Mark," she cried, waving.

"You have a radio on your boat?" her brother called.

"Yeah," Emile told him.

"Well, turn it on and go ahead. We'll hit the Gulf maybe an hour after you."

"Emile," Mr. LeBlanc hollered. "You got any idea where to look?" He bent down and adjusted his glasses so Emile would not be in the lower part of his bifocals.

"We gonna start west, along the marsh. You saw the Larousse boys go by a minute ago?"

"We saw something bounce by look like a wing fell off a jet plane."

"That's them. They gonna go east, but they got a lot of territory to cover with all those inlets. You want to go out fifteen mile and turn east, make a ten-mile pass, then turn around west and keep working in, like you mowing a lawn?"

Mr. LeBlanc threw his cigar overboard. "Let's go."

Colette's brother leaned over the rail. "You want to ride with us, and I'll go in the crew boat?"

She turned toward Emile, who shrugged. Her brother, old uncle, and Paul's brother watched her quietly. "I'll go with speed and somebody's daddy every time. We'll see you in the Gulf." She saw Emile's reluctant smile at the edge of her vision as he stooped into the cabin. They left the tug behind in a whopping roar of a stainless-steel propeller as Etienne the giant's father leaned on the throttle lever, wringing every revolution he could out of the diesel hurling away in the hold. They sang across the harbor, mocking with their speed the aspirate old dredge working the point below town. The railroad bridge flicked over them like a big silver wand, and the river broadened magically in the bend, promising the Gulf.

In the time it took to speed past the thinning ranks of willows and cypresses and enter the burgeoning swales of tall marsh grass, her mind buzzed on about Paul, focusing on one idea only: location. It came before everything else. The word swam her mind like a fish testing out a channel. She knew that Paul was not reckless and would be wary of the weather. With a pang she remembered why he would take a risk, but she would not let that get in the way of figuring where, in all this marsh or dull open water he and the crew could be. They had a skiff and new life jackets. The wooden boat, if it had gone down, might not be completely sunk, and they could cling to what floated near the surface.

Etienne, while unkillable in a fistfight, was little match for the Gulf and its midafternoon rain monsters, which could twist the body of a cypress boat like a wet reed. If the boat had gone down, she thought, it would have been on the flight back toward the mainland, and Emile would be right in searching close in. She imagined Paul and the others in the water, or in the skiff, or treading the Gulf without life jackets. The thought give her a tingle of pity and fear that made her shake her head like a spaniel. Then something else occurred to her.

"You said you talked to Alfred LeBlanc about his boat that was caught in a squall?"

"Yeah."

"Were they catching shrimp?"

He looked away, and she asked him again. Glancing over to her and then back at the water, he shook his head. "I don't know."

Colette edged closer to him and put a hand on a big round shoulder. "Please tell me the truth."

Emile blinked hard. "It's what worries me most. Alfred made it back loaded down."

She watched a red buoy come into view. "We'll have to rely on their good sense," she said, knowing even as the words came out that if they'd hit money shrimp, after what she had told Paul on her porch about going back with him, he'd fish in a hurricane.

The trees fell back completely on either side of a broad, calm channel, and the envelopment by marshland was complete—a flat, endless plain of sighing grasses veined with openings of barely a skiff's width. She endured miles of this bland mirage pretending to be land. Putting her head down she stared at her hands, white and still, and thought about Matthew's face, his plastic tools. Time raced with the boat, and eventually she noticed that the sound of the engine changed. She looked up to the open water, which offered nothing for noise to rebound from, and she felt like a toddler escaping alone into an enormous, strange yard.

"My God," she said, looking from window to window. "One way is Mexico, the other is Florida, and to the south is . . . is— I don't even know, some foreign country."

Emile turned the wheel and said nothing.

"I feel so damned stupid." She banged the backs of her hands on her knees and looked again at all the water.

The old man lit a cigarette. "Let's just say we got our work cut out for us. Sit on the roof like a Indian and work both sides with the glasses." He jerked a thumb toward the ceiling and she climbed up, wedging herself between the horn and an antenna just as the boat took on a small trough and rolled ten degrees. They headed west, and she lined up her fine eyes with the old pair of German binoculars that had been her father's, scanning the empty water. She watched north and south for an hour, marshland a mile to her right, the Gulf to her left, and she prayed for something to swim into the eyepieces other than the abandoned oil platforms farther out and rafts of pelicans floating at the edge of her range. Emile slowed the boat to a crawl and came out of the cabin.

"Let me take a turn and you run the boat," he said.

"Fine. I already have a headache."

"I thought you might. Even with the clouds, there's glare." He dug into his pocket. "You take aspirin?"

"Sure."

"Take two of these and chew 'em up to powder. Then wash them down with a Coke." He held up his hand and cocked his head. "I know what you going to say about the Coke not being good for a headache. That's bull. Wash 'em down quick and get in the seat. Run maybe half speed. You can close your eyes awhile if you want. Can't bump into anything out here. Just check the compass every few minutes."

She sat in the cabin, bringing the boat up to about fifteen. After they had run west for ten miles, he banged on the roof and told her to turn into a lap of their pattern, a quarter mile farther from shore. Her headache faded, and she looked over and watched Emile's blocky shadow on the water. The shadow would turn and search, swing the other way and search. After an hour he rapped on the roof with his knuckles—she could hear the flesh and bone on the metal—and he called down to her, "Come on up and spell me. My legs is cramping up." They changed places, and almost immediately Colette saw something floating a half mile ahead. Emile sped up at her call, and soon they were next to a box bobbing and rolling in the waves. He came out of the cabin and looked over the scarred rail to a wooden crate of cabbages, the vegetables bound tight under the slats like a raft of skulls. He looked away. "Musta fell off a ship," he told her, tucking in his shirt and turning slowly back to the cabin.

They streaked in their chosen quarter of Gulf until noon, when the smutty clouds seemed to carry an angry light in them, sending down an eye-stinging glare. The boat wound the same braided route until two, and Colette spotted only a school of arching porpoises, a broken tangle of net floats, and a half-empty drum marked for a pesticide. On the east end of their last pass, they spotted what might have been the tugboat on the horizon. Emile spent fifteen minutes warming up his dusty shortwave and tried to raise someone in the wheelhouse. Finally Mr. LeBlanc's voice began to dominate over the fuzz in the old set. He told Emile to come a couple of miles closer so they could talk, and Colette turned the wheel. In five minutes she could make out a red-and-gray slash on the water ahead. LeBlanc's voice came back on, asking what they had found.

"Not a damn thing," Emile hollered into the mike.

There was a pause in transmission and Colette picked up her head. LeBlanc's voice came back slow and careful. "Well, we found their skiff floating and one life jacket."

Emile rolled a pair of sorrowful eyes over at Colette. "Was the jacket latched up?"

"Yeah."

"LeBlanc, was the rope on the skiff broke?"

"Yes. They never got to untie it."

Emile put down the microphone, looked out the window on his side, then picked it up again.

"What else you got?"

"Nothing. But I think you better come on over this side and help us look."

"We comin'." The engine sounded up and they headed south-east.

Colette sat in the cabin and imagined that the skiff had blown off in a waterspout. The jacket might have been in the skiff. Emile looked at her face, then told her to get back onto the roof. "Go on. What they found don't mean nothing. You gettin' a good suntan up there. Stretch out them field glasses." She retook her position between the tarnished horn and the corroded antenna, scanning the water as though she was looking for a lost ring in a vast grassy yard. Her mind began to drift, and sometimes her imaginings would float into the eyepieces, making her straighten her back with false surprise. She saw a face above every leaden swell.

She pulled a life jacket between her and the aluminum roof. She heard the radio come alive in the cabin as LeBlanc and Emile planned the search. The tug crew would continue their own zig-zag pattern and the crew boat would try to find the Larousses and extend the close-in search to the east. She heard LeBlanc's voice translated over the water. "We saw the wild bastards flying low to the north, and we shined a carbon light after them, but God knows what they were after. If we knew whether they'd found anything, it'd be a help." In half an hour Colette and Emile passed within hailing distance of the tug, then angled away. For the first time she read the boat's name, *Dernière Chance,* visible through the prop spray of the crew boat as they rumbled north in search of the twins.

Twenty-two

The crew boat cut through a light chop in its wide-open run, the waves running under the bow like stones, and when Colette could make out the flat top of the marsh, she pointed and Emile pulled back on the throttle lever. The bow nosed into the water and they went ahead slowly, Emile leaving the wheel and coming out of the cabin holding a navigation chart and a wad of twine with an eight-inch crescent wrench tied to the end of it. He sounded the water, and Colette watched him haul back only eight feet of line. From there they checked every few yards until she sensed the boat wandering into a slow turn to the east, parallel to the shore, which now showed boldly a half mile off. They came to an inlet and Emile swung the boat toward it, slowing. He came out of the cabin and watched the wheel wash until it turned black, then went in to reverse the engine and head back east. There was no use in stranding the boat on a falling tide. Colette watched the plain of marching grassland with her field glasses, praying. A mile back in the maze, a cloud of egrets rose, an explosion of thin crescents, and she wondered what had startled them. She felt the hollowness of despair float up through her shoulders as the marsh wobbled in her lenses, undeniable and heartless, not to be walked on. She felt ignorant because she had lived close to it all her life without learning about it. Turning her gaze, she caught sight of a white object flying toward them in the distance, an apparition that could only be the Larousse twins.

In ten minutes, they were charging across the crew boat's bow, looping around to come alongside.

"Hey, you found anything yet?" Vincent yelled, throwing an empty beer can over the side. He was so drunk that he was standing steadily in the pitching boat. Colette narrowed her eyes, studying the ice chest and Victor's bent smile.

"You have field glasses?" she asked

Vincent whirled left, then right, leaning over to pick up a seat cushion. "Yeah. They right here somewhere."

She leaned out and grabbed his shirt, pulling him halfway out of the boat and close to her face, her sour breath. "How can you search for anything if you don't use your damned glasses, Victor?"

"This is Vincent."

She shoved him hard and he fell on his butt. "We don't need your help if you're going to spin around like a couple of asshole kids playing rescue boat." She stood on the rail, jumped into the *Unsinkabelle*, and kicked the ice chest open. She plucked out four linked six-packs and threw them overboard.

"Colette, baby, what the hell?"

She turned on the men and shook water from her hands into their flushed faces. "I'll tell you what the hell. Paul and his father are out here, your friends are lost, and all you shits can think of is riding fast and getting drunk. If you can't do any better than this, then get out of our way," she yelled. "Go back to town and piss off your wives."

Victor began to plead, "Aw, we was looking for 'em good."

"Yeah, baby," Vincent said, standing up and sitting on the rail. "We been trying these inlets to see if maybe they made a break for one to get out the storm. But they all too shallow," he said, looking past her to the shore.

She stepped back into the larger boat. "You've got to concentrate more," she snapped. The twins looked subdued and watched her like schoolboys trying to talk to the playground beauty. She looked their boat over again angrily. "Have you two had anything to put in your stomachs besides Schlitz?"

"Aw, we don't need to eat." Vincent sat down next to the wheel.

Colette got on her knees in the cabin and began to make them sandwiches. Without food, they would be sick and inattentive, more liable to run over someone than to rescue them. While she spread mustard, she heard a noise overhead and saw a large Coast Guard plane heading out high, due south.

Emile made Vincent discuss a chart with him and Victor banged around the *Unsinkabelle,* turning over paddles and life jackets as he looked for his binoculars. A slow roller came up under the boat, and he capsized against the seat cushions. Colette went over to the rail and handed him a baloney sandwich. "I want you to slow this thing down, cruise as close in as you can, and use the field glasses on the marsh line. Check the inlets as best you can." He bit into the sandwich, smiled a crazy mouthful smile, and she laughed, turning away, holding the back of her hand against her mouth.

In the cabin, the shortwave cracked and sizzled, delivering a call from the tug. Emile listened to LeBlanc make arrangements for a rendezvous at six o'clock near an unmanned oil platform. The cloud bottoms had burned off somewhat, but there was not much good light left. She bent over and put her hand in the Gulf, satisfied that at least it was warm. If one of the men was still in the water, he would have a chance.

"Hey," Victor said. "I see the rig LeBlanc is talking about. It's a little one about three mile out." He had finally found his binoculars.

Colette's head snapped up, a knifeful of mayonnaise in her hand. "Emile, does it say on the chart if there's a light on that rig?"

He pursed his small mouth and studied the pale expanse of lines and numbers spread out on the deck. "No, but there's a lot of water under it. They'd have to have a light on it." He gave the Larousses a look. "Did you boys check it?"

"We didn't get out that far, man. We checked three or four empty platforms close in." He held up an arm. "Over there." He pointed to a cluster of old twelve-legged platforms spread over five square miles of water to the east, probably idle or capped wellheads. If one tried to notice, there were dozens of wells, intermittent dots running to the horizons. Victor rolled the wheels on his binoculars and leaned out toward the Gulf.

Emile got on the radio and raised LeBlanc again, who could barely get his signal.

"What you got?" LeBlanc sounded as if he was shouting.

"Where you at?"

"About a mile south of that platform. We'll keep looking and then come back to it to meet y'all."

"You check it?"

"Aw, no. We passed a mile north of it and gave it the once-over with the glasses. Nothin' on it."

Emile looked again at the chart, which he had dragged into the cabin. He bent his head low, held his breath over the map as though a passage of wind might blow the spidery printed figures off the paper. Colette looked through the cabin door and watched his face become heavy with blood as he studied. When he looked up, his mouth was a tiny oval. "That's the first lighted platform east of where I think they were trawling." He pulled the microphone to his mouth and sat down on the deck. "LeBlanc."

"Yas."

"Get right up on that platform and call us back."

"We done checked it out with the glasses." LeBlanc's voice was tired. Colette imagined the hundreds of gallons of fuel they had burned.

"Well, damn it," Emile yelled, "check it out with your eye-balls."

There was no transmission for two minutes, and she wondered

whether an argument had broken out in the wheelhouse of the tug. Finally her brother's voice came over the set. "We'll turn north right now. Over."

For the next forty-five minutes, the Larousses, one motor picked up for reserve in case they damaged the other in the shallows, cruised close in over the mud and sand flats. Sometimes their boat stalled when they wandered in too close, their engine kicking up a geyser of mud. Colette and Emile worked a half mile out from them, her glasses scanning only lazy vees of pelicans sailing low. Eventually they turned the crew boat south to get in range of the tug's radio, and when they were within three miles, they got a fuzzy signal.

Colette was steering, Emile on the roof. "What did you say?" she hollered into the mike, her fingers slippery with sweat on the instrument.

"I said, we got one." Uncle Lester was on the radio. "LeBlanc and Mark are on the back deck with him."

"Who is it?" she yelled, her voice rattling the window glass next to her.

". . . was sitting on a strut about three feet over the water."

"Who did they find?"

Again the radio went quiet, and she closed her eyes, squeezing the microphone between her knees. Now her brother's voice cut across the water. "Colette, we found Raymond. He's real weak and we're giving him some fluids. Kind of scuffed up."

"And the others?" She imagined she could see the words fly south across the water like thin birds.

"No sign," the radio said.

"What did Raymond tell you?"

"We just got him in the boat."

"What?"

"The light's no good now for looking for anything. You all come in and tie up alongside us," her brother told her.

"Bullshit. I can still see for miles. What did he say? You tell me this minute," she said, her older-sister voice welling out of her, bossing him.

"They ran head-on into the rig in the worst part of the storm and broke the back on the trawler. Etienne was knocked out, and about a mile closer to land, the boat came all apart. Paul and his daddy went into the water, holding Etienne up. Raymond thought he was following them, but he wound up back at the rig they hit. That's all he knows."

She tried to pick up the microphone, but her arm was lead. Emile came down and took it from her. "Hey, did they have jackets on?"

"What?"

"Did they wear life jackets?"

Dead air followed. A horsefly entered the cabin and Emile smashed it against a window with his hand. The set came alive. "Raymond says Paul and his daddy were wearing them, but not Etienne."

"Over," he said, hanging the mike in its cradle and holding his hand there a moment. "That boy never would put on a life jacket. You could almost count on him doing the one thing that would most likely get him killed." He pulled off his hat, holding it with a fist in his lap. "The times that boy scared me to death—the wrecked cars, the fistfights. One night some dumb local cop was shootin' at him in front the house and he was hiding behind the Mary throne. I had to go out and stop that mess in my bare feet. I never been so scared."

"Etienne's a good man," she heard herself saying.

"Yas, but not a good one to have to raise." He put his hat on the back of his head and turned for the door. "We going to the tug?"

"No," she said, her mouth set. "Flag in the twins."

"But why?" He looked at her and saw her dark eyes rocking back and forth but looking at nothing. "What you thinking so hard for?"

"You're going to tell the twins where to look." She pointed to the navigational map curled up on the floor. "How often has Etienne worked this area?"

With a grunt, Emile got down on his knees and smoothed the chart. "A bunch. When he was just starting out, he worked on LaBat's old oyster lugger. They would grapple and sometimes crab somewhere around here. I think in back of an island."

Colette turned her head north. The mainland was not land. It was a labyrinth of grassy rafts, sandbars that shifted with the seasons, peninsulas that disappeared with high tide, islands that built and waned. "We haven't found deep water all day. These inlets are nothing but mud and oysters. Does the chart show a cut with a little water?"

"I see what you getting at." He put his finger down on the depth markers. "Some cut that would have enough water maybe to get out of a storm." His head moved over the map for a long time. Then he got up off his knees and sat in a chair. "Nothing on the chart. The shore changes every year. It falls in, inlets go away, and storms cut new ones." He put a hand over his eyes and Colette saw that he was tired, his eyes cooked by the day's glare.

"Emile," she said, "give me an answer. Tell me where to search." He pinched his eyes and shook his head. "Look," she began, trying to sense the next step. "They went down due south of here, just a mile, maybe a little more. Etienne was the wheelman, damn it. He was heading somewhere."

Emile looked down. "He was a big foolish boy. Reckless. I'm sorry if he caused . . ." He left the sentence unfinished and dangled his hands between his legs, his shoulders rounding down.

Anger welled up in her and Colette reached over and slapped him hard. "If you give up, you can't help me," she told him. He made a fist and drew his arm back quickly, his elbow cracking the window behind him. She took the fist in her hands, unclenched the fingers, and held them. "Listen to me," she said, close to tears. "Have you ever watched Etienne dance?"

"What?" His face was one big question.

"Let me tell you something." She knelt next to his chair. "I never thought I would say this out loud. He is *so* sharp. He has never once run into another pair of dancers. He knows where he's going, six, maybe eight steps in advance. Even when he's talking to his partner, I've noticed that he keeps the whole dance floor in the edge of his vision and sees how everyone else is moving. I danced with him years ago and can tell you that he is the only man I know who can tell a dirty joke, chew a breath mint, feel up and down a girl's back, and dance a two-step on a dance floor with thirty-five couples and not brush a shirt sleeve with anyone else in the room." She squeezed Emile's hand hard.

The man's eyes flared. "So when the boat hit the rig, he wasn't just lost. He was going somewhere." He turned on the cabin light, got down on all fours once more, and hovered above the chart. Colette listened to his labored breathing, looked out to the north, where the light was failing over a plateau of tan grass bordered on the horizon by a pebble of tortured oaks. "Here," he said at last. "We might as well try here. It's a mud hole, but maybe he knew something I don't. It's northeast of that rig, I can see that. They mighta been making a beeline for it."

In twenty minutes the sun was aground, and Colette was with the Larousses, their skiff slowly feeling through the shallows, a motor on dead slow. A hundred yards ahead lay a thirty-foot-wide opening in the marsh. So far they had not struck bottom. A breeze kicked up, and a light chop foamed against the boat. Ten feet into the mouth of the inlet, Victor gave a whoop and sprang over the windshield into the thigh-deep water, skimming to the narrow sand fringe bordering the marsh grass. Lying there was Paul's father, barefoot and wobbly, trying to sit up. Vincent grounded the boat ten feet from shore and slid over, giving Colette a hand. When they reached the old man, they kept him down and made him drink from a plastic water jug. He was shivering. His eyes, bloodshot and staring, fastened on the Larousse boys. They rubbed him over to check for broken bones and to limber him up, to show how glad they were to welcome him back to the world. Colette ran her hands over the white whiskers on his chapped face. She gave him water a sip at a time and soon he sat up.

"Ah, Colette, the squall took the stuffing out that old boat. We was all down in the hull bailing. Etienne was in the wheelhouse, trying to steer with no lights, and then we hit something— a big pipe, I don't know." He put his head down into his hands for a moment, then picked it up, blinking as though his eyes were shedding salt water. "He got us backed off somehow and we headed out again, but the hull was split and water filled the hold. It got up two feet on that engine before it quit and then we went sideways to the wind and turned over."

"Take it easy," Victor said, giving him another sip of water.

"T-Bub had a flashlight and it was hard to tell what happened, but I think the boat broke open like a egg, and next thing we was in the water. Etienne hit his head, seemed like, and we held him up. I could hear Raymond yelling for a minute." He put a hand to his hairline. "God, my head hurts. I'm starving to death."

Colette put her hands under his face and raised it to her. "We've got Raymond. What about the others? Where are they?"

"I don't know," he cried. "We tangled up in a bad surf and got split apart. A big wave hit me, and next thing I knew, my foot touched sand and I started fighting for shore in pitch-black dark. I made it here and started yelling for the others until I got hoarse." He pushed her hands away but held them. "Let me look down, Colette."

"Okay, Papa."

"When the light came, I walked and yelled on this side the inlet all day until I fell down." He stopped, and she knew why.

He knew they had drowned, were out there with the waterlogged hull and lost nets. She raised her face to the twins, who hovered awkwardly over them, their thumbs hooked into the front pockets of their jeans.

She stood up and pointed west. "Jump that inlet," she said too loudly, "both of you, and one run the outside of that bar, one the inside, until the dark turns you back." She grabbed their upper arms and shoved them into the water. Set in motion, they swam across and set off at a jog. After five minutes she could hear their voices over the ruffling grassland as they called out, "T-Buuuuub" and, later, "Ti-enne." She brought Paul's father a pack of cheese crackers from the boat and gave him some soda to wash them down with. Then she ran up the inside of the channel until she sank to her knees in a bitter mud. A lagoon a half mile across festered behind the island, a trapped and shallow place. There were no tracks anywhere, no sign that the reeds had ever been disturbed, just the keening of a pair of gulls and the distant bellow of an alligator. Backtracking through water, she waded the mud from her legs and walked past Paul's father, who stared out over the Gulf. She jogged east over gray sand for a mile, stopping to examine trash washed up in the shallows, until the sun set and the bottoms of the western clouds showed coppery fire. Where she stopped, she turned to the darkening east and filled her lungs, yelling Paul's name with an earsplitting anger, receiving no call in return, her voice going out like the truest of arrows, nothing to stop it, no one to hear. She yelled again, from her bones out, a long blast of pain lost over the uncaring marshland.

Twenty-three

Victor and Vincent had the old man lying down on the deck and the motor idling when she got back. She splashed out to the boat and each twin grabbed an arm and hauled her in.

"Colette," Vincent began, "we didn't find nothing. No tracks, no nothing." His expression was apologetic, a look she had never seen on the face of a Larousse. She sat down on a life jacket, suddenly too tired to think, her throat sore. Victor scanned the Gulf for Emile's running lights and turned the boat around. In half an hour they were all in the crew boat, the *Unsinkabelle* following behind on a towline, heading south for the tugboat's carbon arc light, which LeBlanc was sweeping like a finger of ice on the darkening water, a signal to guide them in, to cast one last look.

After supper in the galley of the *Dernière Chance*, Colette sat at the end of the long serving counter, watching her uncle gather the plates and silverware. LeBlanc and her brother were at the other end of the little room, looking at a chart, talking about currents. The steel walls and ceiling gave off a smell of hot enamel and diesel oil. Most of the men were asleep or getting ready to sleep, rigging hammocks in the engine room or cots on the stern. Colette pushed open the oval screen door onto the walkway, staring at the dim superstructure of the oil platform they were tied against. Her legs ached like sore teeth, and her hair felt like an oiled rag tied to her head. She pulled it into a ponytail and fastened it with a rubber band. Climbing down to the lower deck, she looked into the engine room at the insulated piping, the braided wires brocading the ceiling, the quiet main engines and yammering generator, the fuse boxes, buttons, rheostats, and valves bathed in a yellow, throbbing light. It was impossible for her not to imagine Paul in there, his hands tingling to touch everything, to draw power from the machine and take it home in his pockets. She realized that men who are good with anything generate their own energy along with a type of grace, which is the oil that helps love slide along. She put her arm into the warm electrical breath of the engine room and drew it slowly back, turning toward the dark night as she began to cry with a quiet anger.

At the first gray hint of light, she climbed out of the bunk and listened to the calm breathing of Paul's father above her. Her head was clear at once, and she knew what to do, mounting the steps to the wheelhouse and pulling one giant long drone from the air horns. Her shoes clopped into the galley and she turned on the lights, put on a gallon of grits, fired up the grill, and began frying slabs of bacon and islands of eggs. The men came in one by one, and she gave each a steaming mug of coffee, until everyone was there—LeBlanc's redneck and even the rescued—rattling knives and forks and banging plates. She was the heart of the rescue, powering everyone, getting everything started again.

Soon men were getting the various machines warmed and ready for the day's search. The main engines kicked over below-decks, the crew boat shuddered to life, and the *Unsinkabelle*'s outboards jittered and sneezed, warming up before the Larousses spun off toward the shallows in the northeast. The lack of purposeful talk was frightening, but still everyone kept moving, handling ropes, turning on radar, radios, pumps, compressors. The men spoke about everything but the possibility of finding anyone alive, as though they were doing all this not for a concrete purpose but as a ritual. She untied the crew boat's lines and went into the cabin. Her eyes hurt and already she wanted more coffee, but she settled for two bitter aspirin washed down with a hot cola.

The crew boat bellied into a light chop, wave tips drawn up by the wind, which was brought out by the sun itself. She looked ahead in the distance at the Larousses banging away at the little waves, then back at a puff of black smoke from the stack of the tug as LeBlanc backed from the oil platform. LeBlanc's redneck came out of the engine room wearing overalls and no shirt. She wondered if he was ready to quit. She knew that she and Emile were not, and that was all that mattered.

All day they ran through the Gulf in patterns, as if the ocean were really a logical thing that would yield to geometry. The morning stretched along slow and glaring, and at noon she could tell that Emile was washed-out and glazed in the eye, and once, when she stopped the boat to retrieve him on the roof, she found him asleep. A Coast Guard helicopter hovered over the marsh where they had found Paul's father, flattened the saw grass for a half hour or so, then disappeared in a whopping roar to the west. The Larousses kept to the shallows, beating their brains out in a rocking surf until a blade broke off a propeller. At three o'clock they ran out of gas, and she came upon them dead in the water, Vincent watching her respectfully, holding a towline as if it were a rosary. Still later, she watched the tug parade its winding path on the horizon like a toy as they continued their own route, the *Unsinkabelle* bobbing on a towline in the crew boat's wheel wash, the Larousse boys asleep on its cushions.

She had spotted oil drums, net floats, a few planks that might or might not have been decking. She stood upright on the roof and gave the horizons a surprised stare, as though she suddenly realized that a trick had been played on her. Colette gathered her dark hair and pulled it to the top of her skull until her scalp hurt. All the water looked the same, and she had the plummeting feeling that she had been floating over the same area for two days, drunk on the fantasy that everyone would be found alive. She wondered if the others thought she was a silly, grieving woman, too stubborn to give it up and head for shore. She raised her head to the sky and looked for planes. Where were they looking? What did they think, those navigators?

She knew she was tired, and she went down into the cabin. Emile was seated at the wheel, looking at a photograph he had taken from his wallet, which rested open in his lap. It was a cracked black-and-white photo of a younger Etienne, grinning, of course, wearing a big overdecorated football jacket buttoned up high. Emile was mourning now, and she sat back, afraid. Looking to the stern, she could see Victor urinating overboard, holding himself with one hand, the binoculars with the other, searching north.

The sun came down like a decision they all had to deal with. At dusk they turned for the tug, which had come into shallow water and dropped anchor. The Gulf was as calm as a pond. Emile guided the crew boat around to the big boat's stern and tied off his bow, mentioning lightly to Colette as he handed her onto the rail of the tug that he was nearly out of diesel and would have to be towed back to town.

After supper Colette sat in the wheelhouse alone, thinking of Matthew. She ran her hands over the hydraulic steering levers and admired the bright gauges, handles, pull cords. Outside, the night was black and starless. From the stern came the voices of the younger men, who were gathered around the main towing bitts, lounging on coils of rope. The older men, including Paul's father, who was stopped up with a cold, started a game of bourrée in the galley, a quiet contest in which there was only the snapping of the cards. A gust of wind leaned against the tug and it swung on anchor. She watched LeBlanc come forward on the lower deck, unscrew a four-inch brass pipe cap, and insert a long stick, pulling it out and looking at the fuel mark. He remained on his knees a long time before closing off the pipe. She knew they would go back to Tiger Island at dawn. She also knew that even if they had found no one, the search would have been worth it, because such a group would form for her only one place on earth. She stepped out onto the walk, trying to step out of her feelings, but she thought of Paul's big soft hands and of the times he had talked her out of her fear or guilt, spending his plain mechanical logic freely until she was whole again.

A laugh rose from the stern. Raymond's voice was serious and bright with some exciting idea. "We ought to rent Blanchard's in Pierre Part for the funeral," he was saying.

Then her own brother began: "Etienne would love it. We could hire a French band and put a black box on sawhorses in the middle of the floor."

"We could dance around it, man."

"It's a stupid, crazy idea," intoned LeBlanc's redneck. "But I got to admit, he'd shore like it."

Colette listened and tried to understand, then went to her bunk, said her prayers, and waited for sleep, hearing the old men break up their game, the young men give up their talk. LeBlanc killed the generator to save fuel. Raymond and Paul's father came into the forward bunk room, where she lay, and climbed in, and then there was only the thin sound of breeze in the screened portholes and the slow roll of the mean Gulf under them all, no whistles to interpret, nothing but night. She thought of how hard Paul must have tried to stay alive in all this water, and why.

Twenty-four

During the first morning of the search, *Grand-père* Abadie hobbled up the levee, bound for his daughter's house. His khaki shirt and pants were still warm from his iron, and the dew polished his heavy brown shoes. At the kitchen door he pulled off his cap and called out to Paul's mother, *"Comment ça va?"*

"Ça va," she replied from the little table under the crucifix. She waved him in and rose to fix another cup of coffee. She told him what Colette had done, and he frowned, rubbed his chin absently, looked old and useless. He sat down at the dinette and saw a box of photographs she had been digging through. He picked up a creased shot of an eight-year-old Paul taken in the front yard. He looked hard at the paper. Halfway down the block was his own narrow house, out of focus, a white hen pacing the front porch. In the photo, Paul was a soft, kind-faced boy, leaning on his Schwinn, a smudge of oil on the bridge of his nose. The old man frowned more and drank from a cup of coffee that had appeared at his elbow. He fretted the picture, turning it in several directions to give the paper more light. He touched other pictures of Paul in the box, of Paul's brother, of other children in the neighborhood, most of whom were in other towns now, earning money for their bills. He saw a photo of Paul in diapers and remembered the baby-oiled heat of him in his lap. Abadie gulped his coffee and stood too quickly, holding on to the table. His daughter, who had just joined him, looked up.

"T'a oublié quelque chose?"

"Je crois que c'est ça," he said, turning for the screen door.

In an hour he was wading out to his cypress skiff, a burlap sack on his back filled with six cans of potted meat, six of Vienna sausage, one can of Spam, one large box of crackers, and one jar of Spanish olives. He went back for four gallon-jugs of drinking water and a roll of toilet paper. He spun the wheel on the glossy black Ferro, and it spat to life, pushing the boat out of the shallows and downriver, where he stopped at the ice house for gas.

Berrard Larouquette, a wiry, sharp-featured man in his fifties, passed down the nozzle for him to fill both the tank behind the engine and two flute-sided cans in the bow. "Monsieur Abadie, you going back fishing some more, hanh?"

"Yas, baby, I got me a big one I want to catch." When Berrard was six years old, he had ridden with Abadie to bait lines. "When you haul up this hose, don't bam me in the head, now."

He sat in the skiff with a set of twenty-year-old charts and looked and looked, running his brown forefinger down the Chieftan, around the islands and passes, to its mouth in the Gulf and along the shoreline to the east. His skiff would take no open water, but it drew only ten inches to the propeller tip, so he could stay close to shore and, when the tide was right, go into the maze.

His fingers wandered east like the logic of the searchers already out in the open water. The farther east one traveled, the more porous the marsh became, the map breaking up into a spongelike system of lakes, lagoons, mud holes, bayous, cutoffs, pipeline canals, reefs, shell mounds, *chênières*, and mud flats. He smiled at the names, a list of old friends: Business Bayou, Little Business Bayou, Dead Tarpon Point, Tisdale Cut, Jack Lane Bay, Lake Deux Pied, Fiddler's Lagoon. He studied a ten-mile-long stretch of shore, the southern rim of Isle de Loup, fronted by a mile of two-foot-deep mud flats, a silty area where fisherman seldom tried their luck. The others would search deep water on the Gulf side, but if Paul's crew had made it to Isle de Loupe, they might have decided to wade north through the marsh rather than risk waiting four days or more to be seen by a crab fisherman or alligator hunter braving the flats at high tide. Yes, he thought. If they washed ashore and knew where they were, they might try to slog five miles to Quatre Fils Bay, which would be full of fishermen. It would be easy for them to get lost, but they might try it.

Abadie had read the tides in the morning paper. He looked at his windup wristwatch and bent to untie the skiff, watching his fingers stall on the knot. It would, after all, be easy to turn around and go home. He looked up at Berrard Larouquette, at his face, which was still in many ways six years old. Pulling the knot free of the piling, he pushed off, opened the rough door in the compartment in the bow, and stowed the yellow charts. By the time the skiff had throbbed under the railroad bridge, he had said ten Hail Marys and a good Act of Contrition.

When he rounded the first bend below Tiger Island, he remembered one reason he no longer ran in the main channel with his old boat. His eyes were no good for distance. He pulled out his telescope from its canvas case, looking downriver to a white trawler going out. He decided to follow as long as he could see it, but a rumble at his back signaled a big offshore supply boat coming. It roiled up behind him and he closed his eyes and picked up his shoulders, waiting to be run over or passed. The big boat sliced by and he cut across its wheel wash to keep from shipping water. By the time he got straightened up again, he was across a thousand-foot river near the willows and had lost sight of the white trawler.

He went on, his little engine going *pump-pump* and him trusting perhaps the map of feeling in his head. All day he slid along, zigzagging the channel, dodging speeding crew boats. In his mind was a lifetime of throbbing meanderings, and he daydreamed, memory and present becoming one time. Before long, Abadie found himself in a wide, peaceful waterway, straight and evenly lined by levees. His head turned this way and that, and he stopped the skiff, standing up and looking east and west. "Now, you know," he said. Turning the boat around, he backtracked three miles to the Chieftan and turned south again into the correct channel. An hour later, plodding through a broad stretch of river, he fell asleep, navigating into a dream and waking only when the boat labored into a raft of hyacinth. Killing the spark to the engine, he pulled out his water jug and Vienna sausage, chewing himself awake.

The engine drummed slowly toward nightfall, pushing the skiff along the shore of the Gulf through a chilly wind and low, muddy breakers. He looked for an opening in the shore of his memory, and after a while, a minute or so before the sun set, he found it and steered the boat north into the smooth shallows behind Isle de Loupe. He threaded a narrowing bayou, slowing down the engine until the skiff grounded, and then he stopped it. In the light of his flashlight he read his watch. Low tide. He slapped on 6-12 against the bugs, sat in the skiff, and listened. Collapsing his nose with forefinger and thumb he blew hard, clearing his ears. He closed his eyes and listened harder. A few spiders were grinding, and one distant bullfrog drummed above the rustling of the millions of acres of grass. He clamped his eyes tighter and strained the old machine that was his brain. If they were alive, and if they were in this marsh, and if Paul still breathed, he had a chance to find them. Yards off, a nutria cried out like a baby, and Abadie made a face.

By morning, the incoming tide had lifted the skiff from the mud, and he woke on the floorboards, chilled and stiff. For a long while, he was amazed that he was not in his bed. He sat up and yearned for hot coffee and the closeness of his little house. The sky was clear and the air unnaturally cool. By seven he was under way, the engine pumping along in the middle of the boat. He got into Quatre Fils Bay, a thirty-mile-long shallow area washed out by some great hurricane a hundred years before, and he ran by the south shore, watching the marsh with his telescope, keeping the steering stick between his knees. By ten o'clock he began to see a sport fisherman or a crabber every two miles, but he didn't even waste a wave on them, watching instead for something in his head that should come to his eyes. Then he saw the opening for Bayou Entrelac, a knotty, forking system of dead water and blind meanders leading into Horsefly Bay, an area popular fifty years before with muskrat trappers who were man enough to get to it with only paddles and pirogues. He made the sign of the cross and pushed the steering stick over, passing on the left a grove of live oaks rising like a round green oasis on the desert of marsh grass. In the oaks were dozens of snowy egrets, and *Grand-père* Abadie smiled up at them, letting the light from their feathers brighten his face.

That afternoon he ran the bayou, or what he surely hoped was the bayou, as it widened to small bays and narrowed to deep ditchlike passes stretched full of green water. At sunset he stopped to eat and heard a boat engine, an inboard, starting up in the distance. He pushed on through a shallow run that turned right and developed into a pelican-filled lagoon. Farther on, the lagoon constricted, and he headed for this narrowing, only to see that it lead to the open Gulf. He stopped the engine, listening until he heard the sound, then turned his glass south, capturing in its lens a crew boat towing a large white fiberglass skiff, heading toward what—he couldn't see—a red bump in the distance.

He wanted to get over the mud flat and follow whoever it was, but the Gulf was becoming an open dark hole. He looked back over his shoulder. His work was here. Lighting his lamp, he opened the crackers, poured water, and spread potted meat with his pocketknife, eating over the spread-out charts, chewing into the marsh's design, memorizing, tapping his temple with a crooked finger as though driving the facts inside.

After dark the air became cool again, and he remembered that an impossible front had forced its way down as far as Kansas, last time he'd checked. The forecasters had said the air would never make it to the coast, and again he laughed at the government, because it was the government that made the weather on TV, he thought. He stood up to walk into the bow, and nothing was there, not even a boat. He had a spell. When he came out of it, he was seated next to the engine, his arm over the side, in the water. "Ah," he said, "what in the world I'm doing out here?" It was several minutes before he realized that the singing in his ears was the buzzing of mosquitoes. Crawling to the cabinet in the bow, he fished out his repellent and a battery-powered spotlight, which he fixed to the bow with a rusty C-clamp. He shook out a little blood-pressure pill and washed it down with water from a jug. Soon he was running slowly, weaving around in the marsh night, the engine steaming in the cool atmosphere. Anyone watching him would have sworn he was lost, and maybe he was. He kept a small compass in his hand, checking it with his flashlight, trying to head generally northwest, back into the most tangled part of Bayou Entrelac, which wound around like the ridges of a brain.

At midnight, his engine hiccuped and stopped, and he found that his fuel tank had gone dry. He poured gas from one of the fluted cans, the sloshing sound the only noise around him. The land, if it could be called land, absorbed him in its silence, and he talked to himself to prove he could still hear. "All the bugs is quiet. The frogs done backed down in the mud." He replaced the can and sat on the bench seat. "If T-Bub is out here, he'll hear this old Ferro engine for sure. He'll know it's me, yeah." He swung the flywheel around and the engine whistled through its priming cup, spat, and started running, the skiff swinging left around a grove of palmettos, then drunkenly right into the blackness lit feebly for fifty feet by the battery light. Abadie retarded the spark on the engine so its exhaust would grow loud and slow, would sail across the marsh for miles, the only heavy-flywheel, slow-beat one-cylinder inboard motor in this water for thirty years. The blackness retreated before his light like a wall and closed in behind. Coming around a small island of wind-crippled oak trees, the skiff rode up onto a submerged log, and he reached the kill switch before the boat could roll over. He found the oar and pushed clear, then listened. A mullet splashed once, twice, then jumped into the boat, flipping around on the footboards before accepting that he could not swim in air.

Abadie listened hard. His old ears were still good, pretty good. "I don't hear nothing, me, except my own fool voice." Again he cranked the engine, his back muscles burning into the action, his legs this late in the day a rasping rain of sparks. He set the engine to a booming exhaust, then floated along in his envelope of light, which showed only marsh grass and onyx water as he traveled in the pattern of a lace doily.

Every fifteen minutes he would stop, even though it was painful for his arms and back to sling the cast-iron flywheel for a new start. In the quiet he would listen with his newly ironed khaki soul and hear nothing. At three in the morning, lost and forgetting, he nodded off against the stick, the skiff taking a long curve until it ran into a shell reef. The old man pitched forward and cut his cheek on a nail. The propeller chewed up oysters and the engine sputtered out. "Old fool," he said as he tended to his face, digging through his cabinet for a Band-Aid and Merthiolate. The night was as quiet as the dark side of the moon, and he could see his breath. He lay back against the bow and said a prayer. A pressure formed on his thigh, and he put his hand out on the back of a huge snake crawling into the boat over him. Abadie picked it up like a stray kitten and dropped it back onto the bank. "Fish snake after that damned mullet." Bending down, he felt for the fish and threw it out, too.

He blew his nose and listened, blew it again and listened harder. Turning around, he clicked off his spotlight, as though light itself made noise, and he closed his eyes and raised his head. In his ears was a whine, a musical monotone, far away and singing like an imagined mosquito in the dark bedroom of the marsh. He was afraid that he was dreaming, and he opened his eyes, as if they wanted to hear instead of see. What he heard put rhythm into the air, then disappeared, and the old man swore he'd never heard it. And then like the thinnest slice of birdcall, something was flying above the invisible marshland from the south and landing on his shoulder: *A-ba-dieee. Aaaa-baaa-dieeee.*

Twenty-five

Colette was dreaming that she was gliding soundlessly down a northern California seacoast highway in her Mercedes. The air was cool and dry, and out on the ocean white trawlers sat and rocked like seabirds. She steered over a long bridge and looked down more carefully, discovering that the boats were not moving but were broken and on their sides, some disappearing partially in the white-tipped waves, men bobbing like insects around the spray-tortured hulls.

She sat up and looked around the bunk room in the dark, then eased off the mattress and went quietly to the rail outside the wheelhouse to stare into the blackness. The Gulf was mournfully calm under a sky of stars fading toward morning. She wanted to be with her baby but did not look forward to living in the big house, which now would have a new ghost, another presence standing in the doorways and staring at her tingling back. She had no one who could hold her, no dance partner in light-winking shoes, no flawed and joking man to repair the machinery of her dreams.

Mr. LeBlanc came out on the deck below, a luminous T-shirt floating, and she imagined he looked up at her. "You sleep any, girl?"

"Some."

"What time is it?"

"About five, I guess," she told him.

He stretched and then rubbed his belly, bent over and rested his elbows on the rail. "We gave it our best," he said.

"You could say that."

After a minute he straightened. "I'll go and crank up the generator."

"Wait," she said.

"What is it, baby?"

She shook her head. "Listen for a minute and tell me if you hear anything."

LeBlanc turned toward the Gulf and put his head down. "I don't think so."

"Just give it a minute." She listened for a sound at a great distance—maybe a machine on an oil rig three or four miles away. It disappeared altogether, and she started to turn inside, but suddenly, with a shift in the wind, it drifted back to her. It was a pulse, a fast heartbeat.

"I don't hear much," LeBlanc said. "Might be a drilling engine. They carry ten miles or more." LeBlanc did not raise his head, though. Finally he looked up at her, and she could almost see his face. "I hear something."

"Like what? You tell me." She looked north. "You know what it is, you of all people."

"It sounds . . ." he began. "Nah. It couldn't be. Not way out here."

"Like what? Tell me."

He put his hands in his pockets and looked down again. "Damn if it don't sound like a old one-lung inboard with a pipe exhaust." He laughed at the silliness of the thought. Then Colette saw him bolt into the engine room and start the generator. His heavy feet banged on the steps as he flew past her and into the wheelhouse, grabbing the headlight lever and twisting the rotary switch. The big carbon-arc light fired up and sent a beam like a sword toward the north. "If he's out there, he'll find us now, girl."

The sky began to lighten in the east. In the distance something buglike floated into the spotlight's beam and out of it. LeBlanc yelped and hung on the whistle cord, trumpeting a blast over the Gulf. Colette watched a feeble spark grow into a bow light on the approaching boat and could hear plainly the heartbeat of the engine. Paul's father and Raymond came into the wheelhouse, pulling on their shirts.

"Hey, man." Raymond blinked and scratched. "What's going on?"

LeBlanc turned and pulled him closer to a big square window. "Look at that old thing coming in. It's got to be Abadie."

"Hell," Raymond said, "let's go down and pull him out. The old rooster's probably stiff as a axle." He clopped down to the stern, Paul's father close behind. Colette saw Emile come out of the crew boat's cabin, and she started down, cut off by the bare-foot Larousse twins and LeBlanc's redneck coming out of the galley. Paul's brother and her uncle stepped from the engine room, where they had slept on the catwalk above the engines. Uncle Lester grabbed her elbow. His face showed three days of white whiskers, and his button-down shirt was greasy and pulled out of his pants.

"Colette, what's going on, baby? I can't find my glasses."

"We think old man Abadie came out to help us. Come on." She guided him to the wide stern of the tug and then waited for the incoming sound, now clearly visible as a skiff with one person sitting upright. In two minutes the boat was pulling alongside, *Grand-père* Abadie's "*Comment ça va?*" drifting up to the watching faces. It was then that LeBlanc turned on all the running and deck lights, and everyone could see that there was more than one man in the skiff. Paul and Etienne lay touching shoulders, their heads against the little cabinet in the bow.

Paul's name exploded from Colette's mouth as though she were trying to scream him back to life, and he opened his eyes, raising an arm to shield them. She jumped across three feet of water down onto the little bow and touched the men's faces. Emile stepped from his crew boat onto the tug's stern and looked down into the skiff. "Abadie," he said, "what's wrong with Etienne?"

Abadie put out a hand palm-down and rocked it back and forth. "He comes and he goes. He got him a fever and a bad bump on the googoon." Abadie knocked the side of his head with a fist.

Vincent and Victor began to jump around and whoop. They dove overboard and swam to the skiff, shoving it against the tug. Paul rolled his eyes up at Colette with the expression of one of the tortured saints in their church's stained glass. He seemed afraid to look at her. "Colette, I lost the boat," he said, his voice full of fear and shame.

An explosion of laughter came from all the men, who banged one another about the shoulders and shouted mocking versions of "I lost the boat." Colette stepped down into the rocking skiff and kissed Paul's sunburned face, then raised her head high, laughing louder than the men, showing her fine straight teeth, sitting back hard on the narrow rail and tumbling overboard into the delighted arms of the Larousse twins.

Twenty-six

He was still the kind of man who could wake up in the morning without opening his eyes, letting the new day come to him through sound instead of light. It was spring, the mild days were dry, and sounds, like people, had more carrying power. Paul heard from his bed in the big wooden house the tin doors at the fish dock up the street bang open against the building, one, two, as Nerby Billiot pushed them wide to the sun. In the cane fields across the river, a locomotive honked at a crossing with the diminished voice of a child's toy. In the middle of the rolling Chieftan, chain was rattling onto a steel deck, and from south of town, like the greeting of a relative, came the deep steamy drone of the rebuilt dredge *Gruenwald*.

Colette began to move beside him and he rolled into her back, where they waited like two spoons in a drawer for the Louisiana Sawmill whistle to rasp from north of town and tell them to make breakfast for Matthew and tend to Jennifer, a new girl-child with ebony hair and eyes as dark as a well.

Paul swung his old lunch box as he walked to LeBlanc's Machine Shop, which had reopened to a good trade since the oil business was seeping alive and the local sugar mills were wearing out their engines. LeBlanc had had a bypass operation, was retired, and Paul had been brought back to run everything. The riverside doors were already open, the five-foot fans humming in the roof peaks, *Grand-père* Abadie sitting on the church pew under the oak, pale, trying to remember something.

From the pew Paul could see inside the shop, where LeBlanc's redneck was uncrating a computerized milling machine elaborate with buttons. "Hey," he yelled to Paul. "Come show me how to start working this thing."

"Read the book," Paul shouted. He sat in the pew and the old man handed him the red plastic cup off his thermos of coffee and laughed.

"T-Bub," his *grand-père* said, "you somethin' else. 'Read the book.' Hot damn." They sat for a long time, passing the cup back and forth, Paul watching the morning's clouds rise above his coming labor.

After she took Matthew to school and Jennifer to Miss Guidry's day care, Colette drove to the bank, which had finally rehired her, this time in a better position than her last. She stepped into her cypress-paneled office upstairs, its window showing a wide view of the eddying Chieftan. She sat at her desk, glancing at a picture of her father and mother, loves she had escaped in spite of her best self. A loan application was on her desk. Antoine Templet wanted a new engine for his lugger. This was Antoine senior, not his lazy son. This was the old man who wore out boats instead of letting boats wear him out. She wrote on the forms, lettering in the voids until she heard a noise like steady thunder and looked through the window to see the Sunset Limited, off schedule, rattling back from California. It trundled over the railroad bridge and blew for the station, its whistle still exotic and inviting. For a long time she stared with her quick dark eyes at where the train had come from, at the blue-black rails that trailed off to the west. Then she looked down at the iron roofs of Tiger Island. Some were storm-worn and bent, some eroded and rusty, porous as a ruined soul, and some were scraped clean and gleaming with new silver paint.

TIM GAUTREAUX

The Clearing

'An extraordinary novel, one of the best I've read in years . . . It is set
in a logging camp in a Louisiana cypress swamp in the 1920s. The
characters are entangled in the rough society of the remote and
lawless settlement, afflicted by racial, ethnic and sexual crimes. But
it is also the story of familial loyalty and affection between two
brothers, one a First World War battle-shocked veteran . . . As the
cypress trees fall and create the stump-pocked clearing of the title,
the reader is swallowed into the gut of a ruthless business.'
Annie Proulx, *Guardian*

'Confident, absorbing, monumental'
Alan Warner, Books of the Year, *Daily Telegraph*

'[An] excellent novel'
John de Falbe, *Spectator*

'The relationship between the two brothers is sensitively and
brilliantly drawn; the strength of the women in the book, which is
at odds with the harsh physicality of a land governed by violence,
is deftly depicted . . . *The Clearing* carries an emotional charge far
beyond its pages and does what all great fiction does: gives insights
allowing us to understand human nature and a distant time and
place. I cannot recommend it highly enough.'
Peter Straus, *Literary Review*

'This is a novel so firmly located and vividly realised that you can
almost smell the Louisiana swampwater as you read . . . A
gripping, action-packed tale'
Jem Poster, *Guardian*

'Gautreaux captures the fetid atmosphere of a frontier society
poised to join the modern world with great skill, each sentence
polished to perfection'
Steve Jelbert, *Independent on Sunday*

SCEPTRE